TIDE AND TEMPEST

Books by Elizabeth Ludwig

From Bethany House Publishers

EDGE OF FREEDOM

No Safe Harbor

Dark Road Home

Tide and Tempest

ALSO BY ELIZABETH LUDWIG

Love Finds You in Calico, California

Died in the Wool*

Inn Plain Sight*

Where the Truth Lies*

*with Janelle Mowery

EDGE OF FREEDOM, BOOK THREE

TIDE AND TEMPEST

A NOVEL

ELIZABETH
LUDWIG

BETHANYHOUSE
a division of Baker Publishing Group
Minneapolis, Minnesota

© 2014 by Elizabeth Ludwig

Published by Bethany House Publishers
11400 Hampshire Avenue South
Bloomington, Minnesota 55438
www.bethanyhouse.com

Bethany House Publishers is a division of
Baker Publishing Group, Grand Rapids, Michigan

Printed in the United States of America

Library of Congress Cataloging-in-Publication Data

Ludwig, Elizabeth.
    Tide and tempest / Elizabeth Ludwig.
        pages cm. — (Edge of freedom; Book Three)
        Summary: "In the riveting conclusion to the EDGE OF FREEDOM series, Captain Keondric Morgan believes Tillie's fiancé was murdered two years ago when he died crossing to America. Now can Keondric save Tillie from the same fate?"— Provided by publisher.
        ISBN 978-0-7642-1041-9 (pbk.)
        1. Young women—Fiction. 2. Irish Americans—Fiction. 3. New York (N.Y.)—History—19th century—Fiction. I. Title.
        PS3612.U33T53 2014
        813′.6—dc23   2013034267

14 15 16 17 18 19 20   7 6 5 4 3 2 1

Scripture quotations are from the King James Version of the Bible.

Cover design by Koechel Peterson & Associates, Inc., Minneapolis, Minnesota

Author is represented by MacGregor Literary, Inc.

To Lee
You're my husband and best friend,
the hero of my dreams.

1

"Captain Morgan? Sir?"

Keondric Morgan glared over his shoulder at the deckhand waving furiously at him from the bow of the *Caitriona Marie*. He slowed his steps, halting the rhythmic cadence of his feet against the gangplank. "What now, Donal?"

His fingers beat with irritation against the pouch strapped to his side. He had somewhere to be, and if he had to mind every move his crewmen made, he'd never get there.

"The doctor, sir." Donal shifted from foot to foot and tugged at the collar of his shirt.

Blowing an impatient blast from his lips, Morgan lifted his cap, dragged his fingers through his hair, and gestured for him to continue. "Well? Go on, man, what about him?"

"What . . . uh . . ." Knuckles white as he gripped the rail, he glanced over his shoulder and back, then cupped a hand to his mouth and leaned out over the water. "What should we do with him, sir?"

"He's dead, Donal," Morgan shouted back, raising his voice to be heard above the flocks of sea gulls arguing overhead. "What do you think we should do with him? Contact his next of kin and see about getting him buried!"

Sighing, Donal grumbled, "'Twould have been easier if the man had died at sea."

A lull in the noise clamoring from the vessels along the dock carried his words to Morgan's ears. He paused mid-turn and narrowed his eyes. "What was that?"

Donal's chin lowered. "Nothing, sir."

"Good. See to it, then." Jamming his hands into his pockets, Morgan hunched his shoulders, spun on his heel, and stormed down the gangplank. The doctor's death disturbed him, but not nearly as much as did his dying words.

"I did it, Morgan. God help me, I took the money."

He scowled as he stomped off the wooden slats of the dock onto solid ground. He'd been weeks at sea, but this time there was no pleasure in the earthy scents of soil and horses that filled his nostrils, no marveling at the road stretching before him, straight and sturdy, with no rolling pitch for his legs to adjust to. Instead there was just . . . irritation?

He mulled the thought like a sore tooth. When the truth finally hit him, he growled low in his throat, feeling as though he'd been blindsided.

Nay. It was guilt.

Swinging off the dirt road toward a line of carriages for hire, he withdrew a coin from his pocket and flagged the first driver he saw.

Just what did he have to feel guilty for? It wasn't he who'd greased the doctor's palm. He hadn't even known about the plot until a few hours ago. He hunkered into his coat. Would that he'd remained oblivious.

He paid the driver, grumbling to himself as he climbed into the carriage. Not true. He knew everything that happened on his ship. It was the fact that the *good* doctor's deed had been accomplished under his nose that made his blood boil.

"Captain! Wait up." His first mate jogged down the dock toward him, his dark hair flopping over his brow. Panting, he skittered to a stop and gripped the side of the carriage. "Where you headed?" Before Morgan could answer, he vaulted onto the seat across from him. "You going to see the lass, eh? The one whose husband—"

"Quiet!"

Morgan's low snarl sliced the words from Cass's tongue. He glanced at the driver, then flushed red. "Sorry, Cap."

Morgan waved for the driver to proceed and then settled back against the seat, his arms crossed over his chest. "You know I hate it when you call me Cap."

"Right. Sorry, Ca . . . Morgan."

Morgan glared at his younger brother. "That one was on purpose."

A devilish twinkle lit Cass's eyes, but he neither admitted nor denied Morgan's charge. "So? What about it?"

Now that the rumbling carriage drowned their conversation, Morgan could relax. He shrugged. "Not sure yet. Guess we'll see what happens when I find her."

"Any idea where to look?"

He gave a curt nod. "Ashberry Street. That's where I left her."

"Do you really think she's still there?"

"If not, my problem is easily solved, eh?"

Cass's brow gathered in a skeptical frown. "I know you, dear brother. Remember? You're hardly likely to let this thing go as simply as that." He leaned forward and braced his elbows on his knees, his lithe body swaying with the rocking of the carriage. "I don't like this, Morgan. I still think we ought to bury the doc and say nothing."

Morgan's thoughts flashed to their mother, back home in Dublin. He angled his chin with a grimace. "Aye, and what would Ma have to say about that? You think she'd approve?"

Cass grunted and threw himself against the seat, matching Morgan's crossed arms. "And why would we even tell her?"

"I wouldn't have to. She'd know something was up the moment she caught sight of our faces."

"Yours maybe," Cass sneered, then ducked Morgan's fist and threw his hands high in surrender. "What? You couldn't lie to save your life and you know it."

"Aye, but unfortunately you can. Ma never leaves the confessional, thanks to you. Probably has a candle with your name on it burning right now."

Cass's deep laugh was contagious. With his answering smile, a bit of the tension eased from Morgan's shoulders. Ach, but glad he was that his brother had finally abandoned the wiles of wine and women and joined him on the ship. Maybe he could finally start thinking about—

He cut short the idea of Cass supporting their mother. Nothing that happened after their father's death was his brother's fault. He was the eldest, not Cass. Providing for the family was his responsibility, just as following in his father's footsteps and captaining the ship had been his choice to make.

He eyed his brother, lounging casually against the back of the seat. "Cass, I . . . I'd rather you not get involved, if you don't mind."

Alarm sparked in his brother's blue eyes. "So, you are worried."

Morgan jerked his head to stare at the towering buildings rolling by—so different from their modest cottage in Dublin. "Haven't had time to be worried. I just found out a few hours ago, remember?"

Cass leaned forward and wagged his finger beneath Morgan's nose. "That's another thing. I thought nothing happened on board the ship . . ." Catching sight of the warning glance Morgan shot at him, he broke off and muttered, "Never mind. By the saints, Cap—"

"Watch your mouth."

"Fie! You're as ornery as a goat in your old age."

Morgan bristled. He was only thirty-one, though sitting beside a brother ten years younger tended to make a man feel ancient. "That's beside the point. I promised Ma I wouldn't let you swear."

Cass roared with laughter. "Aye, and I'd like to hear what the other crewmen would say if you tried inflicting your old-maid ways on them."

"The other crewmen aren't my baby brother."

His laughter quieted as a flush crept over Cass's cheeks.

"Besides," Morgan continued, softening the barb with a bit of teasing, "they all know better than to curse in front of me."

Envy shone on Cass's face as he eyed Morgan's muscled torso. "Only because they're afraid of having the life thrashed out of them."

"A lesson you'd do well to learn."

Cass smirked. "You can't beat me to death. Ma won't let you."

Morgan fixed him with a menacing glower. "Doesn't mean I kinna knock some sense into that thick skull of yours."

"Whoa!" Cass held up his hands. "Calm yourself, big brother. I was just fooling."

"Exactly. You're always fooling, which is why I'd rather you steered clear of this mess with Doc, at least until I can figure out what he meant. A man lost his life, and if what Doc said is true . . ." He shook his head. "There be no room for trifling."

The twinkle faded. Without it, Cass appeared contemplative, even solemn—a rarity that Morgan was glad to see happening more and more often.

Cass lowered his voice. "I'm worried about you, brother.

For sure, ain't no one more capable of looking after himself, but this . . . this has me troubled." After a moment, he grinned and quirked an eyebrow. "Just be careful, all right?"

Morgan knew exactly what he meant. He'd felt it too, the moment Doc started ranting about poison . . . and murder.

Avoiding his brother's gaze, he whistled at the driver and motioned for him to pull over.

"What—" Cass sat up and looked at the driver, then at Morgan. "What are you doing?"

"This is where you get off."

Frowning, Cass unfolded himself from the seat and leapt to the ground, keeping one hand braced on the side of the carriage. "Fine, I'll go back to the ship." He offered a salute before stepping away. "But I have to say, Cap, if I didn't know better, I'd think you had ulterior motives for preventing me from laying eyes on this lass of yours."

Tossing a glance heavenward, Morgan sighed and motioned the driver onward, Cass's bark of laughter ringing in his ears.

The cobbled street rumbling beneath him, Morgan raised his fingers and worried the bit of scruff growing along his jaw. His brother wasn't alone in thinking him tedious. Most of Dublin, his crew included, considered him a prude, but since Da died, he simply had no time for social pleasantries.

His thoughts flashed to Moira and the sad smile that had accompanied his last glimpse of her. Perhaps if Cass knew how often that look filled Morgan's thoughts, he wouldn't be so quick to mock.

No. Morgan plucked an extra coin from his pocket. His brother was never intentionally cruel. Reckless perhaps, or even a touch thoughtless, but never cruel.

Some distance later, the carriage rolled to a stop. Tossing another coin to the driver, Morgan disembarked and stood before a three-story structure with stone steps that led to a brightly painted door. Flowers cheered both sides of the walk—uncommon for most boardinghouses, but not unexpected from this one, considering the kind woman who owned it. She'd opened her door when none of the other proprietors along this street would, a fact that had burned the address, and her name, indelibly on his brain.

It wasn't Amelia Matheson he'd come to see, however. Morgan climbed the boardinghouse steps and raised his fist to knock. No, the person he'd come seeking was much younger, and possibly in far more danger.

And her name was Tillie McKillop.

— ❀ ❀ ❀ —

Her fingers tingling with excitement, Tillie counted the last of the coins from a worn leather pouch she kept hidden beneath a floorboard under her bed. Combined with the money she and Braedon had saved before crossing over to America, and what she'd netted from selling her jewelry and a string of pearls left her by her grandmother, she had just about enough.

Grabbing the pouch from the bottom, she gave it one last shake, just in case any more coins lay tucked inside its folds. Instead, a slender gold ring fell out and rolled onto the floor with a thump. Braedon's ring.

As she'd done often in the past, Tillie lifted the ring to examine it more closely. Though the metal was worn with age, two clasped hands were clearly visible—one larger and obviously masculine, the other smaller and more delicate. Female. Twisting slightly, Tillie dislodged the two clasped hands, spreading the ring so it became two distinct bands, and beneath them a third band upon which a glittering ruby shaped like a heart lay hidden. The sight never failed to rob her of her breath. Where Braedon had come by the ring or how much it was worth, she didn't know, but it belonged to him, and she'd vowed never to part with it.

Guilt pricked her conscience, which she brushed aside with a toss of her curls. Braedon would understand why she'd abandoned the idea of moving to far-off Kansas to buy a farm. There was so much need here in New York.

Her heart fluttered as she replaced the money and ring inside the pouch and returned it to its hiding place. To date, she'd breathed not a word of her plan, not even to Father Ed. But now that she was so near her goal, she'd make mention of it. Perhaps he would be able to steer her toward the perfect spot for—

"Tillie?" Amelia's voice floated up the stairs, but it wasn't her usual lighthearted tone. A troubled edge sharpened her words. "Are you up there, dear? There's someone here to see you."

Tillie pushed her bed back into place, catching her skirt on one of the legs and pulling it free only after three attempts. She scowled at the ruffled hem. At least she hadn't torn it. Again.

Frowning, she marched to the door and stuck her head into the hall. "I'll be right down, Amelia."

She crossed to the vanity and eyed her disheveled reflection critically. It was early, and Saturday. Who could be visiting her at this hour? Hastily she withdrew a couple of pins from her hair and replaced them in almost the same spot. How she wished she'd acquired a bit of the practiced ease with which Ana styled her curls. Maybe then she wouldn't always look so tousled.

A couple more pats and a smoothing of her skirt did little to improve the situation. She sighed. Whoever waited downstairs would likely be more affronted by her tardiness than her appearance.

Relinquishing the attempt at propriety, she made her way from her bedroom to the parlor. A low voice, gruff and vaguely familiar, drew her as she neared.

A gentleman caller? The only male she knew who might pay a visit would be Father Ed, and then only if an emergency at the church required her attention.

Her thoughts winged to the two aging nuns who helped run the shelter. Could one of them have taken ill? She quickened her steps.

The pocket doors leading to the parlor had been slid closed—only a slight crack let sight and sound through. As Tillie gave a knock, she glimpsed the hem of Amelia's embroidered gown and the dark blue sleeve of her guest.

Amelia's gown rustled as she rose. "Come in, dear."

Curious now that she knew the visitor was not Father Ed, for he seldom wore anything but black, she slid open the doors and entered. Amelia stretched out her hands, one toward Tillie, the other toward the man who, once standing, towered over them both.

Lassoed by his steel-gray gaze, Tillie faltered on the threshold. Once before she'd felt herself snared by those eyes. A hint of compassion had softened them then, so she did not quake. Not so today.

Today, he stared with an intensity that sent shivers coursing over her flesh. Instinctively she rubbed her hands over her arms.

"Tillie"—Amelia glanced hesitantly at her and then at their guest—"you remember Captain Morgan?"

She swallowed on reflex. Aye, she remembered him. The question was, what was he doing at the boardinghouse?

And what could he possibly want from her?

2

Tillie resisted the urge to stumble back across the threshold as Captain Morgan stepped forward to greet her. Bowing, he swiped a flat cap from his head. Twisted between his large hands, the tortured gray herringbone resembled lopsided z's.

"It's nice to see you again, ma'am."

"The pleasure is mine, Captain, though I must admit, 'tis quite unexpected."

Captain Morgan raised an eyebrow, making her regret her hasty speech. Ever the angel, Amelia stepped forward and spread her hands.

"Captain Morgan and I were just about to sit down for some tea. Will you join us, dear?"

Tillie glanced at the mantel, where a clock made of cherry and fitted with etched glass kept perfect time. It was barely past breakfast. What on earth could be so important that Amelia allowed it to disrupt the proper order of the day?

Amelia ducked into her sight, her normally cheerful gray eyes somber and pale. "I'll fetch the tea. It'll only be a minute."

Unease squeezed Tillie's heart. Amelia was worried about her, and no wonder, considering the ragged state she'd been in the last time the captain had come to the boardinghouse. She gave her hands a reassuring pat and nodded. "Thank you, Amelia."

For a brief moment, her eyes widened, questioning. Though Tillie knew the concern that must be running through her thoughts, she shook her head and straightened. She'd matured since the last time she'd clapped eyes on Captain Morgan, and both he and Amelia would know it.

Sighing, Amelia swept from the parlor. Tillie smiled, infusing it with as much warmth as she could muster and gestured toward a seat near the fireplace. The warm summer temperatures made building a fire unnecessary. Still, she pulled her chair closer to the hearth, as if by the proximity she might soak up the remnants of ghostly heat.

She waited while he situated his cap over his knee and leaned back to rake long fingers through his dark brown locks. His hair was a touch overgrown. It curled at the edges where it brushed his collar. Curious length for a ship's captain, but not a farmer. Braedon's hair had coiled in just the same way.

Her fingers tightened in her lap. "As I said before, your visit is quite unexpected. Not an unwelcome surprise," she corrected hastily, "I just dinna realize you were in New York. Do your travels bring you here often?"

He pushed up on the chair, the ruddy color in his cheeks deepening. "Often enough to make me remiss. I fear I should have inquired as to your welfare sooner."

Tillie smiled as the confusion cleared from her mind. So that was it. And it explained the look troubling his gray eyes. "Remiss, Captain? Certainly not. You did quite enough caring for me as you did. I never would have survived alone in this big city. Grateful I am that you found this boardinghouse and brought me here to recover."

"It was recommended to me." He frowned. "The ship's doctor knew of the place, not I."

She shrugged. "However I came to be here, it has been a godsend." Amelia insisted that the residents of the boardinghouse call her by her Christian name, but Tillie would not disrespect her by addressing her so in front of a stranger. She gestured toward the door through which Amelia had exited. "Mrs. Matheson has been like a second mother to me."

Hurt rose in her chest. Even that was not exactly true. Tillie's thoughts flashed to her parents—to the disapproval sparking from their eyes at their last meeting. It was a look she had never witnessed from Amelia. Gratitude, thick and bittersweet, clogged her throat.

"I'm glad to hear it," the captain said, cutting into her thoughts. He nodded, and though it did not quite reach his eyes, he smiled. Or attempted a smile. The crooked grimace looked forced to his lips. Once more, he snagged his cap and tormented it betwixt his fingers. "And I'm glad to see you are looking well."

"As are you," she said, noting the stark white sweater at his neck against his bronzed skin, and then blushed when she realized her mistake. He'd meant from the illness that had laid hold of her after Braedon died, not her overall appearance. "That is to say," she amended, "it's always good to see someone from home. Ireland, that is."

The tinkling of china sounded outside the door, and Tillie sprang from her seat. "There's Mrs. Matheson with the tea."

Indeed, it was not Amelia who waited in the hall with the tea cart, but Laverne, the boardinghouse's cook and housekeeper. She ducked her head to whisper, "We've a situation in the kitchen, I'm afraid. Amelia sends her apologies, but she won't be joining you."

She pressed the cart into Tillie's hands, the lines of strain on her otherwise plump features attesting that she was anxious to return to the kitchen to face whatever problem had detained Amelia.

Tillie bowed her head and lowered her voice. "That's quite

all right. Laverne—" she caught the housekeeper's hand before she could flee—"have you seen Meg?"

Laverne nodded, dislodging the mobcap covering her gray curls so that it flopped over her forehead. "Had to send her after eggs. The hens still aren't laying, though I've tried everything to figure out what could be wrong." She clucked her tongue like one of the hens she disparaged. "There's an added expense we could do without, and no doubt." Sighing, she turned for the hall. "If you need anything, I'll be in the kitchen. Otherwise, don't hesitate to ring for Giles." She cast a narrowed glance at Captain Morgan. "He's outside fashioning new shoes for the mare. She went lame last week." She cut her eyes back to Tillie. "But he'll come in a hurry if you call."

"Thank you, Laverne."

Jerking the mobcap back into place, she gave a nod and strutted off, her back stiff and shoulders square. A grin quivered on Tillie's lips. So, she didn't like the captain. Yet she'd only just glanced at him. What on earth had put her out?

Smoothing the surprise from her face, Tillie lifted the tea tray from the cart and carried it to the table where Captain Morgan waited. "My apologies. Laverne is not normally so gruff."

Mirth shone from his countenance. "Trouble in the kitchen, I gather?"

Tillie offered a shy smile and poured the captain a cup of tea, which she handed to him and afterward poured a second cup for herself. "Nothing the two of them can't handle, I'm sure."

Captain Morgan took a swallow of tea and then replaced the cup on its saucer and set the two aside. "I dinna mean to keep you. Truly, I just wanted to see how you'd fared and perhaps inquire after the little one."

Startled, Tillie rattled her cup in its saucer, then set it

down on the polished silver tray. Of course he didn't know. He couldn't. He'd left before . . .

She took a breath and forced her gaze to his curious face.

He leaned forward, one hand clutching the gray cap, the other reaching toward her. "Mrs. McKillop? Are you all right?"

McKillop. Braedon. She hadn't told him.

"I'm fine, Captain. Your words surprised me is all. I'd forgotten that I was . . . that at the time I left the ship . . ."

He went still, his eyes changing from bluish gray to steely blue. "Mrs. McKillop?"

Heat swept up to enflame her face and neck. Shame, thick and stifling, draped over her like a shroud. She clenched her jaw and forced the words through gritted teeth, "My name be Miss McGrath, Captain. I was never married."

The captain's face registered shock, then concern.

"As for the child . . ." She lifted her chin. Even now, two years after the fact, hot tears burned the back of her eyes. She held them in check with iron will. "It pains me to say she never drew a breath. My daughter was stillborn."

3

Though she'd spoken the words with a steadfastness any seafaring man would envy, Morgan read a wealth of conflicting emotions in her eyes. She wasn't the unaffected, impassive portrait she portrayed, sitting there so perfectly rigid, with only the tension in her knuckles giving her away. Still, he admired the attempt and measured his tone to the same careful tenor she'd used in addressing him.

"I'm verra sorry to hear of your loss. You have my deepest sympathy, as well as that of my crew."

Most of his crew, he corrected silently, upbraiding Doc anew. But surely one man's actions weren't to blame for the death of the *bairn*? He set aside his cap and leaned forward to brace his elbows on his knees.

"Your illness . . ." He cleared his throat. "Did your illness have anything to do with the child being stillborn?"

She gave a curt shake of her head before rising to her feet and crossing to a long window stretching up the wall alongside the fireplace. "Your pardon, please, Captain, but this is not a subject I am comfortable discussing. I'm sure you can understand why."

He rose when she did, though he maintained his place at the sofa. "Of course. Forgive me. I dinna mean to pry."

Of course he'd meant to pry. It was why he'd asked. This was getting him nowhere. He circled the coffee table and crossed to stand next to the window adjacent to the one Mrs.—Miss—McGrath occupied. He'd yet to take in completely that new revelation, but one thing at a time.

"I only hope . . . that is . . ."

She looked at him, a sort of waif-like vulnerability and strong determination he found both daunting and irresistible in her gaze. He gave himself a mental kick. "I pray the conditions on board my ship dinna contribute to the loss of your child. 'Twas a difficult crossing to be sure, but I hope you know that I . . . that my crew and I did everything we could to ease the passage."

The words rumbled like stones across the hollow space between them, for they were only partly true. Her expression darkened a split second before she turned her face away—long enough to see that she was reliving painful portions of the voyage in her thoughts.

Her fingers shook as she clenched both hands to her midriff. "Do not berate yourself, Captain. I find no fault in the actions of you or your crew. Truly, I fault no one but myself."

He mulled the words a moment. What cause could she have for blaming herself? He shook his head and gestured toward the chairs. "Will you sit? I'm anxious to hear how you have fared since arriving in New York. Besides a place to stay, you were able to secure employment?"

If his persistence troubled her, it didn't show. Instead she appeared relieved by the change in conversation. She placed her fingers in his palm and allowed him to lead her back to the fireplace.

"Aye. I have a position with a fine milliner now, though that too was thanks in part to Mrs. Matheson."

He assisted her to sit and then reclaimed the chair opposite hers, casually lifting his cooling cup of tea as though chatting with a lady in the parlor of her home were a common occurrence. Once maybe, he thought, his mind dashing to Moira, but not since Da's death. Not since he'd left home and taken over the family's shipping business.

After downing a steadying swallow, he replaced the cup on its saucer. "A milliner? That requires some talent."

Her cheeks colored as she looked away to reach for her own cup. "I've always been quite skilled with a needle."

"But . . ." He paused to phrase his words with care. "Providing for yourself must be difficult. You've never considered returning home to your family?"

Once again her lashes swept down to cover her deep brown eyes, but not before he saw them spark with anger.

"My family is here, at the boardinghouse."

As she spoke, a vein tightened along her neck, creasing the otherwise flawless skin. Was it his prying that ignited such a response or something else? He angled his head for a glimpse of her rosy cheeks. "Miss McGrath—"

Her eyes flew to his, and once again he felt himself at a loss, a condition that was both foreign and unwelcome. He cleared his throat and growled, "I . . . I feel I owe you compensation of a sort for . . . well, the trouble you endured aboard my ship."

Her brow furrowed in bewilderment. "Captain, I'm sure 'tis quite commonplace for people to take ill while making their passage to America."

Fool. She isn't an imbecile.

If he wasn't careful, he was going to give away his secret whether he wanted to or not. He offered a contrite shrug. "True enough, but my lack of communication with you afterward is without excuse. I had a duty to fulfill, a moral obligation as my mother would say, and I fear I've failed. I'm here to make amends in whatever way I can."

She still looked confused, if the tiny wrinkle between her arched brows was any indication, but at least she didn't appear suspicious. "Your mother?"

That was the word she'd lighted on? He gave a slow nod. "Aye. She was quite distressed when I told her about you . . . that is, about your situation," he amended, shifting in his chair. "She has a kind heart, and it troubled her that I'd left America without determining your fate."

Her lips turned in a frown. "Surely she kinna expect you to attend so diligently to all of your passengers?"

No. Likely it had more to do with his incessant talk of a beautiful, frail lass that had spiked his mother's interest so.

Discomfited, he leaned forward, causing his chair to creak. "Truth be told, there aren't that many passengers. Mine is more of a cargo vessel, as I'm sure you noticed, and my crew more accustomed to dealing with freight than people. My mother is very tender-natured, so when she heard about your husband's passing . . ." He paused, but she didn't flinch at his use of the word *husband*, so he pressed on. "She was concerned for you and troubled over your welfare. I promised her I would look in on you the next time my travels brought me to New York."

That much was true enough, though it was a half-mumbled promise he'd made in Dublin. The real fact of the matter was that Doc's confession had prompted this visit, not Ma's concern.

Not for the first time he rebuked the desperate straits that had forced him into accepting the fare of the woman and her "not husband" in the first place. He then rebuked his own meddlesome interest after her companion took ill and died.

Why couldn't he have heeded Doc's advice and just left her in New York . . . ?

Doc's advice.

Morgan grimaced. Miss McGrath was certainly not to blame for the events that had taken place aboard his ship. In fact, had she chosen another vessel, her circumstances might be very different.

Guilt crashed over him, as cold and crushing as the sea. "Now that I'm here," he continued, "I can't help wondering, Miss McGrath, why you never returned to Ireland?"

Her head dipped, and a loose curl tumbled to cover half her cheek. "There was no going back, Captain. This I knew the moment Braedon and I set foot aboard your ship. Besides, my parents died not long after I left Ireland. My future, my family 'tis all here now, and that be simply the way of it."

The way of it? Wondering at her choice of words, he narrowed his eyes to peer at her. She stared back, her eyes wide and guileless. She was an innocent, this one, whatever her circumstances.

He felt a surprising wash of protectiveness surge through him, similar to the emotion he'd experienced the day he took her to see the dying man he'd presumed was her husband. He'd acted against ship's protocol. Passengers quarantined for illness were not allowed visitors. Even Doc warned against it, though of course now Morgan knew why. Still, compelled by compassion, he'd taken her to the dying man's quarters, allowed her to sit by his side as he breathed his last, then watched over her as she sobbed into the wee hours.

All that and more were his blame to bear.

Snapping his mouth closed, he tugged at the collar of his suddenly too-tight sweater. "I know 'tis very little recompense for all you've endured, but I would like to offer you passage back to Ireland. It would be free of charge, of course. My crew and I will be departing for the Carolinas within the next week or two, for a shipment of tobacco. After that, we'll make for Liverpool, and then home to Dublin. You'd be most welcome to accompany us, if you so desire." He paused to clear his throat. "I will personally see to your safety while we travel."

She had gone very still as he spoke, her features even more pale. When he finished, she bit her lip as if considering. Finally, she gave the barest shake of her head.

"Two weeks would hardly be enough time to prepare for a trip of this sort."

Morgan did a quick calculation in his head. The supplier in Liverpool needed the tobacco by early October. It was now late July. He lifted one shoulder in a shrug. "I suppose I could push the date back a bit if you needed more time."

"I couldn't ask you to do that."

He grimaced. "My crew would likely be grateful. I've pushed them hard these last few months. We've scarce had any time in port. The respite will do them good."

Though perhaps not his pocketbook. He'd pushed the crew because he'd hoped to stash enough in his savings to purchase a small farm outside of Dublin, but what use was that? It wasn't as if he could work the land anytime soon. If he were honest, maybe not ever.

He lifted an inquiring eyebrow to Miss McGrath, after which she gave another, more definite shake of her head.

"I appreciate the offer, Captain, but my home is in New York now, and my plans . . ." She lifted her chin and spoke with as much confidence as he'd yet to hear from her. "I volunteer at a church shelter nearby. It has taught me to see beyond my own needs. As long as I can be of service, of some sort of use . . ." Silence seized her as a rosy flush bloomed on her cheeks. "Forgive me. I do not make it a custom to speak so liberally." She got up from her chair and held out her hand.

"My thanks to you for your visit. Please give my regards to your mother when next you see her, and tell her I appreciate her asking after me."

Regret rippled through him. Despite himself, he'd begun to envision her aboard the *Caitriona Marie*, only this time without the weight of sorrow stooping her shoulders.

Morgan loosed the grip of befuddlement with a toss of his head. Rising, he clasped her outstretched hand. "I'll do that."

"And while I am grateful for your offer of transport back to Ireland, I'm afraid I kinna accept," she continued, sliding her hand out from his too quickly.

He gave another slight nod before turning to go. "Of course. I understand, and I wish you well."

For the first time since he'd arrived, a genuine smile tipped her lips.

"Thank you," she said. "God never closes one door but He opens another."

Morgan froze. Oft he'd heard the same words spoken by his mother, but never had they struck him with such conviction. Indeed, Miss McGrath looked as surprised as he at the words that had slipped from her mouth. He jammed his hands into the pockets of his trousers. "It's been a long time since I've heard that saying."

She nodded and clasped her hands before her. "Must have been the talk of returning to Ireland what stirred up them old words."

"I suppose so." Donning his cap, he placed a touch to the brim. "It was a pleasure to see you again."

"And you, as well, Captain."

She waited for him to go, and still he hesitated, his insides jumping. "Miss McGrath?"

"Aye, Captain?"

"You will call upon me if ever you have need of anything?"

She looked confused for a moment, and then she nodded. "I will. Thank you."

Move. Now. He forced his feet to shuffle forward. "All right, then. I'll show myself out."

He exited the parlor and made for the front door. The strange mix of emotions he felt where Tillie McGrath was concerned was a mystery, and no doubt. Unfortunately, despite his apparent freedom from obligation toward her, he was no less troubled than before he'd paid her a visit, and no more certain in which direction he should proceed.

4

The *Caitriona Marie*'s loud groan rumbled up through the soles of Donal's feet, as though even she had tired of the argument that had broken out in the hold. Ach, but he'd be glad to leave this infernal yammering crew behind.

A scowl twisted his lips. With the exception of Captain Morgan, the crew was lazy, unorganized, and stupid. He skirted a row of crates stacked haphazardly across the bow—more evidence of the crew's ineptitude—but dodging them only brought him closer to the bow of the ship and to the rows of freighters moored side by side at the dock. At least at sea a stiff breeze swept away the odor of sweat and rot and fish. Here in the harbor, with the sun beating down on the decks and no wind to riffle the waves, the stench was almost unbearable.

He hopped the last few rungs on a ladder leading to mid-deck and landed with a thump on the solid wood planks—a good sound, the reliable, unyielding echo of quality and craftsmanship. Despite her crew, the *Caitriona Marie* was a fetching vessel.

He paused at the rail, letting his fingers trail the length of cool, hard metal. A ship like this could provide an ample living for him and, perhaps someday, his family.

"Donal!"

He snapped a glance over his shoulder at the ship's boatswain. "Aye? What is it?"

"Ain't ya supposed to be seeing to the unloading of them there crates?" The man, Bozey by name, jerked his chin at a stack of cargo plugging the same spot on the deck since they'd anchored.

Donal snorted. "And where do you think I be heading, if not to the harbor master's office?"

Bozey shot him a dark frown. "You mean the off-load crew ain't here?"

"You don't see 'em about, do you?"

Leaning back, Bozey folded his pudgy arms over his chest. "Does the captain know?"

"Ain't had a chance to tell 'im. He and that first mate of his have been gone since early this morning."

Bozey gave him a nod and then swung in the direction of the cargo bay. "Fine, be about it then. Infernal . . . slow as a late dinner," he muttered. At the hatch, he paused and jabbed his cap back from his forehead. "What about the other thing? The mess with the doctor. You seen to it yet?"

The muscles in Donal's midsection tensed. Aye, the deed was done, no thanks to Bozey. By asking around the harbor, Donal had managed to track down the name of a distant cousin who would be coming to collect the body, but not from here. Not from the *Caitriona Marie*. 'Twas bad luck to keep a dead man aboard a ship for so long. He stifled a chuckle. Even if the cause of death wasn't unknown as the crew assumed. Better to send the cousin to the morgue for his kinsman's remains and let him ask his questions there.

Donal tipped his cap in a feigned sign of respect. "All taken care of."

Bozey grunted and ducked belowdecks. With him out of

the way, Donal resumed his pace toward the dock. True, the harbor master was on his list of stops, but not first. First, he'd take a swing through the city and make his report to the real man in charge.

On a day like today, with the sun bright overhead and the weather balmy and warm, some men might have preferred the countryside. Not Donal. His veins hummed with excitement as he pushed through the throng crowding the wharf. With each creak of rope he felt more alive. Each whistle and barked order along the pier made him hungry for the lure of the sea.

But instead of heading for the row of ships and the open water glinting between flapping sails, he turned and veered down a busy cobbled street. Soon his strides lengthened, and before long the harbor lay far behind. Ahead squatted row upon row of run-down houses and grease-caked pubs. Donal navigated the twisting streets, cutting through their center until he reached a more reputable neighborhood, where he hailed a hack and then settled back for the ride.

In time, grime gave way to grace. Litter along the streets transformed into trimmed hedges and brightly painted fences.

'Tis a façade only, he reminded himself as the hired carriage rolled to a stop in front of one of the more lavish residences. The respectable pretense was a necessary evil to protect the man ensconced inside.

After climbing from the carriage, Donal paid the driver and hurried up the bricked path to a broad door painted green and fixed with a shiny brass knocker. He lifted the ring and dropped it thrice. The resulting bump echoed within, giving indication of the expansive hall on the other side. Before long a black-coated butler opened the door.

Eyeing Donal warily, he said, "May I help you, sir?"

The old fool was too well trained to show his disregard,

but his sharp tone said he'd already examined Donal from head to foot and found him lacking.

Hiding a sneer, Donal dragged the cap from his head and clutched it in both hands. "Good day to you, sir. My name's Donal Peevey. I'm here to see the master of the house."

The man's nose rose higher. "Is the master expecting you?"

"Not exactly." Donal frowned. "That is to say, not right at this moment." He then dropped his voice to a conspiratorial whisper. "He will, however, be glad of my arrival, if you ken my meaning."

The man's wrinkled lips puckered into a glower. "No, sir, I do not *ken* anything. Do you have an appointment or not?"

Donal squared his shoulders and jutted out his chin. "None needed. Tell your master I'm here and I've news to report." When the old goat refused to flinch, he added a sharp, "Now!"

Inclining his head, the man strode down the hall and disappeared through a set of molded pocket doors. He reappeared a short time later with a larger, more imposing figure in tow.

Donal turned to watch him approach. At first glance, The Celt was a kind-looking fellow, with broad shoulders and a full mustache. It was only after one had known him some time that one saw behind the twinkling eyes and jovial smile.

And Donal had known him some time now.

He swallowed reflexively and extended his hand.

Ignoring it, The Celt turned and dismissed the butler with a curt nod. "That'll be all, John." To Donal, he said, "In here."

He gestured toward a parlor off the main hall and strode inside to a sideboard where a crystal decanter filled with amber liquid waited. He lifted it toward Donal, who shook his head. He didn't want brandy. Not at this hour and not when he needed to keep his wits about him.

Shrugging, The Celt poured a drink from the decanter, then

gestured toward an ornate writing desk. Seating himself, he took a swallow and motioned Donal toward the chair opposite the desk. "I wasn't expecting you this early."

Donal hesitated. He'd learned to beware that polite tone. "Aye, sir, but I figured it best to move quickly."

The Celt's glass lowered to the desk with a soft click. "*You* figured it best?"

For a brief moment, fear squeezed Donal's chest. Had he been mistaken by acting with such haste?

The Celt leaned back in his chair and laced his long fingers over his midsection. "Suppose you tell me what you've been up to, Donal, me boy, and let *me* decide what's best."

Ire rose in Donal's throat. Hadn't he always done everything The Celt asked, even this last thing?

Clasping the edge of the desk, he pulled forward on the seat until he sat erect with both feet planted flat on the floor. The Celt watched but said nothing.

"The deed's done." Donal scanned the room and then lowered his voice. "You've no more cause to worry about the doctor. He won't be talking to anybody ever again."

The Celt's head tilted to one side, and his fingers plucked lightly at his mustache. "Really, Donal, did I seem worried to you?"

Again he found himself backtracking. "Well, no. That is . . . I just meant . . ."

The Celt laughed, and Donal flinched when the man rose from his chair and circled the desk to clap him on the shoulder. "Calm yourself, lad. You've done well, better than I could've asked. I'm pleased."

Why then did the hair on the back of Donal's neck rise up and his flesh crawl? Not for the first time he wondered if he'd been wrong to toss his allegiance in with this man.

The Celt then pulled something from his waistcoat pocket

and handed it across to Donal. The wad of bills was thicker than he'd expected. Curious, he lifted his eyes.

The Celt's smile broadened. "It's all there—the agreed upon price and then some. I think you'll find I'm most generous with those who do their job well."

Resisting the urge to lick his lips, Donal shoved the money into his pocket and stood. Now that their business was concluded, he couldn't wait to leave. "Me thanks to ya, sir. I'll be going now—"

The Celt's hand lifted, halting Donal at the door. "Before you go, there's another matter I'd like to discuss with you. If you have a moment?" He gestured back toward the chairs. Reluctantly, Donal joined him there.

"There's a good lad." The Celt braced both elbows on the table and leaned forward to peer at him intently. "Now, what can you tell me about Keondric Morgan?"

— ✳ ✳ ✳ —

For some time after the boardinghouse returned to stillness, Tillie sat watching Amelia, who watched from the window as the captain withdrew. At long last she pulled her hand from the drape, allowing it to fall back into place, and turned to inquire of Tillie.

"Well, we certainly never expected to see him again, did we?"

"No." She drew a deep breath and blew it out. "We certainly did not."

Grabbing her embroidery hoop, Amelia joined Tillie on the settee. "Did he say what brought him, dear?"

Tillie poured a cup of tea from the pot Laverne had provided and passed it across a flowered tray to Amelia. Though she had no reason to doubt him, something about Captain Morgan's impromptu visit troubled her. Realizing Amelia was watching her, she shrugged. "Just that he hoped to inquire after my welfare."

Amelia took the cup and lifted it to her lips for a sip. "Odd, that, after so many months, don't you think?"

Aye, 'twas very odd, to say the least. She turned toward the tea tray. Apart from the pot and a small bowl of sliced lemons, the tray was empty. She stood. "It appears Laverne forgot to add the sugar bowl. I'll fetch it."

Amelia's cup rattled against its saucer. "Don't bother."

Startled by her haste, Tillie paused.

"It's just . . ." She laughed and patted her slender waist, but her cheeks colored and not with mirth. "You don't take sugar in your tea, and I could stand to lose a few pounds."

Tillie retook her seat.

Setting her cup aside, Amelia reached for her embroidery hoop and pulled the needle free of the fabric. "I thought the captain very striking, didn't you?"

She laughed again, but this time it was high-pitched and unnatural, and Tillie had no doubt it was meant to distract her attention from the tea. She leaned forward. "Amelia—"

"I remembered him as being handsome, but today, well, I can't say as I recall him looking quite so distinguished. The past two years have been kind."

"'Tis not only kindness what adds silver to a man's sideburns or lines to his face," she said quietly.

The flashing of Amelia's needle slowed, and her eyes met Tillie's over the hoop. "Yes, I suppose that's true enough."

Pushing the captain from her thoughts, Tillie focused on the friend seated across from her. Amelia looked tired, and strain marred her normally peaceful features. Why hadn't she noticed before? She reached out to clasp Amelia's hand, stilling her fingers.

"Is everything all right? Are you well?"

Though she smiled, her fingers trembled. "Of course. Why do you ask?"

Tillie thought back over the last week. "I thought I heard you stirring last night, after everyone else went to bed."

"Oh, that." She gave a shrug that was surely meant to appease, but to Tillie, it appeared feigned. "Just my old joints giving me trouble, what with all the rain we've been having."

Tillie had not noticed an inordinate amount of rain, but she let the comment pass. "I'll speak to Dr. Kingsley. Perhaps he could prescribe some liver salts."

Amelia tugged her hand free. "No need, dear. It's probably nothing more than a bit of the rheumy. One of Laverne's lemon toddies will fix me right up." She chuckled softly. "All these years and I still can't coax her into telling me what she puts in them."

"I'll make sure she has plenty of fresh lemons, then."

"Thank you, dear."

Amelia went back to her stitching, but the way her lip quivered made Tillie think she had more she wanted to say. She took another sip of her tea and waited.

Finally, she cleared her throat. "Tillie, Laverne and I have been talking. Do you realize winter will be upon us in just a few short months?"

"Aye, and it'll likely be a long one if the predictions in the almanac hold true."

Amelia's needle slowed. "Exactly, which is why we were thinking . . . perhaps the priest at Our Lady of Deliverance—"

"Father Ed?"

Amelia nodded. "Perhaps Father Ed and a few of the other local ministers would be interested in purchasing extra vegetables for their stores. Maybe even a few canned goods."

Tillie hesitated, her suspicion growing. "I didn't realize we had goods to spare. Doesn't the garden normally supply just what Laverne needs to run the boardinghouse?"

"True," Amelia said, averting her gaze, "but you know we haven't had as many residents since Ana and Cara left, not to mention Breda and . . ." Her voice lowered. "Well, Deidre."

Tillie shivered as she recalled the mystery that had hung over the boardinghouse last season. Since then, both of her friends had been forced into hiding and Breda had moved, which meant that of the six rooms Amelia let out for rent, only two were filled. She held in a sigh. Perhaps soon it would be safe enough for her friends to return. She hoped so. She had much to tell them. In the meantime . . .

Her stomach sank as the realization of Amelia's situation struck. "I planned to go by the church this afternoon," she said. "I can make inquiries then."

"That would be grand. Thank you." Smiling, she resumed her stitchwork.

Tillie bit her lip, thinking. "Perhaps I can see about drumming up boarders, too. There are plenty of able-bodied women at the shelter, many of whom would be glad of a situation such as this, only . . ." She paused. The women at the shelter faced the same problem as Amelia. "Most have had a difficult time securing employment in these hard times. What jobs there are to be had are filled by men."

Amelia's mouth turned in a scowl. "And after all that natter during the presidential election of tariffs boosting our country's industry. I'd have thought by now they'd have taken effect."

Hoping to ease the frustration in Amelia's voice, Tillie smiled. "There now, it is only July. President McKinley has barely had time to settle into his office. Things will get better, for sure and for certain."

But would they? Even as she spoke, worry brewed in her

stomach. McKinley's campaign promises might hold true, but perhaps not in time to help Amelia, and not if she lost another boarder.

For the first time, Tillie considered what her plan of opening an orphanage and moving out of the boardinghouse would do to her friend. It left her anxious and unsettled as she collected her bonnet and gloves and set out for the church. The feelings intensified when she passed the land office with an advertisement for a six-roomed farmhouse taped to the window.

She looked away. For now, she'd forget about the orphanage and focus on helping Amelia. That meant talking to Father Ed and the women at the shelter. But only briefly, she told herself. Only until she'd found a way to help Amelia.

Even with her mind made up, a niggle of disappointment tightened her throat. Ignoring the sentiment, she lifted her chin and quickened her pace. Before long, she'd left the land office with its window advertisement far behind.

5

A briny wind lifted the tips of Morgan's hair and whipped it into his face, stinging his eyes. He raked it away with an impatient tug of his fingers. Blast the length! He was determined to have it trimmed by the end of the day, even if he had to whet a knife and cut it himself.

Reaching up toward the gunwale, he closed his fist around a length of rope and swung himself onto the deck of the *Caitriona Marie*, ignoring the ladder slapping against the bulwark. The resulting thump of his boots against timber bolstered him, reminding him that solid footing wasn't only found on land.

Belowdecks, the cries of his crew echoed from the bay. He turned that way and then halted midstride. Donal hurried along the dock from the direction of town. The morgue perhaps? Morgan shoved closer to the ship's rail. With any luck he'd been able to wrap up the details of Doc's burial.

"Well?" he asked when Donal scrambled aboard. "What news?"

For a split second a glimmer of distress widened Donal's eyes and creased his forehead. But then he stood up straight, his feet braced apart, his lips parted in a wide grin, and Morgan wondered if he'd imagined it.

"The deed's done, just like you ordered, Captain." He jerked his thumb over his shoulder toward the rail. "Just come from the morgue. They'll be sending someone to collect the remains." He shuddered and ripped the cap from his head and jammed it into his pocket. "Foul place. Wouldn't want to be going there again anytime soon."

Morgan pulled a watch from his jacket pocket and flipped open the lid. Five o'clock. Plenty of time for Donal to have accomplished his task. "You were able to find kin, then?"

"Aye, sir," Donal said. "Went by the harbor master and asked a few questions first. That's how I come by the name of Doc's cousin." He lifted his chin, almost defensively. "Weren't easy, though. Took me quite a while to track him down."

Morgan took his time returning the watch to his pocket. Donal fumbled with his shirt, where beads of sweat rolled from his cheek and neck to dampen his collar. Now, what reason could he have for appearing so nervous?

"If, uh, if you'll not be needing me, sir—" he cleared his throat and pointed over his shoulder at Cass, who was emerging from the cargo bay—"I'd best see to helping the crew."

And since when had Donal ever been anxious to attend to his duties? He was capable, all right, and he did what he was told quick enough, but he'd never been one to hasten to his responsibilities. No, it was Morgan's own presence he was anxious to be shed of, that much was clear.

Morgan searched Donal's face for clues. Finding none, he shrugged and waved him off. "Be about it, then, and see to it you tend belowdecks. I want the *Marie* fit and scrubbed before nightfall."

"Aye, sir." With a nod and a scurry, Donal disappeared belowdecks.

"Hello, Morgan!" Cass's voice boomed from midship. In his hand he carried a stack of logbooks. He thrust his chin in the direction Donal had taken. "What was all that about?"

Morgan frowned and took the books Cass shoved at him and tucked them under one arm. "Not sure yet. I don't like it, though. He was nervous as a scalded cat and twice as ugly."

"I could say the same about you." Cass snorted through his nose and crossed both arms over his chest. "Where were you all afternoon? I 'bout got all the log sheets finished and balanced."

"You *could* say it," Morgan said, responding to the first part of Cass's sentence and ignoring the rest, "but then I'd have to wallop you." Fighting a grin, he sauntered down the deck toward his quarters.

Cass loped at his heels. "Are you forgetting the last time you and I fought? I nearly bested you then. You're older and slower now."

"You forgot wiser." Morgan shot his boot out and nudged a crate into Cass's path, causing him to stumble and nearly fall trying to avoid it.

"Mugger!" Cass cried.

"Toad!" Morgan retorted, ducking into his cabin but leaving the door ajar.

Cass followed him inside, his mirth fading as he eyed Morgan across the crowded berth. Morgan took his time stripping off his coat and hanging it on a hook fastened to the wall. Under his feet, the ship rocked gently on the waves of the harbor, a far cry from the rolling, pitching troughs they'd forged crossing over from Liverpool, but still not the *terra firma* for which his legs, and soul, longed.

"Well?" Cass folded his lanky length into an overstuffed chair Morgan had given to their father as a joke. "Did you find her?"

He dropped onto the hard edge of his bunk, the troubling conversation with Miss McGrath replaying in his head. "Aye. I found her."

"And?"

He offered a one-shouldered shrug.

"Morgan—"

"How long before we finish the off-load?"

Cass blinked and pushed up in the chair. "A day, I guess. Maybe two. Why?"

"And then?"

"We'll refresh our supplies and see to any needed repairs."

Morgan did a quick calculation in his head. "So, a week or more before we're ready to set sail?"

"I suppose so."

He stood and crossed to a teak cabinet, where he removed a metal mug. He filled it with water from the pitcher on the sideboard. The tepid drink hardly refreshed, but it did give him time to clear his thinking. Turning back to Cass, he said, "Get with Bozey. Have him go over the inventory with you and order any supplies you think we'll need."

Cass lifted an eyebrow. "Isn't that normally your job?"

Morgan shot him a scowl. Aye, it was his job, and under normal circumstances, heaven help Cass or any other mate who dared tread anywhere near the inventory. But these were far from normal circumstances. He set down the heavy mug with a thud. "Haven't you been hankering for a taste of running the ship? Well, I'm going to need you to oversee a few things while I finish up in town—unless you're not sure you can handle it, in which case I can always get Bozey—"

Cass rose to the bait as eagerly as a trout to a worm. "I can handle it."

Aye, he could. Morgan felt a niggle of surprise at the realization. It was quickly replaced by another rush of gratitude at having his brother on board. He reached over and clapped Cass's shoulder. "I knew I could count on you."

A corner of his mouth dipped in a frown. "Did you?"

"I do now."

Giving a snort, he shrugged from Morgan's grasp and veered for the hatch. Before he reached it, Morgan called him back and motioned toward his desk. "Cass, a moment more, if you dinna mind."

He purposely added the last. As ship's captain, he could order that Cass remain, but this was a conversation he'd been meaning to have with him as his kin.

Cass returned to sit at the desk, his fingers steepled and resting against his lips. "I've seen that look before. You and Da always did wear your worries on your face. Is it that bad?"

Morgan slid into the chair opposite his brother. "Actually, 'tis a good thing."

Cass merely grunted.

"It's the bottomry," Morgan continued. "I know you were opposed to it."

Cass sat up quickly. "Only because Da would never have approved using the ship as collateral to finance this trip. Not because I didn't trust your judgment."

He acknowledged this with a nod. "I didn't have much choice, finances being what they were."

"Is that what has you so troubled?"

"No, it's not—"

Cass jerked to his feet and began pacing. "I have some money stashed away. It's not much, but it will help until we can—"

Morgan held up his hand. "Cass!"

He drew to a halt, his brow furrowed.

"It's not that," Morgan said. "The cargo should fetch a handsome price, plenty to pay off the bottomry and then some."

Cass returned to his chair. "Then why the worry, Morgan?"

"Because I have a request, and as my brother—" he paused and looked Cass in the eye—"and my partner, you should have a say in it."

He explained the details of his visit with Tillie, and his offer to provide her with passage back to Ireland. "I should have spoken to you about it first," he said, "but at the time, I thought it better to keep you from getting involved."

"And now?" Cass lifted an eyebrow. "Why bother sharing it with me if she's already told you she wants to stay?"

Heat crept up Morgan's neck into his cheeks.

Cass drew back in his chair. "I see. You still want to help her."

"I owe it to her, Cass. It's my fault she's even in this mess."

"So, now it's our fault? What happened to it being Doc's fault?"

Though Cass's use of the plural gratified him, Morgan frowned.

"Right," Cass said, a trifle apologetically. "You're the captain. *Everything* that happens aboard this ship is your fault."

"That's how it must be. Our passengers and crew have entrusted themselves to me. Their lives depend on the decisions I make."

Even as Morgan spoke the words, the weight of his responsibility bore down on his shoulders. He took a deep breath and squared his chin. "Which is why I think we should use some of the profit from this trip to help Miss McGrath. She told me today she intends to stay in New York and volunteer in some kind of church shelter. Surely we can help her cause."

Skepticism creased Cass's face. "From what you've told me so far, this woman doesn't seem the type to accept charity. What makes you think she'll allow your help?"

Morgan scratched his head. The same thought had occurred to him. "I'll have to find a way to give her the money without her seeing it as a gift."

Cass's eyes narrowed as he peered at Morgan across the desk. "Exactly how much are we talking?"

He shrugged. "I won't know until after the final tally. But don't bother yourself about the money." He rose and circled the desk. "I'll take it out of my share, no one else's. You and the crew—"

It was Cass's turn to raise his hand. "You know I wouldn't have that. I've known you my whole life. I understand about your taking responsibility for the crew. That's what you do, what you've always done."

By the look in his eyes, Morgan knew he was referring to their father's death and his subsequent care of the family.

"What I don't understand," Cass continued, "is why this girl? You barely know her."

Turning from his brother's questioning stare, Morgan directed his attention to the scuttles. "I explained that, Cass."

"No, you explained why you felt obligated to visit her in the first place. What I want to know is why you keep wanting to help her even after she turned your offer down." He came around to stand at Morgan's shoulder. "'Tis more than just that you feel responsible for what happened to her, big brother, whether you care to admit it or not."

Though he opened his mouth, the answer he readied failed to come. Instead he kept his back to Cass and shook his head. A moment later, the hatch groaned as Cass stepped through and shut it behind him, leaving Morgan to wonder what his brother knew, and what he himself refused to recognize.

6

"Careful!" Sister Agnes hurried across the kitchen and rescued the pot of cooked carrots from Tillie's limp fingers. "That there pot is heavy. Wouldn't want you scalding yourself." She slanted her a questioning look. "You all right?"

Tillie rubbed the crook of her fingers. Truthfully, she didn't know. Since Captain Morgan's visit that morning, her thoughts had been scattered, plagued by memories she'd believed long forgotten.

"I'm sorry, Sister. Just a little tired from working all day, I guess," she muttered. By way of apology she grabbed the bowl of freshly churned butter and began spreading a thin layer over a tray of steaming biscuits. Not even these tempted her, despite the fact that she'd skipped lunch.

"And no wonder." The nun snorted and set the pot of carrots down with a thump. "This makes the fifth time this week you've been by to help with supper. And that after your regular duties at the milliner." She dipped her head to peer at Tillie from under her wimple. "Not that we don't need the help, mind you."

Tillie eyed the massive bowl of potatoes yet to be mashed and simmering water waiting to be made into gravy. Aye, they needed the help, which was exactly why she made the effort to come day after day. Guilt nudged her heart. Well, perhaps that wasn't the only reason.

Finished with the biscuits, she set them aside and began carving a ham into thin, even slices. "How is Father Ed coming with the plans for the parsonage? Has he found anyone to do the work?"

No doubt, the wily nun wasn't fooled by the change of topic, but today at least, Sister Agnes was inclined to play along. While she spooned the carrots into a large bowl, she clucked her tongue and gave a sad shake of her head.

"There's another thing what could use a bit of prayer. We sure do miss Eoghan and his skill with a hammer."

The door from the washroom flew open, and the much younger—though still advanced in years—Sister Mary barged through, balancing a basket stuffed with linens. Lye assaulted Tillie's nose.

"What's this?" Sister Mary demanded. "Who misses Eoghan? What are we talking about?"

Tillie winced. While the nuns were privy to the truth behind his disappearance along with Ana and Cara, Sister Mary did sometimes forget herself and say more than she ought—even in the relative safety of the church.

Sister Agnes shot Sister Mary a withering glare. "Hush now. Mind your tongue."

Tillie rounded the table and patted Sister Agnes's arm. "We were just saying 'twould be nice for Father Ed to have someone he could depend on helping him with the plans for the new parsonage."

Sister Agnes's scowl lessened slightly. She raised the spoon and waved it at Sister Mary, paying no heed to the carrots that plopped on the table and floor. "Whatever made that man think he could take on such a task is beyond me. In fact"—she dropped the spoon and crossed herself—"the man's stubbornness is enough to drive me to confession."

Sister Mary snorted. Shuffling to the closet, she deposited the linens, then went to stand next to Sister Agnes. "And I'd have to join ya there."

With their heads together and both of them cackling, the two resembled a pair of giant blackbirds. Tillie dipped her head to hide a smile.

Sister Mary ambled to the pantry and took down a jar of pickled beets to add to the supper. Seeing them reminded Tillie of Amelia's predicament and her promise of help. She grabbed a bowl and carried it to Sister Mary. "Will this hold them?"

"Aye, that'll do the trick." Sister Mary opened the jar, releasing a fragrant cloud of pickling and spices. Closing her eyes, she took a deep whiff. "Ach, but the smell of these beets fairly makes me mouth water. They'll go well with our ham."

"We were running low, last time I checked," Tillie said.

"We'll have fresh soon enough," Sister Agnes said. "The harvest will be here before we know it."

Tillie nodded. "True, but in the meantime, if you're needing anything for the pantry, would you mind letting me know? Amelia has a few things she'd like to sell."

Sister Mary's eyebrows disappeared into her wimple. "From Laverne's kitchen? Aye, we'll let you know. No offense, Agnes."

Sister Agnes scowled in her direction. "Right. I'll remind you of that the next time you're stuffing yourself with me biscuits." She turned to Tillie. "What's Amelia doing selling canned goods? Everything all right at the boardinghouse?"

Tillie shrugged, her thoughts troubled. "Aye, far as I can tell. I know she could use a couple of boarders. It's not good for a boardinghouse to have empty rooms."

"True enough." She motioned toward Sister Mary. "We'll ask around the church."

"Thank you, Sisters." Tillie went back to the table, picked up the knife, and resumed carving the ham.

The nuns' banter continued for some time, but with her thoughts preoccupied elsewhere, Tillie paid them little heed. Gradually, however, the conversation quieted and a floorboard creaked behind her.

Sister Mary broke the silence with "What's up with her? She feeling all right?"

Sister Agnes's spoon stopped dragging across the bottom of the pot she was stirring. "Well, she has been a touch distracted most of the afternoon."

"Did she say why?"

"Wouldn't I say so if she did?"

Tillie looked up at them.

"You all right, lass?" Sister Mary asked.

Both nuns peered at her, worry drawing their brows into identical peaks.

She started to nod, then stopped and shook her head. No longer able to contain her unhappiness, she put down her knife. "May I ask you something?"

Their heads dipped in unison, and then Sister Agnes circled the table, clasped Tillie's hands, and drew her to a stool near the counter. "Ask anything you'd like."

Embarrassed, Tillie swallowed a lump that rose in her throat. "Well . . . uh, neither of you ever married, ain't that so?"

They glanced at each other and shook their heads.

"But if you had, if you'd married and then decided you wanted to become a nun . . . could you have still done it? I mean, would that have been allowed?"

"Ain't no rule against it." Sister Mary gave a puzzled frown,

49

then shot a questioning glance at Sister Agnes, who tightened her grasp on Tillie's fingers. "Why are you asking, dearie?"

Her gaze bounced back and forth between the two sisters. "Oh no, it's not . . . I mean, I'm not—"

"Not thinking of making your vows anytime soon?" Sister Mary gave a bark of laughter and smacked Sister Agnes on the arm. "Relax, Agnes. No novices here."

"As if you weren't assuming the same thing," Sister Agnes retorted, though it appeared a bit of the hopeful gleam in her eyes had faded. She released Tillie's hands and claimed a stool next to her. "So, if it's not the order you be thinking of . . ." She trailed into questioning silence.

Tillie's shoulders drooped. Now what? She'd unwittingly dashed their hopes, and her real question still lingered unasked on her tongue. Her thoughts went immediately to Braedon and the fact that they'd never married. "What I really meant to ask . . . uh, I guess what I want to know is, if God wasn't your first choice, and you didn't . . . well, how much is He willing to forgive?" She blurted the last, sensing rather than seeing the two nuns exchange a glance.

Sister Agnes's voice lowered to a soft murmur. "Something in particular you'd like to talk about?"

Tillie fidgeted uncomfortably on the stool. Much as she loved these two women, she'd never found the courage to tell them about Braedon or the child she'd conceived out of wedlock. Fear snaked up from her belly. What if they felt differently about her once they learned the truth?

Sister Agnes's chin jutted slightly while Sister Mary retrieved her basket. "I'd best be about my chores."

The door closed behind her with a quiet click. Though Tillie hadn't expected her to go, she was grateful. Her shame was easier to bear with only one nun present.

"Why don't you tell me about it?" Sister Agnes said.

Compassion shone from her face, but instead of taking comfort in it, it brought tears to Tillie's eyes.

"We had a visitor today, at the boardinghouse. Someone I met a long time ago, before ever coming here."

"And his presence stirred up painful memories for you?"

Her thoughts winged to Braedon again, to her parents' refusal of him, and the desperation that had driven them to flee in order to be together. She sighed. "I've made some poor decisions in my life, Sister. They've affected more than just me." Pain stabbed her heart as she thought of her child.

"Bad decisions usually do, despite what we tell ourselves when we make them."

"But . . . when it comes time for punishment for our sins, surely it's only the person who's done wrong who's expected to pay?"

Sister Agnes smiled. "Not even them, if they've accepted the Savior."

Confusion muddied her thinking. She'd done wrong, that much she'd accepted. To think she'd not be expected to suffer was too much to hope for. She grasped her guilt and held tight.

"But," she continued stubbornly, "if we accept our penance and carry it out without complaint, God is satisfied, aye? His law is met and no one else . . . no one . . ."

Sister Agnes's gnarled hands closed around Tillie's and squeezed. "Is that why you're always about, working dawn till dusk, day after day? Lass, what is it you've done to think you deserve such a penance?"

Tillie licked her dry lips. Maybe she could still enjoy their acceptance if she told her some things . . . about Braedon. But not the baby. Not her child.

"I left home and disobeyed my parents to be with a man."

"You loved him?"

"Aye."

"And they objected?"

"He was a Fenian. They were afraid for me, especially when so many of them were imprisoned or executed for trying to free their comrades."

Sister Agnes's mouth firmed into a thin line. "Is that why you left Ireland?"

Tillie nodded. "Braedon thought we could come here, possibly help organize the efforts in America."

"And you?"

She bit her lip against a rush of pain. "I just wanted to be with Braedon."

To her relief, no judgment welled in Sister Agnes's eyes. Only tears. "But without your parents' blessing."

And without vows. Though she left it unspoken, Tillie knew she understood. She lowered her head in shame.

Sister Agnes rose, fetched a towel, and held it to her nose, then offered the other corner to Tillie, who took it with a sniff.

"Child, I'm going to tell you something that I hope you will accept as coming from someone with a wee bit more experience."

Seeing the twinkle in her eyes, Tillie smiled. "All right."

Her lined face softened, and her voice, like a balm, soothed Tillie's spirit.

"Sometimes, talking about our sins makes them easier to bear. Have you considered making your confession? It may be the penance Father Ed prescribes is much less wearisome than the one you've laid upon yourself."

Tillie shuddered inwardly. She didn't want a less wearisome penance. Sister Agnes only thought so because she hadn't told her everything. If she had . . .

No. Braedon's death, and that of her baby, were her punishment, and no penance, no matter how severe, would ever be enough. Wasn't Captain Morgan's reappearance proof of that? What other reason could there be for his coming except that God wanted to remind her of her guilt?

Thinking of the brief happiness she'd enjoyed while imagining herself buying the orphanage brought a wave of fresh shame. The orphanage was just one more way of repaying God for what she'd done. It was not meant to make her happy, for that was an emotion she'd never be blessed with again.

Ever.

7

Pushed by a light breeze, the *Caitriona Marie* bobbed gently on the waves in the harbor. Outside the ship, sea gulls called to one another. Their voices, normally a cacophony, were today a pleasant symphony. It might have been enough to coax Morgan to slumber, if his thoughts hadn't left him in such a muddle.

Abandoning his bunk, he set off belowdecks in search of Cass and found him in a spirited debate with one of the other crewmen over a game of cards. At his appearance, the men around the table straightened, and all but one quieted—his brother.

"Admit it, Fisher. You're too thick for this game, and for me."

Fisher shoved back from the table, his sinewy arms flexing. "Why, you—"

"Cass, a minute if you don't mind."

One glimpse of Morgan's face and the twinkle disappeared from Cass's eyes. He tossed his cards to the table and rose, his chair scraping the deck. "Donovan, you're in. Mind you don't lose all my winnings." He turned and wagged his finger in the face of the unhappy crewman with whom he'd been arguing. "That's two weeks' worth of dishes you owe me now, Fisher."

Fisher nodded. "All right, all right. Go on with ya now." Picking up his cards, he looked around at the men still seated at the table. "Where were we?"

Play resumed as Morgan and Cass made their way to the galley. Though Morgan didn't allow the men to gamble their wages, they were permitted to ante their chores, so long as the work aboard ship didn't suffer.

Clear of the hallway's narrow passage, Cass swung alongside Morgan and raked the hair off his forehead. "You look troubled, big brother. What ails you?"

Morgan held up the scorched remains of their morning coffee. Cass shook his head. Just as well. The brew had been sitting on hot coals since dawn and likely was as thick as tar. He poured himself a cup anyway and took a hasty swallow.

Cass frowned. "Things that bad?"

"Maybe not," Morgan replied. "I made a decision."

"About the girl?"

"Yes, the girl."

"And?"

"I'm going back to speak to her today."

"I see." Pulling up a crate, Cass took a seat. "Have you thought about what you're going to say to her?"

Indeed, he'd thought of little else. Wound too tight to sit, Morgan paced the length of the galley, the mug in hand. "I think you're right, Cass. She doesn't seem the type to accept charity. That being the case, I think my best bet will be to express an interest in the shelter she spoke of."

Cass cocked his head.

"She'll have a much harder time declining financial help if she thinks I'm making a donation."

"Like an investor of some sort?"

"Aye, like that."

"Well, before you go transforming into a philanthropist . . ."
Morgan turned to look at him. A frown marred Cass's brow,
and he gave an almost apologetic shrug. "You remember those
repairs we made before we left Dublin?"

"The bilge?"

"Aye. Well, there's water coming in through the hull. Even
with the repairs, 'tis more than the pump can handle. I'm
thinking it's going to need a closer look."

Which meant more repairs, more time in port, and more
overall outlay. He drained his mug, then scowled at the bitter
aftertaste. "We'll make it work somehow, even if I need to
wire Dublin for a little extra cash."

Cass narrowed his eyes. "From your own private funds,
you mean."

He shoved his sleeves to his elbows and said nothing.

"Morgan—"

"It's all part of running a shipping business, Cass. Repairs
and overhead come with the job."

"And donations to women you barely know? Where does
that figure in?"

Stifling a grunt of frustration, Morgan turned his back.
"I explained all of that to you."

"Not quite. You explained what happened, but you left out
the part about how anything Doc did makes you eternally
obligated."

Morgan faced his brother again, arms crossed. "Don't be
ridiculous. I'm talking about a one time offer, something to
help her get on her feet. And then I'm done."

"Really? Are you certain about that? Because even after all
this time she still seems to have a pretty firm hold on you."

He leaned back on the crate, balancing on one edge. The
slightest push would have sent him crashing to the deck,

which was something Morgan was wont to do when next Cass opened his mouth.

"You gonna tell me what it is about this lass that has you so jiggered, Cap?"

"Watch your mouth."

The crate thumped to the deck. "She's a bonnie thing, is that it? Eyes the color of a cornflower and all that?"

Just the opposite. Tillie McGrath's eyes were brown with bits of gold shimmering in their depths—especially when they were awash with tears.

Cass rose and sauntered around the table. "And I suppose she has waves of russet hair that hints of lavender when stirred by a breeze."

Unwilling to be provoked by his brother's blarney, Morgan bit his tongue and watched him approach. "You got the color right, but I have no idea what her hair smells like, nor do I care to know."

Cass snorted. "Ah, brother, 'tis the jewel that can't be got that is the most beautiful. Isn't that what you're always telling me?"

"And the man without eyes is no judge of beauty—that's usually how you respond."

Cass chuckled. "Fine. If it isn't her looks, then what?"

The two stared at each other in the uneasy silence that followed, and then Cass sobered and went to stand at arm's length from Morgan. "You're thinking to tell her the truth about how her husband died, is that it? Is that why you're so set on returning to the boardinghouse?"

It wasn't often his little brother could make him uncomfortable, yet Morgan found himself fidgeting beneath his stare. By all rights he should have already told him what he'd learned about Tillie McGrath's "husband," and yet . . .

"I haven't decided yet. Telling her the truth could be dangerous."

"Why?"

"Because whoever killed him, whoever ordered him killed," he corrected, "isn't a dullard. If the truth were to leak out, if anyone were to find out that I broke quarantine and brought her in to see him before he died, that she spoke to him and that he—"

A creak from the hallway cut his words short. He shot a glance at Cass, whose eyes had gone as wide as portholes at the sound. Morgan looked down at the floor. A shadow drifted in the crack between the bottom of the door and the deck, but the owner made no move to knock.

A murderer and now a spy? Never before had he felt so threatened aboard his own ship. Putting a finger to his lips, he rounded the table.

"Well, I still say you're worrying about breaking your shin on a stool that isn't in your way, big brother."

Though he continued talking as casually as before, Cass picked up the crate and crouched into position opposite Morgan. "After all . . ."

He nodded once, and Morgan held up one finger.

". . . it's not like we'd ever be able to prove . . ."

Two fingers.

". . . who Doc was working with . . ."

Three!

Morgan flung open the door, a growl ripping from his throat. The sound, combined with the sight of Cass wielding the crate, was enough to startle the eavesdropper into ducking, his hands curled defensively over his head.

"Whoa! 'Tis me, Captain. 'Tis Donal."

"Donal." Cass lowered the crate. "By thunder, what are you doing out here?"

Reaching around him, Morgan grabbed Donal by the collar and dragged him into the galley, then slammed him flat against the wall. "Eavesdropping, Donal? Why? What were you hoping to hear?"

"Eavesdropping?" A deep flush crept over Donal's cheeks. "No, sir. You got that wrong—"

Morgan bunched both fists around Donal's collar and lifted until his feet skimmed the deck. "Were you skulking outside this door or not?"

"Morgan—"

"Aye . . . I mean, no, sir. Not skulking." Donal sputtered and clawed at Morgan's fingers.

"Morgan!" Cass grabbed Morgan's fist and squeezed until he tore his gaze from Donal to look at him. "Hear him out."

Reluctantly, he loosened his grip. Donal's face slowly returned to normal color, but anger burned in his eyes. "I was looking for *you*, Captain. The lads said I could find you here."

"Looking for me, why?"

"The undertaker's come to collect Doc's body. Said they'd charge us to keep him iced until the family came, but that it wouldn't be more'n a day or two." He rubbed the scarlet marks on his neck. "I figured you'd want to know."

Deep down he sensed that wasn't the only reason Donal had been looking for him. He didn't trust the man, didn't like the way his seedy eyes darted over every part and parcel of the ship. But he was a solid crewman, and he came with good references, so unless he had reason to dismiss him . . .

Disgusted, Morgan waved him toward the door. "See to it, then. Have the charges made out in my name and bring the bill to me."

"Aye, Captain."

"And, Donal?"

"Sir?"

"I catch you lurking about unannounced again, I'll have you put off this ship. Understood?"

Donal squared his jaw and gave a curt nod before striding from the galley.

When he'd gone, Cass exhaled and rubbed his palm over his chin. "What do you suppose that was about?"

Morgan rolled his shoulders, releasing a bit of the tension that bunched the muscles along his neck and back. "I don't know. Could be I'm wrong."

"But you don't think so."

He eyed his brother, so much like their mother in temperament and disposition. It was fortunate Cass had been present to calm an otherwise volatile situation. Who knew what he might have done otherwise. He shook his head. "No, I don't. One thing's for certain, however."

"And that is?"

"From now on, I think we'd best watch our backs."

"Aye," Cass said.

Morgan motioned toward the exit and the direction Donal had taken. "And be verra careful about what you say."

8

Rage roiled up from Donal's belly as he stepped from the dock onto the street. Oh, but he'd have liked to cut the smugness from the captain's face as he'd threatened to toss him from the ship.

He'd not attempt it in broad daylight, though. He rubbed his fingers along his neck where his flesh still tingled. No, he'd felt the strength in the captain's hands for himself, sensed the power there. He'd not stand a chance man to man. But under cover of darkness? Well, that would prove a different story. The thought sparked a smile.

"Will you be riding along or what?"

The man from the morgue peered down at Donal from his perch on the wagon seat. He was tall and thin, just like an undertaker should be, but he walked with a swagger and spoke with a distinct accent that scraped Donal's already raw nerves.

He glanced at the stark wagon carrying Doc's wrapped body. On its side were painted the words *Steven R. Ramsey, Sexton and Undertaker*. He scowled. The last thing he wanted was to be a fellow passenger in *that*.

A bark of laughter from the undertaker cut into his thoughts. "He's dead, you know. Not like he's going to sit up and ask for a cup of tea." He gathered the reins and gave a tilt of his head toward the vacant seat next to him. "Well?"

"I'm coming."

Bracing his foot on the hub, he swung into the wagon. He grabbed hold of the side when the undertaker gave a chirp and set the vehicle in motion before he was fully seated.

"Easy!"

"Sorry." The man lifted his chin and eyed him from beneath the brim of his tall hat. "Name's Ramsey."

"Donal Peevey."

"Just got into port?"

He grunted.

Ramsey loosened his grip on the reins and settled against the seat. "Figured so. We don't usually get asked to collect bodies from ships like that."

"I wouldn't have asked this time. 'Twas the captain's idea to go looking for the lad's family." He turned a narrowed stare toward the undertaker. "Would have suited me to dump him in a pauper's grave and be done."

Clearing his throat, Ramsey focused on the road ahead. 'Twasn't long before Donal noticed that carriages and pedestrians naturally moved aside for them. Those that didn't, Ramsey gave a sharp whistle to. He peered down his nose at them when, startled, they gaped at the words painted on the side of the wagon.

Donal realized then what it was he didn't like about the man. 'Twas the same arrogant stare that he'd scuttled from as a poor lad when a lord's or lady's coach went rumbling by.

Fortunately the wagon clattered to a halt a short time later in front of a plain brick building with ivy growing over its walls. Waiting near the walk was a low wooden gurney. Donal jumped from the wagon and reluctantly helped Ramsey wheel the body through a black door.

"Through here." Ramsey pointed down a wide corridor toward a room that opened off the end.

Inside was a long, narrow table. In one corner sat a row of wide lockers stacked one atop the other. Ramsey flipped the latch on one. The door, about three feet wide by three feet tall, swung open with a rusty groan. Donal pinched his nose at the odor that followed.

"In here."

The confines weren't much bigger than a coffin, Donal realized with a start. A very chilly coffin when packed with ice to keep a body from decay. Or . . .

His mind whirled with the possibilities as he watched Ramsey finish the task and then slam the locker door shut with a bang. He motioned toward the locker. "How long can a body keep in one of those?"

Ramsey shrugged. "Depends. Gotta keep the ice fresh and all that, but otherwise they're pretty airtight."

Donal knew right then what he'd do with the information he'd overheard between Captain Morgan and his brother.

He fidgeted from foot to foot while Ramsey made out the writ and signed the bottom with a flourish. Jamming the paper into his pocket, Donal spun and left the morgue, a new determination in his footsteps.

For sure and for certain, 'twould be of interest to The Celt to learn that someone besides Doc had sat with Braedon McKillop when he died. He might even care enough to pay Donal to take care of the problem for him.

Aye, and he'd name his price for the service. Cash, that's what. Lots of it. And the *Caitriona Marie*. Then they'd see who put whom off the ship.

And the woman? She was naught but the key to wealth

for him. He could ill afford to see her as anything more. He would show pity, however. He'd make sure she was actually dead before he laid her in the locker next to Doc.

— ❈ ❈ ❈ —

Tillie put the finishing touches on a bonnet made of more ribbons than satin and held it up for examination. Across a wide table used for cutting and measuring fabric, Mrs. Wilford Darby narrowed her eyes as she scrutinized the final flower Tillie had crafted and fastened to the brim.

"You made this?"

"Aye, ma'am."

"From a pattern?"

"No, ma'am, from memory. I saw one like it recently, in an advertisement for *Harper's Bazaar.*"

"I didn't realize this establishment followed *Harper's Bazaar.*"

"No, ma'am. Mrs. Van Rensselaer saw my interest and gave me a copy."

Mrs. Darby's thin brows rose, and tiny lines formed around her lips. A moment later, she beckoned to the millinery shop owner, Mrs. Ferguson. "Box this for me."

As the woman hastened after her bidding, she turned to Tillie. "And from now on I'd prefer it if you saw to my orders personally."

Sensing her employer's eyes upon her, Tillie caught her lip in her teeth.

"Will that be a problem?"

Mrs. Ferguson hurried back, a large hatbox clutched to her chest. "Not at all, Mrs. Darby. Tillie will be happy to see to your requests. Isn't that right, my dear?"

Tillie swallowed and ducked her head. "Of course, ma'am."

"Good. Thank you, Mrs. Ferguson." Mrs. Darby motioned

to her footman, who accepted the box from Mrs. Ferguson and carried it back to her carriage. "I'll need something in purple. My husband and I will be attending a fund-raiser later this month and I'm having a gown specially made. I'll send James with samples of the fabric."

Tillie nodded, already envisioning an array of possibilities. After signing for her purchases, Mrs. Darby left the store, a host of exhausted shop employees in her wake.

Mrs. Ferguson shuffled past a flustered seamstress, who fanned her face with a swatch of muslin, then pulled a handkerchief from her apron pocket and mopped her brow. "I can't believe it. This has to be the first time that woman has left the store satisfied with her purchases."

She pushed off the counter and ambled to Tillie, a wide smile creasing her plump cheeks. "I'll never know how you managed it."

"'Twas nothing. A wee bit of prodding is all. Mrs. Darby prides herself on being up-to-date with the latest fashions."

"*And* a distant relative of the Van Rensselaers," Mrs. Ferguson said. "A stroke of genius bringing her name into the conversation, my dear. Simply genius."

When the laughter quieted, she motioned for the staff to resume their responsibilities, but to Tillie she extended her hand. "Come. There is something I've been meaning to speak with you about."

Tillie scooped up the ribbons she'd used for Mrs. Darby's bonnet and replaced them in a drawer fitted with a glass front, then followed Mrs. Ferguson to her office.

As she shut the door, Tillie's thoughts flitted to the look she'd glimpsed when Mrs. Darby requested she oversee her projects. She twined her fingers tightly at her waist. "I hope I've not done anything wrong."

"On the contrary, my dear." Mrs. Ferguson crossed to a

tea cart and poured two cups. "I've been quite satisfied with your work for some time now."

She grasped one of the cups and extended it toward Tillie, which she accepted gratefully. So, if she wasn't displeased . . .

Mrs. Ferguson sat on a small rose-covered settee positioned beneath a paned window and beckoned for Tillie to join her. "Tillie, you know that when you first came to us, I wasn't certain things would work out."

She nodded. And no surprise, considering the sad, broken lass she'd once been.

"Since then, however, I've been quite impressed with your progress. You always complete your orders on time, and I've never once heard your customers complain. Indeed, I've grown to rely on you to help the others when they have a particularly troublesome request." She set aside her cup and folded her hands primly in her lap. "Tillie, would you be interested in assuming additional responsibility?"

She waited, and Tillie motioned for her to continue.

"I'd like you to supervise all the orders, not just Mrs. Darby's. That would mean overseeing the fittings, taking measurements, even offering suggestions as you did today. It would involve less of the actual sewing, especially when it comes to shirts or waistcoats and the like, but I think your time and talent will be better served in the long run." She paused and leaned toward Tillie expectantly. "What do you think?"

She looked away, thinking. Added responsibility at the millinery would certainly mean spending less time at the shelter. "I think 'tis a grand offer, but . . ."

"Of course, I would increase your wages. I would never ask you to add to your responsibilities without compensating you for the effort."

Tillie lifted her head. "Ma'am?"

Mrs. Ferguson continued with enthusiasm, "Business has been sound in recent months, my dear, and I have no doubt it is thanks in part to you. I can offer . . ." She leaned forward to whisper in Tillie's ear.

Upon hearing the amount, Tillie's eyes widened. The raise would mean moving the purchase of the orphanage up several months. Her only quandary was weighing the need for help at the shelter with the need for an orphanage, which she simply could not do without first speaking to Sister Agnes.

She drew a deep breath. "I'm honored that you hold my work in such high regard, Mrs. Ferguson. Might I perhaps have a day or two to ponder your offer?"

Mrs. Ferguson's eyes shone, as if she already sensed Tillie's answer. "Of course. No hurry." She lifted her cup, saluted her with it, and then took a sip.

Tillie lifted her cup as well, but her thoughts were far from the tea. A thrill raced through her at the notion that she might soon see her dreams realized. After finishing her tea and withdrawing from Mrs. Ferguson's office, she dashed through her remaining orders and then gathered her reticule and bonnet and said good-bye for the day.

Outside, the brightness of the afternoon matched the cheerfulness inside her. While it would have been unseemly for her to skip, she couldn't help but hurry her steps in the direction of the church. Ach, but she couldn't wait to tell Sister Agnes her plans. She only hoped she wouldn't be leaving the nuns in a bind—

"Miss McGrath?"

Upon hearing her name called, she halted and looked up the street. Weaving through the crowd of shoppers and children, a large figure hastened toward her. It took her a moment to realize who it was. She drew back her shoulders, resisting the urge to also smooth her skirt.

"Captain Morgan?"

He removed his cap as he drew near and dipped his head. "Good afternoon."

"This is an unexpected surprise."

"I hope you don't mind," he said as he replaced the cap on his head. "I went by the boardinghouse this afternoon. I was hoping to speak with you. They told me I could find you here."

"Actually I was just on my way to the church. Our Lady of Deliverance," she clarified, "the shelter I told you about."

"I see." The troubled frown cleared from his face, and he swept his hand toward the sidewalk. "Do you mind if I accompany you?"

Indecision held her motionless. He was nigh a stranger, after all, no matter how kind he seemed. No, that wasn't really fair. She'd been witness to his kindness firsthand. Her cheeks warmed as she nodded and set off again toward the church.

Though the sun still shone brightly, it wasn't with the blazing heat of midday. Indeed, a pleasant ocean breeze stirred the hair on her neck, and twice she saw the captain turn his gaze toward the harbor, as if lured by the scent of the sea.

Not that he was inattentive company. They hadn't walked far before she realized she rather liked having the handsome captain strolling by her side. He directed the conversation with a skill that set her at ease, asking questions about the church and shelter and volunteering stories about his Catholic upbringing that made her smile.

When they reached the corner near the land office, she slowed, of habit searching for the sign in the window and sighing with relief when she saw it hadn't moved.

"Something wrong?" The captain's deep voice pulled her thoughts away from the orphanage.

She shook her head. "No. Forgive me. We should be going."

He moved past her toward the land office window. "What is this?"

Tillie's heart pounded. The orphanage had been a secret dream for so long, she almost feared giving voice to it. "'Tis . . . uh . . ."

Reflected in the window, his eyes sought hers. "A house?"

He turned. This time when he looked at her, his gray eyes gleamed an almost steely blue. "You be thinking of moving? Of leaving the city?"

"Not leaving, exactly. The house is located in the Lower East Side, near the church."

"Have you been to see it?"

It had seemed too bold, too presumptuous to visit. "Not yet."

"But you've considered purchasing it."

His questions were too direct, and they reminded her of her parents. She stiffened her spine and glared at him. "May I ask why it matters to you?"

Her retort only served to sharpen the intensity of his gaze. He closed the gap between them, and though he towered over her, she refused to step back, despite the shaking of her knees.

Thankfully, when next he spoke, his voice and his manner were gentle. "I pray you forgive my impertinence. Truly I mean no disrespect, but I must know. Miss McGrath . . . are you betrothed?"

9

The moment he'd asked the question, Morgan wanted to bite off his tongue. Tillie looked angry enough to slap him, and well she should. He wasn't her suitor, nor kin with familial responsibilities to uphold. Yet the query hung in the air between them unanswered.

Confusion clouded her brow. "Betrothed? Why on earth would you ask such a question?"

The obvious answer was that he was concerned for her welfare. The truth went much deeper.

Her attention drifted to the flyer with the picture of the house for sale in the window. "Oh, you thought . . ."

Embarrassment burned his face and neck. None of this was going as he'd planned. How in blazes had he let the situation get so complicated? Bunching his fists, he retreated a step. "I beg your pardon. 'Tis none of my concern. I shouldn't have asked."

"No, it was a fair assumption." She frowned and bit one side of her lip, as though she wanted to say more but didn't. Finally, she motioned toward the sidewalk. "Shall we go on?"

Surprised she'd even consider allowing him to stay, he nodded and swung into step beside her. "I suppose now that we have the awkward questions out of the way . . ." At her quiet laugh, he went on. "Will you tell me why you're interested in that old house? It's far too large for a single woman living alone."

A shy smile flitted across her lips. "Aye, I suppose you're right. Then again, my plans aren't to live there alone."

Surprisingly, her remark birthed resistance in his gut.

She cast a searching glance at him. "May I ask *you* a question?"

Given that he'd made such a muddle of things, how could he say no? He motioned for her to continue.

"Have you never thought about giving up the seafaring life and settling down?"

His steps faltered. Give up the *Caitriona Marie*? He cleared his throat. "My ship is essential to my family's livelihood, that much is certain, but—"

"But?"

Instantly he was transported back in time, and it was Moira who asked the question.

"Have ya never thought of settling down?"

His answer that day had broken both their hearts.

"Captain Morgan?"

He blinked. They had come to a stop on the sidewalk, and irritated gentlemen steered their ladies around them on either side. Just a few yards away, the land office with Tillie's dream pasted to the window beckoned.

"Aye, I thought about it once," he said. "Even dreamed of marrying my childhood sweetheart and raising a passel of bairns."

Sorrow darkened her eyes. "Why didn't you?"

He grimaced. "Life interfered."

She nodded. "It has a way of doing that."

Aye, for she was one to testify to that fact, thanks to him.

The crowds had thinned with the onset of evening. What carts remained to pack the streets were pitifully low on supplies. It amazed him how so much business was conducted in so little time. Very different from life aboard the *Caitriona Marie*, where days could fade into weeks when the wind and sailing were slow.

Next to him, Tillie lifted her face to catch the last few rays of sunlight seeping over the rooftops. The orange glow brought out the burnished highlights in her hair and made her skin shine with health and innocence.

So sweet.

Just like that she'd put her worries and outrage behind her to find pleasure in the day. Did he have any right to take that from her? What reason could he give to fill her life with pain and anguish anew?

"You never told me," he said, drawing her eyes back to him, "what it is about that advertisement that fascinates you so."

He pointed at the land office, then offered his arm so they could continue on their way.

"The advertisement for the house says 'tis vacant now, but it shouldn't be. I imagine it filled with children and laughter."

Her children?

She blushed and averted her eyes. Aye, and hadn't he had similar dreams once, before Da died and the responsibility for providing for the family fell to him?

"I see," he said, and he did.

A gentle breeze wafted over them, sweeping the last vestiges of doubt from Morgan's mind. Tillie McGrath deserved to live out her days free from the torment of knowing that her lover had been murdered and never, ever knowing why. Perhaps she'd even find happiness, and if buying that old house and filling its many rooms could give her that, mayhap he would find peace, as well.

But not until he knew the truth. Not until he knew who had ordered Braedon McKillop's death and why.

And whether or not Tillie would be safe.

Like it or not, he'd never be free of his obligation to her unless he knew for certain that whoever had claimed McKillop's life wasn't after hers, as well. But to uncover that, he'd need help.

He needed Cass.

His mind made up, he deposited Tillie at the church and then made the long trek back to the wharf at a rapid pace. Cass was working alongside the rest of the crew on the deck, his chest bare and red from the heat of the day. Morgan motioned to him from the dock.

"Fetch a shirt," he yelled, cupping one hand to his mouth. "You're going to need it."

"Where we going?" Cass asked once he'd dressed and scrambled down the side of the ship onto the dock. As they walked, he tucked the tails of his shirt into the waistband of his trousers.

"Someplace where we can talk."

"You've never been afraid to talk aboard the *Marie* before."

No, and he'd never had to worry about who heard, either. That he did now set him on edge. He motioned to a pub down the street, whose door swung open and closed with patrons entering and exiting.

"Hungry?"

"Always," Cass said, "but especially after unloading crates all day."

Inside the pub, loud music and voices made conversation difficult. They wound past the crowded tables to a secluded corner. Once they were seated, and their orders of roast-beef sandwiches taken, Cass dragged his cap from his head and motioned to Morgan.

"You going to tell me what happened today or aren't you?"

He did, beginning with the first time he'd laid eyes on Tillie McGrath, and ending with their visit earlier that day. "She's alone, Cass, and whether she knows it or not, my allowing her in to see McKillop before he died may have put her in danger."

By now, the food had arrived but still sat untouched on their plates. Cass picked absently at a wilted piece of lettuce before lifting his head to look Morgan in the eye.

"Well?" Morgan said. "What do you think?"

Cass sighed. "I think you're right. We owe it to this girl to try and found out who Doc was working for. But you should know I have no intention of letting you do this on your own."

Morgan hid a grin. So accustomed was he to looking after his younger brother, it was quite amusing to be on the other end—and if he were honest, a trifle humbling. Leaning forward, he lowered his voice so only Cass could hear. "I have no intention of trying. But we're going to need to stay in New York longer than we'd planned. Do you think you can arrange it?"

Cass hesitated a moment, then nodded. "Aye, should be simple enough. The off-load's been a touch tricky this time around, anyway. I think I can delay it a couple more days."

"And the repairs to the bilge," Morgan said. "I'll go ahead and order them in the next day or two. That should give us at least a week without raising any suspicions."

Cass matched Morgan's whisper. "Mind if I ask whose suspicions you're worried about raising?"

Morgan's thoughts turned quickly to Donal. He didn't fully trust the man, but that wasn't enough to accuse him. He picked at the rim of his cup with his nail and said, "I'm being cautious is all. I thought I could trust Doc, and we saw how that turned out. No, 'tis better if we hold our cards close, at least until we understand what it is we be dealing with."

Cass agreed with a slow nod. "Right. So? After we get the repairs ordered, then what? Have you given any thought as to how we should proceed with the girl?"

"I dinna know, Cass. This entire business sets me flesh to crawling, like something terrible may be coming."

Cass shifted in his chair. "What do you mean?"

Morgan paused. How to explain the roiling in his gut that had started the day Doc told him about what he'd done and had continued to grow ever since? He shoved his cup back and laced both hands. "What was it about McKillop that made someone want to kill him? Have you thought of that?" By his blank expression, Morgan knew he had not. In fact, the notion had only just occurred to him. "I mean, if a man were willing to go to all that trouble to hire someone and then keep it a secret . . ."

Cass's eyes grew rounder as he spoke. "Are you saying you don't want to go through with finding out who done it?"

Morgan shook his head. That part had been determined the moment Doc breathed his last, but involving his brother, only now did it occur to him how dangerous that could prove, too.

"You're my brother, Cass. Hard as I am on you, I dinna desire that any harm should befall you."

"Aye, and you're mine. So what are we going to do?" He didn't even blink as he made the matter-of-fact reply. Indeed, renewed determination carved lines about his eyes and mouth. "Well?"

"I'll see about renting a room at the boardinghouse where Miss McGrath lives," Morgan said, swallowing a swell of pride at his brother's courage. "I think 'twould be easier to keep an eye on her, make sure she's in no danger whilst we be about asking our questions."

"I agree. What about the men?"

"Do what you can to set their minds to rest. And give them a couple of days' shore leave. Tell them 'tis because we'll be setting sail soon, and they're to see about their business while we make ready."

"Done. Except . . ." He hesitated, his throat working.

"What?" Morgan asked.

"I think we should leave the off-load to Bozey. You could use an extra man at the boardinghouse to keep an eye on things when you aren't around. Think on it. If this lass is in as much danger as you say, it might not be wise leaving her on her own, especially with you going around stirring up trouble by asking questions."

Fie.

Much as he hated to admit it, Cass was right. He couldn't be in two places at once, and if he held off on telling Miss McGrath the truth, then he had to do something to make sure she was safe.

He took a swallow from his mug and then gave a curt nod. "Fine. We'll swing by the boardinghouse in the morning and speak to the owner. But remember"—he tossed a wary glance around the pub, at the mass of strange faces peering back—"keep quiet about all this to the men."

Cass snorted. "One of these days, you're going to realize I stopped being a bairn a long time ago."

True enough, Morgan thought as he watched Cass rise and stride from the pub, his broad shoulders clearing a path to the door. Until then, he was concerned with one thing only, and that was making sure his little brother met with no harm.

10

Tillie took her time rising the next morning, even though the bright sun streaming through her bedroom window teased her eyelids and coaxed her toward wakefulness. Stretching her arms over her head, she reveled in the promise brought by the new day.

Her eyes snapped open. Aye, 'twas a promise, for both Sister Mary and Sister Agnes had bestowed a blessing upon her plans once she'd told them of her desire to open an orphanage.

"To think," Sister Mary had said, tears springing to her eyes, "all them bairns will have a place to call home. Ach, 'twould be a blessing to us all, and no doubt."

"Don't you go worrying about how it will affect us," Sister Agnes had added. "We'll get along, sure enough. Always have."

Sighing, Tillie slipped from her bed and hurried to wash and dress. Before she went downstairs, however, she paused to slide Braedon's ring from its leather hiding place and pressed a kiss to it. "I know you'd be proud, me sweet lad," she whispered, closing her eyes. "I know it."

Surprisingly, Braedon's name didn't bring a wash of tears as it had in the past. Instead she moved with a new lightness down the stairs. At the bottom, the scent of bacon and freshly baked bread drew her to the dining room—that and the hum of male voices. Visitors at this hour? She peeked into the room.

Amelia sat at the head of the table, the morning papers ironed, folded, and laid neatly at her elbow. Across from her, Meg, the only other resident of the boardinghouse, stood at the ornately carved sideboard, a plate in her hands and a smile upon her lips for the gentleman pouring a cup of coffee to her left.

Tillie stifled a gasp, for though he wasn't nearly as striking as Captain Morgan, they so closely resembled each other that she had to look twice to realize it wasn't him.

Meg's lashes swept down at something the tall stranger said, and her cheeks flushed red.

Across the way, Amelia motioned. "Tillie, come in, dear, and have some breakfast."

At this, all eyes turned in her direction, including the stranger's and the captain's, whom she'd first thought the man to be.

Captain Morgan stood from a place near the end of the table, next to the seat she normally occupied. "Miss Mc-Grath."

"Captain."

Her attention shifted to Amelia, who rose at her entrance and gestured to the men. "Tillie, come in and meet our guests. Captain Morgan you know, but this is his brother."

The stranger rounded the table to stand before her and dip in a gallant bow. "Cass Morgan, at your service."

Captain Morgan had a brother? Her head swimming, Tillie returned the nod. "A pleasure."

Rather than respond, he shot a most quizzical glance at his brother, who merely looked away.

At that moment, Laverne bustled in, a platter of scrambled eggs in one hand and crisp, fried bacon and sausage in the other. "Here we are. All ready. Can't tell you what a pleasure it is to cook for a houseful again."

To Tillie's shock, Laverne sent a wink flying at Cass as she deposited the food onto the sideboard, then bustled back to the kitchen after a bowl of jam.

As though he'd been doing it all his life, Captain Morgan pulled out her chair and waited to seat her in it. While taking the chair, Tillie set her jaw and peered at Amelia, as if by staring she could somehow read the thoughts swirling inside her graying head.

"Toast?"

She blinked and turned her attention to the plate Captain Morgan extended. "Aye, thank you."

Somehow she managed to keep her voice light, but her mind whirled. What was the captain doing here, and with his brother no less?

She lifted a slice of toast and laid it on a small bread plate next to her tea. 'Twas slim repast, but anxious as she was to speak to Amelia, it seemed ample. She waited impatiently as the rest of the meal was served and grace said before gulping her tea and motioning for Amelia to join her in the hallway.

"All right then," she said, sliding the dining room door closed, "what exactly be going on here this morning? Gentlemen at the breakfast table? I'm beginning to think I've lost my mind."

Amelia lifted her chin, and though she kept her tone bright, lines of tension formed around her mouth and eyes and around her clasped fingers. She shrugged. "What on earth do you mean, dear?"

Tillie noted Amelia's white knuckles. There, at least, was evidence of her true state. She pressed her hand to Amelia's. "I know something is wrong. Will you tell me? Please?"

Seconds ticked by, marked by the old grandfather clock

Amelia had brought with her from England. Finally she breathed a sigh, which seemed to let the air out not only from her lungs but from her spine and shoulders. "You know we've been experiencing a bit of trouble recently, what with so many of our rooms empty."

She nodded. "Aye."

Amelia continued, "I didn't want to worry you or Meg, but since Cara left, and then Ana and Breda, running the boardinghouse has gotten much harder."

Tillie's thoughts winged to Giles and Laverne. The boardinghouse was their livelihood. "I'll speak to Sister Agnes and Sister Mary again. Perhaps they can suggest something."

Amelia shook her head. "Actually, another solution has presented itself, which I think will suit quite nicely." She gestured toward the dining room doors. "Captain Morgan and his brother are going to be staying with us while repairs are made to their ship."

"Staying with us?" Tillie repeated. What could they have possibly said to change Amelia's stance on male boarders? Only women were allowed, apart from Giles, and he because the boardinghouse couldn't do without a handyman.

"Yes, dear, while their ship is being repaired."

"I don't understand."

"From what they shared with me this morning," Amelia said, lowering her voice, "they're going to have to make some extensive repairs before they depart for the Carolinas later this month. Captain Morgan said it may delay them by two weeks or more."

Panic, irrational in its intensity, stirred in Tillie's stomach. "But wouldn't it be more feasible for them to stay on board while the repairs are being made? What if a situation arises that requires their attention?"

"Captain Morgan insists that isn't possible," Amelia said,

plucking at the lace that rimmed her sleeve. "Something about the nature of the damage." Tilting her head, she peered at Tillie anxiously. "Do you have an objection to the captain and his brother staying with us?"

Other than the uncomfortable fluttering that occurred in her chest every time she laid eyes on the captain? Tillie bowed her head and swallowed the lump in her throat. "No objections." At least none that she could think of. "I thought you were reluctant to take in male boarders."

"That's true, I suppose," Amelia admitted.

Fighting to control her nervous quivering, Tillie clasped her arms around her middle. "What about the Dickersons? They've rooms for rent, and from what I understand, they house mostly men employed by the shipping companies down on the wharf."

A shadow flickered across Amelia's face. Was it desperation? Just how dire was the "bit of trouble" she had referred to earlier?

Tillie paused. "Amelia?"

She bit her lip. "The truth is, I am most grateful for their coming. Giles has been so overworked lately, and Captain Morgan's brother has offered to help with the chores while they are here."

Her eyes pleaded for understanding. Something was wrong, more than she was saying. Tillie opened her mouth to speak, but her words were cut short by the sliding of the door.

Captain Morgan emerged, a puzzled frown upon his face. "Is everything all right?"

Amelia immediately brightened. She left Tillie's side and crossed to clasp his arm. "Oh my, yes. We were just discussing boardinghouse business, isn't that right, Tillie?"

Left with little choice, she nodded agreement.

"Come then, we mustn't let Laverne's breakfast get cold. Captain, may I get you some more coffee?"

Tillie followed as Amelia led the way back into the dining room and then bustled to the silver coffeepot. She continued her lively chatter as she refilled first his cup and then that of his brother, but to Tillie's ears, the talk was little more than a ruse to end an uncomfortable line of questioning.

Fine, but the discussion wasn't over. She retook her seat at the table next to the captain. Now that she knew how deep Amelia's worry went, she'd press until she found out what she could do to help.

Conversation around the table resumed, with Cass Morgan regaling Amelia and Meg with tales of life at sea, and Giles piping in to add a quip from his own seafaring days. How quickly the younger of the Morgans had made himself at home.

At her elbow the captain's low tone interrupted her thinking. "Amelia tells me you're quite a skilled musician."

She played a tune or two on the pianoforte, but skilled? Tillie shook her head. "Only what I learned by listening, back home in Ireland. I kinna read music."

He tapped his ear. "Ach, but to hear and replicate the sound *is* a skill."

She frowned. "Do you play?"

He chuckled, a most pleasing sound, being that she'd not heard it from him before. "Not at all, though I've always admired those who can. I used to sit and listen to my ma for hours."

His voice warmed at the mention of his mother, and Tillie felt a surprising surge of envy. While her own mother was quite learned, she never played for pleasure. "She must have a love of music."

"That she does." He lifted his fork and took a hearty bite of egg and sausage, savored it, then gave a nod. "The rumors are true. Laverne is a good cook. I'll have to see if she'd be willing to pass a tip or two on to Sully."

She paused with her cup aloft.

"The ship's cook," he said in response to her unasked question.

She nodded.

"So, what is it you do at the church?"

An innocent question that Tillie found herself reluctant to answer. Before she could ask herself why, he shrugged.

"Just curious."

Of course. She took a deep breath. Whatever it was about the captain that set her nerves to tingling was of her own imagining.

She laid her napkin across her lap and lifted her chin. "Odds and ends mostly. Sometimes I help with the cooking. Other times I clean or sew—whatever they need."

"Are there many women at the shelter?"

"Thirty-five perhaps, or forty. It varies."

Captain Morgan's eyebrows lifted. "That many? Where do they come from?"

She shrugged. "Overseas mostly. Single women. Or widowed with children. They have their own reasons for coming to America, but all have one thing in common. They're hoping to find a better life."

Her breath caught on the last part of the sentence as Braedon's promise of what they would find once they left Ireland rang in her head. To cover her discomfort, she reached for her tea and took a sip.

"Is that why you go?" Captain Morgan asked softly. "Because you have something in common with these women?"

Tillie looked around the table at the others, who were all engrossed in their own conversations and so paid them no mind.

She swallowed with difficulty. "In part, I suppose. Mostly I just want to fill a need."

And to have a need filled.

She fiddled with the handle of her cup. The thought wasn't new, but never had she felt the weight of it as keenly as she did under the captain's intense scrutiny. Fighting the urge to squirm, she finished her tea and replaced the cup on the saucer.

"And speaking of the shelter—"

"Do you go there often?" Captain Morgan said in the same moment. He inclined his head, his long fingers stroking the stem of his water glass. "Forgive me. You were saying?"

"Just that I should be going," Tillie said, her cheeks warming. "I'd like to get started at the millinery early so I can stop by the shelter this afternoon." She took a deep breath and looked up at the captain, meeting his eyes. "I want you to know, I am glad that you and your brother have come. 'Twill be a help to Amelia. Good day, Captain."

She moved to rise, but to her shock he stayed her with a touch to her hand. "Miss McGrath, before you go . . ."

She resumed her seat, resisting the temptation to rub her fingers where his touch had warmed her skin. "Aye, Captain? What is it?"

"I was wondering, how often do you make the trip?"

"To the shelter?"

He nodded.

"Three, perhaps four times a week. It depends, I suppose, on how many women they have staying. Why?"

"And . . ." He appeared uncomfortable, his Adam's apple working as he swallowed. "Do you often walk alone?"

Tillie nodded. "I wouldn't get far if I waited for a chaperone to escort me everywhere I needed to go, now, would I?"

"No, I suppose not."

Though he fell silent, she sensed he wanted to say more. Tension bunched the muscles in her shoulders. "Is something wrong?"

"Don't mind the cap," Cass said from across the table, drawing her startled gaze. "It be in his nature to worry, especially since our *daed* passed away. I don't know what he'd do with his time otherwise."

He stared at his brother, and though he smiled, she sensed caution. Why? She looked back at the captain, who lifted his head and acknowledged the others at the table with a nod.

"'Tis true, I'm afraid. Inherited from me mother. There's not a moment goes by that I'm not pondering on what bad thing might happen to endanger my crew."

"Not such a bad trait," Amelia said from the head of the table. A smile brightened her face. "I've always found it quite admirable for a man to look after the people placed in his charge." Her smile widening, she lifted her coffee cup and saluted him with it.

"You haven't suffered under one of his protective tirades," Cass protested, laughing. "Or had to listen to one of his speeches. Though I will admit, it is one of the things that makes him such a good captain." He angled his head toward Meg. "For instance, do you know that before this crossing, my brother here warned me that he thought the bilge would be needing attention?"

Meg's eyes widened. "Really?"

"Didn't even have to look at the pump to know it, either. Ain't that so, Morgan?"

Tillie marveled as his bronzed skin reddened under the praise. Shyness from a ship's captain? What other surprises were there to know about this man?

She tamped the thought a second after it rose. Ruined as she was by the choices she'd made, she had no business learning anything about any man, but particularly not one as handsome and noble as he.

She slid back from the table, and this time she didn't

hesitate as she made her excuse to Amelia and then hurried to the hall.

Work and the shelter—those two things alone would she allow to occupy her thoughts. And the captain?

He, she told herself as she tossed her shawl about her shoulders, would be difficult to avoid, seeing as how he'd be staying at the boardinghouse while the repairs to their ship were being tended.

Pressing her lips together firmly, she stepped out onto the street and closed the door behind her. 'Twould be difficult, but that did not mean she didn't intend to try.

11

Donal was right—the morgue *was* a foul place.

Morgan stifled a wave of distaste as he ducked through the outer doors and into Steven Ramsey's cramped office. Despite his height, the man looked small hunkered behind an enormous desk. Great ledgers filled the shelves above his head. Papers spilled from the open cabinets onto his desk, where, on one corner, a molding crust of bread and cheese drew flies. How did the fellow work in such a mess?

Morgan sidestepped a pile of boxes stacked haphazardly on the floor. "So you say this cousin, this James Finch, came by to collect the doctor's remains this morning?"

Ramsey gave a little shrug. "That's what I said." He narrowed his eyes. "You have business with him?"

Business? Aye. Like finding out who Doc's enemies were, and the kind of people with whom he associated. "A bit," he replied.

Ramsey's brows bunched into a dark line. He patted the stacks of paper and receipts scattered along the desktop. "I do think I have his address around here somewhere, though it could take me a moment to find it, I'm afraid."

A process that could no doubt be hurried along with a coin

from Morgan's pocket. He gritted his teeth as he withdrew a piece of silver and dropped it on the desk.

"Ah, here it is." Ramsey hoisted a soiled scrap of paper and waved it under Morgan's nose. "Knew I'd find it sooner or later."

The man's scrawny shoulders hunched as Morgan snatched the address from his fingers. Morgan pointed to the street name. "Mangham. Where is that?"

"Upper East Side. Near Lexington."

The name meant nothing to him. The address memorized, Morgan returned the paper to Ramsey. "Any idea how far?"

"Well . . ." Ramsey scratched his head and stared at the ceiling as if thinking.

Sighing, Morgan retrieved another dollar from his pocket and flipped it into Ramsey's waiting palm.

"Not far. Maybe twenty or thirty minutes by carriage."

A moment later, Morgan exited the morgue, glad to be shed of the place and even more so its proprietor.

Outside, the day had turned sticky and hot. For a split second he longed for the ocean's cool breezes and expansive rolling waves, especially when after just a few steps he found himself jostled along the teeming street.

He shuddered and sidestepped onto the walk. Why people would choose to live packed together like rats was beyond him. Giving a sharp whistle he hailed a carriage and recited the address to the driver before climbing inside.

Unlike Ashberry Street, or even Woodrow Boulevard, where Ramsey the undertaker conducted business, Mangham Street was a collection of tidy row houses with small patches of neatly kept yards. They rolled past, door after painted door, until finally rumbling to a stop outside a particularly narrow structure with tall windows that stretched upward on both the second and third floors.

"Here you are, sir," the driver called, "2416 Mangham Street."

The carriage pitched as Morgan climbed down and circled to the front. He held up a dollar. This trip was getting expensive. "Can you wait here?"

The driver's eyes gleamed. "Aye, sir. For another coin I can wait."

Grunting, Morgan tossed him the money and then strode through a wrought-iron gate, up a bricked path to a set of broad steps. At the top, a great oak door with leaded-glass sidelights and matching fanlight beckoned. He lifted the brass knocker and let it fall once, twice, then stood back to wait. After a moment, a black-coated butler swung open the door.

"May I help you?"

He had no card to present. Morgan merely gave his name and explained the purpose of his visit.

The butler's stoic expression remained fixed as he listened. "If you will follow me, I will see if Mr. Finch is available." He indicated a wide hallway with polished wood floors and strategically positioned benches. A hall tree with curved arms supported a variety of hats and coats. The butler motioned to Morgan's cap, which he relinquished with an inward sigh. "I'll be back shortly," the butler said before depositing the cap on the hall tree and disappearing up a flight of stairs.

The home of James Finch was understated but impressive, with curtains that pooled on the floor at every window, and gleaming silver frames that boasted photos of a large family on every table. Farther down the hall, a striped settee invited guests to linger. Mrs. Finch was indeed a woman of refined taste.

Like Moira.

He clenched his jaw as he turned toward a painted mural brightening one wall. The work had taken talent, he decided, with its many swirling patterns and shaded planes. He moved closer for further study just as footsteps sounded on the stairs behind him.

James Finch was a short older man with thinning hair that grayed at the temples. He balanced a pair of gold-rimmed spectacles on his nose, and his mustache twitched as he approached Morgan with his hand extended.

"Captain Morgan?"

Morgan clasped the hand Mr. Finch offered and was pleasantly surprised to receive not a flaccid shake but one purposeful and firm. He instantly liked the good doctor's cousin. "You must be James Finch."

He nodded, waving toward a small parlor. "John is bringing tea. I hope that is all right?"

His brow lifted in question, which Morgan answered with a subtle shake of his head. This was no social call.

"Then perhaps our business would be better conducted in the library," Mr. Finch said as he led the way past the parlor and dining room. Once again, the room they entered was designed with care and taste. Elaborately carved bookcases held row upon row of leather-bound books. Opposite the door stood a large marble fireplace, and just inside was a table bearing a vase of flowers and the family Bible. Beyond that were a desk and two large chairs, which was where Mr. Finch led them.

"My butler tells me we may have some unfinished business regarding my cousin." He waited until Morgan claimed one of the chairs before seating himself in the other. "I don't understand. I thought everything was accomplished earlier today at the morgue."

He withdrew a box of cigars from a desk drawer and offered one to Morgan, who declined.

"As far as his burial is concerned, you are correct. Our business is most definitely concluded," Morgan said. "I'm afraid I've come on another matter, equally as unpleasant, but indeed quite vital."

Mr. Finch lit his cigar, filling the room with the scent of tobacco and cherry, and motioned for Morgan to continue.

"Sir, how well did you know your cousin?" Morgan began, trying discreetly to gauge the man's reaction.

Mr. Finch's face disappeared behind a smoky cloud, but through the haze Morgan saw his eyes narrow.

"Being near in age," he said with a wave of the cigar, "we were quite close growing up. That changed as we grew older, I'm afraid, after Lionel took up the medical profession. His travels took him far from home, as I'm sure you are aware."

Lionel. Morgan was startled to realize that he'd only ever known him as Doc. He cleared his throat. "But before that, would you say you knew him well? His friends? The people he associated with?"

Mr. Finch said nothing. After a moment he laid the cigar in a marbled tray and folded both hands atop the desk. "This is perhaps an odd line of questioning, Captain Morgan."

Indeed it was, and Morgan felt ill at ease with the task he'd undertaken. Comfortable or not, however, uncovering the man who'd paid to have someone end Braedon McKillop's life had fallen to him. He pushed forward in the chair. "I'm afraid I have some rather shocking news," he said, clipping his words so that they rattled like stones in the quiet room.

Mr. Finch neither wavered nor blinked beneath Morgan's hard stare. "Go on."

Rather than mince the truth, Morgan let the words fly like a lash. "It has come to my attention that your cousin accepted payment in exchange for poisoning a passenger aboard my ship. I want to know why and who it was that paid him."

There. It was said. He waited while Finch processed what he'd heard.

The man sighed heavily. "How long ago?"

Morgan gripped the arms of his chair. That was it? The question with which he'd responded showed no doubt. No outrage. "Almost two years."

Again he waited.

"Just after Josephine and Oleta took ill." Finch's lips turned down in a frown.

"Beg your pardon?" Morgan said. "Who?"

"His wife and daughter. You didn't know he had a family?"

"To my shame, I did not."

The frown lifted from Finch's face, and he dismissed Morgan's words with a wave. "Do not berate yourself, Captain. I'm not surprised that Lionel never told you about them. His wife was colored, and the child did not belong to him. Lionel met them while practicing in a small town outside of Atlanta." He picked up the cigar and resumed puffing. "Though there was never any doubt that he cared for them, we all thought it was a matter of charity that he brought them to New York and gave them a place to live. When he married Oleta, however . . ." He directed a stare at Morgan. "Well, let's just say there were some in our family who did not approve."

Irritation raced through Morgan's veins. "And when the woman and her daughter took ill, you didn't offer to help."

"Condemnation, Captain?" The two looked eye to eye until finally Finch directed his eyes upward, thinking. "Yes, I suppose the sentiment would be warranted, though at the time our concern was for the family. We never guessed the kind of straits Lionel was in. He . . . he became quite desperate."

"Desperate enough to kill a man?"

While he didn't say it aloud, guilt and grief twisted Finch's features. "I think, Captain, that you already know the answer to that."

Perhaps he did. Pity filled him, as did remorse, that he'd not known Doc better. And the crewmen who still lived? How well did he know them? He thought of Bozey, who'd joined the crew of the *Marie* almost three years ago, and then trickled over the rest of them, settling at last on Donal.

"Any idea who might have known about Doc's circumstances and used the information to bribe him?"

Finch's shoulders rose. "He wasn't shy about seeking odd jobs in order to raise enough money to move his family out of the city and into a warmer climate. I suspect it could have been any number of people. Although . . ." He tapped the desk with his forefinger. "There was a man, Irish, I think, who spoke to him concerning a job. It was right about the time he went to work for you, if I remember correctly. We were all surprised that he would consider leaving his wife and the child to become a ship's doctor."

Morgan dug through his memory, searching the days and weeks surrounding the period when he'd been without a doctor. Just before leaving New York to return to Dublin, Doc had approached him saying he'd heard Morgan was looking.

He gave himself a mental shake. Impossible. It wasn't until the next voyage to America that Braedon McKillop had come aboard the *Caitriona Marie* as a passenger. How could Doc—or anyone—have known? Unless . . .

McKillop's coming hadn't been by accident.

He clenched his jaw, a blast of anger rushing through him at the thought that someone would use his ship to accomplish their sinister purpose. A second later, reason replaced the anger.

Composing himself, he stood, shook Finch's hand, and thanked him for his time. After informing him of the address of the boardinghouse and how long he'd be staying, he asked him to kindly get in touch should he remember anything he thought would be helpful, and then he left.

Free to reflect on what he'd learned once he left Finch's home, Morgan scowled and hurried his steps toward Ashberry Street and Cass.

If what Finch had told him was correct, if someone had paid Doc to take a job on the *Caitriona Marie*, then somehow convinced McKillop to board the ship for America, the plot, and the danger to him, Tillie, and his brother, was far greater than he imagined.

12

Business at the millinery hastened now that Tillie had accepted the position Mrs. Ferguson offered. Having received Sister Agnes's blessing, and Sister Mary's hearty approval to boot, she'd been happy to inform Mrs. Ferguson of her answer and begin with her new responsibilities.

She lowered the wick on an oil lamp until it went out, then carefully set it aside and stooped to remove her reticule from a cubby beneath her worktable. The shop was quiet now that the last customer had left and all the employees had gone home. Only she and Mrs. Ferguson remained, the latter approaching with a jingle as she held her keys aloft.

"So, my dear, what did you think of your first day?"

Tillie gave her tired eyes a rub. The stress to her fingers had been far less, but her mind was far more fatigued than on a normal workday—as was her back from bending over the table as she'd examined the orders being prepared for delivery. "I never realized how many ventures we had going at once."

Mrs. Ferguson chuckled merrily. "Just wait. The summer season is almost over, but come fall, when people submit their orders for the holidays and Christmas, we'll see our numbers double."

Tillie shook her head. "How have you managed it on your own all this time?"

Separating one of the keys from the ring in her hand, she shrugged. "I had little choice after Mr. Ferguson passed away, but things are different now. Business is better, and I can afford the extra help. Good thing." She patted her graying hair. "The pace of running this place is rapidly becoming too much for this old lady."

Tillie smiled. Mrs. Ferguson's advancing years had proven to be good fortune for her. "I'm glad I can help." She motioned toward the windows, which had been propped open to allow a breeze while the women worked. "Shall I help you lock up?"

Mrs. Ferguson turned the key in the front door lock. "That would be nice, dear. Thank you."

Once the shop was snugged for the night, Tillie bid Mrs. Ferguson farewell and turned her steps toward the boarding-house. It was odd to be going home at this time of the evening with the sun already dipping behind the tall buildings, causing long shadows to stretch over the sidewalks. In the distance, a woman's voice echoed as she called her children to dinner. Tillie knotted the strings of her bonnet and set off down the street. Come winter, it would be dark by the time she quit the shop and made for home.

But not now. Now she could enjoy the cooler air that made strolling a pleasure. Perhaps she could even explore a couple of the fruit-vendor carts that lined Ashberry Street on her way home, pick out a nice melon that Laverne could add to their supper.

She smiled, picturing the woman's delight, and just as quickly wiped it away when a prickling at the nape of her neck slowed her steps. She paused and turned to look. The streets were not crowded this time of day, though there were still plenty of pedestrians bustling to and fro to make her wonder what it was that made her wary. Biting her lip, she continued on her way, relieved when she spotted a melon cart not far from the boardinghouse.

"Good evening, miss," the owner said, tipping his cap. "Something I can help ya with?"

Again the prickling. Tillie cast a glance over her shoulder at the thinning crowd, then back at the proprietor. Though she couldn't explain it, longing to be back within the safety of the boardinghouse walls filled her. "No . . . I suppose not."

"That one looks nice."

Tillie startled at the voice at her elbow. Cass Morgan stared down at her, a rakish grin fixed to his lips.

Tillie shifted the reticule to her wrist as she dipped in greeting. "Mr. Morgan, you surprised me."

He held up his hand. "Just Cass. Morgan is my brother."

As if he might materialize, she looked past Cass to the street.

"I'm alone. Thought I'd do a bit of exploring before supper. Never expected to run into you."

Why then did his speech sound so hasty to her ears? Was he the reason she'd felt such unease?

Cass motioned to the cart and its selection of fruit. "What about that one?"

She followed his gaze to a large watermelon.

"I can carry it for you, if you like. We be going the same way, after all." He pointed over his shoulder with his thumb. "Well?"

She checked the dwindling passersby on the street one last time, looked back at his smiling carefree face, then swallowed and nodded. Whatever had caused her discomfort, it wasn't him. "Aye. That would be fine."

She reached for the strings on her reticule, but before she could unfasten the bow, he plucked a coin from his pocket, dropped it into the vendor's waiting palm, and hoisted the watermelon to his shoulder.

"Here's hoping this one is as good inside as it looks out." He thumped the end with his thumb. "I don't have the same touch for picking the sweet ones as Morgan does." He started toward the sidewalk. "Ready?"

Tillie set off again, preceding him down the street. "So, Captain Morgan has a hand for gardening?"

"When he's not figuring out how to save our family." Cass swung into step beside her, one hand bracing the watermelon, the other held out from his body, elbow extended to her. She accepted the proffered arm and rested her fingers lightly against his forearm. Though he was of slighter build than his older brother, there was no doubting his form. The taut muscles beneath her touch ignited a memory she'd thought long buried.

Braedon's gentle smile, his hand reaching to her, the feel of his strong arms gripping her waist as he helped her to rise. *"Come, lass. Let me help you up."*

She shook her head, dislodging the recollection and the flood of emotions that accompanied it. "You were out exploring the city?" She croaked the words from a dry throat.

His attention slid from her to the street ahead. "Aye. I've not been to New York before. Morgan has, of course, but not me. 'Tis a fascinating place. Did you know the city was once the nation's capital?"

"It was?"

"Briefly. From 1785 to 1790." He paused. "Is it true they're thinking of dividing New York into boroughs? I've heard talk of it around the city."

She'd heard the same rumors. "Aye, there's been talk of it. True or not remains to be seen."

He continued chatting, but to Tillie's thinking it was more

a way of keeping her from asking questions than to entertain. Why she should feel so, she couldn't explain.

The boardinghouse lay just ahead. "I'll be glad to get home and rest my legs. Too much standing at the millinery made for a long day."

Cass glanced sidelong at her. "Do you always work so late?"

"Not usually. I've a new position with Mrs. Ferguson, helping her manage the orders and such. It's more pay, but it will mean later hours."

"It doesn't bother you walking home alone?"

Under normal circumstances she'd have answered no, but today the unease she'd felt earlier crept back on tenacious fingers. "Let's go inside, shall we? Laverne will be most pleased to see what we've brought home."

She led the way up the boardinghouse steps and held the door wide for Cass to pass through. Very wide. His broad shoulders took up nearly the entire frame. What was it about these Morgan men that made them so very large?

Cass patted the watermelon on his shoulder. "To the kitchen?"

"Aye. That way," Tillie said, pointing down the hall to a door that opened off the end. "Can't wait to see Laverne's face. It's her favorite."

Indeed, upon catching sight of the large watermelon, Laverne welcomed them with a smile. "We'll have our fill of the canned fruits once the cold months set in," she joked, patting a spot on the counter and then bending to take a long whiff of the fruity rind. Rising, she gave a satisfied smile. "That's a good one, and no doubt."

"You can tell by smelling it?" Cass's brow crinkled. "How? What's the difference?"

Laverne's eyes twinkled. "The good ones always have a sweet aroma about them."

Cass cocked his head and grinned. "Ma used to say the same thing about men." He leaned toward Tillie. "What do you think, lass? Am I sweet?"

"Enough, Cass." The low voice startled them all. Tall and glowering, Captain Morgan made a formidable figure lingering in the doorway. He beckoned to Cass with one finger, then nodded to Tillie and Laverne. "Cass, the library, if you please. Ladies."

He bowed before exiting, leaving Tillie to wonder about his sour appearance.

"As different as night and day, those two," Laverne said, giving voice to the thought hammering in Tillie's head. She grabbed a long knife and plunged it into the melon rind, releasing an aroma as sweet as she'd predicted. "One of them without a care in the world, and the other with all the world's cares." She clucked her tongue as she sliced the end off the melon and set it aside. "One would think a gal could find a man with the right balance of both."

Lowering her eyes, Tillie grabbed a bowl and carried it to Laverne to receive the slices of fresh fruit.

She had found such a man. Braedon. Only she'd lost him. And ever since then she'd doubted she would ever be content with anyone else.

Worse still, she doubted anyone else would ever be content with her.

13

Donal swung off Broad Street and onto a less traveled side street, where a black carriage with a matching set of black horses approached at a brisk clip. Flat on top and trimmed in gilt, the carriage might have made a spectacle were it not for the locale and the sheer number of fine rigs passing by. This one rumbled to a stop alongside him, and one of the beveled glass doors swung open.

At last. He'd wondered how long he would have to meander this stretch of road before The Celt showed up. Donal climbed aboard and snapped the door shut behind him as the carriage lurched into motion.

Settling back against the plush velvet seat, he was about to give a respectful nod to the passenger sitting opposite when he realized there was another man in the carriage besides The Celt. The man seemed to be studying him, his eyelids hooded beneath a gray flat cap.

Donal forced his attention back to The Celt. "Glad you could meet me."

"Your message said it was urgent."

Aye, that it was. He licked his lips and glanced at The Celt's companion and back again. "I thought you would be alone."

He shrugged. "Does it matter? My associate here is privy to most of my conversations, isn't that right, Mr. Dunahoe?"

The man gave a tip of his cap, a leer stretching his thin lips into a semblance of a smile.

Resisting the urge to lean forward to get a better look at the man, Donal remained where he was and folded his hands in his lap. "Your orders were to keep my eyes and ears open, no? I'd say I've done that."

"Well?" The Celt's eyes gleamed in the filtered light of the carriage. "What have you learned that made it so important we meet?"

Careful, lad. Don't want to make him angry with the messenger.

Again, Donal licked his lips. "It's the lass. The one McKillop insisted he bring with him to America."

Almost imperceptibly The Celt's grip on his pearl-handled walking cane tightened. In fact, were it not for the whiteness of his knuckles against the burnished wood, Donal might not have noticed at all.

"What about her?" The Celt growled.

Donal drew a breath and squared his shoulders. If he were to win The Celt's favor and thereby get his hands on the *Caitriona Marie*, it would have to be now. He swallowed, then lifted one shoulder in a shrug. "Turns out getting rid of the good doctor wasn't as tidy as we'd hoped. Turns out he left behind a few loose ends."

The Celt's eyes, already narrow, formed slits.

"What I mean is," Donal continued, looking from him to the man seated next to him, "the captain let someone in to see McKillop before he died."

"You know this for certain?"

Donal nodded. "Overheard the captain and his brother talking about it me own self."

To his relief, The Celt released him from his unyielding stare and looked down at the carriage floor. Just then it jostled to the left, but The Celt swayed with the movement, barely having to adjust the way Donal did with a hand to the wall to brace himself.

"What else did you hear?" The Celt asked at last.

Anxiety bubbled in Donal's gut. If ever The Celt were to lose his temper, it would be now. Instinctively he inched away from the end of the cane, which he'd heard rumored housed a steely blade. It had run red more than once, so the story went.

An involuntary breath puffed from his lips. "They said . . . before Doc died . . . he must have told them he'd been paid to murder McKillop." He couldn't help himself; he fidgeted under The Celt's cold glare. "Leastwise that's what I reckon since they both admitted they knew McKillop had been murdered."

"And?"

"That's when the captain said he feared it might be dangerous for the lass if anyone were to find out she'd been in to see McKillop before he passed."

Donal waited, holding his breath and searching The Celt's face, but the man absorbed the information like a sponge, no expression. More important, no word of thanks.

He clutched the edge of the seat where it hit the backs of his knees. "If I may, sir?"

A nod was his signal to continue.

"The captain and his brother, well, 'tis true they're now privy to Doc's part in McKillop's dying, but so far as they know, it could have been anyone what ordered the deed done. The lass, however . . ." Donal paused, rubbing the dampness from his palms on his trousers, then stammered on, "There be no telling what was told to the lass before McKillop passed. I say she's a thistle to you, sir, one that needs be plucked out before she causes any more damage."

"Indeed."

"Aye, sir. And I know just how to go about it—getting rid of her, I mean. I took it upon myself to follow her around the city this morning and last. Got a good feel for her comings and goings, I did. Figured the knowledge might come in handy."

For the first time, Donal thought he saw a glimmer of appreciation shining from The Celt's eyes. So much for his glowering companion. He lifted his nose. "I can take care of this problem for you. Easily, in fact. And I won't ask much for me trouble, either. Just say the word and it's done."

"Like it was done after I gave you the word to get rid of Doc?"

His mouth dry, Donal said, "What?"

The Celt lifted his cane and rapped on the carriage's roof. The man beside him cupped one fist inside the other and cracked his knuckles, the sound loud in the cramped space of the carriage. What was his name? Dunahoe?

"Like it was done when I asked you about Keondric Morgan and you told me I had nothing to fear from him?" The Celt continued.

Sweat formed on Donal's brow. "That was hardly my fault. How was I to know Doc would do all that talking before the poison set in?"

"I paid you to know," The Celt barked, his sharp tone sending shivers over Donal's flesh.

He shot his hand to the carriage wall as they came to an abrupt stop. Through the window, tree limbs swayed, pushed by a breeze that blew off a winding stretch of the river nearby. He swallowed hard and looked at The Celt, then at Dunahoe. How far had they driven? "I don't recognize this place. Where are we?"

To his relief, The Celt stretched out his cane and pushed open the door next to Donal. "I won't be needing your services, Mr. Peevey. This is where you get off."

Wouldn't need his services? After the information he'd just provided? He formed a retort, then glanced out the carriage window and thought better of voicing it. Solitude rang from the place they now occupied. Dense trees lined the riverbank, and the rutted road they'd traveled looked barren.

He jerked his chin up. Fine. The Celt wouldn't pay for his assistance, but he knew someone who would. No doubt Captain Morgan would be glad of the information he possessed.

Edging from the seat, Donal reached for the door handle and prepared to disembark. Maybe he wouldn't get the *Caitriona Marie*, but for now that could wait. After all, what were a few more weeks?

Just as he placed one foot on the rung hanging below the carriage, Donal felt a sharp thump on his back, directly between his shoulder blades. Almost as though he'd been struck. Almost . . .

He fell forward, surprised to realize that his legs felt very weak, his knees refusing to hold him up. He pitched forward, caught himself with both hands when he felt it again—a sharp, stabbing pain.

"What—?"

"As I said, Mr. Peevey, I'll no longer be needing your services."

A buzzing in his ears deadened The Celt's voice, made it sound as though it carried from a great distance. It was then that he knew. The blackguard had betrayed him!

He opened his mouth wide, fighting to suck air into lungs that felt hard and flat. The f-filthy rat had stabbed . . . stabbed him in the back!

It was the last thought he had before he flopped into the dirt and everything around him went dark.

14

The day dawned clear and bright the following Saturday. Despite what she'd told herself about avoiding Captain Morgan, Tillie took special care getting dressed and even gave her cheeks a pinch before descending the stairs on her way to breakfast. Catching sight of the captain, handsome in a dark cotton shirt that pulled at his shoulders, she hesitated at the doorway and took a deep breath before entering.

Immediately, Cass rose from his chair and met her at the door. "You're looking quite fit this morning, competition for a fine day."

Bending over her hand, he gave a kiss to the back of it before leading her to the table, where she was met by a chorus of good mornings—except for Captain Morgan, she noted, whose expression had gone sour.

Taking extra time in choosing the blue cotton dress she wore had made her the last to arrive. She spoke her apologies while Cass slid back her chair.

"Not to worry," Amelia said, beaming her approval of Cass's gallantry. "We haven't even had our coffee yet."

On cue, Laverne bustled in holding a silver pot and set it on the table near Amelia's elbow. "Breakfast will just be a moment," she said.

"And not a moment too soon," Meg said, grabbing the pot and pouring both herself and Amelia a cup. "This weather makes me hungry."

"It makes me lazy," Giles said. He opened his napkin with a snap and laid it across his lap. "Barely got anything done in the stable yesterday." He tilted his head toward Amelia. "Hope you don't mind, I went ahead and started planting them extra rows of peas for a fall crop like you wanted."

Extra rows? Tillie breathed her thanks to Cass as she took her place at the table. She reached for her water glass and took a sip. What need had Amelia for extra vegetables? As it was, there'd proved to be an abundance since Cara and Ana had vacated the boardinghouse.

Despite her concern, all rational thought fled her mind when, a moment later, Captain Morgan placed a light touch to her wrist.

He held the silver pot aloft. "Coffee?"

Somehow she managed to swallow. "Please. And thank you, Captain."

Ach, but she sounded like her mother. Lowering her eyes, she set aside her glass and folded her hands in her lap while the captain poured her coffee.

"Cass is right."

He'd spoken so softly, she had to look up to be sure. "I'm sorry?"

He filled his own cup, then set the pot aside. Averting his eyes, he said, "You . . . uh . . ." He gestured toward her dress. "The color suits you."

She ran her palms over her skirt self-consciously. All that, and he'd yet to actually look at her. Her cheeks warmed. "Thank you again."

"You have plans for today?" His eyes, appearing steely blue against his navy shirt, shone with genuine interest.

"Some shopping." She lowered her voice. "Laverne's birthday is coming up." Surprised she didn't stammer, what with the clumsiness of her tongue, she hid a portion of her face behind the rim of her cup.

Though he said nothing, the glance he shot at his brother prompted an immediate response.

"Perhaps I could accompany you," Cass said, setting aside his glass. He pressed his napkin to his lips and cleared his throat. "I . . . um, need to purchase a few supplies for the ship, ain't so, Morgan?"

"Aye." He turned to Tillie. "'Twould be a great help if you would show Cass around the city, help him find the things we need. If it's not too much of a bother," he added.

Spending an entire day accompanied by the handsome Cass? No, she wouldn't say 'twas a bother. The only thing that might make it better would be if the captain himself . . . She cut short her wayward thoughts and nodded. "'Twould be my pleasure."

Cass raised his glass. "Good. We'll leave after breakfast. Meg? Amelia?" He shifted in his chair to address them. "Would either of you like to come along?"

Meg frowned. "I can't. I promised Laverne I would help in the garden."

"And I have a meeting of the Ladies Auxiliary," Amelia said.

Cass nodded. "Well, it looks like it's just you and me then, Tillie."

"What are your plans for this morning?" Tillie asked the captain.

"He is—" Cass began, only to be interrupted by his brother's upraised hand.

"I've me own errands to run, and then I need to swing by the dock and see how the repairs are coming." To her surprise, he leaned close and whispered, "You'll be safe with Cass."

Confusion muddied her thinking. Safe? Did he think she

doubted his brother's honor? Was he concerned because they would be without a proper chaperone? Perhaps it was his own brother's reputation he was concerned for, and he looked down upon her for the mistakes she'd made in the past.

"The city is a large place, and while I know you be quite accustomed to wandering it, I'll feel better knowing you aren't alone."

Her guilt eased, for it wasn't any of the things she'd feared. "Thank you, Captain. Your kindness is appreciated, though you needn't have bothered. I've lived in New York long enough to know which streets to avoid."

Instead of alleviating, the intensity of his countenance burned even brighter, robbing her of breath. Fortunately, Laverne appeared with their breakfast and the conversation turned to more pleasant topics.

Once the meal was finished and the dishes cleared, Tillie joined Cass on the street in front of the boardinghouse, glad for the sunny day, the mild temperatures, and the affable lad strolling by her side. Though he favored his brother in appearance, he was far less intimidating, what with his quick wit and easy laugh, and she found herself thankful for the good fortune that had sent him into town after supplies.

"Any idea where you'd like to go?" Cass asked, offering his arm and then moving with her down the crowded street.

"There's a jewelry store nearby," Tillie said. "Not too expensive. If we have time, I'd like to look for something there."

"Jewelry? For Laverne? She doesn't seem the type."

Tillie smiled. "Do not let that gruff demeanor fool you. Inside, she's as soft as a lamb. Besides, what woman doesn't enjoy pretty things now and again? Laverne would never think to buy anything for herself, which is why I thought I'd see if I might find a bracelet or a pair of earrings—something to remind her of her gentler side."

Cass's lips curved in what could only be construed as a devilish grin. "Nice sentiment."

She nodded as they approached a cheerful building with striped awnings over both windows. "That's the one."

Dropping her arm, he hastened to open the door, which pushed a bell that jingled merrily as they entered. Despite the hour, several patrons were shopping, and Tillie had to wait her turn at the counter. Unfortunately, though there were several items in her price range, nothing caught her eye. Some time later, she left the store disappointed.

"How about a bottle of perfume?" Cass suggested, indicating a shop across the street that had the name of the place painted on the door in wide, curving letters.

She bit her lip. Though she hadn't thought to give Laverne perfume, it might prove a fine substitute and still fit within her budget. "Aye. Perfume would be nice . . . but what about your supplies?"

He shrugged. "Plenty of time for that. Shall we?" Once again he offered his arm, but this time, when she took it, he covered her hand with his own.

Tillie drew in a breath. While she sensed Cass to be the sort who made friends easily, and his gesture was intended as nothing more than amicable, it still felt odd to be in the care of a man.

A very nice, very handsome man.

Normally she traveled the streets unobserved. But today, several gazes followed them as they passed, most of them feminine, all of them envious. Tillie found herself walking with her shoulders drawn back, even lifting her chin ever so slightly.

Inside the perfumery, scents from spicy and robust to flowery and delicate wafted on the air. She almost expected Cass to wrinkle his nose and beg to wait on the street. Instead he picked up several bottles and sniffed. Finally he gave a satisfied nod and held one of them toward Tillie.

"This one. It's perfect."

Indeed, the exotic fragrance was exactly what she would have chosen for Laverne. Though she could only afford a small bottle, she was excited when she slid the package into her reticule.

"I can't wait to see her face. Thank you so much for helping me choose, Cass."

He tipped his cap. "My pleasure, ma'am. And now . . ." He pulled a package from behind his back and held it aloft. "For you."

Tillie stared in confusion. "Me? What? Why?"

Cass bumped his cap off his forehead with his thumb and scratched his temple. "Why not?"

"But . . . it's not my birthday." The words sounded trite even to her own ears, yet she could think of no other reply.

Cass laughed, a completely abandoned sound that startled and then transfixed her. How long had it been since she had felt free enough to laugh so? She couldn't remember.

Plucking her by the wrist, he deposited the package into her palm. "I'm sure you'll have a birthday eventually, eh, lass?"

She couldn't help but smile at the merriment in his eyes. "I'm sure. Thank you."

"You're welcome."

"And now," she said quickly, before he could see how his token of kindness affected her, "we should see to your errands. I've a feeling your brother will not appreciate it if I keep you busy buying trinkets all day."

He snorted. "Ach, my brother. He should spend the day just so once in a while. It'd do him good."

He escorted her back outside, where the press of shoppers had thickened. Several times they were jostled as they walked, until Cass drew her to his side and moved with her closer to the street, where the crowd was thinner.

"So, your brother," Tillie said, fidgeting with the string on her reticule, "has he always been so . . . somber?"

"You mean ill-tempered? Belligerent? Cantankerous?" He waggled his brows.

Tillie giggled. "I was thinking more like stern. Solemn. Serious-minded."

"Ha! Good for you." His grin changed, became wry. "To be fair, I suppose I'm to blame for some of that."

"You?"

He nodded, his fingers absently patting the back of her hand. "He wouldn't have worked so hard, given up his dream of staying home and running a farm, if he hadn't had to provide for me and Ma after Da died."

Her smile faded. "How old were you?"

"Ten. Morgan was nineteen. Of course, I didn't bother making things easy." Regret thickened his voice.

"I'm sorry."

A carriage rumbled by, drowning anything else she might have said. When it passed, he pointed to a dry-goods store on the opposite side of the street. "Mind if we go there? Looks like it'll have most of what I need."

"Of course." She hitched her reticule higher on her wrist and prepared to step out into the street.

"Have a care," Cass warned, holding out his hand. A large wagon loaded with barrels rattled toward them at a brisk clip. "That fellow must be mad, driving like that."

In truth, the wagon made quite a sight rumbling and lurching as it did down the busy street. The driver seemed not to notice the pedestrians scattering in various directions before him. If he wasn't careful—

Before she could finish the thought, Tillie felt herself pushed from behind—a hard shove that sent her sprawling past Cass's outstretched arm and into the busy street.

Straight into the path of the fast-approaching wagon.

15

Morgan grabbed the last of his gear and stuffed it into a leather satchel before sliding the strap through a worn loop and securing it over his shoulder. Under his feet, waves rocked the *Caitriona Marie*, pushing her from side to side like a cradle beneath a mother's gentle hand. Times like this, he didn't mind so much the life his father's passing had compelled him into, though the ship did feel oddly lifeless with all the crew members except for Bozey gone ashore.

Morgan stepped from his cabin and made his way to the stern, where Bozey was totaling up the last of the off-load and entering the figures into a log.

"So? How does it look?"

Bozey handed him the ledger, a broad smile creasing his plump face. "Good, Cap'n. Better'n we'd hoped."

Morgan scanned the page. He wasn't a man given to much praise, but when it was warranted . . .

He handed the ledger back and clapped Bozey on the shoulder. "Good work."

"Thank you, sir."

Morgan turned to go.

"Cap'n, have you got a moment?"

He paused. "Aye?"

Though he wouldn't have thought it possible for a sailor as salty as Bozey, the man actually blushed. He looked to be working up the courage to speak.

Morgan crossed his arms and stared. "What is it, Boze? Speak up."

Bozey cleared his throat. "It's the men, sir. They've all gone ashore, but with orders to return in two days. I figure that would give me plenty of time to line up the repairs you asked for and see to the stocking of the galley."

"And?"

"It's Donal, sir. I've not seen him since . . ."

"Since?"

His chin lifted. "The crew overheard the skirmish between you and him the other day. I know you wasn't pleased, so I'd understand if you told Donal not to come back."

"I wouldn't do that without telling you."

Bozey reached up and scratched the top of his head. "Right, but ain't none of us laid eyes on the lad since he stormed off. If you didn't fire him, where in blazes could he be?"

Morgan shifted the satchel on his shoulder. "Has he any kin in New York?"

"None that I know of."

"What about his gear?"

"I checked his berth this morning. It's all still here. He hasn't been by to collect anything."

That *was* odd. Morgan nodded his thanks. "I'll check into it. Thank you, Bozey."

Morgan stowed the information, then made his way off the ship and down the length of the dock. Two figures waited at the end: one large, the other short and slight, both wearing the same black wool coat and twill trousers. On their heads were tan dome hats, and fixed to belts around their waists were black wooden nightsticks.

The smaller of the men stepped forward to meet him. "Keondric Morgan?"

Morgan nodded. "Aye, that's me. What can I do for you?"

"Police, Captain Morgan."

Police? Though the man continued talking, Morgan's thoughts flashed to Tillie and his brother. But he shook his thoughts free of this grip of fear. "Beggin' your pardon, what . . . what did you say?"

The smaller man gestured toward the street. "I said we're going to need you to accompany us to the morgue. I'm afraid there's been an accident and, well, unfortunately we're going to need you to identify the victim."

— ✳ ✳ ✳ —

For several seconds, Tillie could do nothing except will air into her burning lungs. She'd scraped both palms when Cass shoved her out of the way of the oncoming wagon, but it was the blow to her back when they hit the cobbled street that had left her dazed and breathless.

"Are you all right?"

Cass rolled into her vision, his face a worried mask and his eyes smoldering copies of the look she'd witnessed from Captain Morgan earlier that morning.

"I . . ."

He gripped her shoulders. "Tillie?"

"Aye." She squeaked the word through tight lips and then, with his help, managed to push upright. She cast a bewildered look at the people gathered around them on the street. "What happened?"

Now that she was talking, the color seemed to return to Cass's wan cheeks. He stood and bent to grasp her forearms.

"You tripped. 'Bout scared me to death, too. You could have been killed stumbling out into the street like that."

Lifting gently, he helped her to her feet. Tillie eyed the wagon that had rocked to a stop just a few feet from where she and Cass had landed. "Was anyone else hurt?"

"Not yet," Cass growled, shooting a blazing glance at the driver, who slouched alongside his horse.

She shook her head. "No, Cass. I'm fine. Really. Let's just go."

Indeed, she was most anxious to get away from this particular corner, but not because she hoped to keep Cass from a fight.

It was because she was most certain she had not tripped.

She scanned the faces surrounding them again. One of them belonged to the person who'd pushed her into the path of the rushing wagon. Why? If it was an accident, why did they not speak, if only to offer an apology?

She shuddered. "Come, Cass. I'm not feeling well. Please help me back to the boardinghouse."

The crowd seemed satisfied now that they saw she wasn't seriously injured, and they slowly began to disperse.

Despite Cass's glowering face, the wagon driver straightened and took a hesitant step in their direction. "You all right, ma'am?"

"No thanks to you," Cass shot back. "What if it'd been a child who stumbled out in front of you? Did you think about that?"

"Sorry," the man mumbled. He tipped his cap to Tillie, then turned to go. "Glad you're all right, miss."

"Wait."

Cass started toward him, but Tillie grabbed his arm and held him back. "Let him go."

Seconds ticked by before he finally relented. Grabbing his cap from the street, and her reticule from the sidewalk where it had flown from her wrist, he turned from the driver and led her away from the scene. He hunched protectively over her all the way back to the boardinghouse, admonishing her as they walked to watch her step.

Ach, but she must have looked a sight for him to hover so. And though she tried to reassure him, she wasn't quite able to control her trembling, even after they'd arrived home and Laverne had deposited them in the parlor and then went to fetch tea.

Meg wrung a towel in a bowl of fresh water and laid it gently over Tillie's scraped palms. "Tell me again how you fell into the street? Tripped, you say? On what?"

Tillie shrugged. "I don't know. I dinna look."

"Not like you to be so clumsy," Meg said, not unkindly but in her typical blunt way.

"It wasn't her fault," Cass said. "It was very crowded today. We were probably much closer to the street than was safe. I blame myself for what happened."

Tillie's heart warmed at Cass's defense. She flashed him a grateful smile, then turned to Meg. "Don't listen to him. 'Twas an accident, nothing more."

But inside, she wasn't so certain. 'Twas no careless jostle that had sent her skittering into the path of the wagon. It had felt more like two hands thrust against her back in a calculated manner meant to cause her harm.

She shuddered.

"You're cold," Cass whispered. He eased closer on the settee and clasped her wrapped hands.

Laverne entered bearing a silver tray. "This'll warm her right up. Chamomile, your favorite."

Setting the tray down, Laverne glanced at Tillie's face and tsked softly. "Poor dear. Got quite a fright, I expect."

Was it her imagination or did Cass appear reluctant to let

go of her hands as he rose to make room for Laverne? Her heart gave an odd little flutter.

"All right, let me see those wounds," Laverne ordered. She gave the scrapes on Tillie's palms a cursory investigation before grunting in approval. "Looks a sight better. Good job, Meg."

She poured a cup of tea and then pressed it into Tillie's shaking fingers. "Drink this. It'll fix you right up. You'll be back to normal in no time."

Normal? Tillie took a hesitant sip. She didn't think so. Something had happened today that had shaken her to the core, and she doubted Laverne's tea, or Cass's defense, or even Meg's concern would ever be enough to make her feel normal.

Indeed, she wondered if she'd ever feel normal again.

16

Unbelievable. The morgue. Again. Would things never return to normal?

Morgan hunched his shoulders and ducked inside the place. The two policemen who'd met him at the dock led the way down a long hall.

The knot of dread that had formed at their appearance tightened in his gut. They'd already told him the victim was a man, someone they suspected to be a member of his crew. Could it be Cass?

He clenched his fists tighter. No. He wouldn't let himself consider such a thing. His breathing turned shallow as they approached the examination room, where Ramsey waited at the table next to a sheet-draped figure.

The undertaker dipped his head. "A pleasure to see you again, Captain Morgan."

He couldn't claim likewise. Instead, Morgan tipped his cap and kept his eyes fixed on the examination table.

"We found some papers in his coat pocket. No identification, but we were able to make out the ship's name. Looked like a work order of some kind."

Fear stabbed Morgan's heart. He waved toward the head of the table. Lips tight, he said, "Who is it? Let me see."

Ramsey's hand moved toward the edge of the sheet, then hesitated. "You should know, Captain, the body was found floating in the harbor. He was trapped in the pilings below Liberty Pier. The waves, the pushing against the rocks . . . well, it's a gruesome sight, I'm afraid. By the look of him, he may have fallen in quite a ways upriver and floated downstream. You may want to prepare yourself."

As though the place itself had not already sparked the worst possible imaginings? His stomach rolled. Sweat trickled down his back and neck. He clenched his jaw and shot Ramsey a glare. "Enough. Pull back the covering or I'll do it myself."

Bit by agonizing bit, Ramsey complied. Slowly, dark hair appeared.

Morgan sucked in a breath and took an involuntary step from the table. The man's hair was black, like Cass's. Or was it just that the man's hair was soaked that made it resemble his brother's so?

Forcing himself to look at the man's face, Morgan let go a sigh of relief that sapped the strength from his shoulders. It wasn't Cass lying on the table.

It was Donal.

"Do you know him, Captain?" one of the policemen asked.

Gradually, his heart calmed its wild racing. Though he was by no means glad to see another member of his crew dead, it did mean his brother was safe, and for that he couldn't help but be grateful.

Morgan gave a curt nod. "Aye, his name is Donal Peevey. He was one of my crew."

"How long has it been since you've seen him?" the other officer asked.

"A couple of days." He fell silent as Ramsey replaced the

sheet over Donal's bloated face. Along with numerous bruises, jagged cuts and scrapes marked him from brow to chin. "Any idea what happened to him?"

"It wasn't the water that killed him," Ramsey announced matter-of-factly. "That much was obvious."

"What do you mean?"

"He had multiple stab wounds to his back and shoulders, all pretty vicious gauging from the depth of the blows. Bloke probably never saw it coming."

"And the river?"

"No water in his lungs that I could tell. Looks to me as though the killer stabbed him and then dumped him in the river to get rid of the body."

Disbelief slowly replaced the fear that had gripped Morgan. Two members of his crew murdered? Why? Worse yet, who was next?

The shorter officer rounded the table, thanked Ramsey, and then dismissed him. The door to the examination room closed behind him with a soft click.

The officer looked at Morgan. "Any idea who could have done it, Captain?"

He thought briefly about telling the officers about Doc, then shook his head.

"What about enemies? Did the man have any?"

Obviously. But were they Donal's enemies, or his? "None that I know of," Morgan said, his throat dry. That much was true.

"What about the rest of your crew? They get along pretty well?" the taller officer asked.

"They get along just fine."

"Mind if we ask them?"

Unease spread through Morgan's belly. The questioning didn't feel right, as though the policemen were looking for clues to Donal's killer among the *Caitriona Marie*'s crew. He frowned. "Aye, you can ask them, but it might take a while to round them all up. Gave them all a couple days' leave while I have repairs made to the ship."

"What kind of repairs?"

Morgan eyed the smaller officer critically. "Does it matter?"

He shrugged. "I suppose not."

The taller officer stepped forward. "Mind coming to the station, Captain? We've a few more questions we'd like to ask. Besides that, we'll need to gather any information you have regarding the man's family. Where he's from, things like that."

He signaled toward the door quite congenially, but Morgan sensed it wasn't a request. A man had been murdered, and the two officers standing across from him were determined to figure out who'd done it.

Unfortunately, they were both staring at him, and if he wasn't mistaken, the look in their eyes said they'd already formed a few suspicions.

And that couldn't be good. It would be worse when they found out that Donal was the second man from the *Marie* to be housed inside one of Ramsey's cold lockers, if they didn't know already.

Morgan cast a glance at the shorter officer. If they'd spoken to Ramsey . . .

Who was he kidding? Of course they had. Which explained why they were both watching him so intently.

No. Following these men to the police station for questioning wasn't good. Not good at all.

17

The opening of the front door woke Tillie from a light slumber. She sat up on the settee, confused for a moment as to where she was and the time of day. Long shadows crept along the swirling rose carpet. The sun hung midway down the tall parlor windows. Late afternoon . . .

Her hands began to throb, reminding her of the events of that morning. On the table next to the settee sat two cups of tea—one partially empty, the other untouched. Hers. She remembered now.

Rising, she eased into the hall to see who had entered. Captain Morgan lowered his hand from the hall tree, where he'd hung his cap. With his shoulders bent and his face lined with worry, he looked as tired and careworn as she felt, but the moment he spied her, he straightened and crossed to meet her.

"Good afternoon."

"Hello, Captain."

"Have you seen my brother?"

She motioned toward the parlor. "He was with me a bit ago. I'm not sure where . . ."

Perhaps it was the disorientation from having awakened to find herself alone, or perhaps it was a last vestige of the fear she'd felt when she looked up and saw the wagon bearing down on her. Whatever the cause, a trembling started in her limbs she was helpless to control.

The captain moved toward her. "Miss McGrath? Are you all right?"

Reaching behind her, she felt for the wall and used it to steady herself. "I'm fine. A bit out of sorts is all."

"Perhaps you should sit down."

"No, I'm sure it will pass. I just need a minute to collect myself."

Despite her assurances, she knew that to move from the wall would not be wise. Her knees felt as soft and unstable as melted butter. And strangely, the fact that the captain now stood beside her did not help the situation. He was like a massive oak, looming over her with his feet braced apart and his hand outstretched.

"Let me help you."

The command felt warm and familiar. She placed her hand in his.

"Are you ill?"

Before she could answer, Cass appeared from the kitchen, a thick slice of Laverne's freshly baked bread in his hand. "Tillie, you're awake. Good. How are you feeling? Did the nap help?" He didn't wait for a reply but turned to look at his brother. "So? How'd it go in town?"

Morgan only spared Cass a cursory glance before returning his attention to her. "So you *are* ill."

She shook her head.

"Who? Tillie?" Cass lowered the bread. "I thought you were resting after . . ."

"After what?" Morgan demanded, his brows lowering.

"We . . . uh, we had a little accident," Cass said.

"What!"

Though he ground the word out, he could have shouted for the reaction it spurred from Cass. He dropped the bread on the hall table and rushed toward them.

"She never left my side. I swear, Morgan. 'Twas an accident, nothing more. And she's not hurt, besides a few scrapes and such."

Morgan sucked in a breath as he shifted back to her. "You're hurt?"

She swallowed and hid her hands in the folds of her dress. "Like Cass said, 'tis only a few scrapes. Nothing serious."

Despite her assurance, the scowl on his face grew. He pointed toward the parlor, and even with the shaking of her knees, it did not occur to her to disobey. Or Cass either, it seemed. He followed behind her and then took the seat next to her on the settee.

"Tell me what happened—what you did, where you went—everything leading up to the accident."

Morgan paced as he listened to Cass explain in detail the events of that morning. The unease Tillie had been feeling since she awoke blossomed into dread. The interest the captain displayed was inordinately intense.

Something had happened.

When Cass finished, so too did Morgan's pacing. He paused at the window, his tall figure nearly filling the frame.

She rose and went to him. "What have you not told me?"

His eyes met hers, bluish-gray and as cold and roiling as a storm-tossed sea. "When you woke, you were afraid. Why?"

She bit her lip. "No . . . I . . ."

He turned so he was facing her and caught her by her shoulders. "Tillie, tell me."

His use of her name caught her off guard, added an intimacy that absorbed every thought and action so that she forgot anyone else was in the room.

"I . . ."

His fingers tightened. "Aye, lass? Go on."

"I don't think I tripped."

"What!" Cass exclaimed.

"I'm sorry I didn't tell you," she said, then pressed on when the captain's hands fell away. "Just before I fell into the street . . . I thought I felt someone push me. But it was crowded and we were walking along the outside of the sidewalk," she added quickly, whether in defense of Cass or her wild claim, she wasn't certain. "It could have been an accident."

As she spoke, the captain's eyes took on a fierce quality that at once frightened and enthralled her. He moved closer to bend over her as Cass had done, only with him the peace she felt was immediate.

"'Twas no accident, Tillie. Someone meant you harm, and it was only Cass's quick action that prevented it."

Someone wanted to harm her? Confused, she put up her hand and retreated a step. "No . . . that kinna be correct. Why would you assume such a thing?"

Cass had risen to stand, and though his face was pale, he did not look surprised by anything his brother had said.

Suspicion formed in her chest. "What is it the two of you know? What haven't you told me?"

The brothers exchanged a look, and then Morgan crossed to a chair and indicated that she should resume her place on the settee. She did, for now that the trembling of her limbs had returned, she doubted she could have stood any longer. The captain sat in the chair closest to her.

"When you were aboard the ship, Tillie," he began, "do you remember a man treating your . . . Braedon McKillop?"

He'd been prepared to say her husband. She swallowed a knot of shame, unable to look at either him or Cass. "The doctor? Aye, I remember him."

"And had either you or McKillop met him before?"

She shook her head and looked up. "No. Why do you ask?"

It was the captain's turn to look away. A muscle ticked near his jaw, and his fingers had curled into fists.

Cass spoke from his place near the window. "Tell her, Morgan. She needs to know."

"Know what?" So dry was Tillie's mouth, the words squeaked out with a sound akin to a door on rusted hinges.

She held her breath as the captain heaved a sigh and put out his large hand to cover hers. "First, you should know that my crew and I . . . that none of us had any idea what happened until just a few days ago."

And she still didn't. Her breathing quickened. "Go on."

Captain Morgan appeared to chew the words. No, she realized a second later, he was mulling them, choosing with care the ones he would use.

"There's no easy way to say this," he said at last, his voice a rumbling bass that shook her insides. "There are no words to express how verra sorry I am to tell you that . . . Braedon McKillop's death was no accident."

Shocking as the news was, what followed left her even more dumbstruck.

"We believe he was murdered, and now . . . Tillie, I'm afraid you might be next."

18

It took every ounce of self-control for Morgan to resist sweeping Tillie into his arms. Her dark hair curled around her pale face, and her lips were tightly clenched, but despite all of that, she stared up at him with a touch of defiance shimmering in her goldish-brown eyes.

"Murdered." She blinked as she said the word, as though unable to process such a horrendous concept. Morgan tightened his hold on her hand.

"Just before Doc passed away, he called me into his cabin. I think perhaps he knew his end was near and he wanted to go to his Maker with his conscience clear."

Her eyes narrowed. "What do you mean 'clear'? What did he have to feel guilty for? What had he done?"

Though he sought with all his might to find a way to soften the blow, there was none. He grit his teeth. "Doc was paid to kill Braedon, Tillie."

Instantly she jerked her hands away as though she'd been bit. "What?"

Morgan gave a slow nod. "He poisoned him and then made it look as though he'd taken ill."

"But . . . why would he do that?"

Cass drew near to her shoulder as they spoke. She looked up at him, her eyes wide and confused.

"Cass?"

Morgan's heart gave a jolt. She looked to his brother? But he shoved aside the selfish thought and motioned for Cass to resume where he'd left off. If it was Cass she trusted, perhaps the rest would be better coming from him.

"Morgan went to see Doc's cousin," Cass said, "a man named James Finch. He told him that Doc had a family—a wife and adopted daughter, both of whom took ill just before Doc came to work for us—for Morgan," he corrected, tossing an apologetic glance his way. Morgan dismissed the slip with a wave. Cass cleared his throat and resumed. "According to Mr. Finch, Doc was in desperate need of money."

He placed his hand on Tillie's shoulder, a move that made Morgan's stomach tighten. Unable to watch, he stared at the floor while Cass went forward with what they knew right up until they'd returned to the boardinghouse.

"And that's it," Cass said when he'd finished. "That's why Morgan came looking for you, and why we both felt it best we keep an eye on you, at least until we could figure out who paid Doc, and why."

Morgan flexed his fingers. "Actually . . ."

"What?" Thankfully, Cass removed his hand from Tillie's shoulder. "What's wrong?"

He'd hoped to share the news with his brother alone, but now that they'd told her the truth, he couldn't see holding back. Indeed, 'twould be better if she understood the full extent of the danger. Morgan rose and crossed to his brother.

"It's Donal, Cass. The police found his body floating in the harbor early this morning. I've already been by the morgue to identify him."

"He drowned?" Disbelief rounded Cass's eyes.

Morgan shook his head. "He was stabbed and his body tossed in the river."

"Donal?"

He glanced at Tillie. Her features had gone unnaturally white, and for a moment he feared she'd faint, until he saw the determination blazing in her eyes. Just what was going on inside that head of hers? He turned to face her. "One of my crew."

"Did he know Doc?"

"Only from working with him aboard the *Marie*. At least we think so."

"So you dinna believe the deaths are related?"

He shook his head. "At this point we kinna be certain of anything beyond what we've told you."

"Which is nothing besides the fact that my fiancé was murdered while on board your ship."

Morgan drew back, surprised. Of course she'd be distraught. He even expected to receive a bit of recrimination. But anger?

Nay, not anger. It was stronger than that. Fury flashed from her eyes, her white lips, and her tightly curled fingers. She stood as he advanced a wary step toward her. She stood toe-to-toe with him, even though she had to look up to peer into his face.

"When were you going to tell me?" she asked.

"I'd hoped to have more to tell," he said quietly.

Her head shook. "You had no right to wait. I could have been searching, asking questions—"

"Which is exactly what we wanted to avoid," Morgan interrupted.

"What?"

"Without knowing who paid Doc, you would only be placing yourself in further danger by asking questions. It was far safer for you this way."

"Obviously not," she snapped, throwing both fists to her hips, "or I would not have been nearly killed today."

"Tillie—" Cass began.

His gaze still pinned to Tillie, Morgan put up his hand to stop him. "Are you implying that what happened today was somehow my fault?"

"Not at all. What I am saying is that had you warned me earlier, I might have been on my guard."

"All right. Say I had told you the truth; what would you have done differently?"

"I . . . I . . ." Her face flushed and she looked away. "I don't know."

Compassion softened his heart. It could not have been easy for her to admit her vulnerability, given the situation. He'd battled with it himself. But one thing he did know: letting word get out that she'd spoken with McKillop before he died was not a good thing.

"Tillie?" His mouth went dry as she looked up at him, a pained expression on her face. Swallowing, he continued, "You have no reason to believe this other than what you know of me, but I hope you realize that I acted to protect you. I had no other cause to keep the truth from you than that."

To his relief, she gave a slow nod, a relief that flickered and died when next she opened her mouth.

"What will we do now? Keep trying to find out who paid Doc?"

"*I* will keep trying." Morgan set his jaw against the resistance flashing in her brown eyes. "You will keep to your normal schedule and allow Cass to accompany you when you go out."

"'Tis a sweet sentiment, but I hardly think so."

Unaccustomed to having his orders disobeyed, Morgan could only stare, dumbfounded. "Miss McGrath—"

Her chin lifted. "You've already called me Tillie. I daresay 'twould be silly to revert to formality now, given the circumstances."

Refusing to be distracted, Morgan nodded. "Fine. Tillie, then. I don't think you understand what you're up against."

"Neither do you, seeing as you've no idea who hired Doc in the first place, ain't so?"

"Aye, but—"

"What about this man Donal—how long has he been in your employ?"

If she thought he was going to give her even more information that could put her in further danger—

"Ten months. Maybe a little more."

He glared at Cass, who lifted both hands and gave a sheepish shrug.

"Ten months . . ." she repeated.

He turned back to Tillie, who had begun pacing in front of the window, her index finger lightly tapping her lower lip.

He took a deep breath and braced both hands on his hips. "Now wait just a minute. Donal was a decent enough crewman, but he was also a firebrand who liked to gamble. We've no cause to think his death is tied to Doc's. Could be he got himself into trouble over a game of cards and it wound up costing him his life."

"Not likely, given what happened to Tillie today," Cass said.

Resisting the urge to grab him by the collar, Morgan ground his teeth. "One more word out of you, little brother, and you'll end up joining Donal in the river."

"Except he's not in the river; he's in the morgue with Doc." Tillie drew to a halt at the window and glared at him. "We need to find out why"—her hand flashed to her chest—"I even more than you since it was likely my fiancé's death that caused—"

She got no further. Over her shoulder through the glass, Morgan saw a man standing, his arm raised. He didn't stop to think, but flung himself at her and drove them both crashing to the floor. A second later, a blast shattered the window and sent broken glass showering over them both.

19

Tillie tensed as she fell, expecting to have the air driven from her lungs by the solid wood floor as it rushed up to crush against her spine. Instead she found herself cradled in Captain Morgan's strong arms. It was his back that had absorbed the fall, his lungs that expelled a sharp breath in a *whoosh*.

And then he was rolling, pulling her along with him until he lay atop her, his long form covering her completely, his arms and hands shielding and protecting her face.

"Cass!" he yelled.

"Here!"

"Where is he? Can you see him?"

Glass crunched beneath Cass's feet as he eased toward the window. "No. He's gone. The street's clear."

The words instantly released the tension from the captain's muscled frame. His eyes as he peered at her were pools so deep she felt herself drowning. "Are you all right?"

Still breathless, she nodded.

She felt him relax, and then he moved off her and gently helped her to stand. And then helped her to sit, for as soon as she was on her feet, her knees gave way and she sank to the settee.

"Did . . . did someone . . . ?"

Tears flooded her eyes, washing away the sight of him. She felt him leave her side, and through blurred vision she saw him striding to the window and drawing the curtains shut.

"Cass, go take a look. See what you can find, but be careful."

"Aye."

She only heard Cass leave. The tears were coming too hard now for her to see the door close. A second later, the cushions on the settee dipped as the captain sat beside her and pressed a handkerchief against her palm.

"Someone tried to shoot me!" The words burst from her lips and with them a fresh onslaught of weeping. "Why? What have I done?"

"Nothing. You've done nothing."

His arms wrapped around her, gently this time, instead of hard and powerful like the steel bands she'd felt before. The effect was no less traumatic. For several minutes she could do nothing more than soak the front of his shirt with her tears.

"I do . . . not . . . understand."

Each word was punctuated by a catch in her throat, which made it almost impossible to breathe, much less speak. Despite this, the questions struggled for release. "Why? Who?"

Captain Morgan caught her chin and lifted her face to his. "Tillie, listen to me. The others will be coming soon. 'Tis imperative that you be verra careful how much you say, for their sake as well as your own."

"What?"

"I promise you, I will explain what I think is going on here, but for now—"

"Tillie?" The door to the parlor burst open, and Amelia hurried in, with Laverne and Giles close on her heels. "Captain Morgan!"

Rendered speechless by the sight that met them, the three skittered to a halt.

Only Meg, who entered behind them, found her voice. Eyes wide, she scanned the shattered glass strewn across the carpet. "What on earth happened?"

The front door slammed, and Cass joined those already assembled. "No sign of him, Morgan. No one on the street seems to know what happened, either. Lucky for him, most of the vendors had already gone home for the night."

"'Twas hardly luck," Morgan growled.

Raring up like a great shaggy bear, Giles stomped across the parlor and motioned toward Cass and Morgan. "I think you lads had best explain what in the blazes is going on."

"We will," Morgan said, "but first I suggest we move to the back of the house, away from the street."

"The library," Amelia said, a quiver in her voice.

"But the window . . ." Tillie began.

Morgan directed a sharp glance at Cass, who took up position next to the window, one hand guiding the curtain aside so that he could watch the street. One by one, the others filed toward the library, with Morgan bringing up the rear. Once they were all seated, Tillie listened while he explained what had happened earlier that morning, and then later in the parlor.

"But why?" Meg asked. "Why would anyone want to hurt Tillie?"

Her defense melted a bit of the frost from Tillie's bruised heart. She shot her friend a grateful smile.

"All of this took place in broad daylight." Amelia's fingers shook as she pressed them to her temples. "It's all so unbelievable."

Tillie looked around at the faces gathered near—Meg, Laverne, and Captain Morgan. Reflected there, she saw the same sentiment Amelia expressed. Indeed, it resonated deep within her own heart. Were it not for the steadying glance Captain Morgan flashed her way, she might have burst into tears.

Circling to stand before Amelia's chair, he clasped both hands behind his back and dipped his head. "I'll let Tillie fill you in on the rest. For now, I think it best if I help Cass keep an eye on the house. In the meantime, we'll need to send someone after the police. Giles?"

"Going." He whirled and strode for the door.

Lowering her hands to clutch the mangled handkerchief in her lap, Amelia said, "I can't tell you how thankful I am that you and your brother were here to keep Tillie safe."

Instead of accepting her thanks, he grimaced, and why not? Thanks to her, both he and his brother had been forced into the path of danger. No doubt he was already regretting the decision that had led him to check on her in the first place. Before he left, he paused at her side.

"Are you sure you're all right?"

The words were hardly more than a whisper, yet they reached to Tillie's soul. "Aye, thanks to you," she whispered back. "I kinna thank you and Cass enough. I owe my life to the two of you."

A shadow flitted over his face—regret and something more. Her breath caught as he reached out to clasp her shoulder.

"Keep to the rear of the house, either here in the library or the kitchen. It's safer than the front. The others, as well. Do you understand?"

"And what about you? Or Cass and Giles?" she added. "What if whoever tried to shoot me . . ."

The words withered on her lips. There was no doubt now. Someone had tried to kill her . . . twice. Likely they'd be back. Could she live with herself if they killed him instead? Or anyone in the boardinghouse, for that matter?

She drew a shuddering breath, cut short by the touch of his finger below her chin.

"It'll be all right, lass. We'll give our statement to the police and then figure out where to go from there."

He spoke with such confidence she was tempted to believe him. Almost. His next words squelched the flicker of hope as nothing else could have done.

"Tillie . . . say nothing about speaking to Braedon before he died, to the police or anyone else."

She frowned. "What?"

"When you tell the detectives what happened, be cautious in how much you reveal." He drew closer, shielding her from Amelia's sight and lowering his voice so only she heard. "Please. I promise you, I will explain everything."

Only when he moved away did she release the breath trapped in her chest. Immediately, Amelia and Meg flocked to her side. Even Laverne, who seldom hovered, pulled a handkerchief from her sleeve and waved it in Tillie's face.

"Poor, sweet lass," Meg crooned.

"Had to have scared the wits out of ya," Laverne said.

"Yes, yes." Amelia grasped Tillie's arm and led her to a nearby chair. "Now, what else isn't the captain telling us? Anything?"

She shook her head. Despite their concern, she knew the captain was right. For their own safety, the less they knew, the better.

She grimaced at the irony of the thought. She hardly knew more than they. But Captain Morgan?

Her only hope would be to follow his lead and pray that somehow they would discover who was harboring a vendetta against her.

Her life depended on it.

20

Morgan waited until the detectives had left and everyone had gone to bed before seeking out Tillie. Like him, Cass figured it best if they took turns guarding the boardinghouse, at least for the first few nights, and had agreed to take the first watch. As Morgan walked down the hall from the library to the parlor, he thought once again how glad he was to have his brother by his side.

Especially now, when very little else made any sense.

Tillie made a wraithlike figure, standing with her hand to the boarded-up window. By the light of an oil lamp, unshed tears sparkled like jewels in her eyes. For several seconds he could only stare, his feet rooted to the floor outside the door. And then she moved, releasing him from her spell.

He blew out a breath. "I thought I'd find you here."

Her hand fluttered to wipe her eyes before she looked at him. Somehow, knowing she didn't want him to see her vulnerability made her all the more endearing. He gave himself a mental kick. The last thing she'd need or want was to have a man ten years her senior thinking of her in that way—or any way.

He squared his shoulders and crossed to meet her. "How did it go with the detectives?"

She shrugged. "As well as could be expected, given what little I could tell them." She widened her eyes. "What's happening? What have I done that would make someone want me dead?"

He sighed and motioned to the settee. Her hands trembled as she sat. She clasped them tightly in her lap. "Well?"

Morgan struggled for words. Finally, he said, "I kinna be certain."

"But you said—"

He covered her hands. "That is, I think I may know why someone has been sent to kill you, I just dinna know *who*."

Closing her mouth, she drew back and motioned for him to continue.

"Tillie, you remember I told you that someone had paid Doc to poison Braedon? And later, I told you that before Doc died, he confessed all of that to me?"

"Aye?"

He shook his head. "What I didn't tell you was that Donal overheard Cass and me talking—at least I think he did."

"But I thought you said his death and Doc's weren't related."

"That was before we knew someone really was trying to hurt you."

Bewilderment cast a shadow over her face. "I don't understand."

Of course not. It hardly made sense to him. He drew a slow breath. "I think all of this goes back to the day Braedon died. I think my letting you in to see him is what put everything into motion."

"What harm could it have possibly done for me to be at his side when he passed? Unless . . ."

"Unless he possessed knowledge that someone wanted to keep hidden. Someone powerful. Someone wealthy."

"Wealthy enough to hire Doc," she finished, realization dawning on her face.

Morgan nodded. He'd drawn the same conclusion, only the attack at the boardinghouse had kept him from sharing it.

"And then Donal overheard and went to that same person to tell them what he knew?"

"I think so."

She sank back against the settee. "So they figured they had to kill me, in case Braedon had shared the secret from his deathbed."

"That be my reckoning."

She shook her head, as though unable to fathom such a heinous plot. "But he didn't tell me anything."

"They don't know that." Morgan turned to face her. "Tillie, something Braedon knew was worth killing over. Have you any idea what that could be?"

"No. He was a farm boy, from a poor family and with few connections. He didn't have any enemies . . ."

Her hand flew up to cover her mouth.

"What is it?" Morgan asked. Then, remembering why they'd left Ireland in the first place, he clenched his jaw. "Was it his family?"

"No, not them. They didn't always agree, but they loved him, of that much I'm certain."

"But you thought of something else, didn't you?"

She lowered her hand. Before she spoke, she cast a glance over her shoulder, almost as if she expected a figure to materialize from the shadows gathering in the corner of the room. "Braedon . . ." She swallowed and lowered her voice. "Braedon belonged to an organization called the Fenians. Have you heard of them?"

He frowned and wracked his brain for what little he knew of the group. "Only in passing. Something about establishing home rule?"

"Aye." She rose and began pacing, her long dress rustling

in the quiet room. "It started a long time ago, before you or I or Braedon were even born."

"The famine?"

She nodded. "People were starving. They looked to the English for help, but when others started grumbling that it was too slow in coming, they rebelled and fought to be free. When the uprising failed—"

"They came to America, like Braedon."

"And me," she added. "But not just America, Canada and South America, too. I think they thought once they were free from the fear of retribution, they'd be able to redouble their efforts against England."

"It worked?"

"Somewhat. The opposition of the church proved a hindrance."

"Why?"

"People were afraid to join their ranks, afraid of what the church would do to those who showed support of the Fenians."

Suspicion took root in his brain. "People?"

She sighed. "My parents."

That explained why she'd left her family behind. They hadn't approved of Braedon's political ties. He motioned for her to continue.

"Rumors of actual plots against the British government began to circulate as the movement became stronger. They had no choice but to take steps to crush it. Many Fenians were imprisoned, including Braedon's older brother." She winced. "It was after he was executed as a traitor that Braedon joined the group."

Morgan drew a long breath and then expelled it. While it didn't explain why Braedon had been killed, or why that same person had now set his sights on Tillie, at least she'd given him a lead to follow.

He left the settee and went to stand beside her. "Tillie, do you remember what Braedon said to you before he died?"

Her eyes took on a faraway look. Finally she gave a slow nod. "He told me that he loved me."

The hitch in her voice tore at Morgan's heart. "What else?" he prompted.

"He gave me a ring and told me . . ." She paused and looked up at him, her eyes wide and frightened. "He told me if I ever needed anything, to sell it."

He gave a curt nod and moved to turn. "All right—"

She grabbed his arm before he could finish. "Wait. That's not all."

"Aye, lass?"

She dropped her hand, and he could see that she was shaking.

"What is it, Tillie? What else did he say?"

His eyes moved to the pale line of her neck, which convulsed as she worked to swallow.

"He said if anything happened, if I were ever in danger . . . I was to take the ring to an old friend of his—a man named Jacob Kilarny."

— ✳ ✳ ✳ —

Speaking Jacob's name again after so many years left a bitter taste on Tillie's tongue. Memories washed over her of late nights spent gathered around tables in dimly lit rooms; cryptic messages that caused Braedon to be secreted away for days on end; fear that rose and fell like the tide every time she knew he'd been sent on another mission from which he might not return.

Worst of all, the worry that he'd meet the same fate as his brother.

She shuddered.

"Are you cold?"

Reminded of Morgan's presence, she ripped free of the grip of the past and raised her eyes to his. "Not cold. Just . . ."

His lips curved in the barest of smiles, yet the sight drove all else from her thoughts.

"No need to explain, lass."

Seconds passed, and then she dipped her head in thanks.

With no light penetrating the boarded-up window, the parlor had grown dark earlier than normal. Morgan turned up the wick on the oil lamp and then motioned her back to the settee. "Please, tell me about this Kilarny. Who is he and how well did you know him?"

"Truth be told, it's been years since I've seen him, long before Braedon and I left Ireland. As for who he is"—she blew out a heavy sigh—"I suppose the best way to explain would be to say that he was one of the most outspoken of the Fenians. He became verra powerful within the organization."

"So he was one of their leaders?"

"You could say that."

A frown wrinkled Morgan's brow. "And Braedon told you to go to him? Why?"

She bit her lip. Why indeed? It wasn't as though the two men had been particularly close. They'd been more like business associates. "I have no idea," she admitted finally. "I'm sorry."

"No, dinna apologize. None of this be your fault."

As he spoke, his eyes darkened to a deep blue. Ach, but how she wished for the ability to read the man's thoughts. He braced both hands on his knees. "I suppose our next move will be to search out this Kilarny. Do you have any idea where I might find him?"

She shook her head. "'Tis been so long since I even gave a thought to the Fenians. When Braedon died, my ties to them died, too."

Instead of the disappointment she feared, he set his jaw

and lifted his chin. "Then finding him will be our first order of business. In the meantime, do you think I might see this ring Braedon gave you?"

"Of course." Rising, she went to fetch it and, a few moments later, returned with the ring clutched in her palm. Entering the parlor, her breath caught. In her absence, Morgan had removed his coat and rolled the sleeves of his white cotton shirt to his elbows. With the seams pulling slightly at the shoulders, he was a sight to turn a woman's head.

But not hers, she reminded herself grimly. She'd not allow any man to turn her head again. Not now or ever.

Grimacing, she bore the ring to where Morgan stood and laid it on the table. "There. That's the ring Braedon gave me."

Morgan's long fingers curved around the gold band as he raised it high to examine it by the light of the lamp. Concentration furrowed his brow. "Unusual design."

Tillie nodded, then plucking the ring from his fingers she showed him how it opened.

His reaction was similar to hers the first time she saw the ruby heart tucked inside. His lips parted in amazement. She handed it to him so he could once again examine the ring more closely. "'Tis beautiful." He lowered it to look at her. "And yet you do not wear it."

"No."

He stared at her, unblinking. "Was it because Braedon died before the two of you could be wed?"

Guilt and sorrow for the decisions she'd made pressed like a stone upon her heart. "No, that's not it. I think Braedon always intended to give me a ring to wear, but not this one."

She frowned, remembering the urgency in his voice and the fevered pleading in his eyes as he pressed the ring into her hand.

"Not this one," she repeated. "I do not wear this ring because on the night Braedon died . . . he asked me not to."

21

Even at ten thirty in the morning, a solid line of people pushed in and out of the swinging door of Shanahan's Pub, a squalid place in a seedy corner of the Lower East Side. Morgan grasped Tillie's elbow and pulled her to one side, out of the line of sight of two men whose leering made him itch for a fight.

He lowered his head to whisper in her ear, "You're sure about this?"

She gave a quick nod and lifted her chin. "Aye. If there's anyplace he's apt to be in a city this big, it's here."

He had to admit, he admired her pluck. Yet admiration or no, the idea that she might be putting herself in further danger sent an uneasy tremor racing along his flesh. "I mean about talking to Kilarny alone. How do you know you can trust him?"

Her chin trembled and then fell just a bit. "He doesn't know you. If I'm to have even a chance of speaking with him, I have to go alone. Besides, Braedon trusted him. That's enough for me."

But it wasn't enough for Morgan.

He eased to stand before her, both hands clutching her

shoulders. Though he felt her trembling through the fabric of her dark blue dress, she met his gaze steadily. "I'll be right here," he said at last. "Try and stay where I can see you, and if you need me—"

"I'll call out," she finished, repeating what they'd said before leaving the boardinghouse. She looked past him, over his shoulder toward a table near the window where Cass sat nursing a tall mug.

Reluctantly he dropped his hands from her shoulders. "One of us will have an eye on you at all times. You remember what you're to do if the situation becomes uncomfortable?"

He bit back a grimace. The situation was already uncomfortable. He'd chosen the word hoping to calm her fears.

She pulled a fan from her reticule and flicked it open with a snap of her wrist.

"Right." It was time. They were beginning to draw attention, yet Morgan found himself unwilling to let her venture further.

She put her hand to his chest, effectively blocking the air from entering his lungs. "I'll be all right. Braedon would never have sent me to him otherwise."

Fie.

Dipping his head, he shuffled aside and allowed her to pass. The moment she was out of arm's reach, however, he wanted to call her back, to carry her to the *Marie* and lock her in his cabin, where he knew she'd be safe.

Morgan, lad, what in the world is wrong with you?

Except for Cass, it had been some while since he'd been so acutely aware of the well-being of another. The feeling was not altogether welcome. Morgan wrestled with it as he yanked a chair from a nearby table and dropped onto the seat. He was accustomed to looking out for his crew, but somehow this was different. It had to be simply that she was female—a very small, very vulnerable female—that stirred such protective feelings.

"Get ya something?" A redheaded barmaid brushed his shoulder suggestively as she leaned to clear the table of dirty dishes.

Morgan craned his neck to see around her. Tillie had wound through the bar and was approaching a table near the back. A large man in dark trousers, white sleeves, and suspenders rose to meet her. Hands braced against the table, Morgan prepared to rise, then relaxed when the man nodded and pointed toward another table away from the bar.

"Well?" the barmaid said.

"Coffee. Black," he snapped, glad when she moved away to fetch his drink. He slipped a coin from his pocket and tossed it onto the table so they'd not have to speak when she returned.

Slow down, he commanded silently, willing Tillie's steps to slacken before she passed through a door at the rear of the pub and out of sight. He cast a glance at Cass, who was also straining to keep an eye on Tillie's retreating back.

But she didn't stop, didn't even hesitate as she walked through the door and closed it behind her. The muscles in his stomach clenched. This wasn't good. Hadn't he just told her to stay within sight?

Grinding his teeth, he pushed away from the table and made to stand. A flick of Cass's wrist caught his attention.

Wait, his brother mouthed.

For what? Until it was too late?

Cass glanced around the crowded room. Morgan caught his meaning. What could Kilarny do with so many people present?

Growling low in his throat, Morgan plopped back into his chair. Five minutes. That was all he'd wait, and if there was still no sign of her, well, not even the door would keep him from getting to her.

— ✳ ✳ ✳ —

Tillie passed through the doorway into a long hall, resisting the urge to cast one last glance at Morgan before it shut behind her. Three doors opened off the hall just as the man at the bar had said—one to her left, one to her right, and one straight ahead. She made for the one straight ahead.

Two knocks, then wait.

Her hand shook as she raised it and pounded on the door twice. After a moment, the door opened a crack and a rather ugly man with a long face and pointed chin poked his head out.

"Well?"

She pressed her damp palms against the fabric of her skirt. "I'm T-Tillie McGrath. Braedon McKillop was my fiancé. I'm here to see Jacob Kilarny."

It was the same line she'd given to the man at the bar, yet it had nowhere near the same effect. The man's eyes only narrowed further. "He expectin' ya?"

"No, but if I could just—"

"Ya got the wrong place. No Kilarny here." The man shut the door with a firm click.

Tillie's brow furrowed in consternation. If she'd been wrong, why then had the man at the bar pointed her toward this door?

Drawing a breath, she lifted her fist and knocked again. This time the door flew open, startling her so that she stumbled a step and nearly tripped over her dress.

The man with the long face strode out, his brows dark slashes across his forehead. "Look here, woman, I told you once already, ya got the wrong place."

"But if I could just tell you why I need to see him—"

"Get out before you get yourself hurt!"

The man stopped inches away and thrust his face close to hers. Though she feared her shaking knees would fail her, Tillie stood her ground.

"Please," she whispered. "My life depends on my talking with him."

The man didn't move, but neither did he speak. She pressed on.

"My fiancé's name was Braedon McKillop. He and Jacob knew each other years ago. Braedon told me if ever I was in trouble, to seek him out and . . ."

She hesitated to tell this man about the ring.

Behind the man, the door swung wider. "Let her pass."

Tillie recognized his voice the moment she heard it. When Braedon was alive, it had haunted her dreams and filled her waking moments with fear. She shivered as the man blocking her path moved aside and swept his hand toward the open door.

Heart thumping, Tillie eased around him. The room she entered was furnished with a couch that looked as though someone had slept on it, along with a table and two chairs. Against one wall stood a large bookcase, and on the opposite wall a clock kept perfect time.

Jacob Kilarny stood next to the clock.

The pendulum swung back and forth several times before he finally stepped toward her, his hand outstretched. "Matilda? It is you."

She licked her dry lips nervously. "Jacob."

He grasped her hand and drew her to the table. Pulling out one of the chairs, he seated her and then swung the other around so he sat facing her. "The rumors be true then. Braedon's dead."

She clasped her hands in her lap and nodded. "On the ship crossing over from Ireland."

He shook his head. "I'm sorry, lass. That must have been hard for you."

She searched his eyes for traces of derision and found none. Instead she read compassion in the lines of his face.

"You look older, Jacob."

"As do you. I reckon the world has been less than kind to us both."

How much did he know? "Aye, I reckon that be so."

"And is that why you've come?"

The wild racing of her heart returned. She looked around the room at the rumpled blankets scattered over the arm of the couch and the dirty dishes stacked high on one end of the table. This hardly looked like the quarters of a man wielding power enough to protect her. What if Braedon was wrong and Jacob wasn't the man to help?

Rather than look at him, she picked at the edge of her sleeve. Wrong or not, he was the man Braedon had told her to turn to.

She drew in a breath to steady herself. "What happened all those years ago, Jacob? What drove you and Braedon out of Ireland? He never would speak of it, but I know it must've been something terrible."

Ignoring her question, Jacob replied with a question of his own. "I thought you said you were in trouble?"

"I am."

"And your questions, what have they to do with it?" He jerked up from his chair. "You want my help, lass, you're gonna have to trust me and quit your prying."

Though her heart beat like a hammer against her ribs, she rose and planted both palms against the table. Sticking out her chin, she said, "Aye, I want your help, but I'm not a fool, and you're wrong if you think I'm going to stumble in here blind."

Surprise flickered in his eyes, and then a whisper of admiration. Tillie forged on, quieter than before.

"Braedon might still be alive if he'd stayed in Ireland. I have a right to know what it was that drove him to go. What drove us both to go. Tell me, Jacob."

His jaw worked as he stared at her, measuring. Outside the door, muffled laughter swelled, but he seemed not to hear. Finally he indicated the chairs they'd vacated. When they sat, he said, "How much do you know?"

She shook her head helplessly.

He grunted and laced his gnarled hands, which made him look much older than he was. "Doesn't surprise me. All Braedon ever wanted was to protect you, you know."

She swallowed a lump in her throat and nodded.

He sighed. "You didn't have to come to me. Anyone inside the Fenians could have told you what I'm about to share. Probably would've been a lot less trouble for you, too."

"Like I said, Braedon told me who to find."

His eyes narrowed. "Right. I suppose we'll get to that." Leaning back in his chair, he eyed her steadily. "So you want to know what happened, eh? Fine, I'll tell you. But then I'll have a few questions of me own."

He waited a moment, and then at her nod he began, "There was a group of us lads from Derry what joined the Fenians around the same time—me, Sean Healy, Eoghan Hamilton, and Braedon. I suppose if you asked any one of us why we joined, we'd give a different answer, but the bottom line was we all believed that Ireland needed to be free to rule herself, independent of England, and by force if necessary."

Her chest tightened. For just a moment, she heard Braedon's voice speaking the exact same words.

Jacob went on. "That meant we were all willing to use drastic measures to accomplish what we wanted. Sean came to us, said he'd heard of a politician named Daniel Turner who might be influenced with just a little pressure. Turner was opposed to home rule. The plan was to kidnap him, scare him into voting with us, and then let him go free."

"That wasn't what happened?"

Jacob leaned forward and laid both arms atop the table. "I've heard two different sides to what happened that night. Truth is, I kinna be sure. Not really. All I know is what was supposed to put a scare into Turner ended up killing him. Sean Healy, too."

"And Braedon? What part did he have in all of this?"

Jacob settled back against his chair. "When Sean realized Turner wasn't going to be cowed into reversing his stance, he pulled a gun and threatened to kill him. A fight broke out. Eoghan stepped in to protect Turner and wound up killing Sean instead."

Everything he said fit with what Tillie had learned last summer. What she didn't know was which side Braedon had chosen. She held her breath.

"Some of the lads thought Sean was in the right," Jacob continued. "Others picked Eoghan. I don't know that Braedon sided with either, but he knew we had to stop the fight before anyone else died. He pulled out a pistol and fired it into the air. Took me a second to realize where the shot came from. When next I looked around, Eoghan was gone and Sean was dead."

"But so was Daniel Turner."

He nodded. "Sometime during the fight, Sean's gun went off. The bullet hit Turner in the back. Me and Braedon . . . 'twas me and him what carried Turner back into town."

Tillie drew a shaky breath. "So that was it? That was why the two of you thought you had to leave?"

"Not thought, lass. We *knew* the Turner clan would be

bent on hunting down the men responsible for killing their kinsman. Parliament too was bound to go after any Fenians who'd had any part in murdering one of their number—and we knew that's how it would be seen, regardless of whether we'd planned for him to die or not."

Covering her face with both hands, Tillie battled a rush of hot tears. So, according to Jacob, Braedon had been a part of the terrible event that nearly destroyed Cara and Rourke, and later forced Ana and Eoghan into hiding.

"Ya all right, lass?"

Surprised by the concern in his voice, Tillie lifted her head. The fiery passion that once burned in his eyes had become less intense, less destructive to those on the fringes. Instead he seemed a gentler soul, one who'd suffered enough to have compassion when he saw suffering in others.

"I'm glad I know the truth."

He dipped his head.

But what would she do with the knowledge? Her thoughts winged to Morgan. She pushed back from the table. "I should be going—"

Jacob's hand flashed out to fasten around her arm. "Not quite yet, lass."

At the strength of his grip, she startled. "What . . . ?"

A slow grin spread across his thin lips. "You still haven't told me why you came." Jacob's fingers tightened like ropes around her wrist. "And I still have me own questions to ask."

22

Ten minutes. Morgan stared at the pocket watch in his palm. It had been ten minutes since Tillie disappeared behind the door on the opposite side of the pub. Since then, it had remained tightly closed, a scowling tree of a man barring the entrance.

Morgan caught Cass's attention and tipped his head toward the giant. They'd have to be careful. One swing of those fists could fell a man like a sledgehammer. Cass gave a slight shake of his head.

He thought they were moving too soon.

Ignoring his brother's warning, Morgan stood, his chair scraping the wood floor.

"Another drink? Maybe something a wee bit stronger this time?"

The barmaid's return only irritated him further. "No, thanks."

He moved to sidestep her, but she sidled to stand in his way, her hand to his chest. "Aww now, what's your hurry? Why not sit with me a while?"

Morgan directed a pointed stare at her long, painted fingers. "I've got somewhere I need to be."

She pouted. "Too bad. Maybe another time?"

He didn't think so, but he gave a tip of his cap as he dodged the fabric of her fitted silk skirt.

The giant had spotted him. The muscles of his biceps flexed as he sent a sharp glare winging across the pub at him. No doubt he knew who Shanahan's regulars were, and Morgan wasn't one of them.

"Say, before you go . . ."

Morgan bit back a growl of frustration as he looked over his shoulder at the barmaid.

She held up his pocket watch. "This belong to you?"

His hand went to his jacket pocket. He'd have sworn he replaced it before he got up. How . . . ?

She was distracting him.

The realization hit him so hard he nearly reeled. Whirling, he strode across the pub straight for the giant. The man uncrossed his arms and waited with feet braced.

Before Morgan reached him, Cass stepped into his path and hissed, "Hold up there, Cap."

"Not now, Cass."

"We don't know that she's in any trouble."

His voice rose. "Get out of my way, Cass."

Cass grabbed his arm. "Would you simmer down? 'Tis only been a few minutes." He threw a glance over his shoulder at the giant. "If she did find him, she's hardly had time to explain what she's doing here."

Though the argument made sense, Morgan could see nothing past the scowling figure blocking his path to Tillie.

Cass shook his arm. "Morgan!"

Sucking in a breath, he forced himself to relax, his knotted muscles to loosen. "Fine."

Behind them, the barmaid stepped closer. "He all right?"

Cass clapped him on the shoulder. "Aye, he's all right. Ain't so, Morgan?" Though he smiled, his brows lowered in warning.

"Aye," Morgan grumbled at last.

Turning, he saw as Cass took the pocket watch from the barmaid's outstretched hand.

"Our thanks to you, Miss . . . ?" He scratched his temple. "Dinna figure I caught your name."

Her smile broadened until a dimple appeared on one of her pale cheeks. "Catherine."

"A pleasure, Miss Catherine." Cass bent low over her hand and pressed a kiss to the back, then gestured to the table he'd vacated. "Can I buy you something to drink?"

Morgan grunted. Ach, but the lad could layer on the charm. Still, the offer seemed to defuse the situation. Catherine followed him to the table, and the giant crossed his arms again and resumed a more relaxed stance, though he continued to watch them warily. Left with little choice, Morgan claimed one of the chairs while his brother delighted Catherine with tales of boyish escapades.

After what seemed an eternity, the door behind the giant opened, spurring Morgan from his seat as if he'd been jabbed. When at last Tillie emerged, he let the air loose from his lungs in relief.

She was all right. A little pale perhaps, but none the worse for it. He cut the distance between them to fasten onto her arm and lead her outside.

"Well," he demanded once they'd walked some distance and the fresh air had had a chance to fan the fogginess from his brain. "Did you find him?"

"Wait up!" Dodging horses and pedestrians, Cass jogged to meet them. Wiping sweat from his brow, he peered at Tillie. "How'd it go?"

"Can we go somewhere private to talk?" she asked.

Her cheeks puffed in and out as she spoke, and Morgan regretted dragging her up the street. He motioned toward a carriage for hire. "First, let's get you out of this neighbor-hood to someplace safer."

Letting go of her arm, he hailed the carriage, helping her up after the driver circled around.

"Ashberry Street," he ordered the driver before climbing up after Tillie.

And after Cass.

The sneak had scurried in and claimed the seat next to Tillie while Morgan's back was turned. Unwilling that either should sense the turmoil roiling inside him, Morgan settled against the leather seat and let Cass do all the talking.

"So, was it him?" he began, eyes snapping with excitement.

Tillie pulled a frilly lace handkerchief from her reticule and pressed it to her mouth. "Aye, it was him." Her eyes darted to Morgan. "I had no idea that seeing him again after all these years would affect me so. He and Braedon worked together a long time."

Either he didn't see her trembling or didn't realize what it was that caused it, for Cass continued rambling while Morgan was hard-pressed to remain in his seat. Just what had happened in that room that had unnerved her so?

"What did he say when you showed him the ring?"

Morgan put up his hand. "Slow down, Cass. Let her tell it from the beginning."

His heart rate quickened at the look of gratitude she flashed his way. Bit by bit, she explained how she and Braedon had come to know Jacob Kilarny and what their relationship to him had been since. She finished by clutching her reticule to her chest.

"He wanted to keep the ring, but I wouldn't let him. I told him it was all I had of Braedon, but if he needed to see it again, I'd bring it by."

"And you have no idea why he was so interested in it?" Cass asked.

She bit her lip. "He didn't say."

Morgan gnawed the inside of his cheek. The ring was definitely the key to something or Kilarny wouldn't have been so interested. "Tell me again what he said when he saw it."

Curiosity gleamed in Cass's eyes. Morgan flashed him a look meant to say *later*.

"Well?" Morgan said, turning to Tillie.

The rumbling carriage hit a bump, throwing Tillie sideways. Though he put out his hand, he could only watch helplessly as she fell against Cass's chest . . . and Cass's arms went up to encircle her waist.

For a second they only looked at each other, and then Cass chuckled. "You all right?"

A rosy flush colored her cheeks and neck. "I'm fine. You?"

"What, having a bonnie little thing like you fall into me arms? Aye, I'm right as rain."

A spark of something he'd never experienced toward his brother ignited in Morgan's belly—anger, and mixed with it a draught of jealousy. 'Twas not a good meld. Though he fought not to let it show, it was several blocks before he dared turn his face to either Tillie or his brother, and a few more before he was able to unclench his fingers from around the handle on the door.

"The ring," he choked at last, cutting into Cass's lighthearted jesting. "What did Kilarny say when he saw it?"

Tillie's gaze fastened to his, a hint of frustration rippling in its depths. Perhaps she wasn't as taken with his brother as he thought. Or was it him she was frustrated with, for breaking the mood with Cass?

"He didn't say much, but I think he recognized it the moment he saw it. He held it up to the window, almost as though he were checking to make sure the stone was real. Then he sort of sucked in a breath and asked if I knew where Braedon had gotten the ring."

"Do you?" Morgan asked.

She shook her head. "I always assumed it was a family heirloom."

"And what did Kilarny say to that?"

"He grumbled something about hanging on to the ring, told me to keep it in a safe place and not let anyone else see it."

As she spoke, her fingers tightened around the reticule. Just what in blazes made the ring so significant? And if it wasn't an heirloom, where had McKillop gotten it? More to the point, why had he kept it?

These questions and more pummeled Morgan's brain as they approached Ashberry Street. Even as he instructed the driver on where to leave them off, he couldn't help believing that if he uncovered the truth about the ring, he'd find the answers he sought regarding Braedon's death, and later, Doc's and Donal's.

In the meantime, he was wont to follow Kilarny's advice. He'd keep both Tillie and the ring in the safest place he could find.

Close by his side.

23

Tillie undid the last button on her boot and let it slide from her foot to the floor with a thump. Laying aside the hook, she stretched out on her bed, content to let the stress of the day trickle from her limbs.

Had it only been one day since she'd learned the truth about Braedon's death? Or since she'd almost lost her life . . . twice? It hardly seemed possible.

A light knock broke her from her thoughts. She sat up in the bed. "Aye?"

Meg poked her head around the door, her long hair rolled in rags. "Still awake?"

"I am." She gestured for Meg to enter. "Please, come in."

Meg closed the door tight and then went and sat down on the bed beside Tillie. "The captain is downstairs. I saw him keeping watch at the parlor window. Giles repaired it this afternoon." Her green eyes widened as her voice lowered to a whisper. "I still kinna believe that someone tried to shoot you."

"You and me both." Tillie pulled her legs up and smoothed her skirt over her knees. "I feel like I'm in a bad dream from which I kinna wake. Every time I think on it . . ." She shuddered.

Meg's lips drooped in a sympathetic frown. Wriggling close, she patted Tillie's knee. "What can I do to help?"

The last thing she wanted was to endanger Meg or anyone else at the boardinghouse. She shrugged. "For now, I'd appreciate your prayers."

"Tillie . . ." Meg bit her lip, then leaned forward, her face earnest and pale. "Have you thought about speaking to Rourke?"

"Cara's husband?"

The rags on Meg's head bobbed. "After you got back this afternoon, I thought about what you and the captain said, how you both thought it would be wise to lay low until you could figure out who wanted you dead. With Rourke's connections here and at home, maybe he could help. It be worth a try, no?"

Tears glistened on the tips of Meg's lashes, and for the first time Tillie considered how worried she would be if the situation were reversed. She gave Meg's hand a squeeze. "Aye, it be worth a try. I'll speak to Captain Morgan in the morning."

Relief washed over Meg's features, and just as quickly a bit of teasing lifted her lips in a smile. "That captain . . . he's dreadful handsome, wouldn't you say?"

"Meg," Tillie scolded.

"He's also verra concerned about you. I've noticed how he watches you. In fact, he never lets you wander from his sight. Him or his brother, for that matter." Her brows rose. "I suppose Cass Morgan is closer to our age."

"None of that is of concern to me," Tillie said, grasping the covers and giving them a firm tug. "They're here because they want to help, nothing more."

Meg's scowl said she didn't agree, but she let it pass. Instead she cupped Tillie's hand in both of hers, the sleeves of her nightdress swallowing them up so only Tillie's arm showed.

"Promise me you'll listen to him—Captain Morgan, I mean. I've a good feeling about him, Tillie. I think maybe God sent him here to take care of you."

Heat suffused her cheeks. "Don't be silly, Meg. The captain's arrival here was a fortunate coincidence. It has nothing to do with me."

"Eh," Meg said, standing. "Think what you like. I'm inclined to believe 'tis because he's had a hard time ridding his thoughts of a bonnie young miss who stepped aboard his ship two years ago." Winking, she ducked through the door, her merry laughter ringing along the empty hallway.

Despite her protest, the beating of Tillie's heart did quicken at the idea that Captain Morgan's concern might be personal. Could it be true? Was he purposefully keeping an eye on her, as Meg claimed?

The possibility kept her lying awake atop her covers well into the night. Knowing he stood vigil mere yards away was an even greater temptation. Finally, she pushed her feet into a pair of worn slippers and made her way downstairs. As Meg had said, the captain was standing watch at the parlor window, his tall form a rather imposing figure in the light of the half-moon. At his elbow a single candle cut the gloom of the shadowed room.

Tillie paused at the entrance. "Captain Morgan?"

He turned. His long hair was tousled, and a day's growth of beard roughened his chin. With his jacket removed and his sleeves pushed to his elbows, he was as fetching a sight as any she'd ever seen. Her breath caught.

Letting the curtain fall, he left the window and crossed to her. "Tillie? It's late. Is everything all right?"

If one counted a heart that was beating too fast and a

163

mouth that was too dry as being all right, well, then she supposed so. She nodded. "I couldn't sleep. Forgive me for bothering you at this hour, but may I speak with you, Captain?"

"Of course. Wait there a moment."

Easing to the window, he checked outside one last time and then arranged the drapes so that the view inside was fully covered. Afterward, he pulled two chairs away from the hearth to a wall farthest from the windows. Motioning for her, he indicated one of the chairs. After she was seated, he claimed the other.

"You look upset," he said, his dark brows bunched and his mouth turned in a frown. "What's wrong?"

Tillie searched his face. Though she read genuine concern in the etched lines on his face and around his mouth, it went no deeper. Meg was wrong. He probably would look exactly the same if it were one of his crew in trouble.

She sighed. "Captain Morgan—"

His hand lifted. "Please, just Morgan is fine."

She swallowed and offered a tight-lipped smile. "Morgan. Aye."

"You were saying?"

The room, the candle, the time of night—the entire setting felt too intimate. Tillie swiped her damp palms over her skirt and rose. "Forgive me. I shouldn't have bothered you. It's nothing that kinna wait until morning."

In the span of a blink, he too was on his feet. "Tillie, wait. You're here now. May as well confess what keeps you from sleep. Perhaps I can be of help."

Giving in to his gentle urging, she sank back onto the chair. "I spoke with Meg. She thinks I should talk to Rourke, get his opinion on what Kilarny told me."

"Rourke?"

"Cara's husband, and Daniel Turner's son."

"The politician whom Sean Healy accidently killed."

She nodded. In the dim light of the candle, his face was awash with concern, doubt, maybe even a bit of frustration. All things she herself had wrestled with before coming downstairs. "You dinna agree?"

He ran his hand over his face in a weary gesture that broke her heart. Surely he regretted having gotten himself involved in her troubles. Rourke, on the other hand, had a vested interest in the outcome. Better she should rely on him than to ask Captain Morgan to further embroil himself in a mess not of his making.

Before he could answer, she laid her hand upon his arm. "I want to thank you for all you've done to help me. 'Twas more than I had any right to expect."

He looked down at her hand, then up to peer at her. "Nay. 'Tis my fault any of this ever happened."

She withdrew her hand. "No. I learned one thing by speaking with Jacob Kilarny, which is that all of this goes back much further than either of us thought. You had no way of knowing Bracdon was involved with a plot that went wrong all those years ago."

His eyes narrowed as he stared at her for a long moment.

She bit her lip nervously. "What?"

"Something else is bothering you. Something you didn't talk about earlier."

She looked down, afraid he'd read the truth in her eyes, more than she was ready to reveal. "I'm not sure I understand what you mean."

"No?" His long fingers wrapped around hers, warming her hand, thrilling her heart. "Tillie, look at me."

She did, though somewhat reluctantly. His eyes were dark pools in the low light, his face a shadowed veil behind which myriad questions lay.

"You said you realized this went back much further than you thought. What did you mean?"

She'd had plenty of time to think upstairs. One question in particular had risen time and again to invade her thoughts. But to share it with him would only involve him deeper than he was already.

She shook her head, and though she tried to pull her hand away, he refused to let go. "Captain Mor—"

"Morgan."

"Morgan," she repeated, "you are a kind man. Grateful I am that God saw fit to put Braedon and me aboard your ship when we left Ireland."

He made to cut her off, but she pressed on before he could speak. "None of this was your fault. After meeting with Jacob, I'm certain of that. Tomorrow I will speak with Rourke, and we'll figure out what we should do, where we should go. In the meantime, I want you and your brother to get clear of this and be about your business—"

Morgan's hand went to her cheek, slicing the words from her tongue as effectively as any knife. "I'm not leaving, Tillie. Not until I know you're safe and we both know what happened to Braedon and my crew."

The warmth of his callused palm against her skin, the look of affection and concern welling in his eyes—both spurred a response in Tillie's chest that she had no right to feel.

She held her breath as he drew closer. She wasn't so naïve as to not know that he meant to kiss her, but was surprised when he ended up pressing it to her forehead instead of her lips. When he drew back, a wry sort of grimace twisted his features.

He lumbered to his feet, drawing her with him. "Go to bed, Tillie. Try and get some rest. Tomorrow we'll talk about this more, and if you still think it best, we'll seek out this Rourke Turner."

Helpless to argue given the dryness of her mouth, Tillie turned and fled the room, her feet taking her up the stairs and down the hall to her bedroom. Resting her back against the closed door, dismay filled her.

Despite her intentions, despite all her precautions to the contrary, one thing had become clear. What she'd meant to say or hoped to accomplish were of little consequence. What mattered was what had actually happened.

And that was that somewhere along the way, be it when he'd pushed her from the parlor window and saved her life or just now, when he'd cupped his hand to her cheek and vowed to remain by her side . . .

She'd fallen in love with Captain Morgan.

24

Long after the sound of Tillie's steps faded from his ears, Morgan stared after her, his heart thumping inside his chest and his thoughts in turmoil. What had he done? He was nearly ten years her senior.

Nine, his conscience argued. *He was only nine years older.*

Giving his shoulders a shake, he stalked to the window and pulled back the drape to peer outside. Did it matter? She was a child.

His thoughts drifted to the tantalizing softness of her cheek and the sweet tilt of her mouth. Nay. She was young, but she was no child.

But she *was* young.

The reminder firmly in place, he stared out through the glass at the eerie street. With the gas lamps casting flickering shadows, every movement drew his eyes—from a cat leaping off the steps of the tenement across the street to the bent figure of a beggar woman scrounging for scraps among the piles left by the vendors.

Ach, but 'twas a helpless feeling to do naught but stand guard, waiting for something that might not happen and someone who might not appear. Perhaps Tillie was right.

Perhaps seeking out Rourke Turner was the wisest move. At least it involved action.

Grabbing the chair he'd vacated earlier, he spun it to sit near the window. From this vantage he'd be able to keep one eye on the street and the other on the front door. It wasn't the first time he'd stood vigil thus.

His gut tightened. One eye on the street, watching for the doctor to come, the other on his parents' bedroom door . . .

At the memory of his failure, he sighed. Da had passed away because he could do nothing. He'd not let Tillie meet the same fate. Somehow he'd find a way to help her.

The vow rumbled round and round inside his head, keeping him awake until the dawn's first rays peeked over the city's rooftops. Down the hall he heard Laverne stirring in the kitchen. Somewhere a rooster crowed, and then the back door opened and closed with a snap.

At a creak on the stairs, Morgan looked up and saw Cass rubbing the sleep from his eyes.

"How'd it go?"

Morgan stood, stretching the stiffness from his limbs and stifling a yawn. "Quiet. Too quiet. I'd rather we were at sea on the *Marie* battling a storm than sitting through a man-made storm on land."

Cass lingered at the entrance, one hand half raised to scratch his temple and one eyebrow quirked. "Blimey, Morgan. How long did it take you to come up with that?"

Blimey? He'd been listening to Bozey. Or maybe Laverne. Grimacing, Morgan strode past him and made for the stairs. "Never mind. Keep an eye on things for me while I wash up."

Once again, Cass's laughter rang behind him. Would he never cease to be a source of amusement for his brother?

Racing up the stairs, Morgan washed and dressed before heading to the dining room for breakfast. By the time he returned, the other residents and Amelia had assembled, but it was to Tillie's place at the table that his eyes landed.

Dark smudges colored the skin beneath her eyes. Her hair, normally a bit tousled, today looked neatly combed, as though she'd taken pains to arrange it, or she'd not slept and so had plenty of time to smooth every hair into place. She did not look up when he entered, neither did she glance in his direction when he slid into the chair next to hers amidst a chorus of good mornings. He opened his napkin with a flick of his wrist. The question on his tongue itching to be spoken was for her welfare. Instead he waited until breakfast had begun in earnest and the conversation flowed before he said, "Still want to talk to Rourke Turner?"

She did look at him then, her wide brown eyes so deep and dark, a man could lose himself in their depths. "I do," she whispered.

Scooping a forkful of scrambled eggs, he brought it to his mouth and pretended to eat. "We'll go after breakfast."

So slight was her nod, he almost missed it. But staring at him from across the table was Cass, and there was no mistaking the determined gleam in his eyes or the thrust of his chin signaling he wanted to talk in the other room.

He set down his fork, but not before Cass pushed aside his plate and stalked from the dining room.

Meg's eyes rounded, and she set down her cup with a clatter.

Amelia lowered her own cup and set it much more delicately in its saucer. "Is everything all right, Captain?"

"Everything is fine. Please excuse us," Morgan said, following his brother into the hall.

Cass paced from the front door to the stairs. At Morgan's appearance he strode to him and stood with fists planted on his hips, glowering. "What was that all about?"

Morgan crossed his arms. "What?"

Cass jerked his chin toward the dining room. "In there. Since when do you go making plans without talking to me about them first?"

"You're not my mother, Cass."

His expression darkened. "I thought you said we were partners."

"When it comes to the *Marie*, we are."

"But not when it comes to looking after Tillie?"

Morgan paused. So that was it? The catalyst behind Cass's anger this morning was jealousy over Tillie? "Cass—"

"I care about her too, all right? I want to help her as much as you do."

"Fine," Morgan said. "You can do that by remaining here."

"And you? What will you do?"

He straightened and looked his brother in the eyes. "That's none of your business. You'll do as I say or you'll go back to the ship. Understood?"

Anger shadowed Cass's features, but at last he nodded.

"Good, then let's go back to breakfast."

"I'm not hungry," Cass muttered, spinning on his heel and striding for the kitchen and the back door. "I'll be in the barn if you need me."

"Fie," Morgan growled as the door slammed shut.

Maybe someday Cass would understand that what he was doing was for his own good, but not today. Today, his irritation and arrogance only proved what Morgan had known all along. He was still a lad in many ways.

"Morgan?"

At the sound of Tillie's gentle voice, he spun. She looked at him and then in the direction Cass had taken. "Is everything all right?"

His heart heavy, he sighed. "Cass and I had a wee bit of a spat is all. Brothers fight on occasion. He'll get over it."

His breath caught as her eyes drifted back to him. "Are you ready to go?"

She motioned toward the hall tree. "Let me fetch my bonnet and a shawl."

She moved to get them, but before she could swing the wrap around her shoulders, Morgan caught hold of it and spread it wide. "Allow me."

It was a foolish gesture, and one he'd probably regret later, but for the briefest moment he took great pleasure in the scent of Tillie's hair and the nearness of her body. Finally he let the shawl slip from his fingers onto her shoulders.

"Thank you."

Did he imagine the warmth in her voice? She turned, but he was already moving to open the door, averting his eyes before she read an uncomfortable truth in them.

The walk to the office where Rourke Turner worked was brief and accomplished without incident. With every step, Morgan gave thanks for the protection of the tall buildings that lined the street to their right. On their left, people hurried to work or chores. Still, he kept his guard up and Tillie close. No time for idle chatter, but given his mood, that was probably a good thing.

"There it is."

Tillie waved toward a three-story brick building with an imposing set of arched doors. On the side of the building, metal stairs wound like a snake, providing escape in the event of a fire, or a hasty exit in an attack. Morgan took note of their position before ushering Tillie up the steps to the entrance. Gilt lettering on the glass read *Harmon and Barrow, Attorneys at Law*.

Scowling, Morgan reached for the brass door handle. "He's a barrister?"

She shot him a playful smile. "Among other things. Rourke does a lot of work for city hall."

He snorted. Politicians were no better than barristers in his book.

Inside, gray marble floors led to an expansive lobby, in the center of which sat a large desk and a balding receptionist. He looked up when they entered, adjusting his spectacles so he could peer at them through the lenses.

"May I help you?"

Tillie stepped forward. "We're here to see Rourke Turner."

"Is he expecting you?"

She shook her head. "I'm a friend of his wife."

The man nodded, then rose and skirted the desk. "Your name?"

"Tillie McGrath." She gestured toward Morgan. "And this is Captain Keondric Morgan."

At the sound of his full name on Tillie's tongue, Morgan startled. He'd never heard her speak his Christian name before. Surprisingly it wasn't unpleasant. Then again, his refusal to use it had nothing to do with any aversion to the name itself.

"A moment, if you please," the man said, tugging on his vest to straighten it. "I'll see if Mr. Turner is available."

Turning smartly, he disappeared down a narrow hall and reappeared a few moments later with another man in tow.

"Tillie? What a pleasant surprise."

The second man, as tall as Morgan and handsome in his pleated trousers and coat, instantly set him on guard. He approached with outstretched hand, and were it not for the fact that Tillie knew him, Morgan might have been tempted to intervene.

Was tempted, he realized, stiffening when Turner wrapped her in an embrace.

The bloke's married, he reminded himself. No threat here. He kicked himself mentally. Not that he had a right to feel threatened.

"My thanks to you for seeing us, Rourke. Forgive me for not sending word first."

Turner shook his head. "You never need hesitate stopping by, Tillie. You know that." He turned to face Morgan. "Captain Morgan."

Morgan nodded and extended his hand. "A pleasure to meet you."

Not exactly true, he reasoned as he shook Turner's hand, but for Tillie's sake he'd make it appear so.

Turner motioned back the way he'd come. As they followed, the receptionist resumed his place behind the desk, his attention already on something else.

Turner's office was much like the man himself: neat, sparsely furnished, but with a bookshelf stuffed with volumes. His desk, while large, was not ornately carved or cluttered. He did not sit behind the desk but motioned to a set of leather chairs near a coal stove for Morgan and Tillie, then drew up the swivel chair from his desk to join them.

"How are Cara and Ana?" Tillie asked, removing her bonnet and shawl and passing them into Rourke's waiting hands.

His face grew troubled as he hung them on a coat-tree situated in the corner of the room nearest the door. "Eoghan is looking out for them. He sends me word now and again when he can, but not often enough."

Sorrow filled Tillie's eyes. "And the baby?"

"Due in less than a month. I was hoping we'd have more resolved by now so we could bring them all home." Sighing, he sat and motioned toward them. "So, what can I do for you this morning?"

Grateful for the questioning glance Tillie shot him, Morgan tilted his head and indicated that she should be the one to fill him in.

Beginning with the journey from Ireland, Tillie explained

how she knew Morgan, and finished with his visit to the boardinghouse less than two weeks prior.

Had it really only been two weeks? Sitting back in his chair, Morgan cleared his face of disbelief. She'd filled so many of his thoughts, it felt like much longer.

Turner locked eyes with him. Caught off guard by the look of understanding that flashed between them, Morgan cleared his throat. "When Doc told me what he'd done, I realized I had to find Til . . . Miss McGrath." A flush heated his face, though it appeared to go unnoticed.

Turner nodded. "I agree. We should look into this deeper, see if we can't figure out who it was that hired him, and why."

Tillie put out her hand and laid it over Turner's arm. "There's more."

"Why do I get the feeling that all of this is somehow tied to me?" Turner said.

Her fingers twisted in her lap. Though she drew a shuddering breath, no words emerged. Unable to resist, Morgan reached for her hand and gave it a squeeze. She looked at him gratefully.

"Tillie went to see an old colleague," Morgan said, "someone Braedon was acquainted with back in Ireland. He told her . . ." He hesitated, but after receiving an encouraging nod from Tillie, he forged on. "He and Braedon were present the day your father was killed."

The second the words were out, Turner's expression hardened. Before he could speak, Morgan leaned protectively toward Tillie.

"She didn't know any of this before."

Turner's throat worked. After a moment, his lips parted and he drew a deep breath. "So, Braedon was . . ."

"A Fenian," Tillie whispered, "and responsible in part for your father's kidnapping and death."

Morgan clenched his fists. Tillie seemed certain this Turner fellow was a friend, but just in case, he'd be ready.

Turner's head shook, but not in anger. Deep sorrow twisted his features as he leaned forward to peer into her face. "I'm verra sorry, Tillie. Sorry for what happened, but most of all, that it touched you."

His answer was surprising. No outrage? Even a trace of bitterness would have been expected. Instead, the man extended understanding.

The two of them reached out to each other, Tillie's hand swallowed by Turner's much larger one.

"This man," Turner continued, "can you tell me his name?"

"I can, but first . . ."

She hesitated, and her chin trembled, making Morgan long to smooth away the worried wrinkles.

She squared her shoulders. "Rourke, I must have your word that his name and identity go no further than this room. I owe him that much." At Turner's nod of agreement, she drew a deep breath. "His name is Jacob Kilarny. We think he may have answers about what happened to your father."

Pulling her hand away, she explained in detail how her conversation with Jacob Kilarny had gone and then finished with, "So? What do you think?"

Rising, Rourke paced the room. "I think this Kilarny might be able to answer a lot of questions except the most important one: how these two events are connected." His pacing ceased and he spun on his heel. "And they are connected, of that I have no doubt."

"That's why we're here," Tillie said, "to tell you what we've learned and to ask your advice."

"My advice?"

"On how best to proceed."

Turner looked at Morgan. Returning to his seat, he said,

"You should know, I spent many years trying to track down my father's killers and not because I wanted justice. It was revenge I sought, pure and simple."

Well he understood the concept of revenge. Most men lived by it, especially on the sea. Morgan clenched his jaw and said through gritted teeth, "Ought not your father's death be avenged and his murderer brought to justice?"

"Justice? Aye. But revenge? That is the Lord's."

The humbleness of his speech pricked Morgan's conscience. Another time and place, he might want to learn more about this Rourke Turner. For now . . .

He jerked his chin toward Tillie. "And what think you of the matter at hand? Any ideas of how we can go about uncovering if and how these deaths are connected?"

Turner scratched his head. "Possibly, but it will mean speaking with Kilarny—something he'll not likely consent to, save with someone he trusts."

Tillie's brows rose. "Like me?"

Morgan's guard rose. He hadn't liked that she'd gone to see him the first time.

"Not you," Turner said. "Someone like Eoghan."

"Cara's brother?"

At Turner's nod, Morgan relaxed against the back of his chair.

"I'll send word to him in the morning and see about making other arrangements for Ana and Cara and the baby."

Concern flooded Tillie's face. "Cara's days are too close to being accomplished. Traveling won't be good for her or the baby. And Ana won't leave Cara alone now."

"No," Rourke agreed. "I'll have to send someone to them." He reached out and patted Tillie's hand. "Dinna worry. I've still got family here who can help."

His reassurance seemed to appease Tillie, but Morgan was

nowhere near as certain that they could trust Rourke Turner. The man had already admitted he'd spent years trying to assuage a thirst for vengeance. Who was to say his thirst would not be revived once they came nearer to uncovering the truth about his father's death?

And if that truth involved Tillie . . .

Eyeing the man across the way, Morgan made a silent vow. He'd let Turner do whatever plotting he thought necessary, but only if it would not pull Tillie into further danger.

And there was only one way to accomplish that. He'd have to keep her close by his side. Very close. In fact, he intended to keep a watchful eye on her every minute until the threat against her life was resolved.

He studied Tillie's upturned face and there read courage, determination, even a bit of impertinence. But hemming all those emotions was a ragged fringe of fear, enough to stir up every protective instinct he possessed.

Lowering his eyes, Morgan sighed. Sure, keeping her close was the only way to guarantee her safety, but the threat to his heart? That had never been more real.

25

The days from Sunday to Sunday sped by, with the routine becoming at once familiar and familial. Tillie enjoyed leaving the stresses of her new job to find Cass waiting to walk her home each evening. His lighthearted banter made the trip enjoyable, and she found she could chat easily with him about the challenges of work and her ideas for the orphanage. Today, however, he had agreed to accompany them to Mass, an idea she found both exciting and amusing.

Dressed in her finest muslin with ruffles that capped her shoulders and tapered down to fit snugly at her wrists, she felt stylish, even attractive. Her navy skirt fit closely over her hips and flared just above the knee, while the braided bodice and high neck made her look taller than her five-foot-four inches. The dress had been an extravagance, and the stitching had taken her weeks to complete, but it was the one bit of finery she possessed, and she wore the dress proudly every Sunday.

At the bottom of the stairs, Cass waited for her, his face upturned and smiling as he watched her descend.

"Ach, but you be a vision." When she reached him, he held out his hand and helped her dismount the last stair, but instead of letting go of her fingers, he kept a tight grasp and motioned toward the door. "Ready?"

Tillie looked around them in confusion. "What about Amelia and Meg? Or Laverne and Giles?"

"Already gone ahead." Cass's smile broadened. "I told them I'd be happy to accompany you, and they agreed not to wait, as Mrs. Matheson had something she wanted to discuss with the priest."

Amelia wanted to talk to Father Ed? She hadn't mentioned needing to speak to him before, or had she said something and Tillie was too preoccupied at the time to realize it?

Determined to seek her out the minute they returned to the boardinghouse, Tillie clenched her jaw as she reached for her bonnet and shawl.

"Allow me to help you."

Cass's steps carried him swiftly to her side. He lifted the shawl from her fingers and laid it over her shoulders. Though he lingered, she felt no flash of excitement the way she had when Morgan had acted the same. Instead, her face heated with discomfort and she moved away, adding to the space between them.

"Tillie."

Startled by the hoarseness of his voice, she looked up at him. "Aye, Cass? Is something wrong?"

His head shook. "Not wrong. Just . . . I'd like to speak with you this afternoon, after we get back from the church. If you're not opposed to the idea, that is."

Why on earth would she be opposed to talking? They did that every day. She shot him a wry grin. "No, I'm not opposed."

"Good."

Her answer seemed to spur too much elation, but she thrust the thought away and glanced back over her shoulder toward the kitchen. "I dinna suppose . . ." Clearing her throat nervously, she adjusted the buttons on her cuff. "Has Morgan already left the house, as well?"

"Aye, he left early this morn. Said something about seeing to an errand."

Disappointment at his answer flooded her heart. Ever since leaving Rourke's office, he'd been attentive, even protective of her, and she'd come to appreciate his quiet, careful ways. It was because of his concern that Cass walked her home, she was sure of it, and deep down a part of her had wanted him to see her in her finest dress.

Smoothing the frustration from her face, she lifted her chin and forced a smile. "Shall we go, then?"

Laying hold of his proffered arm, she allowed him to lead her into the warmth of the sun outside. A light breeze blew the length of Ashberry Street, stirring the striped awnings above many of the shop windows and sending bits of paper scuttling along the cobbles.

Before they'd gone far, curiosity drove her to glance sidelong at her companion. "Cass, tell me about you and your brother. You've only recently joined him aboard the ship, at least that be what I've gathered from your conversations with him."

Shoving his cap higher on his forehead, he grimaced and gave a rueful nod. "Aye, that's true."

"May I ask why?"

For a lengthy span he stared at the clouds drifting lazily between the buildings. "I always thought it was because I was too busy having fun with the lads. Now I realize I was angry."

"With Morgan?"

He shook his head. "With Da for dying and leaving us to fend for ourselves."

Sorrow squeezed her chest. "And Morgan? Did he feel the same way?"

181

"No. At least I dinna think so. He never let his emotions show."

Ach, and was he any different now? She didn't think so. She pressed Cass's arm. "Why doesn't your brother allow anyone to call him by his Christian name? Seems odd, given you are both Morgans."

"Keondric was our father's name. I suppose Morgan doesn't use it because he doesn't feel he measures up." Tilting his head to her, he reached out and covered her hand. "He's never said as much, but I know. Ma's the only one who still calls him Keondric, even though it grieves him."

The sorrow Tillie felt curdled into a deep and familiar ache. Well she knew the guilt Morgan carried, and it pained her to think he was as acquainted with shame as she.

Gone was the brilliance of the summer morning. Cass seemed to sense her mood and walked with her in silence the rest of the way to the church. Once they were inside, they found their place on the pew next to Meg and the others from the boardinghouse, but it was only after the final prayer was said that Tillie felt a bit of her peace return.

Spying Sister Agnes, she begged Cass's leave and scurried over to greet her.

"Tillie McGrath, it be good to see you, girl. You've been missed at the shelter."

"I've missed you, too," Tillie said, gripping the older nun's hands. "Please tell me everything here is all right."

Sister Agnes's lips spread in a kind smile. "Everything is fine. Dinna worry your pretty head. That doesn't mean we dinna long for a familiar face now and again." She then lowered her head to whisper in Tillie's ear, "How come the plans for the orphanage? Any luck?"

"Not yet," Tillie whispered back. She'd not told the sister about Braedon or the plot against her life out of concern for her and Sister Mary. She glanced over her shoulder toward the door where Cass waited. "I should be going."

Sister Agnes clasped her arm and gave a nod toward Cass. "That your young man?"

"No . . . just a friend."

"What about the other one, the one with the broad shoulders and ruddy skin? He looks a wee bit older, but they favor one another just the same."

"Morgan? How do you know him?"

Her brows formed surprised peaks. "Why, he's been by, lass. Twice, in fact. Both times he asked to speak to Father Ed, and both times he left a generous gift for the ladies at the shelter. Figured you'd know that."

She didn't. Tucking the information away, Tillie wrapped Sister Agnes in a hug and bid her farewell. "And tell Sister Mary hello for me, too, will you?"

"Of course," Sister Agnes said, giving her arm a pat. "Come by when you can. We miss you."

After assuring her that she would, Tillie turned and made her way down the long aisle toward the rear of the church. Most of the parishioners had gone, but a few lingered, and one figure in particular caught her eye. Though the man wore a tweed coat and a cap pulled low over his ears, something about the set of his jaw seemed familiar.

She looked to the door. The spot where Cass had stood a moment earlier was now vacant. Neither was he among the people clustered around the prayer candles. Her eyes darted back to the figure in the coat and cap. For a brief moment he lifted his chin, and she thought she recognized him.

"Jacob?"

Once again, his head lowered, hiding his face from view. He half turned as if to leave. Moving quickly, Tillie skirted the last row of pews and crossed toward him. "Jacob, wait."

She had nearly drawn even with him when he whirled around. Grabbing her arm, he dragged her into a room off the vestibule.

"What are you doing?" Tillie demanded, more than a little frightened by his strange behavior.

Once the door was shut behind them, he turned and tugged the cap from his head. One eye was purple and swollen. Above the other, a long gash ran from his eyebrow to his ear.

Tillie gasped. "What happened to you?"

"The ring, do you still have it?" he growled.

Eyes wide, she nodded.

"Good. There's something I need you to do." He stepped closer, his eyes wild with excitement. "The pub where you met me the other day, you remember it?"

"Aye," she rasped.

"Just down from there is an apothecary shop owned by one Patrick Bligh. I want you to find him and show him the ring just like you showed me."

He shoved from the door and strode toward her. Tillie stumbled back. She resumed breathing only when he halted a couple of feet from her and jammed both hands into his pockets.

"This is important, Matilda. You must not leave the ring with him, but 'tis verra important that he see it in case . . ." His features hardened, and the one eye he could still see out of twitched.

"Jacob," Tillie whispered, "what happened to you?"

The breath he drew whistled between his lips. "Be verra careful, lass. Dinna be alone if you can help it, and watch what you say and to whom you say it."

"Why?" she insisted.

He motioned to his bruised eye. "So the same thing doesn't happen to you."

"What?"

He shook his head and put a finger to his lips. "Someone saw the two of us talking. This was the result."

Remorse washed over her. "Oh, Jacob . . . I'm so sorry."

"No apologies. It wasn't me they was after. Just what you told me."

"They?"

"I didn't recognize them," he said.

"Then I dinna understand. How do you know it was me . . . ? Oh." She eyed the ugly bruises once more.

"Dinna trouble yourself, lass. They didn't get anything out of me, and I got in a few licks of me own before the cowards ran off."

Assaulted by a bout of trembling, Tillie reached for the wall, found it, and inched sideways to rest her shoulder against it. "You want me to show the ring to someone else in case something happens to you, or to me."

"Aye."

So curt was his reply, she blinked.

"You know who this ring belongs to."

Jacob neither confirmed nor denied the accusation.

"Do you know who is after us?"

"Not yet."

Outside the door, Tillie thought she heard someone call her name.

"But you're looking?" she pressed.

"I am now."

Again, the voice calling her name sounded, only close enough now that she recognized it as Cass's. "I have to go."

Jacob nodded. "Remember what I said. Be careful, and show the ring to Patrick as soon as you can."

"Tomorrow," Tillie promised, opening the door a crack and then sliding through.

"There you are." Cass strode toward her, his face a thundercloud of worry and fear. "What were you thinking, disappearing like that?" He eyed the closed door. "I thought Morgan and I made it clear that you weren't to be alone."

"You d-did," she stammered. "I was looking for you." It was partly true, enough to appease her conscience.

"I went outside to help Giles with Meg and Amelia."

Her face grew hot. "Oh. Sorry."

Cass heaved a sigh and offered his arm. "You ready to go?"

Aye, she was more than ready. He accompanied her outside, but even with his confident presence by her side, she couldn't help looking over her shoulder. That, combined with angst over how she would accomplish the orders Jacob had given her, made for a very long walk home.

26

Monday morning, Morgan departed the boardinghouse early and made for the dock. After speaking with Bozey, he left the noise of the shipyard and veered left toward a crowded part of town. Crowded, and far more dangerous.

Reaching inside his coat, he adjusted the harness over his shoulder so that the pistol fit snugly against his side. At least Bozey knew where he was going, or where to look if he disappeared.

He quickened his pace. Some twenty minutes later he arrived at Cherry Street, which Bozey insisted was the best place to ask the kinds of questions for which Morgan needed answers.

Cutting straight through the Lower East Side, Cherry Street was home to hundreds of immigrants, many of them Irish. They lived and worked in the bricked tenements and shops packed side by side and stretching in all directions. Metal fire escapes snaked up the walls, their barred landings forming ready-made clotheslines on every floor. On the street level, people teemed around businesses of every sort. One brightly painted window boasted butter and eggs. Next to it, a ragged awning fluttered over a sign touting custom-made coffins. Farther down, women dressed in suggestive silk dresses lounged around the entrance to a dimly lit pub.

Easing into the flow of human traffic, Morgan wandered until he spotted a run-down hotel with a battered door that swung from rusty hinges. Inside, the lobby swarmed with men and women of all ages, many of them still looking inebriated from the night before.

"We're full up," the proprietor grunted from behind the counter. Hefting a basket stuffed with soiled linens, he propped it on his hip and circled the counter.

"Not looking for a room," Morgan replied, crossing to him.

The proprietor lifted a snowy eyebrow. "What're you doing here, then?"

"Hoping you can help me." Morgan reached into his pocket and pulled out a picture he'd begged off James Finch from among Donal's things. "Have you seen this man?"

The proprietor spared only a cursory glance. "Nope."

"You sure?"

"Yeah, I'm sure." Shifting the basket higher on his hip, he squinted up at Morgan. "Who is he?"

"One of my crewmen."

"Jumped ship, did he?"

Morgan returned the picture to his pocket. "No, he died. Someone killed him."

"Sorry to hear that. Can't help you, though."

He scurried away with clipped, mincing steps. Morgan followed. "Can you tell me where I might ask—?"

"Nope."

Pushing through a swinging door, the proprietor ducked his head and disappeared.

Morgan caught the door as it swung back. Even had the man known something, he wouldn't have been willing to help, a conclusion Morgan drew from having made several such visits yesterday. Disgusted, he turned and left the hotel.

Two more stops yielded similar results. The third place—a noisy restaurant catering to a distinctly Irish crowd—was only slightly more hopeful, with a waitress who claimed she thought she remembered seeing Donal but who was unable to pinpoint how long ago or who he'd been with.

His frustration growing, Morgan thanked the woman and returned to the street. He'd gone only a few steps when he felt something prod him from behind.

"Dinna turn around."

Morgan tensed. The pressure against his ribs increased until he felt the uncomfortable pricking of a blade.

"Up there. Green door on yer right. Take the alley next to it and keep walking."

Away from observing eyes? Not likely.

And yet the man wasn't a pickpocket or he'd have lifted Morgan's money pouch and disappeared into the crowd. What then did he want?

"Who are you?" Morgan hissed, resisting the painful prompting of the man's knife.

"Walk or I slit ya open where you stand."

For a heart-pounding second, Morgan debated the wisdom of obedience, but to confront the man on the street would mean risking injury to innocent bystanders. He started walking.

The door the man indicated belonged to a butcher. The alley alongside it reeked of slaughterhouse remains. Crates and boxes leaned at odd angles. A little push would send them toppling. Fingers flexed, Morgan sucked in a breath and entered the alley by three paces. One more and they'd be out of the sight of passersby.

The man behind him had inched closer, tension rippling from him in waves. He'd asked no questions, made no demands.

Probably not a good thing and certainly not something Morgan was willing to leave to chance.

He curled his hands into fists and feigned the last step. The man moved with him, but faster. Too fast.

Instead of walking straight ahead, Morgan ducked to his right and whirled. The man's arm flashed downward, the knife clutched in his hand grazing Morgan's arm.

Palm out, Morgan struck the man's nose and sent his head flying backward. Blood gushed over his lips and chin, but that only slowed him for a moment. Eyes watering, the man crouched low and circled Morgan, the knife swaying in lazy circles.

"You'll pay for that."

"Who are you?" Morgan demanded, his confidence returning now that the field had been leveled a bit.

"Somebody that wants you dead."

"Why?"

Barely had he spoken when the man lunged at him again. This time, Morgan thrust both hands out. With his right he caught the man at the crook of his elbow, buckling his arm. His left he balled into a fist and landed a punch on the man's back just above the kidney.

The man let go a yowl of pain and dropped to his knees. Grabbing hold of his wrist, Morgan twisted until the knife fell to the street with a clatter. Kicking it away, Morgan wrenched the man's arm around his back and up until he squealed.

"I'll ask you again. Who are you?"

"McDermott. My name's McDermott."

"Why were you following me?"

"I was paid to kill you."

"By who?"

Screwing his eyes shut, the man grunted and thrust himself forward.

"Who!" Morgan demanded, increasing the pressure against the man's wrist until he groaned again.

"Don't know who. Some bloke met me in a bar last night and offered me fifty dollars."

Tempted to snap the man's wrist, Morgan drew a shuddering breath and leaned hard over the man's shoulder. "Liar. Yesterday was Sunday. The pubs were closed."

All trace of surrender melted from the man's face. Sweat poured over his brow, and a snarl rent from his lips. Craning his neck, he peered up at Morgan. "Go ahead, break it. I'll hunt you down anyway. You and that sniveling brother of yours. And the girl? I'll take me time with her—"

He broke off, and for a moment Morgan thought it was from pain, but then his eyes widened, and Morgan realized he wasn't staring at him but at something behind him. The hair on his neck rose. Instinct took over. Flinging the man's arm away, he dove for the stack of crates piled along the wall of the alley.

A second later, a barrage of hot lead split the air.

27

Wearily, Tillie slid her shawl from her shoulders and hung it over a peg in the hallway. Once again, business at the millinery had been heavy. Cass had attempted cheerful banter, but with her heart grieved over the trouble Jacob had encountered because of her, and her thoughts preoccupied on how she would separate herself from Cass long enough to show the ring to Patrick, she'd hardly paid attention.

Tugging the knot free on her bonnet, she deposited it on the peg next to her shawl. Down the hall, Cass's laughter rang, and Giles and Laverne's echoed back.

Good. Perhaps he'd be engrossed elsewhere long enough to give her time to think through her dilemma.

Behind her, the door banged open, letting in a burst of balmy afternoon air. Expecting Meg, she turned and was surprised to see it was Morgan, leaning against the frame. Relief flooded over her. She'd not seen him since yesterday morn, but rather than confess what had happened at the church to Cass, she'd waited, hoping for a chance to speak with Morgan alone.

She stepped toward him, her hand outstretched. "You're home—"

Morgan slammed the door shut, then whirled to face her. "Where's Cass?"

Recoiling, Tillie yanked her hand back. "In the kitchen. Why?"

"Away from the door," he said. Then, grabbing her arm, he pulled her toward the rear of the house and the library.

"Morgan, what's happened?" Tillie demanded.

Only when they were inside the library and the drapes drawn did he slow down enough to look at her, and still he gripped her arms tightly. "Are you all right?"

"Of course."

"And Cass? The others?"

"All fine, so far as I know. I just got home myself."

She glanced down at his fingers where they pinched into her flesh. Blood stained the back of his hand. Her heart leapt to her throat. "You're bleeding."

"A scratch. I'll be fine." He pulled her closer. "Tillie, did you see anyone today? Anyone unusual?"

She shook her head.

"What about at the shop or on the walk home?"

"No one."

At her response, a bit of the tension drained from his face, and his hold slackened until finally he released her. "Wait here."

He reached for the knob, but this time it was she who grabbed his arm. "Morgan."

For several heart-pounding moments, neither of them spoke but only stared into each other's eyes. At last he took her hand from his arm and walked with her to Amelia's favorite settee in an alcove left of the door. When they sat, he kept hold of her hand, a fact that both frightened and thrilled her.

Lines of worry creased his brow. But it was the intensity in his expression that held her bound.

"I went into the city today," he began.

Her fingers tightened around his. "Why?"

"I was searching for someone who might have seen Donal before he died." Pulling a picture from his pocket, he leaned forward to show it to her.

She took the picture, studied it, then returned it to him and clasped her hands in her lap. "And? Did you?"

He grimaced. "No."

"Was that where you went yesterday, too?"

"Aye. I was hoping I might find some clue as to who he was meeting."

Unable to argue with the logic of his quest, she turned instead to the danger he'd faced. "But why go alone? Wouldn't it have been better to let Cass or Rourke . . ." She paused. Though she couldn't say it, the thought that she might have lost him filled her with dread. Unbelievably, he seemed to sense the feelings stirring within her, but she read no revulsion in the gentle touch he placed against her cheek. His warm palm loosed the tears gathering in her eyes so that they streamed over her cheeks and chin.

"Tillie," he breathed, pulling her to his chest.

Though she longed to savor his embrace, she resisted, bracing both hands against his shoulders until he looked at her, surprised.

"You . . . you have to tell me the rest." She forced her eyes to the crimson stain on his jacket. "What happened to your arm?"

He blew out a sigh. "I was asking around Cherry Street. Someone came up on me from behind with a knife."

She widened her eyes, unable to breathe, unable to speak.

"He forced me into an alley."

Her hand flew to her mouth. "He was going to kill you."

"Either that or he wanted to ask me some questions."

He seemed reluctant to voice the rest, and deep down she was reluctant to hear it. Wrapping her arms around her middle, Tillie squeezed her eyes shut. "'Tis my fault."

"No."

"It is. Yesterday, Jacob Kilarny met me at the church. A couple of men waylaid him, too. Beat him and almost killed him. He said it was because they saw him talking to me."

He did pull her to his chest then, even though she resisted, even though at first she would not allow her arms to encircle his waist.

"It's not your fault."

"I should never have gone to Jacob."

"Shh."

"I should never have let you help me."

"No, Tillie." Pulling away, he slipped his fingers beneath her chin and tilted her face to his. "You couldn't have stopped me."

"But—"

Laying a finger to her lips, he shook his head. "I lied, Tillie. It wasn't my ma what convinced me to come. I wanted to help you. Wanted to see you. And when I did, when I knew that someone . . . that you . . ."

He trailed off, but she knew there was more he wanted to say, and more she wanted to hear. His gaze fell to her mouth.

She held her breath, waiting.

He drew closer.

She let her eyes drift closed and lifted her chin.

"Tillie?" The library door banged open and Cass's voice boomed in the quiet room. "You in here?"

In the span it took for her to jerk her eyes open, Morgan had pulled away and stood to his feet. She stared up at him, her heart pounding as he raked one hand through his hair. A second later he snapped his mouth closed and dropped both hands to his sides.

"We're here, Cass." He spared her one last glance before stepping from the alcove.

Cass dipped into her sight, his brow wrinkled with confusion. "You're back?"

"Aye. I got back a few minutes ago."

"What'd you find?"

Morgan looked at her and then his brother. "We need to talk. Can you sit with Tillie while I fetch the others?"

"Aye, but—"

Before he finished, Morgan disappeared out the library door.

"What was that all about?" Jamming his fists to his hips, Cass peered down at Tillie. "Say . . . are you all right?" He frowned, dropped onto the settee next to her. Collecting her hand, he pressed it between both of his. "Your fingers are cold, and you're trembling."

She could only shake her head.

"Tillie, what happened?" he demanded. "Was it Morgan? Did he say something?"

"No—"

Standing, Cass stalked the length of the library and back. "That brother of mine, so thickheaded. Always trying to draw blood out of a turnip. I told him not to push you."

"Cass, wait. That's not what happened."

"No? Then why are you so upset?"

"Because something happened today. And yesterday. Oh . . ." She pressed her fingers to her temples.

His eyes widened. He strode to her and, clasping her hand, lifted her fingers up to see them better. "You're bleeding!"

"What?"

"Your hands. You've been hurt."

Indeed, dried blood stained the tips of her fingers, but it wasn't hers. She shook her head again. "No. I'm fine."

"Then whose blood is that?"

"Someone's hurt?" The questions piled up as first Laverne, then Meg and Giles filed into the library, followed by Amelia and Morgan.

"No." Tillie rose to her feet. "That is, Morgan's hurt, but I'm not."

"Morgan's hurt!" Amelia spun to stare at him. "You didn't tell us you were wounded. Laverne, fetch some bandages."

Before she could leave, Morgan held up his hand to stop her. "A scratch only. I'll be all right."

She didn't argue, but it was Cass's response that Tillie found surprising. He said nothing but stood with his arms crossed, glaring at his older brother.

Morgan motioned toward the various chairs scattered about the library. All were situated so as to create cozy reading nests, but right now, Tillie knew he'd want them gathered close. She grabbed one and drew it closer to the settee. Soon the others followed suit. Except for Cass. He remained standing at the window.

"So? What happened, lad?" Giles asked, propping both elbows on his knees.

As concisely as he'd explained to her, Morgan told the others about his venture and how it had evolved. Having been interrupted before he could tell her of the shooting, Tillie was as shocked as the rest.

"And the bloke who attacked you?" Giles said. "What happened to him?"

Morgan's face reddened and he looked at neither Tillie nor Cass. "Killed by a stray bullet."

Amelia's soft gasp resounded in the silent room.

"And the shooter?" Meg asked, her eyes wide.

"He ran off before anyone could stop him."

"Anyone get a good look at him?" Cass said, his clipped words making Tillie wince.

Morgan nodded. "A couple of witnesses. None had seen him before. They gave his description to the police."

"Heaven help us," Amelia whispered, pressing both hands to her mouth. "Thank God you were not seriously injured."

"Might have helped if you'd told someone where you were going," Cass said.

"I did," Morgan grunted. "Bozey."

Whether he realized it or not, his answer only seemed to infuriate Cass further. Inhaling a deep breath, he shook his head and then strode from the room. Silence reverberated in his wake.

Finally, Tillie rose to her feet. "Rourke should know what has happened."

"You're not going anywhere," Morgan snapped. "Not alone. 'Tisn't safe."

Amelia crossed to wrap her arm around Tillie's waist. "I agree."

"I'll go." Giles flashed a quick glance at Laverne, who nodded.

"I'll fetch me cape."

Meg's eyes widened. "You're going, too?"

"Someone's got to keep an eye on him." She jerked her thumb at Giles and grinned. "I'd like to see anyone try and lay a hand on him while I'm around."

"No, Laverne," Morgan said, rising. "Better if Cass or I go."

"Right, and ain't you and him the ones they're after?"

"She's right," Amelia said. "Besides, your arm still needs tending." Crossing to Laverne, she grabbed one of her hands and one of Giles's and held them tight. "Hurry back."

When they'd gone, she bade Meg to ready the bandages while she went into the kitchen to heat water, leaving Tillie alone to wait with Morgan.

She motioned to his coat. "You should take that off. Meg and I will see that it gets laundered and repaired."

To her surprise, he did as she asked without argument, wincing when it came time to slide his arm from the sleeve.

Tillie hurried to help, her eyes widening at the width and depth of the cut on his arm. "I thought you said it was a scratch," she scolded through tight lips.

"'Tis less than it could have been," he replied.

"And more than it should have been," she retorted. Her fingers shaking, she laid his still-warm coat over her arm.

As though she had not spoken, he moved to stand before her. "I meant what I said earlier. You couldn't have stopped me from trying to help."

She would have formed a reply had not his next action robbed her of logical thought. Bending low, Morgan claimed her free hand and brought it slowly to his lips. She held her breath as he pressed a kiss to the back.

"Guess I'd best see about getting this thing tended to." Releasing her, he hitched his shoulder and walked to the door, pausing there with one hand on the jamb. "You'll fetch me when Giles and Laverne return?" At her nod, he ducked out of the library.

Her heart racing, Tillie stared for several seconds as the door slid closed. It was only then—when he'd gone and his steps had faded down the hall—that she realized she still hadn't drawn a breath.

28

With the ache in his arm somewhat lessened by the snug bandage Amelia and Meg had placed there, Morgan slid into a clean shirt and tossed the ripped and bloodied one into the trash. Fastening the buttons on his cuffs, he left his room and walked down the hall in search of his brother. His room was empty, but from his window, Morgan spied the open stable door and grunted.

So, Cass had gone in search of solitude, just like when they were younger. What in blazes had him so twisted up, anyway?

Jamming a cap on his head, Morgan hurried down the stairs and out the back door. Thumping and scraping came from the stable, accompanied by the outraged clucking of chickens.

Skirting them, Morgan wound past the stalls toward the rear of the stable. He found Cass huffing and sweaty as he tossed several hay bales down from the loft. One landed particularly close, thudding hard against the floor and raising a cloud of dust and chaff.

Waving his hand in front of his face, Morgan scowled up at Cass. "That one was on purpose."

"So?" Cass heaved another bale over the side, then braced

both hands on his hips, a satisfied smirk on his face as Morgan jumped out of the way.

"One more like that and I'll have to climb up there and toss *you* down," Morgan threatened.

"What's stopping you? It's not like I'm doing you any good sitting around here."

Morgan pushed his cap off his forehead with his thumb. "That what has you so riled up?"

"What do you think?"

"I think we need to talk."

At first, he doubted Cass would comply, but then he scrambled down the ladder, landing with a solid *thump* on the floor next to him.

"Good—" Morgan began, only to have Cass cut him off before he could finish.

"I want to know why you didn't tell me where you were going yesterday, or today, for that matter. I want to know why you're always the one taking risks and I'm left baby-sitting the crew."

Each accusation was punctuated by a jab to the chest by Cass's finger. Clamping his lips on the sarcasm he felt brewing, Morgan whirled and paced the width of the stable.

"Well?" Cass demanded. "You said you wanted to talk." He lifted his hands, palms up. "Let's talk."

Morgan studied his brother from below lowered brows. This perhaps was not what he'd had in mind. Cass had never been easy to reason with, but especially when he got his ire up.

Sighing deeply, he willed his feet to stop, then grasped the top of the nearest stall door. "I could tell you that you're my responsibility . . ."

Cass crossed his arms and glared at Morgan across the stall wall.

Morgan extended a peace offering with his lifted hand. "But I won't because it's only part of the reason."

Cass remained rooted and glowering. "What's the other part?" Uncrossing his arms, he stepped around the stall to stand next to Morgan. "It's Tillie, isn't it? That's the part you're not telling me."

Morgan turned to look at his brother. Cass was still angry, given the whiteness of his lips and his clenched fists, but there was also hurt mingled in his expression.

And something else.

"Cass . . ." It took Morgan a minute to realize what it was that Cass hadn't said, but when it finally hit him, it struck like a blow. He gave a light shrug. "Aye, I'm worried about Tillie's safety, and finding out who has set out to harm her, nothing more."

A bit of the anxiety cleared from Cass's face. Letting go a sigh, he clapped Morgan on the shoulder. "Of course you're worried about her, brother. We all are, me included. But I'm worried about you, too. You could have been killed today. Tillie and I wouldn't want that, no matter what good you hoped to accomplish by going off alone."

Cass didn't know it, but with each word he spoke, he delivered a blow more punishing than any Morgan had felt that day. "Tillie and you?"

"That's right. We talked about you, Morgan. I told her how important it is to you to live up to Da's memory. But this isn't the way, brother. You'll only wind up getting yourself killed."

Morgan gritted his teeth. They'd talked about him. Tillie and Cass. And why not? They'd spent enough time together. He was closer to her age. Likely the two of them had much in common.

More than he could hope to have with her.

Tamping down a burst of jealousy, he swallowed hard and jammed both hands into his pants pockets. "What can I say? You're right this time."

"This time, eh? So you admit it?"

Relieved to hear a bit of the blarney returning, he lifted his head and grinned. "Dinna let it go to your head."

The smile faded from Cass's lips, but so too did the anger and hurt. Backing up a step, he said, "Well? What do we do now?"

"I'll need you to stay with Tillie. If you can, try and talk her into taking a day or two off from work."

"And you?"

"I'll speak to Rourke Turner, see if he's got a couple of men we can use to try and track down some information on Donal."

"You don't want to use the crew?"

"Not if I can help it."

Nodding, Cass moved toward the stable door. "I'll talk to Tillie." He motioned with one hand. "You coming?"

Morgan shook his head. "In a while. I've got some thinking to do first, and 'tis better done out here."

Cass looked as though he meant to speak, but then thought better of it. Instead he turned and disappeared out the door.

Once he'd gone, Morgan blew out a sigh and dragged the cap from his head. What a fool he'd been not to see it sooner. Cass was in love with Tillie. More than likely she loved him, too. And to think, there in the library, he'd nearly kissed her!

Ach, and what a mistake that would have been. Not only would she have not welcomed his kiss, it might have irreparably damaged his relationship with his brother, a relationship that was only now inching past the tumult of their youth. Cass blamed him for much of the trouble between them, and rightfully so. But this?

No, he'd not risk hurting Cass in the same way he'd been hurt all those years ago. Tillie too deserved better than a grumpy old sea captain with naught to offer but a broken-down vessel and her salty crew.

It was Cass she deserved. Cass with his playful, teasing ways who would coax the laughter and cheer from her.

Leaving the stable, Morgan strode outside and slammed the door behind him. Aye, Tillie and Cass belonged together, and he would do everything in his power to see to it that they ended up so, no matter how much he wished it could be otherwise.

No matter how much it pained him.

— ❈ ❈ ❈ —

The light of the setting sun warmed the back of Neil Dunahoe's shoulders. He'd been sitting so long in one attitude, he'd likely have a burn, but better that than the punishment he'd receive if he failed to carry out The Celt's orders.

Shifting, he rose from his position betwixt the boardinghouse stable and the building next door. At least he'd have something of note to report this time, instead of admitting to a failed attempt on the woman's life followed by a dismal stab on Keondric Morgan's.

He scanned the area for prying eyes and then sauntered away from the boardinghouse onto the street. The Celt wouldn't be happy about McDermott. For sure and for certain he'd have a bit of explaining to do in that area, even if it was an accident. But at least he could say the man had died before giving away anything of importance.

He scowled as he hailed a cab, then waited for the driver to pull around. Was it his fault The Celt's men were such feebleminded idiots? After all, how much trouble could one lass be? Had The Celt been patient, Neil could've had the job done and had the woman's body floating in the harbor by the end of the week. The captain and his brother, on the other hand . . .

He rubbed his chin.

That Morgan was one to watch. The way he'd dodged McDermott's knife 'twas no easy task.

Perhaps the wily old Celt had been right to enlist his four most trusted henchmen. Maybe he'd just see to the woman and let the other two take care of the Morgans.

Warming to the idea, Dunahoe settled against the carriage seat to wait out the ride. Tonight he would tell The Celt what he'd overheard. And tomorrow . . .

Tomorrow he would introduce himself to Tillie McGrath.

29

An early morning chill greeted Tillie as she slipped from the boardinghouse before the sun's rays had even begun to pink the sky. Clutching her shawl about her shoulders, she scurried down the steps and hailed the first cab she spied.

The driver's eyebrows lifted when she gave him the address. He scanned her garments from bonnet to hem. "You sure you wanna go there, miss? It's not exactly a fittin' place for a gal such as you to be roaming all by yourself."

"I'm sure," Tillie said firmly. She'd already broken her promise to Jacob by one day. She'd delay her visit no longer. She settled on the seat and arranged her skirt over her knees. "Drive on, please."

Shrugging, the man gave a cluck to the mare and set the carriage in motion. The long ride gave Tillie ample time to think over what Jacob had told her.

"The pub where you met me the other day . . . just down from that is an apothecary shop owned by one Patrick Bligh. I want you to find him and show him the ring just like you showed me."

A shudder took her at the memory of Jacob's battered face. Though she knew Morgan would be irate when he found out she'd gone alone to meet this Bligh, she couldn't bear the thought of him or Cass or anyone else coming to harm on her behalf.

Squaring her shoulders, she clutched the pouch containing Braedon's ring. Whoever Patrick Bligh was, Jacob trusted him. She had no choice but to trust him, as well.

The address she'd given the driver was to the pub where she'd met Jacob. Climbing from the carriage, she handed him the fare and then waited until the horse and carriage rumbled away before walking the short distance to the apothecary shop where Jacob had told her she would find Patrick Bligh.

Indeed, the shop was where Jacob had said it would be, but a sign on the door told her it would be nigh unto an hour before the store opened. She tried the handle anyway, grimacing when it failed to surrender to her prodding.

Heaving a sigh, she pressed her back to the door and scanned the street in both directions. Even now, her presence had begun to draw curious stares. She eyed the pub. Though it was open, she dared not set foot in that place alone.

She pushed from the door and walked a few paces down the street, then changed her mind and returned the same way. Passing the apothecary, she kept going until she reached the pub. As she'd suspected, the door swung open with just one shove.

Inside, the scent of stale cigar smoke hung heavy on the air. Thankfully, the table nearest the door was empty. She eased toward it, pulled out a chair, and sank down onto it. Perhaps if she didn't look at anyone, they'd leave her alone.

A rough voice at her elbow snuffed the dim hope.

"Well, well. What have we here." The chair next to her scraped the floor and then two thick knees bumped hers under the table. "You're a bonnie enough lass. Haven't seen you around before. Must be me lucky day."

"I'm waiting for someone," she mumbled, keeping her eyes downcast.

"As was I. Looks like I found her."

The suggestive drawl raised goose bumps on her flesh. She risked a peek, then wished she hadn't when the leering gleam in his eyes matched the tone of the man's voice. He was unkempt and unshaven, but what frightened her most was the wolfish smile curving his lips.

Pushing back her chair, she moved to rise. "I should go—"

The man's hand flashed out, catching her wrist before she could dart away. "What's your hurry?"

"I told you." Tillie stiffened and injected her words with more courage than she actually felt. "I'm waiting for someone. Now, please let go of my wrist."

She had no time to wonder whether the man would comply, for no more had the words left her mouth than a familiar voice drifted to her ears.

"You heard the lass. Let her go. Now."

Tillie jerked her head around, wild relief rushing through her veins. "Morgan."

Indeed, Morgan stood just a few feet away. At his shoulder stood Cass, his scowl only slightly less threatening than his much larger brother. Tears leapt to her eyes at their appearance, for though they were sure to be angered with her, she no longer doubted her safety. She directed a pointed stare at the fingers still twined about her wrist. Reluctantly, the man let go. A second later, she found herself escorted outside, a glowering Morgan at each elbow.

Cass pulled her to a stop on the sidewalk. "Tillie, what in heaven's name were you thinking, coming here alone like this?" He maintained his grip on her elbow.

Morgan, she noted, did not. He'd dropped his hand the moment they set foot outside, then paced a short distance away, occasionally shooting her a withering glance, but mostly just stalking a hole in the sidewalk.

"I . . ." she began.

"You what?" Cass rubbed his hand over his face. "Do you have any idea what could have happened in there?"

"I know 'twas dangerous, but—"

Morgan stepped closer. "I thought I made it perfectly clear you weren't to leave the boardinghouse."

An onset of ire gave her courage. She matched his posture and thrust out her chin. "*You* made it clear?"

He glared at her. "Well, didn't I?"

"Since when am I a member of your crew?"

Under his furious scrutiny, Tillie's boldness melted quickly. She lowered her head, though a stubbornness she hadn't known she possessed kept her from taking the words back.

She clenched her jaw and refused to look at him, directing her attention to Cass instead. "How did you know where I'd gone?"

"Morgan figured it out." He gave an apologetic shrug. "Said you'd mentioned something about seeing Jacob Kilarny yesterday. He reckoned you'd—"

"It seemed reasonable when you didn't come down to breakfast that you'd left in search of him . . . in direct opposition to my orders," Morgan interrupted.

One corner of Cass's mouth lifted in a wry grin. *See?* he mouthed.

"That's not exactly right," Tillie said, sounding somewhat like a petulant child even to her own ears. "Jacob did come to see me at Mass, but he told me to show the ring to someone else, a man by the name of Patrick Bligh."

The brothers shared a quick glance, and Tillie forged on.

"That's his shop there." She pointed at the apothecary's door a few stores down. "But he wilna be open for business for a while yet."

"Kilarny told you to show the ring to this man?" Morgan asked.

Tillie nodded. "I think he was afraid something might happen to him. Or to me."

At this, the smile faded from Cass's lips. He looked at Morgan. "What do you think?"

"I think we should figure out why that ring is so important that Kilarny would see fit to tell another of its existence." He turned to Tillie. "Do you think this man Bligh might be able to tell you who it belonged to?"

She bit her lip. "I suppose. Could be that's why Jacob wanted him to see it."

Morgan waved toward the increasing number of people moving about the street. "I'd rather we not wait around out here for the store to open. Cass, there's a diner not far from here." He pointed. "That direction. Take Tillie and wait for me there."

"What are you going to do?" she asked before Cass could respond.

"I'll go by the apothecary, check it out, see who he has loitering about. If it looks safe, I'll come back for you."

Though she didn't like being ordered about, again, his plan made sense. Drawing an irritated breath, she turned to Cass. "C'mon, then. Let's go sit until Morgan tells us it's safe to come out."

Without waiting for Cass, she stomped off, though who she was angry at—herself or Morgan—was yet unclear.

The diner Morgan indicated was a busy place, even for this hour of the morning. The aroma of frying bacon filled the air, along with eggs, potatoes, and freshly baked bread. Tillie regretted having left the boardinghouse without first breaking the fast.

Cass secured them a table against a far wall. Though she

would have rather watched for Morgan, he claimed the chair facing the door.

"Coffee," he told the waitress hovering nearby.

She brought it promptly, a bitter brew that slid down Tillie's throat like tar. Cass too grimaced at his first sip. Neither of them drained their cup, or had to, for Morgan appeared a short time later.

Dropping a few coins on the table, he nodded to Cass, then moved to hold Tillie's chair. "Let's go."

"You've seen him then, this Patrick Bligh?" Cass asked as they exited the restaurant.

"Aye, I've seen him." He turned to Tillie. "You have the ring with you?"

She held up the pouch.

He hesitated. "Tillie, I think 'twould be best if I took the ring to Bligh."

"What?"

He closed the gap between them and lowered his voice so only the three of them heard. "There were several men milling about the shop. Salty-looking lot, all. I dinna think it wise to let them see your face."

"But Jacob—"

"'Tis for your own safety. Cass?"

"I agree," he said, squelching her argument before she could give it voice. He pressed her hands between his, his eyes earnest and pleading. "Morgan wilna let anything happen to the ring, and it might be safer if he goes in alone."

Tillie's heart thumped inside her chest. She'd felt better when it was only her own welfare at stake. She shuddered and finally gave in with a nod. "What will we do?"

Morgan gestured to a shoe store across the crowded thoroughfare. "There. The windows face the apothecary. I think you'll have a decent vantage if you stay to the front of the store."

"Done." Cass looked at Tillie. "You ready?"

She slipped the pouch into Morgan's waiting palm, any anger she'd felt disappearing like steaming mist beneath a hot sun. In that instant, when his fingers grazed hers and his hand closed around the ring, she experienced a moment of paralyzing panic.

"Morgan . . ."

He peered down at her, his eyes piercing.

"Please be careful," she whispered.

His mouth twitched, the faintest of smiles. He then glanced at Cass. "Take care of her."

In response, Cass claimed her arm and led her away from the sidewalk, toward the shoe store.

The distance seemed so much farther than it had appeared from the other side of the street. Twice they paused to let a carriage or wagon rumble by. Several times they had to dodge scurrying pedestrians. Tillie was grateful for Cass's steadying hand against her back, for she was hard-pressed to concentrate on their destination, not when every thought was focused on the man they'd left behind.

30

A small bell welcomed Morgan as he sauntered into Patrick Bligh's apothecary shop. Brown bottles and jars of varying sizes filled the shelves along the walls. There were sundry goods in the bins and barrels stacked on the floor, as well. He took note of those that could be used to his advantage should he have need for a hasty exit.

A loud voice boomed from the rear of the store. "Welcome, sir. Can I help you?"

Morgan motioned toward his neck. "Throat drops?"

"Aye, right away."

A portly man, as large as his booming voice, snagged a paper bag from a shelf and circled a long oak counter. He motioned toward a metal bin. "How many would you like?"

"Just a few." Again he touched his neck.

"Ach, summer colds are the worst kind."

He didn't correct his assumption.

Lifting the lid on the bin, the man eyed Morgan's clothes. "Just off the sea?"

Morgan shrugged. His dark blue coat and brass buttons usually gave him away. Nothing suspicious there.

"Where are you from, if ya dinna mind me inquiring?"

"Dublin."

The man's head bobbed. "I've got family there. Ya been gone long?"

"Long enough," Morgan said, taking the bag the man proffered.

Replacing the scoop inside the bin, the man wiped his hands on his apron. "That'll be fifty cents, please."

Morgan removed the coins from his pocket and dropped them into the man's waiting palm, then followed him to a shiny cash register that jingled as he rang up the purchase.

"Will there be anything else?" the man asked, his shaggy eyebrows lifting with his friendly smile.

Morgan cast a glance about the store. Except for an elderly man who looked intent on choosing the right elixir, the place was vacant. He turned back to the proprietor. "Actually, I wonder if you could help me. I'm looking for the owner of this store. Patrick Bligh, I believe his name to be."

The man straightened, his smile fading. "I'm Patrick Bligh. Do I know you?"

Morgan lowered his voice. "Jacob Kilarny sent me."

If the name meant something, Bligh didn't let it show.

Morgan slipped the pouch containing Tillie's ring from his coat pocket and laid it on the counter.

"Say, Mr. Bligh," a wavering voice behind them called, "this potion here, is it good for arthritis?"

Bracing his hands against the counter, Bligh leaned to peer around Morgan. "Not that one. That one's for ague. Try the one next to it." He returned his attention to Morgan and the pouch on the counter. "What's that?"

"Something Jacob wanted you to see."

Bligh's gaze bounced between the pouch and the figure at the shelves. "No, no, Mr. Collins, on the other side."

He darted—an odd feat for such a large man—around the counter and rescued a bottle from the customer's shaking hand and replaced it with a much smaller jar. "This be the one I was referring to. It's a balm now, not an elixir. Rub it on the affected areas. Usually you can expect relief in just a couple of hours. Would you like me to wrap it for you?"

The man's graying head bobbed, and both returned to the counter, Bligh's hand steady on Mr. Collins's elbow. Watching them, Morgan slid the pouch out of the way and waited while he rang up the older man's purchase. When they'd finished, Bligh turned to Morgan.

"Now, you were saying?"

What he'd been saying and what he'd been thinking were two vastly different things. Surely this could not be the same Patrick Bligh that Kilarny had meant. Morgan shook his head. Grabbing the pouch off the counter, he made to leave. "Nothing. Sorry. I must have the wrong place."

"I was expecting a woman."

Morgan paused near the door and looked back. "Pardon?"

Bligh gestured toward the pouch. "He told me it would be a woman bringing that there ring by—assuming that be what you have in the bag."

Morgan let go of the doorknob and returned to the counter. This time it was Bligh who looked about the store. "Let's see it. Make it quick."

Sliding the pouch to him, Morgan watched while Bligh shook the ring into his palm and gave it a cursory glance. His face twisting, he reached below the counter, took out a magnifier with a slender black handle, and held it to the ring. With a flick of his thumbs he separated the rings, exposing the ruby heart and giving it careful study.

Shock registered on Bligh's face. "*Memento mori*," he breathed.

"What?"

Bligh shook his head as though to clear it. He dropped the ring back into the pouch and handed it to Morgan. "Put it away before someone comes in."

Morgan did as he was told and pushed the pouch into the pocket of his coat. "Well?"

Bligh sucked in a breath. "Aye, I've seen it before."

"You know who it belongs to?"

The man's eyes narrowed. "Don't you?"

They stared at each other across the counter for the span of several seconds.

"Where's the woman Kilarny told me would be coming?" Bligh asked at last.

Morgan shrugged. "Thought it would be safer if I came alone."

"Safer, eh?"

The way he spoke the words sent a shiver coursing down Morgan's back.

"Aye, then," Bligh said, "I suppose you're right, especially if that ring belongs to the person I think it does."

Morgan clenched his jaw. "And who is that?"

Another glance around the store, and then Bligh leaned forward, drops of perspiration rolling down the sides of his face. "Have a care with that there ring. It belongs to a very important man. How your girl managed to come by it . . . well, I'd be interested to know that myself."

"The owner," Morgan snapped, growing impatient, "what's his name?"

Bligh drew back, his head shaking. "I dinna know his name. I reckon there's not many who do. But around here—" he stopped, took another quick glance around the shop— "around here he's known as The Celt, and he's the leader of a brotherhood made up of Irish."

"The Fenians."

"Aye, lad. The Fenians."

— ※ ※ ※ —

Tillie's pulse quickened as the door to the apothecary's shop swung open, but instead of Morgan, an old man hobbled out, his back and shoulders stooped and a small bag clutched in his fist. She let go a sigh.

Cass's voice rumbled in her ear. "Easy now, no sense drawing attention to ourselves."

How could she help herself when she so badly wanted to rush to Morgan's aid? Her fingers shook as she replaced a white kid slipper on the shelf.

A harried salesman scurried to her side. "Can I help you with that, miss? It's a fine shoe. Note the toe and the narrow strap on the instep, both embroidered with white and gold beads. Makes for a fine evening slipper."

Indeed it would, though it would take weeks for her budget to recover. Never had she owned such a fine shoe, nor would she have need for such anytime soon—not in the millinery or the orphanage.

She'd been so wrapped up in her recent troubles, she'd hardly given a thought to the orphanage.

She glanced at Cass, who slipped his arm about her waist and smiled at the salesman. "We're just looking for now, but we appreciate your attention."

The salesman looked doubtful as he turned to assist another customer, but then he was gone and Tillie could concentrate on the shop across the street once more.

"You all right?" Cass whispered.

As he led her away from the shoes, he nodded at two women who watched them from beneath large feathered hats. Taken with his infectious grin, one of the women giggled and hid behind a lace fan. The other merely deepened her scowl.

"I'll be fine just as soon as—" Tillie began, then cut her words short when the door across the busy street swung open again. This time it was Morgan's broad shoulders that filled the frame.

Grabbing Cass's hand, she yanked him toward the door. "There he is. Let's go."

Her feet could hardly keep up with her heart as she dropped Cass's hand and raced out of the store. She skittered to a stop at the curb and waited impatiently for a black phaeton to whir past before resuming her trek toward Morgan.

He met her midway across the street. Seizing her hand, he led her back to the sidewalk, then raised his arm to hail a carriage for hire.

"Where's Cass?"

"Here," Cass replied, huffing as he caught up.

"We need to get Tillie away from here."

When the carriage rolled to a halt, Morgan's hand fell to her waist to help her up. She sat, then didn't wait for Cass but held out her hand to assist Morgan.

This time, he didn't let go.

A second later, Cass joined them, and the carriage set off with a lurch.

"Did you find him?" Tillie asked, a trifle breathless.

It was the excitement that constricted her chest so, yet she couldn't help but be aware of the tingle in her fingers where the warmth of Morgan's skin touched hers.

Reaching inside his coat, he withdrew the pouch and gave it to her. "Aye, I found him."

"And what did he say?" Cass leaned forward, his eyes gleaming.

A trickle of disappointment filtered into Tillie's thoughts. It was the danger and mystery Cass found so exhilarating, not concern for his brother. Not concern for her. She directed her attention to Morgan.

"He remembered the ring. Said it belonged to someone called The Celt."

Tillie stifled a gasp.

"You know him?"

She took a deep breath, tugged loose the strings of her bonnet. Morgan gave her fingers a reassuring squeeze.

"I only know *of* him," she replied. "He's the leader of the Fenians, the group Braedon belonged to. Very powerful and mysterious."

"So how did Braedon get his ring?" Cass asked.

Tillie looked at Morgan. "I don't know, but I think we should tell this to Rourke as soon as possible."

Leaning out of the window, Morgan barked new instructions to the driver, then dipped back inside and resumed his grip on Tillie's fingers. Cass's eyes followed and, a second later, drifted up to meet Tillie's.

Morgan too appeared to notice the direction Cass's attention had taken. He slid his hand from Tillie's and clasped both of them in his lap. The rest of the ride was carried out in silence.

Barely had the carriage shuddered to a stop than Morgan leapt to the ground, one hand on the door and the other toward the driver. "If you'll hold for a moment?"

The driver nodded. Morgan then poked his head back into the carriage. "We don't all need to go inside, and it's safer for Tillie back at the boardinghouse."

To her dismay, Cass agreed.

She reached out to clasp the door handle. "But—"

"No arguments, Tillie. Better if you wait at the house with Amelia and the others. Also . . ." His face darkened in a frown. "I think it's time you told them everything so they can be on their guard."

Her stomach sank. She settled against the seat. "All right. And Mrs. Ferguson?"

Morgan looked at Cass. "Send word through Giles that Tillie won't be returning to work for at least a couple of days. Dinna tell her why, but let her know it kinna be helped."

As he finished, he shot a questioning glance at Tillie. She nodded.

"Good. I'll get back to the boardinghouse as soon as I finish here."

She leaned forward to tell him to be careful, but before she could, the door closed and he was striding away. Too quickly the carriage set off again, and all she caught of Morgan was one final glimpse out the window as the carriage rounded a corner.

Several buildings and businesses sped by before Tillie realized that Cass was still watching her. A look of sorrow flashed across his features and then disappeared, replaced by a wink and a too-brilliant smile.

"He'll be all right, you know. Morgan's always been able to take care of himself. It's looking after others that he's lousy at."

The attempt at humor only heightened the foreboding growing in Tillie's stomach. It was a feeling she was only too acquainted with—the knot of dread that felt like it had taken root and would soon spread to every limb and nerve.

She'd felt it the day she left Ireland.

And again the day Braedon died.

A third time when she'd lost her baby.

And now . . .

Gripping the side of the carriage, Tillie clenched her teeth and forced herself to concentrate on what Cass had said about Morgan taking care of himself, but one thought kept intruding, kept fanning to life the embers of doubt and fear.

She'd fallen in love with Keondric Morgan. And that meant

he was in greater danger than he knew, because God would never allow her love for him to exist. Not when she had done something so frightfully wicked she deserved whatever punishment the Almighty decided to hand down.

Her only hope was in God's mercy and Morgan's own goodness. Surely God would not rob their family of Morgan's provision. Surely He knew how much Cass and their mother needed him?

The thought was of little comfort, as was the simple prayer that repeated itself over and over inside her head.

God, dinna let anything happen to Morgan. Let your wrath fall on me instead. Please . . . bring him back safe.

— ❊ ❊ ❊ —

Frustration and rage simmered in The Celt's gut and licked like fire along his veins. Even the gentle rocking of the coach taunted him, reminding him that while all seemed secure on the outside, on the inside, one slip, one misspoken word could spell his downfall.

His grip tightened on the head of his pearl-handled cane, a gift he'd received long ago from a person he barely remembered. How could it be that after everything he'd been through, every move he'd made to ensure his success, one tiny lass could be his undoing?

No. He lifted the cane and drove it against the floor of the coach. No, he'd not let some foolish child rob him of everything he'd worked so hard to achieve. Too much blood had been spilled to let her spoil things now. Even his own son . . .

Regret washed over him and then faded.

His son had always been aware of the stakes. His death had been unfortunate and untimely, nothing more. Given the chance, he'd no doubt lay down his life all over again if it meant they would move one step closer to their goal. Despite his flaws, his rash and idealistic ways, his son had always been loyal. A good and brave lad.

"We're close," he said, willing the whispered words across the ocean to a narrow grave and his son's lifeless ears.

But first, there was something he needed to do, needed to know.

The coach slowed, its wheels rumbling over the cobbled street. At last, it stopped altogether, and his driver peered at him over his shoulder.

"Here it is, sir, 1364 Ashberry Street."

The home of an old friend and acquaintance. Reining in his emotions, The Celt rose, adjusting for the pitch of the coach as he climbed down. By the time he'd traveled up the walk and mounted the stairs leading to the front door, he no longer shook from struggling to contain his rage. By the time the door swung open in response to his knock, he had a pleasant smile fixed to his lips.

"Surprised?" The Celt said, opening his arms wide and inviting a hug. "It's been a long time."

Amelia Matheson stared, her eyes wide and unblinking, and her lips parting in a slow, pleased smile. "Well, for heaven's sake, look who's here." Her hand fell from the knob as she stepped from the entrance into his embrace.

After a moment, she pulled away, her hands gripping his arms, and tipped her head to peer up at him. "Douglas Healy, you old goat. Why didn't you tell me you were coming?"

31

Weariness began to surface from somewhere deep within Tillie—not just weariness but a great deal of worry mingled in, as well.

At least the boardinghouse was peaceful, with everyone either ensconced in their rooms as they changed for dinner or not yet home from work. Tillie made her way down the hall toward the stairs. Maybe she could catch a quiet moment alone in her room. To think. And pray.

Low voices drifted from the parlor. She paused with her hand on the banister. One belonged to Amelia, but the other was most definitely masculine. Giles?

No, this voice was much deeper.

She left the stairs and eased toward the parlor door. It opened before she reached it, and Amelia stepped out.

"Oh, Tillie. I thought I heard someone stirring."

"I thought I heard voices."

"Yes . . . ah . . ." She glanced behind her at the partially open door. "That was just . . ."

A flush crept over Amelia's cheeks, startling against her cap of snowy white hair. Yet it wasn't a pleased flush or even the pale pink of shyness. She was embarrassed.

"Amelia," Tillie said, grasping her friend's arm, "is everything all right?"

"Of course." Lifting her chin, Amelia stepped back into the parlor and pushed the door open wide. "You remember Douglas Healy?"

Tillie's breath caught. Aye, she remembered him, and his daughter-in-law, Deidre, who last year had tried to kill Rourke and Cara.

Hiding her trembling hands in the folds of her skirt, Tillie gave a curtsy. "Welcome back, Mr. Healy."

"Thank you, Miss . . . McGrath, is it?"

"That's correct."

Mr. Healy's full mustache wiggled as his lips turned in a broad smile. "Mrs. Matheson and I were just about to indulge in a cup of tea." He gestured to a tray sitting on the table in the center of the parlor. "Will you join us?"

Tillie directed a glance toward Amelia. Despite his jovial air, she still seemed flustered. Her fingers were red from wringing, and damp tendrils had escaped from her normally perfect bun to cling to her temples and neck.

Turning her back to Mr. Healy, Tillie lowered her voice and clasped Amelia's fingers. "Are you all right?"

Amelia's attention shifted to the figure looming over Tillie's shoulder. "I . . . would appreciate if you helped with the tea." She smiled weakly and moved toward the table. "Shall we?"

"There are only two cups," Tillie said.

Amelia rang a small bell on the table. "I'll have Laverne fetch another."

Tillie marveled as Amelia poured first a cup of tea for Mr. Healy and then one for Tillie. Though there was no doubt that she was upset, the cup barely rattled as she pressed it into her waiting hands.

Amelia removed the lid from the sugar bowl and held it high for Mr. Healy. "Still like your tea sweet?"

Such a benign question, yet every word, every syllable, seemed electrically charged. How did Amelia know how Mr. Healy liked his tea? Catching him staring at her, Tillie shifted uncomfortably in her chair. Why had his gaze been pinned on her since the moment she'd entered the room? She barely knew the man.

Lifting her cup, she took a sip, allowing the warm liquid to calm her frayed nerves. A light knock sounded on the parlor door, and Amelia rose to answer.

"Another cup, please, Laverne," she said, "and some of those marmalade cookies I like so much."

Her quiet murmur faded as Tillie's eyes locked with Mr. Healy's over the rim of her cup. She lowered it slowly. "So, Mr. Healy, how long are you in America?"

"That depends," he said, reaching for a pearl-handled cane resting against the arm of his chair and worrying the tip of it between his fingers. "I've some business that needs attending before I can think about going back."

"Business?"

He brought his cup to his lips and took a sip, yet his eyes remained fixed on her. "Aye. Unpleasant, and all that, especially since I thought it was something I'd taken care of long ago, but that is the way of things now and then I suppose."

Tillie replaced her cup in its saucer with a clatter. It wasn't the words he spoke, for truly he made lighthearted chatter. It was his steady stare she found so unnerving and . . . threatening.

Setting aside her cup, she stood. "I should help Laverne with dinner."

She glanced at the door, where Amelia stood holding the empty cup and saucer Laverne had supplied.

"Forgive me for not staying. I hope you dinna mind."

"Not at all." Amelia looked past her toward Mr. Healy.

He too set aside his cup and rose. "I think it's about time I was going, as well." Picking up his cane, he went to Amelia and took the cup from her loose fingers. "So nice to see you again, my dear. You will think on what we discussed?"

"You know I will, Douglas."

Though she smiled, it wasn't the kind to reach her eyes. Tillie noted lines of strain around her mouth, and a stiffness to the set of her shoulders.

Leaning slightly, Amelia stood on tiptoe to wrap Mr. Healy in a hug. "Good-bye, Douglas. Come and see me again soon."

"I will. Good day, Amelia." Rescuing his fedora from the ladder-back chair where he'd hung it, he plopped it onto his head and bowed first to Amelia and then to Tillie. "Ladies."

Only when he'd let himself out did Tillie feel free to breathe again. Amelia also let out a long sigh.

"What was *he* doing here?" Tillie asked.

Reaching for her empty cup, Amelia shook her head and shrugged. "Douglas and I are old friends." Tillie followed as Amelia carried the cup to the tea tray and deposited it next to the still-steaming pot. "Despite what happened last summer, the two of us share a history. It is difficult to explain."

"Did you speak about what happened?"

"Only briefly. The loss still grieves him."

"Why then did he visit?"

A worried frown creased Amelia's lips. "To be honest, Tillie, I'm not sure."

"What do you mean?"

Amelia motioned toward the chair Mr. Healy had vacated. Tillie took it while Amelia sat opposite her.

"He was very charming as always, very warm and friendly, but this time he asked so many questions."

"What kinds of questions?"

Her frown deepened. "About the boardinghouse, who I have staying here and the like, but then . . ."

"Aye?"

Amelia lifted troubled eyes to Tillie. "He asked about Cara and Rourke—if I had seen them and whether they corresponded with you."

"With me?" Tillie pressed her hand to her throat.

"Yes. I thought that was odd, but then Douglas has always tried to look out for me. . . ." She trailed off, her thoughts apparently shifting to some faraway time.

Tillie leaned forward to clasp her hand. "Amelia, how long have you known Mr. Healy?"

Slowly her eyes came back into focus. "Thirty-five years or more. Ever since I was a young woman."

"And how did the two of you meet?"

As though driven by a stiff wind, a shudder closed over Amelia's expression. She averted her eyes and clasped her hands in her lap, but even so, Tillie read tension in the white skin stretched across her knuckles.

"Amelia?" she prodded. "Is something wrong?"

When Amelia finally looked at her again, tears glistened in her eyes. "I've been lying to you, Tillie. Douglas Healy is more than just an old friend."

Tillie's throat tightened, yet somehow she managed to push the words past her stiff lips. "What do you mean, you've been lying? If he's not a friend, what is he?"

Her hand limp, Amelia gestured around the room. "This . . . the boardinghouse. I suppose you could say he's a benefactor."

"What do you mean, Amelia? What did Mr. Healy do?"

For several long seconds, she merely stared. When she did speak, the words were almost impossible for Tillie to comprehend.

"Douglas Healy brought me here, to America. Tillie, he paid for this boardinghouse."

32

"The Celt. Bligh said the ring belonged to The Celt?" Rourke paced the length of the library and wound up back at the fireplace, where Morgan sat with two of his kinsmen. The older one, a crusty old soldier named Malcolm, held up a gnarled hand.

"Hold on, lad. We still dinna know what any of that means to us, if anything."

"He's right," a younger version of Malcolm added. "Given Braedon McKillop's connection to the Fenians, it does seem likely, but we've come too far to act rashly now."

"But if they were involved, Clive . . ." Rourke dragged his hand through his hair, then lifted his head to stare at his uncle. "If the Fenians killed Da . . ."

Malcolm rose, unfolding his length like a wave that grew and built until it crashed upon the shore. Morgan watched him warily. Rourke's admiration for the man was obvious. He suspected it was his counsel that would determine Rourke's course of action.

"Dinna forget, we accused someone wrongly of that same crime once before. What would that bonnie wife of yours say if she were here listening to us now?"

A heavy sigh ripped from Rourke's throat. Morgan's gaze

bounced among the three men. Finally he stood and crossed to Rourke.

"Do you think your uncle and your cousin can help me keep an eye on the boardinghouse?"

Rourke glanced at his uncle, who nodded.

"Aye, we can see to that." Malcolm motioned to Clive. "Round up a few of the lads; have them take turns staking out the place. Tell them to report back to us if they see anything suspicious, and be careful, son."

There was no hesitation in his step as Clive moved to clasp his father's shoulder and then slipped out to do his bidding. Watching them, Morgan felt the smallest flicker of regret fan to life. He missed his own da, missed that they'd never had the opportunity to work side by side as men.

He shook the notion aside and focused his attention on Rourke. "What about your wife's brother?"

"Eoghan is on his way," he said. "I expect him tomorrow or the day after."

"Good. And Kilarny? Any word?"

The two men shook their heads.

"No one's seen him since he spoke with Tillie," Rourke said.

Malcolm gave a low growl. "Kinna be good. We may need to scour the morgues."

"I'll see to it." Rourke scribbled something across a sheet of paper, folded it in half, and stepped into the hall and handed it to his butler. With a few whispered words, the man was off.

When he returned, Morgan shoved his hands into his pockets. "Well? What now?"

Rourke and Malcolm exchanged a glance that sparked a troubled ember in the pit of Morgan's belly.

"Now," Rourke began, "we talk about how we're going to uncover who this Celt is and what ties he has to Father."

"I thought you said you and your uncles have been trying

to figure that out for a while. What makes you think it'll be any different now?"

Again, a shared glance. Morgan set his jaw. "What?"

"She could be the key," Malcolm said, his voice low.

Rourke's head bowed. "I know."

"Know what?" Morgan removed his hands from his pockets and crossed his arms. Shooting a sharp glare at Rourke, he said, "What is he talking about?"

Worry clouded Rourke's countenance. "Morgan, I think . . . we need to talk to Tillie."

The muscles in Morgan's gut clenched. "Why?"

"We have an idea, but it may require her help."

"What kind of help?"

"She may be the only one who can reason with Kilarny. He trusts her or he never would have sent her to Bligh."

"So?"

"So, if we can find him, get him to talk to her, he may be able to point us to The Celt."

A bit of the tension eased from Morgan's body. "And that's all you need from her?"

"For now," Malcolm interjected with a shrug. "Later, who knows? We'll have to see where this lead takes us."

Morgan turned on his heel and paced the room. He didn't like using Tillie even if it was only to glean information, but at least he could appreciate the man's honesty.

"She has as much cause as either of us to want these questions answered, lad," Malcolm continued. "Perhaps you should leave the depth of her involvement up to her."

The words bit like iron into Morgan's flesh. Gritting his teeth, he turned to glare at the two Turner men. "I'll not allow you to use her as a pawn. If I think she's in any danger—"

"Neither of us would risk her life unnecessarily," Rourke cut in. "You can count on that."

Morgan frowned. While he didn't know Malcolm, what he'd come to learn about Rourke was that the man could be trusted. He relented with a nod. "Fine. We'll talk to Tillie, see what she can find out."

A look of understanding passed between him and Rourke. Morgan moved toward the window, hiding his face before either of the Turners wrested any more secrets. For now, all they knew was that it was important to him that they keep Tillie safe. That's all they would know, so long as he kept his blasted emotions under control. It was all anyone would know. Except for him. He could no longer lie to himself.

He loved Tillie. More than he'd ever loved anyone. More than he'd loved Moira.

His back to Rourke and his uncle, Morgan's hands closed into fists.

Well he understood the Turners' loss, even felt a twinge of kinship in that both he and Rourke had lost their fathers. But if protecting Tillie meant shielding her from the Turners, that was exactly what he'd do.

Smoothing the concern from his features, he turned to face Rourke. "Now that we're done with your questions, I have one of me own."

Rourke nodded and motioned for him to continue.

Morgan drew a breath. "You've quite a collection of books."

Rourke followed his gaze to the rows of shelves and back. "Aye?"

"Inside them, have you ever found any mention of the phrase 'memento mori'?"

— ※ ※ ※ —

Tillie rocked back on her heels as the meaning of Amelia's words penetrated the fog clouding her brain. Pacing did nothing to dispel the confusion her confession had caused, and yet it was all Tillie could do.

"It was many years ago," Amelia continued, holding out her hand and inviting Tillie to sit. "Please, dear, allow me to explain."

Dragging her heavy feet across the floral rug, Tillie sank back into the chair she'd vacated. "Why have you said nothing about this? Even last summer, after we found out who Deidre was, how she and Mr. Healy were connected, you said nothing."

Sorrow lined Amelia's face. "Douglas asked me not to, but even if he hadn't, I owed it to him to protect him."

"Owed it to him?" Tillie widened her eyes. "Why?"

Amelia sighed. "I will tell you," she said, her chin quivering, "but first I must know about the danger to you, Tillie. Who is trying to hurt you?"

Tillie hesitated a moment before revealing everything she and Morgan knew—from her final conversation with Braedon to Doc's recent death.

"The poor boy," Amelia said, shaking her head when Tillie explained the details of his murder.

"Braedon was a Fenian," Tillie finished. "Morgan thinks all of this may somehow be tied to them."

"A Fenian!" Amelia's mouth fell open. "I thought . . . I knew your parents did not approve, but I never thought . . ." She trailed into silence and covered her face with one hand. "It seems we have more in common than I knew."

Tillie drew back, confused. "I dinna understand."

When she pulled her hand away, Amelia's face was pale. "My husband was a Fenian—that is, he supported their cause."

"But your husband was British."

Amelia nodded. "It all started when Henry was a boy. I don't know all the details, just that they met the day Douglas saved Henry from drowning. The Mathesons were so grateful to him for saving their son, they took him in as one of their own. The two became great friends after that, hardly left each other's side, despite their differences. When the potato famine struck, so many died of starvation during those terrible years, but the Mathesons never forgot what Douglas did. They saw to it that he and his family survived. It was shortly after that Henry and I were wed."

She blinked as if struck by an onslaught of painful memories. "I always knew there was more to their relationship than Henry was telling."

"What do you mean, Amelia? What didn't he t-tell you?" A quaver she could not control shook Tillie's voice.

Amelia drew a sharp breath. Despite the trembling of her chin, her expression remained steady. "Henry became a spy for the Fenians. He frequented various London circles and reported what he learned back to Douglas. It was during one of the Irish uprisings that Henry was killed and I finally learned the truth about his activities."

"From Douglas."

"Yes."

The tension in Tillie's chest made breathing difficult. She tugged at the buttons of her high-necked collar. "And the boardinghouse?"

"Douglas knew when the authorities found out about Henry's involvement, suspicion would be cast upon me. He was determined to help, said he owed it to Henry to protect his widow."

"So he brought you to America."

"It was the only way to keep me from facing an inquisition, one we both knew I would not survive, at least not socially. No one would believe I had no knowledge of my husband's actions. I would have been viewed as a traitor to England, just as he was. At least here"—she encompassed the room with a wave of her hand—"I could live peaceably, even earn a living for myself and Laverne."

"Laverne came with you from England?"

"She refused to leave me, even after she learned the truth about Henry."

For several seconds, Tillie said nothing as she struggled to absorb all that Amelia had said. Finally she lifted her head. "Today . . . Mr. Healy . . ."

Amelia refused to meet Tillie's gaze. "He checks on me from time to time—when he can, when he's in America." Pulling a lace handkerchief from the sleeve of her blouse, Amelia proceeded to wring it between her shaking fingers. "I was surprised to see him this time. I thought . . . I simply thought that somehow he had heard and . . . come to help."

"Heard what?"

"Why, that—"

Amelia broke off. Deep furrows slashed across her brow, and a troubled frown tugged at her lips. At last her shoulders sagged, and she gave a weary wave of the handkerchief. "The financial situation here at the boardinghouse is far worse than I've let on, I'm afraid. Laverne is the only one who knows. I didn't want to worry you or the others."

"Amelia, what are you saying? How bad is it?"

Fear, deep and agonizing, brimmed in Amelia's eyes.

"Oh, Amelia." Leaning forward, Tillie pulled her into a hug. "You should have said something."

A tremor shook Amelia's frame. "I wanted to, even started to once or twice, but you and Meg were working so hard. And then I heard about your plans from Sister Agnes."

The orphanage.

Tillie swallowed back a lump in her throat. She'd planned and scrimped and saved for so long. The idea of surrendering her dream stabbed like a physical pain. Clenching her teeth, she gave herself a shake and lifted her chin. "None of that matters now. What matters is helping you—"

Amelia shook her head before she could finish.

"Now, Amelia, surely you dinna think I could let—"

Amelia rose from her seat and, taking both of Tillie's hands, pulled her up. "Absolutely not, my dear. I simply refuse to accept your money, not when you have such worthy plans for it. Besides, Douglas's coming could not have been more timely. Surely his visit was provision from the Lord." She sniffed and drew a few deep breaths, calming herself. "Douglas has offered to help before when business was slow. I know I can count on him now."

But did she want him to? Unease crept up through Tillie's midsection. "Amelia, a man like Douglas Healy . . ."

"Yes?"

Tillie ran her tongue over her dry lips. "The two of you share a past, this much I understand, but what do you know of Douglas Healy now? Who he is and the kind of business he runs, I mean? Are you sure you can still trust him?"

Amelia crossed to the window and stood looking out.

Watching her, Tillie said, "You *are* worried, aren't you?"

Amelia turned from the window, her features strained. "Deep down, Douglas is a good man, I'm sure of it. He never would have helped me after Henry's death otherwise."

"That was many years ago. People change." She sucked in a breath, gathering courage. "Do you know if he's still involved with the Fenians?"

She shook her head. "I've never asked him about his dealings, business or otherwise. Just like Henry. I suppose I didn't want to know."

She looked so fragile outlined in the glow of the afternoon sun streaming from the window. Tillie went to her and pulled her into a hug. "Amelia, promise me you'll wait to speak to Mr. Healy. Let me talk to Rourke first, see if there's anything he can do to help. Maybe he can suggest another way to help you raise the money you need to keep the boardinghouse running."

Uncertainty bunched the skin around Amelia's eyes. "I don't know . . ."

"I'll speak to him this afternoon," Tillie said, lifting her chin. "In fact, I'll have Cass drive me over in the wagon right now. What do you say? Will you wait?"

Though she still appeared doubtful, Amelia nodded her agreement.

"Good." Tillie pasted a cheerful smile to her lips. "You'll see. We'll get this sorted out soon enough, and then things will be back to normal around here."

She gave Amelia one last squeeze before hurrying out into the hall after her shawl.

She would talk to Rourke about Amelia's dilemma, but first she needed to find Morgan so she could fill him in on everything she'd learned about Douglas Healy. Deep down, she had a sneaking suspicion that his visit today had not been by accident, or that his involvement with the Fenians didn't have something to do with his sudden interest in her.

Shawl in hand, she scurried out of the kitchen toward the barn, where Cass was still working. She found him with currycomb in hand, brushing down Amelia's mare.

"Put the brush away, Cass." She strode toward the tack room where the mare's bridle was kept. Looping the reins over her wrist, she turned and lifted them up before his widened eyes.

Cass held up his hand. "Hold on there. Morgan told us to wait here, remember?"

"Never mind what Morgan said. We've got an errand to run."

33

Morgan lengthened his stride as he swung onto Ashberry Street. Ahead lay the welcoming façade of the boardinghouse. At least the walk had afforded him ample time to ponder what he would say to Tillie and how he would say it.

We need you to speak to Jacob Kilarny again—that is, if he's not already dead.

Even in his head, the words sounded harsh.

"Fie." Morgan slapped his cap against his thigh. "Better if we could just leave Tillie out of it." And hadn't he said the same thing in Rourke's house? And hadn't they determined there was no way around it?

A shadow separated from the trees, and Morgan reached for his dagger. Realizing the shadow was the kinsman Rourke had ordered to watch the boardinghouse, Morgan nodded to him and mounted the steps.

Morgan knocked, waited, then reached for the knob. The door swung open with just one twist. Poking his head inside, he called, "Cass?"

No answer. He frowned. Hadn't he been explicit in his instructions about leaving the front door locked and guarded? He dropped his coat and cap on the hall tree and rounded the corner toward the parlor.

"Mrs. Matheson?"

She met him in the hall, her apron in hand. "Captain Morgan, you're back. Are Tillie and Cass with you?"

"With me? I told them to wait for me here."

"Yes, but then Tillie said she needed to speak to Rourke. I assumed they would have ridden back with you."

Morgan cast a quick look about the empty boardinghouse. "So, you're saying they aren't here?"

"Why no." She lowered the apron, deep lines of worry marring her forehead. "They left some time ago, headed to Rourke's house. Didn't you see them?"

Foreboding rooted in Morgan's gut. "No, I didn't." He glanced toward the kitchen, where Laverne was noisily preparing supper. "I'd best go out looking for them. Will you let Laverne know?"

"Of course, if you don't think you'll be back in time?"

Morgan shook his head, already reaching for his coat and cap. "I doubt it."

Like a small bird, she flitted toward the kitchen and then skittered back, her hand nervously twisting the hem of her apron. "Perhaps you should give them a few minutes. It may be that they're already headed home."

Morgan slid his arms into the sleeves of his coat. "I've got an unpleasant feeling about this. I think it's best if I went out looking."

"Captain, wait."

He paused mid-turn and looked at her over his shoulder. She peered at him, her eyes rounded saucers in her small face. She clutched both hands beneath her chin, the ruined apron twined between her pallid fingers.

Lowering her hands, she took a tottering step toward him. Instinctively, Morgan reached out to steady her.

"Before you go," she said, clasping his arm, "there is something I must tell you."

— ※ ※ ※ —

"There is something I must tell you." Cass glanced sidelong at Tillie. "Before we talk to Rourke, I mean."

Tillie twisted on the wagon seat to study his profile. They hadn't gone far, only a half mile or so, and Rourke and Cara's home still lay another fifteen minutes ahead. Still, she couldn't help but be curious at his tone. He was seldom so serious.

"All right. What is it, Cass?"

Rather than look at her, he hunched his shoulders and gathered the reins in close. "I'm worried about you, Tillie. We haven't known each other long"—he glanced at her, then away—"still, it seems like a part of me has known you forever."

She smiled, a bit of the worry she'd felt upon spying his concerned frown melting away. "I agree. You are a dear friend, and grateful I am to have you."

A muscle ticked along Cass's jaw as he hunched lower in the seat. "'Tis more than that. You've come to mean a great deal to me, Tillie. There, I've said it." Straightening, he gave the reins a tap, and the wagon lurched forward.

Feeling befuddled, she looked forward at the oncoming carriages. "Well . . . I . . . you've come to mean a great deal to me too, Cass."

"You don't have to say it," he said. "I'm fairly certain I know in which direction your affections lie. I just had to get it off my chest is all."

Somewhere along the path from the boardinghouse to Rourke's, things had gotten severely skewed. Tillie laid her hand over Cass's arm. "Get what off your chest? I dinna understand what you're trying to say."

He scowled, transforming himself into an exact replica of

240

his brother. Despite his obvious consternation, she couldn't help but giggle.

One eyebrow rose. "What?"

"Nothing," she said, lifting her fingers to cover her mouth.

"You find my confession amusing?"

Convicted by the look of hurt that flashed across his handsome features, Tillie sobered and gave his arm a pat. "Not at all, my dear lad."

"What then?"

Leaning toward him, she bumped her shoulder against his. "Well, with that menacing scowl on your face, you looked just like Morgan."

Instead of erasing the frown from his face, Cass appeared even more glum. Drawing back on the reins, he pulled the wagon off the street and stopped. "My brother again. Ach, I suppose I should have known."

She pursed her lips in feigned irritation. "Whatever are you talking about, Cass Morgan? I declare, sometimes you be almost as perplexing as—"

He raised his palm. "Dinna say it."

Something in his demeanor awakened Tillie to the fact that despite his jovial manner, he was deeply troubled. Her smile fading, she reached out again, but this time when she laid her hand upon his arm, he covered it with his own.

She then became acutely aware of their proximity on the seat. With Cass turned toward her, and she toward him, his face was only inches away.

Mindful of the pain she read in his eyes, her breath caught. "Cass . . ."

"I love you, Tillie."

He whispered the words, so low that for a moment she doubted she'd heard him correctly.

"What?"

His Adam's apple bobbed as his throat worked to swallow. "I've known it for a while now, only I couldn't bring myself to tell you, not with your feelings for Morgan so obvious. Only now . . ." He grimaced. "Forgive me, Tillie. I had to say it, if only for my own sanity—so I could live knowing I'd told you the truth even if you didn't choose me."

She felt herself blanch, felt her fingertips grow cold. "What are you talking about?"

His face became like stone. "You and Morgan. He loves you too, even if he won't let his guard down long enough to admit it."

For a split second she thrilled at his words. And then her guilt and fear returned and drove away her momentary flash of happiness. "Oh, Cass."

She fell silent as his grip on her fingers tightened.

"Promise me one thing, Tillie."

Unable to speak, she simply nodded.

"If things dinna work out between you and Morgan, or if you change your mind, or . . ."

Hot tears gathered behind her eyes. She blinked them back and nodded. "Aye, Cass. I understand. Please, dinna say more."

Though she knew her words hurt him, neither could she bear to hear him pour out his heart. Twisting her hand so that it lay palm up, she gave his fingers a squeeze, then pulled away and turned her face toward the street.

Beside her, Cass gave a chirp and the wagon jolted into motion again. Tillie gripped the side, glad to be moving, to be leaving the uncomfortable conversation behind. Still, the drive to Rourke and Cara's house had never stretched so long. She fidgeted on the seat, wishing she could somehow ease the pain that rolled silently off her companion.

She sneaked a sidelong glance. Cass rode with his eyes

focused straight ahead, his jaw firm and unyielding, his grip tight on the reins.

Confusion tangled her thinking. How had this happened? How had they moved from being friends to tense, uncomfortable strangers?

"Cass?" she pleaded.

He stared ahead as though he had not heard.

"I'm sorry. I didn't mean—"

Cass's chin jerked up. Following the direction of his gaze, Tillie tensed as a horse approached, the rider bent low over the saddle. He made a beeline toward them, weaving in and out of carriages at a pace that made her heartbeat quicken.

"Who is that?"

"I dinna know."

Pulling back on the reins, Cass slowed the wagon and turned off the main thoroughfare onto a less busy street.

Behind them, the clopping of hooves echoed against the sides of the brick buildings. Tillie craned her neck to see. It was the same horse and rider.

"Cass?"

"I see him." He cut Tillie a glance. "Hold on."

Giving a sharp whistle, he urged the mare into a gallop, which propelled the wagon bumping and heaving over the cobbled street. Twice, Tillie almost lost her balance. Only Cass's grip on her elbow kept her on the seat. Once again he veered around a corner, slowing only slightly. Buildings and tenements flew past in a blur. Wind whipped tears into Tillie's eyes, but too frightened to let go of the seat, she let them roll down her cheeks unchecked.

Ahead, wagons and carriages clogged the crowded street.

"Cass!"

Tension stretched the skin across his face as he jammed both feet against the bottom of the wagon and stood against the reins. It rocked to a shuddering halt, narrowly missing a carriage whose driver scowled at them from beneath a wide-brimmed hat.

"C'mon," Cass said, dragging her out of the wagon with him and into a darkened alley.

"Where are we going?" Tillie huffed, hitching her skirts with her free hand and struggling to keep up with his rapid pace.

"Somewhere we can hide."

Her heart already in her throat, panic somehow managed to turn her limbs numb.

Shooting her a glance over his shoulder, Cass tugged on her hand. "This way."

He rattled the knob of the first door they came to. "Locked." He jabbed his thumb across the alley toward another door. "Let's try that one."

Though her feet felt weighted with lead, she scurried to obey. "It's locked."

"Keep trying!"

They rushed down the alley, trying doors. At the last one, Cass pounded with his fist. "Anybody there? Hello!"

A shadow darkened the entrance to the alley. Tillie froze, her eyes wide and fixed on the menacing figure.

"Cass," she whispered.

He rattled the knob and pounded again. "Hello in there. We need help."

"Cass."

Lifting his head, he turned in the direction of her stare.

The rider had spotted them. He slowed his mount with one hand, the other hidden by the flap of his coat.

Determination hardened Cass's features. "Get behind me, Tillie."

Her knees shook. "What?"

"Do it. Now."

Surprisingly, her feet obeyed. "Maybe if we call for help . . ."

"Too much noise on the street. No one would hear." His breathing heavy, Cass squared his shoulders and lifted his chin. "Who are you?"

The man laughed, the sound rasping like razors over Tillie's skin. She felt Cass tense as he stretched out his hand to push her back.

"What do you want?" Cass asked the man.

"You're in possession of a small trinket. A ring. Give it to me."

"What ring? What in blazes are you talking about? I'll ask again, who are you?"

Her fingers tightened on Cass's elbow. His other hand grappled for something at his back. She looked down and saw a knife blade flash in the sunlight streaming between the rooftops.

"I said, what do you want?" Cass demanded a second time. "You—"

He got no further. In an instant, the rider's hand slid from his coat. Almost as though time slowed, he aimed a pistol at Tillie's head.

She staggered back. "Cass!"

He spun and threw his arms around her like a shield. An explosion ripped through the alley. A second later, Cass slammed against her and knocked them both to the ground.

Shock registered on Cass's face, and something else—pain. Blood trickled from his mouth.

The rider's arm lifted again.

Tillie's heart thrashed inside her chest. He'd shot Cass. He intended to shoot her. He was going to kill them both. She threw her arms over Cass's head, protecting him as he had protected her.

And it was then that she screamed.

34

A commotion stirred in the crowd ahead of Morgan.

"Someone's been shot!"

He slowed his steps at the excited cry. Such crimes were not unusual in the city, which was one of the reasons he preferred life at sea. Still, hearing the panicked voices sent sweat rolling down his neck into his collar.

The brick buildings and stone streets trapped the August heat, radiating it onto the swollen crowd. Combined with his brisk pace . . .

He scowled. He wasn't far from Rourke's house. Perhaps he could cut across another street and avoid the mob gathered on the corner.

An older gentleman with a pipe protruding from a corner of his mouth questioned the crowd, "Who is it? Anyone know?"

"A man," another answered. "Heard someone say the woman with him wasn't injured."

Dread came to life inside his chest as Morgan crept closer.

A woman, her flowered bonnet quivering, craned her neck to see over the taller men in front of her. "Was it a robbery?"

"Can't say," the man with the pipe said. He removed it and used it to point down a side street. "Is that their wagon?"

"I think so. I saw them barreling past me. Looked as though the devil himself was on their heels."

"Has anyone called the police?"

"What about a doctor?"

"Heard it was too late for him. Better fetch someone from the morgue."

The chatter continued to roll through the crowd, melding into a steady, quiet drone. A shiver traveled Morgan's flesh. He needed a glimpse of that wagon.

Pushing through the crowd, he emerged on the other side of the street and stopped dead. Amelia's mare stood quivering, her head and back covered in froth and her sides heaving.

His stomach roiling, Morgan grabbed the arm of the man closest to him. "Where are they? The man who was shot and the woman with him . . . where are they?"

The man pointed to a spot where the crowd was thinner. "Down there. In the alley."

Morgan broke into a trot, then a full run. "Cass? Tillie!"

At the mouth of the alley he skittered to a stop. The crowd split before him, like a wave parting around a stone. At the center of it were Cass and Tillie.

For one full, heavy second, he couldn't move, couldn't breathe. Tillie was kneeling next to his brother, her dress soaked in blood.

He staggered forward. She lifted her head, tears soaking her eyes, her cheeks.

"Morgan."

"Cass . . . ?"

"He's been shot. We need a doctor."

Behind her, a figure separated from the crowd. Kilarny.

"Already sent for one." Kilarny motioned toward Cass's prone body. "He's lost a lot of blood. If that doc doesn't get here soon—"

Lunging forward, Morgan dropped to his knees next to his brother, the cobbles cutting into his flesh. "Where was he shot?"

"His back," Tillie said through white lips. "Someone followed us, chased us here."

"Get him up," Morgan barked, jerking off his coat. He glared at Kilarny. "Help me."

Together, they managed to lift Cass's shoulders off the dirty street. Morgan shoved his coat into Tillie's shaking fingers. "Hold that. When we get him to the wagon, use it to slow down the bleeding."

She nodded.

Morgan motioned toward Kilarny. "Grab his feet."

Bracing himself, Morgan carefully lifted Cass's torso. Kilarny gestured toward the crowd. Instantly several more hands came alongside to steady his back and shoulders.

"Out of the way!" someone yelled. "Clear the way!"

In minutes they'd reached the wagon and laid Cass inside. Tillie hunched beside him, Morgan's coat pressed to the wound. Around her, Kilarny's men hovered—a sturdy, rough-looking lot with pistols in their hands and their eyes alert.

Morgan climbed into the driver's seat while Kilarny handed him the reins.

"Where you taking him?"

"Rourke Turner lives nearby. Do you know it?"

"Aye, I know the place." He stepped back from the wagon. "I'll wait here—tell the doctor where you've gone." He got the attention of one of the men in the wagon. "Stay with 'em."

The man gave a curt nod. Who he was, or who any of the men in the back of the wagon were, was of no concern to Morgan. Right now, he was grateful for their help.

Morgan sucked in a breath and gave the reins a snap. Urgency roared through his veins as he screamed for pedestrians and vehicles to get out of his way. Twice, he glanced over his shoulder at Cass's still body, then returned his focus forward and urged the mare faster.

Finally they thundered to a halt at the gate. Morgan vaulted from the seat, his throat and chest aching. "How is he?"

Tillie stared up at him, strain twisting her features. "We need to get him inside."

The front door opened, and Rourke stepped outside. "Tillie?"

"We need your help!"

He ran down the steps. Peering over the side of the wagon, his lips thinned. "What happened?"

"He's been shot," Morgan said.

Rourke waved toward the men. "Quick, get him inside. Follow me."

He led the way through the house, up the stairs, and into a lavish bedroom. Several servants clustered close—a maid, the housekeeper, the butler. Morgan vaguely heard as Rourke barked orders for clean towels, hot water, food for Kilarny's men.

He stared down at his brother's ashen face. "Cass? Can you hear me?"

The maid who'd taken Tillie's place discarded a blood-soaked towel in a bowl on the nightstand, then pressed a clean cloth to Cass's shoulder.

A shudder rumbled through him. So many red towels. So much blood.

The next half hour passed in a blur. The doctor's arrival. The ping of a lead bullet as it dropped into a glass bowl. Cass's groan of pain.

Morgan squeezed his eyes shut at the last. At least his brother was still alive. And Tillie?

His eyes flew open. Rourke was there, and the doctor, but she was nowhere to be found. Rourke crossed to him.

"You all right?"

"Have you seen Tillie?"

He nodded. "She's downstairs with the others." He hitched a shoulder toward the door. "Go check on her. The doctor's almost finished here. I'll send for you when it's over."

At his hesitation, Rourke clapped his hand on his back. "Tillie needs you too, Morgan. Go. I'll stay with Cass."

Leave his brother? Not hardly. He opened his mouth to argue, then snapped it shut just as quickly. Tillie was probably a mess of ragged tears and frayed nerves, wondering if Cass was alive or dead. Added to the attempt on her own life—third attempt, he corrected with a grimace. Puffing out a sigh, he turned for the door.

Downstairs, a quiet stirring and the subdued murmur of voices drifted from the hall. Among them he thought he heard Tillie's delicate tones. He took a moment to steady himself at the rail before descending the stairs, then followed the hum to an expansive library.

All heads lifted at his arrival, Tillie's included. She hovered near the hearth, Jacob Kilarny at her side.

Her eyes widened as she tore herself away. "Is he . . . ?"

Her mouth worked, but no more words came out. The sight of her face filling him with fresh courage, Morgan strode to her and pulled her into a hug. She resisted at first, her back rigid and tense.

"Morgan, is Cass—?"

"He's alive," Morgan whispered against her hair. "He made it through the surgery. The doctor is stitching him up now."

As though a cork had been pulled, all resistance drained from Tillie's body and she sagged against him.

"Thank God. Oh, thank you, Lord."

Morgan's hold tightened as the dam burst and her tears began to fall in earnest. "Shh," he crooned, but she only cried harder.

"Morgan, I'm so sorry. He was protecting me. The man

followed us . . . and then we tried to get away . . . but the road was blocked . . ."

Dropping her head against his chest, she gave in to a fresh round of gut-wrenching sobs.

The sound birthed a new ache in Morgan's heart. Tillie's depth of feeling for Cass was far greater than he'd imagined, for only the thought of losing someone dear could have rendered a person so distraught.

Steeling himself, he reached into his pocket, fished out a handkerchief, and pressed it to her cheek. Her own fingers trembled as she took it from him, then lifted watery eyes.

"I'm sorry, Morgan."

"It wasn't your fault, Tillie. You and I both know that."

"But—"

"Come. I have a few questions I'd like to ask your friend." He claimed both of her hands and led her back to the hearth, where Kilarny waited.

"How fares your brother?" Kilarny asked.

"He's alive, so far." He gave Tillie's hand a squeeze, his eyes on Kilarny. "You discovered them?"

"He saved us," Tillie interrupted, reaching for Kilarny's hand. "We'd both be dead if it weren't for Jacob and his men." She managed a wavering smile of gratitude.

Morgan moved a half step closer to Kilarny. "How did you know where she was?"

His grizzled chin lifted. "We've been keeping an eye on her for several days now. Following her about, making sure she came to no harm."

Morgan motioned toward the fading bruise over his eye. "Is that how you came by that bruise there?"

Kilarny's lips parted in a wry smile. "This here bruise is what made me think I'd better keep me sights on her, no disrespect to you or your men."

Whatever had led the man to be present when Cass and Tillie were attacked, Morgan had no cause to be anything but grateful. He extended his hand, albeit grudgingly. "Thank you."

Kilarny accepted the handshake, then shot a wink at Tillie. "See? I told ya he wouldn't be pleased."

Morgan scowled and stuffed his hands into his pockets. "Is that so? And what else have the two of you been discussing?"

The two exchanged a glance, one that fanned the unease roiling inside Morgan.

"Well?" he said, crossing one arm over the other.

Kilarny ducked his head and motioned to his men. "Think I'd best leave the explanations between the two of you." He paused at the door to look at Tillie, one eyebrow lifted questioningly. "You know how to reach me?"

Morgan watched in fascination as she nodded. "You do?"

"I do now."

Giving one last nod, Kilarny slipped out, his men close on his heels. The front door closed with a click, and then the butler's heavy tread faded down the hall.

With the house restored to quiet, Morgan found himself at a restless standstill.

Fool, he chided himself. So much to say and yet he wasn't sure he could trust himself to speak—not with his emotions running so rampant, and Tillie's tears still damp upon her lashes.

He strode to the window where she stood looking out at the lawn, now washed in moonlight. How could he hope to control what he said to Tillie when he could hardly control his own thoughts? She did not deserve to be burdened with the futile pining of a decrepit old sailor. Just today, hadn't he proved himself as unworthy as he feared? Who had stepped into the path of a bullet for her, had laid down his life in order to protect her? Not him. Cass. His brother, who at that very moment lay upstairs, battling for his life while he struggled just to string together a handful of words.

In the end, it was she who broke the silence.

"I'm glad Cass is all right."

He let go a long breath, the air from his lungs fogging the windowpane for a second before dissipating. "As am I."

He turned. Tillie stood facing him, her small fists clenched at her sides.

"I have to do something, Morgan."

He offered a sad smile. Hadn't he felt the same way? "There's nothing you can do. Nothing either of us can except wait for word."

"No. I mean about . . ." Her lips trembled. She lifted her hand and let it fall. "Morgan."

Hearing the plaintive note in her voice struck him to the core. In spite of his misgivings, he crossed to her. He'd barely reached her before she finished closing the gap. His breath caught as she ran to him and then pressed herself against him, her slender arms like silken bands around his waist.

Reason. If he were to have any chance at keeping his wits, he'd have to seek reason.

She tensed in his arms, tipping her head back to look up at him, exposing the sweet, pale line of her neck and cheek.

Blast. This was hardly better.

The haze cleared from her expression, and fervor claimed her dark brown eyes. She slid her hands up to grip his biceps. "Today, at the boardinghouse, I nearly forgot with everything that's happened."

Like a rusted hinge, his mind slowly began working. "The boardinghouse?"

"Douglas Healy was there, when Cass and I got back from dropping you at Rourke's house. He was talking with Amelia."

Morgan shook his head. "Slow down, Tillie. Who is Douglas Healy?"

He led her to a rust-colored settee and sat listening while she peeled away the layers leading up to her conversation with Amelia earlier that afternoon.

"Douglas Healy was a Fenian, Morgan," she finished, an excited flush blooming on her cheeks. "He had to have known my Braedon was, too."

"Aye, that would seem likely," Morgan agreed. "But what does any of that have to do with what happened to you and Cass today?"

She stiffened at this and drew her shoulders back. Sensing he wouldn't like what she was about to say, Morgan too braced against the settee's plump cushions.

"I think we should try and infiltrate the Fenians, figure out how deep Mr. Healy's ties go."

"Infiltrate! Tillie, do you have any idea . . . Have you considered how dangerous . . ." Morgan sputtered to a stop.

She put up her hand. "Wait. Just listen. Jacob and I were talking earlier and—"

Morgan narrowed his eyes. "So this was his idea?"

"Not just his. Jacob and I both feel Mr. Healy's involvement warrants investigating."

His ire rising, Morgan jumped to his feet. "Dinna be ridiculous. Do you realize what would happen if the Fenians mistook you for a spy?"

"Of course I do." She stood too, and stared at him belligerently, her fists planted on her hips.

"Well then?"

"Do you have a better idea?" she demanded.

"Anything would be better than this."

"Fine." Her fingers drummed against the fabric of her skirt. "Come up with something."

"I will." He crossed his arms smugly.

Silence, broken only by the ticking of the mantel clock, stretched for several seconds.

Tillie lifted an eyebrow. "Well?"

Heat flared on Morgan's face. "Well what?"

"Have you thought of something?"

"I will."

"I'm sure." Grasping her skirts, she spun and made for the door.

"Bah! Arguing with you is like fighting with the wide ocean," he called after her retreating back, though she gave no indication she'd heard him.

Women!

If he'd learned anything from Moira, it was that there was no understanding them. Or reasoning with them, for that matter. Hadn't Tillie just proven as much? Ach, indeed she had, and far better than Moira could have, for though she had been persistent in her own right, she'd never shown an inkling of the stubbornness he'd witnessed in Tillie.

He snorted. And to think he'd fancied himself in love with her—with any woman after that first time. Striding to the stairs, he craned his neck and peered upward just in time to catch a glimpse of Tillie's hem as she disappeared into Cass's room.

Well, he'd not be making that mistake again. Falling in love was out of the question, especially with someone as bullheaded and willful as Tillie McGrath.

— ※ ※ ※ —

Men!

Arrogant and overbearing, every one of them. Well . . . one of them.

Tillie snapped the door closed behind her. It was just like

Keondric Morgan to think he could order her about like one of his crew. And to think she'd fancied herself in love with him.

Both Rourke and the doctor looked up at her entrance. Seeing the concern on their faces, every ounce of irritation left her in an instant. She took a hesitant step forward. "How is he?"

At the doctor's nod, Rourke left the bed and crossed the room to grasp Tillie's hand. "I wilna lie, his situation is dire. He'll need watching, and plenty of rest. Is Morgan downstairs?"

Tillie managed a nod.

"All right, I'll find him. Will you sit with Cass?"

"Of course," she whispered, her eyes settling on Cass's waxen face.

Behind her, the door closed and Rourke's tread faded. Remorse settled over her like a cloud. How could she have thought of anything but Cass right now, especially after what he'd done to save her life? Of course Morgan would be resistant to her idea. Hadn't he just suffered through almost losing his brother? And to lay more concern on his shoulders . . .

She felt selfish and spoiled.

Her cheeks burning, she eased to the doctor's side. "Is there anything I can do?"

"There will be soon enough," he said, pushing a lock of peppered hair from his wrinkled forehead. "That wound will need to be kept clean and fresh bandages applied regularly."

She nodded.

"Also, it will be crucial that someone sit with him for the next few hours, just to make sure no fever sets in. If it does, send someone after me right away." He motioned to several small vials on the nightstand next to the bed. "I've left something there for the pain. The larger bottle is to help ward off infection. Mr. Turner knows the dosages."

"Thank you, Doctor."

Dismissing her thanks with a wave, he bent to retrieve a black leather bag from the floor next to his feet. "Don't thank me. He's a lucky man. If that bullet had struck any lower, he might have lost a lung."

Perhaps not luck, but grace. Tillie bowed her head and breathed a silent prayer of thanksgiving.

The doctor glanced around the bedchamber. Spotting his coat thrown over a chair near the window, Tillie fetched it for him and held it aloft.

"Is this what you be searching for?"

"Just so. Thank you, my dear."

As she helped him into it, she asked, "Will you be coming back soon?"

The doctor patted his pockets, then peered at Cass over his spectacles. "Indeed, I will. I'll check on him first thing in the morning. The medicine I gave him should help him rest comfortably till then." He gave his pockets one last pat before turning for the door. "Don't forget to send for me if his condition worsens."

After assuring him that she'd keep a watchful eye, Tillie thanked him again and saw him to the door.

Moments after he'd gone, a low moan sounded from the bed. Tillie hurried over in time to see Cass's eyelids flutter open. Though overly bright and slightly confused, 'twas a relief to witness the brilliant blue of his eyes. She released a sigh and sank onto a crushed velvet chair that someone had pulled near the bed. "You're awake."

"Tillie?"

"Aye, lad, 'tis me."

He ran his tongue over his lips. "Where are we?"

"Rourke Turner's house."

"Why? What happened?"

She reached for his hand, sorrow gripping her. "Do you not remember anything?"

He started to shake his head, and then his features went even more ashen. "Someone attacked us."

"Aye, that's right." She squeezed his fingers. "You were shot trying to protect me."

His eyes drifted wearily shut. "How . . . ?"

"Jacob Kilarny. He and his men showed up in the alley. One of them fired off a couple of shots, but the rider escaped."

Seeing his throat work, Tillie retrieved a pitcher from the nightstand and poured him a cup of water. "Easy now," she said, holding it to his lips. "Just a sip or two."

He managed to lift his head, but after a moment fell back against the pillows with a groan. She waited while he gathered his strength, then dipped the end of a washcloth into the glass and used it to wipe the sweat from his brow.

"I'm so verra sorry, Cass. Would that it had been me who was hurt instead of you."

At this, his eyes locked on hers, vivid and piercing. "I would do anything for you, Tillie. Surely you know that."

Her heart constricted inside her chest. Laying aside the cloth, she caught his hand and pressed his fingers to her lips. "Aye, my dear, brave lad. I know you would. I only wish I were more worthy of your defense."

Once again he struggled to lift his head from the pillows. "You are worthy, Tillie. One day you'll realize that. Until then, I vow to do everything in my power to keep you safe."

"All right now, lie back down," she urged, pushing gently against his shoulders. "The doctor said you are to rest."

"I mean it, Tillie. I was serious when I said I loved you." He clasped her hand, surprising her with the strength of his grip. "And I would do anything to keep you from harm."

For several nerve-rattling seconds she could do nothing

but sit, transfixed by the pleading in his eyes. Then concern washed over her, and she laid her palm against his forehead.

"Tell me there's a chance, Tillie. Tell me that one day . . . maybe . . . you could love me, too."

The whispered plea was so soft and low, she doubted she would have even heard it had she not been so close. Consumed by pity and feeling more than a wee bit beholden to him, she let her hand fall from his brow to cup his cheek.

"Cass . . ."

"We're already closer than most friends, aye? Would it be such a stretch to imagine yourself feeling something more?"

"More than what I would feel for a beloved brother?" she asked gently. "For that is how I see you, Cass—how I'll always see you. Tell me I've not misled you into thinking it was anything more."

"A brother." He grunted and dropped onto his pillow. After a moment, his face brightened. "So you agree, we are more than friends. That must mean you feel something, ain't so?"

She laughed. "Aye, lad, I suppose." Sobering, she cupped her hand to his cheek. "I do love you, Cass. I'll never forget what you did for me today."

"Ach, well, I suppose that will have to be enough. For now."

Bending low, she pressed a kiss to his forehead, relieved to feel the coolness of his skin against her lips. No fever. Perhaps now he'd be able to rest.

Indeed, his lashes fluttered down to cover his eyes as she straightened. Behind her, a rustling sounded from the door. She turned her head, but not in time to see who stood there. All she caught was the briefest glimpse of someone's hand before the person whirled and pulled the door shut.

35

Dawn's dazzling rays tugged at Morgan's eyelids, luring him from a fitful sleep—and fitful it had been, his dreams plagued with worry for Cass and longing for Tillie. Grimacing, he rubbed a crick from his neck. Perhaps he should have accepted Rourke's invitation and made use of one of the guest chambers upstairs instead of acting as sentry while he waited for Tillie to emerge from Cass's room.

Rising from a stuffed leather chair, he exited the parlor into a wide hall. Sounds of stirring emerged from the kitchen as members of the household staff began preparations for breakfast. Already the yeasty aroma of baking bread tweaked his nose. 'Twas not a fragrance he was accustomed to savoring at sea. This was a fragrance enjoyed by those on land, like Rourke. And Cass.

He glanced up the stairs. Cass was in love with Tillie. Not only had his actions proven that out, he'd voiced it last night. And while she did not now currently return his affections, it wouldn't be long before his charm won her over. That had always been the way of things back in Ireland. A wink of those blue eyes, the disarming smile . . . Tillie was as good as his.

Morgan grunted and turned to pace the hall. Aye, and

wasn't that best for them all? The sea was no fit place for a woman. He had no hope of winning her for himself, not that he'd even try. It wouldn't be fair to her. But Cass . . . Cass was free to do as he pleased. Likely Morgan would be leaving New York one deckhand short.

"Two short," he said, his thoughts flashing to Donal. Three, if he counted Doc.

"Excuse me?"

He wrenched his head up. Tillie slipped out of Cass's room and eased the door closed behind her and then glided down the stairs.

Morgan shrugged. "Nothing. Just talking to myself." He gave an upward tilt of his chin. "So? How be the patient?"

She rubbed her back wearily. "Resting. Finally. I promised him I'd stay until he fell asleep, but that turned out to be well after midnight."

"You could have fetched me. I would have sat with him."

A slow grin melted over her lips. "I dinna mind."

He looked away. Her smile, her eyes, even the way her tousled curls made her look, all sleepy and childlike, were not his pleasures to enjoy. Those belonged to his brother, or soon would, whether he relished the idea or not.

Ducking his head, he veered toward the stairs. "Think I'll sit with him a bit, just in case he wakes before the doctor arrives."

She nodded, her dress rustling as she moved toward the kitchen. "I'll have the staff bring you a pitcher of fresh water so you can wash up."

Shooting her a wry grin, he rubbed the scruff on his cheek with the back of his fingers. "Do you happen to be implying something?"

"Not at all, Captain." She laughed and lifted her hand to smooth her unruly curls. "You've no more need for the basin than I do myself."

She turned then, her skirt swishing saucily as she walked down the hall. In spite of himself, he watched until she rounded the corner and disappeared from sight. His hand clutching the banister, he dragged himself up the stairs. So that would be the way of it then—he always pining for something he would never have and she being happily oblivious to it.

Ach, and was it any different than before, when he'd given up his dream of owning a farm and working the land to produce something good?

Aye, he thought, scowling as he stormed up the stairs. He wrenched the knob and entered Cass's room. It was different. Now it was Tillie he'd be giving up.

A moan came from the bed and all of Morgan's anger fled. Dark curls clung to Cass's temples, and a flush colored his skin. Were it not for the stubble on his cheeks and chin, he could have passed for a young lad.

"Dinna be deceived. You're not giving her up," he whispered quietly to himself. "You kinna surrender something that was never yours."

Cass roused, his dark lashes fluttering. "Morgan?"

He sucked in a breath. "Aye, lad, I'm here."

Cass inhaled and moved as if to stretch, grimaced, and then lay still again.

Morgan smiled and pulled up a chair. "How's the shoulder?"

"Painful."

"You were lucky. The doctor said had the bullet entered any lower, you might not be lying here at all."

"Aye, well, thanks for that."

"You're welcome."

Cass cracked open an eyelid, then two. "Do I look as bad as you do?"

"Worse."

"Doubtful, Cap."

Morgan narrowed his eyes. "Careful. I'm not above slugging a wounded man."

Cass laughed, moaned, then laughed softer. "All right, all right. Mercy."

Oh, but his brother's laugh was a good sound. He shuddered to think of how easily it might have been snuffed out. Settling against the back of the chair, he laced his fingers across his stomach.

"What?" Cass asked, peering at him through slitted lids.

Morgan shrugged.

"I know that look, big brother. What's going on inside that thick skull of yours?"

For several seconds, Morgan said nothing. He didn't regret helping Tillie. It wasn't brave or noble, just right. But Cass . . .

"I was wrong to involve you in any of this. 'Tis my fault you were hurt."

Cass struggled to rise. "Are you daft? How is any of this your fault?"

"I could have left things as they were. Maybe if I hadn't told Tillie the truth, she wouldn't be in this danger. And you . . . you wouldn't be lying there with a hole in your back."

"Right," Cass said. "You honestly believe whoever is after Tillie would have left her alone once they found out about the ring?"

Morgan raised his chin obstinately. "Maybe."

"Bah." Cass snorted. "Even if that were true, I know you. You could never have hidden the truth from Tillie. It isn't like you to lie."

Both heads turned as Tillie entered the room carrying a tray laden with a pitcher and clean towels. She set the tray down on a little table in the corner and then straightened to glower at them both.

"I would appreciate it if the two of you would stop debating about what is best for me and allow me to figure that out for myself."

"Couldn't hurt, I suppose," Morgan said, "considering that everything *we've* tried has been a miserable failure."

Cass smiled weakly and nodded.

"Well, what do you have in mind?" Morgan asked her.

Tillie pointed at the pitcher. "Wash up. When you've finished, I'll come back and help Cass."

"I can see to him," Morgan said. After all, his brother was his responsibility, even if he hadn't done a very good job of looking after him thus far.

Tillie sized him up, then gave a determined nod. "Fine. I'll fetch Rourke. We'll talk up here, if Cass thinks he be up to it."

Shifting in the bed, Cass pushed upright. "I'm up to it. Takes more than a stray bullet to stop me."

Despite his bravado, his lips were white-rimmed, and beads of sweat dotted his brow.

Once Tillie had gone, Morgan stood and rested his hand on Cass's shoulder. "Easy there, brother. No sense killing yourself trying to impress Tillie. She's impressed enough, trust me."

Cass's mouth twisted in a crooked grin, but he sank against the pillows and didn't argue when Morgan pulled the covers up over his chest. Soon enough, he was dozing and hardly stirred when the doctor returned to check his wound.

"Looks good," the doctor declared. He rubbed his spectacles against his shirt as he straightened. "He'll need a day or two more of bed rest, then maybe a week of light activity before he fully heals." He motioned to the bottles on the nightstand. "See to it that he continues with the prescription for infection, however. It's not unusual for a fever to flare up in patients who aren't properly attended."

Morgan had no intention of allowing that to happen. He

gave a little bob of his head and then showed the doctor out. A short time later, one of the maids appeared bearing a bowl of broth and toast for Cass, and a platter of thick-sliced bread and eggs for Morgan. He saw to Cass before devouring his own breakfast and had just laid aside his napkin when the door opened and Tillie and Rourke entered.

By their faces, Morgan knew the discussion had begun without him. He tensed and motioned for the hall. "Perhaps we should talk outside."

Cass wrestled to sit up. "No. I'm fine, Morgan. I'm part of this. I want to hear."

Aye, he was part of this, a fact for which Morgan still berated himself. Grudgingly he motioned the two closer but cast a warning glance at his brother. "You start to feel tired, or if I catch even a hint of you running a fever, I'm tossing everyone out, whether you agree with me or not. Understood?"

"Aye, Morgan. Understood," Cass grumbled, shooting a wink at Tillie.

Morgan's scowl deepened. "I saw that."

Turning his attention to Rourke and Tillie, he waved them toward a carved wooden bench situated beneath the window. It had a high back and arms, and on the sides a gleaming oak crucifix had been scrolled. Most likely the bench was a castoff of some church. He found it fitting that Rourke Turner should own it. The man looked quite at ease seated on the end nearest the bed. Tillie, however, chose to pace the length of the room.

Her fingers worked her bottom lip as she walked. "Rourke and I have been discussing my conversation with Jacob. We've decided we can no longer sit idly by hoping for clues to turn up. It's far too dangerous, especially after last night."

"I agree," Morgan said warily.

"Good." She glanced at Rourke, who encouraged her to

continue with a nod. Crossing to stand next to him, she clasped both hands at her waist and drew in a deep breath. "We've come up with a plan, an idea for figuring out who has been behind the attacks on Cass, me, even Jacob."

Morgan looked from Tillie to Rourke and back again. Her fingers twisted restlessly, and twice her tongue ran over her dry lips. Even Rourke refused to meet his eyes. But it was something else that warned him he wouldn't like what he was about to hear.

Tillie stepped toward him, her stiff posture challenging him to disagree. "Rourke and I believe there is only one way to ferret out the information we need—to find out who among the Fenians is behind everything that's happened."

He almost didn't want to ask, didn't want to know what addlepated scheme Tillie and Rourke had concocted in the wee hours of the morning, and yet he had to know. The words left his lips before he could even think of drawing them back.

"So, what is the 'one way' you came up with to get the information?"

"We need to send in a spy, someone with ties to the Fenians so as not to raise suspicion. Jacob has agreed to help so long as the person is someone he too feels he can trust."

"And that person is . . . ?" Morgan pressed.

Tillie lifted her chin and stared at him eye to eye. "That person is *me*."

36

For several heart-pounding seconds, Morgan said nothing, his face an angry mask of torment and disbelief. When he did speak it was one word only, but uttered with such force that Tillie's knees quaked.

"No."

Rourke half rose from the bench. "Morgan—"

He whirled to him. "How could you even think of putting her in such danger?"

Rourke spread his hands, palms up. "It wasn't my choice to make. She dinna ask my permission, Morgan, and I dinna think she's asking yours."

She steeled herself as his attention swung back to her, a look of disbelief in his eyes. Slowly, she began ticking off the evidence that had led to her conclusion. "We have to identify who The Celt is, Morgan. If indeed the ring belongs to him, we have to know why Braedon had it, and why he was so determined to give it to me."

Though he still glowered, and the unsavory expression on his face had not changed, he said nothing. She forged on.

"I dinna deceive myself. I know asking questions about

the leader of the Fenians is risky. I am sure to run into more than a few who will count my probing a threat."

Seeing Morgan's mouth twitch, she pressed on before he could interrupt. "That's why I had to enlist Jacob's help."

She strode across the room to peer up at Morgan, earnestly pleading for his support, though deep down her decision had already been made. She owed it to Braedon to discover why he'd died. And if this was the only way . . .

"To be sure, Jacob has his faults," she whispered. "But even I know how much he loves his country, how m-much he desires for Ireland to be free."

"And?" Morgan growled. "What has that to do with you . . . or Braedon?"

"Jacob is suspicious of The Celt's involvement with Daniel Turner's death."

Morgan turned to Rourke. "Your father?"

He nodded.

"But Jacob kinna ask questions," Tillie continued. "He's too deep in the organization. Every move he makes is watched. The most he can do is help me to be accepted, smooth any suspicions, and perhaps see to it that I'm included in the meetings."

At this, Morgan recoiled.

"'Tis the only way," Tillie insisted. "You must know we tried to find another, but—"

He cut her off with an upraised palm. "Fine. I'm going with you."

Tillie had already begun to shake her head when Rourke said, "That wilna work, Morgan. The whole point is to insert someone the Fenians already trust. She wilna be able to get close enough to The Celt to do any good otherwise. If we try to bring you in—"

"It's too dangerous to let her try this alone." Morgan

looked at Cass, who lay motionless and silent on the bed. "Well? Do you agree?"

A troubled frown etched lines around Cass's mouth and on his forehead. "If she doesn't do this, if we dinna allow her to take the chance . . . she dies. Probably we all do. Ain't so?"

Tillie looked at Morgan. He'd gone as lifeless as a statue, his face hard and frozen.

Cass panted as he pushed up in the bed. "You said it yourself, Morgan. I'm lucky to be here. I for one . . . am sick of being on the defensive . . . not when we still aren't any closer to knowing who the enemy is."

Drops of sweat rolled down the sides of his face. Tillie hurried to the basin and retrieved a towel, wringing it in the bowl before positioning it on his brow.

"Maybe you should lie down," she urged softly.

Cass glanced up at her. "If we're wrong—" he swallowed, his Adam's apple bobbing—"I'd never forgive myself if you were to come to harm."

She feigned a smile. "You can hardly blame yourself for something that wasn't your decision. Besides, I'll be perfectly fine."

"You dinna know that," Morgan said flatly.

Tillie half turned and frowned at him. "Neither do you know that I'd be any safer sitting in this house. I kinna hide forever. Better I take matters into me own hands and leave me fate to God."

Though she made the claim with more courage than she actually felt, Tillie sensed a glimmer of truth to the words. Perhaps it *was* time she put her life squarely into God's hands. After all, it wasn't like she'd done a fine job of it on her own. At least then she'd be able to rest, knowing she'd accomplished the one thing she never thought to do again—achieve peace with her Maker.

Bending low, Tillie pressed a kiss to Cass's forehead. She then straightened and faced Rourke and Morgan.

"I suggest we proceed downstairs. We can grind out the details of this scheme without Cass. I think it best we let him rest a while now. Agreed?"

She looked to Rourke first, who gave a nod and shifted toward the door. Morgan, however, stood with his hands jammed into his pockets, refusing to meet her gaze. She walked to him and laid her hand on his arm.

"Morgan . . ." She took a deep breath and plunged ahead. "Keondric, please."

More words piled upon themselves inside her head, but with fear clogging her throat, the simple plea was all she could manage. She waited, her heart beating like a surge of tumultuous waves inside her chest.

Finally he looked up, and in that brief glance she thought she read anguish, mingled perhaps with grim determination.

Without another word, he spun and strode for the door.

37

The pub that had been assigned as the meeting place was dark and crowded, even though it was well past the supper hour. Smoke as thick as fog choked Tillie when she stepped inside and stung her eyes as she squinted for a glimpse of Jacob. Several faces turned toward her when she entered, but none were the one she searched for. Nervously she wound her way inside and selected a table near a tall multi-paned window.

"Not there," a deep voice growled.

Startled, Tillie cast about for the owner and spied a gnarled old man with graying beard and a ragged cap tugged low over his ears.

Pulling a pipe from between his lips, he gestured toward a table near the back. "Over there. Someone'll join ya soon enough."

"Thank you," she said. She bumped several tables on her way to the one the man indicated and received several scathing stares in return. Finally she pulled out a chair and slumped into it to wait.

A short while later, a waitress appeared and plunked down a mug. "You'll draw too much attention sitting there without something to drink," she hissed before slipping away.

"Thank . . ." Tillie began, but the woman was gone as though she'd never spoken.

She curled her fingers around the mug. What was in it, she didn't know and didn't care to find out, since she'd never manage to slide anything past the fist-sized lump in her throat. Spying a clock in a dimly lit corner, she checked the time.

Jacob had said he would meet her at exactly eight thirty. He was five minutes late. Worry shook her at the possibility that he'd been detained, or worse.

"C'mon."

The urgent whisper caught her completely by surprise. Liquid from the mug sloshed onto her dress as she was jerked from the table and half led, half dragged out of the pub.

"Jacob—"

"Quiet!" he ordered, glaring at her over his shoulder.

With a heavy wool coat and dark cap on his head, plus a scraggly beard covering half of his face, she barely recognized him. They wound down the street, making several turns through a series of dark alleys until Tillie's head spun. How Jacob was able to keep his bearings, she could only guess, for her sight wasn't nearly keen enough to penetrate the gloom. Finally they emerged onto a less crowded street. Gas lamps cast flickering shadows on the walk, but even that feeble light was better than the stench and murkiness they left behind.

Tillie gulped as she struggled to regain her breath. "Where are we?"

"Better you dinna know." His eyes gleamed in the half-light. "Certain you still want to do this, lass? 'Tis not too late to back out. I wilna be able to promise the same later."

She scanned the brick walls on both sides of the street, the buildings packed so tightly together there was no telling where one began and the other ended. Above, dark windows stared down at her like blank, gaping eye sockets. That's how she would live her life if she turned back now, always feeling like someone was watching but never knowing who lingered in the shadows.

She thought of Braedon, of the orphanage and all the children she hoped to help. She squared her shoulders. "I'm sure."

He grinned. "Good girl," he said, then thrust his chin up the street toward a wooden door, its paint peeling off in strips and littering the threshold. "In there. I'll go first. You come in close behind. Let me do the talking. I'll introduce you about, let the lads know who you are and where your interests lie. If you see something that spooks ya, give me a nod. I'll try and get ya out."

He was turning to go when Tillie grasped his hand. "Jacob?"

"Aye?"

"Why are you doing this? 'Tis not just to help me."

He sobered and drew back his head. "No. It's not just to help you, Matilda. I wish I could say it were."

"Why then?"

He paused, peered up and down the street. Finally his eyes settled back on her. "You know why I came here—to America? It was to carry on the struggle. To find a way, any way, to keep as many men alive as I could, but still fight for Ireland's freedom. But then . . . well, things got all twisted. Motives became clouded, and I was no longer certain who I could trust."

She tried to pull her hand away, but he crushed her fingers until she almost winced.

"I am many things, Tillie McGrath, some not so noble as I'd like." His chin lifted. "But I am not without honor. I love my country and I'd do anything to protect her, even if it's from some of her own."

Her eyes widened. "What do you mean?"

His jaw worked, but he said nothing. Somewhere, a horse

273

neighed. Jacob flinched at the sound. "We should get moving. 'Tisn't wise to linger too long." He moved closer to the wooden door. "You ready?"

Swallowing hard, Tillie nodded.

"Remember what I said. And try to stay close."

Inside, the glow of a half-dozen oil lamps lit the dingy room. What chairs she saw were already filled. Where there was space, crates had been upended and stacked on their sides to serve as seating. Several pairs of eyes looked up at their coming—some questioning, a few most definitely hostile.

One ape of a man, with bulging biceps and eyes that protruded from his skull, stepped forward. "Hold up, Kil. What be the meaning of this?" He jerked a beefy thumb in Tillie's direction.

At his words, an uneasy hush descended over the room. Never had Tillie wanted more to flee. She even doubted her knees would hold her, except that Jacob shot her a reassuring wink before motioning to the men and handful of women that packed the place.

"You all remember Braedon McKillop?" A couple of uneasy nods trickled about the group. "Well, this here be his woman, Matilda McGrath. They were to be wed before Braedon died, God rest 'im."

Hands lifted here and there in the sign of the cross. Tillie's breathing deepened.

"So she's Braedon's girl," the ape man said. "What's she doing here?"

"Braedon and I believed in the same things," Tillie blurted. "I want to help."

Silence filled the room.

"Help with what, dearie?" the ape man asked, his eyes narrowing to slits.

For a moment, only Jacob's glare kept her frozen in place.

Having forgotten his warning, she wanted to bite off her tongue. Instead she pleaded with her eyes for him to continue.

"All right, Seamus," Jacob said, directing his attention to the ape man. "That's enough. I told ya, she and Braedon were betrothed. That in itself is endorsement enough for me."

"Well, it ain't just up to you, is it?"

"What are ya saying?"

"We kinna have people coming in here all willy-nilly. You're the one who's always spouting off about being careful. 'Tell our plans to no one,' that's what you're always saying. And now look at ya, dragging in this here girl without a word to anyone."

Like Tillie, heads rotated back and forth between the two men. By the charged atmosphere in the room, it was obvious that disagreements between him and Jacob were not all that uncommon. Tillie's hand inched toward the waistline of her skirt and the short dagger that Morgan had insisted she carry there.

Jacob drew himself up straight, his clenched jaw and bunched fists a warning to everyone that his mood for trifling conversation was long past. "She's not just any girl, Seamus. Her man was a friend of mine. We fought alongside one another in more places than I can count—more than you've seen in your lifetime. Now, I say she's all right, and if you"—he glanced around the room—"if any of you have a problem with that, speak up. I'll be happy to take this argument outside." He waited a moment, his chin thrust out. When no one answered, he gave a nod. "Good, then I say we get started. That all right with you, Seamus?"

With a bob of the man's bushy head, Tillie's lungs resumed working. Jacob moved to the front of the room while she eased off to the side, into the shadows yet near enough to Jacob to feel relatively safe.

Perhaps Morgan had been right all along. Perhaps she hadn't really taken into consideration the danger she'd be facing, even with Jacob's support and Braedon's reputation as protection. Sinking onto a rickety crate, she pressed her hands against her midsection and willed the trembling in her limbs to cease.

She'd ask no questions tonight, make no move that might cause the people gathered around to take notice. Tonight, she'd simply be thankful that she was alive and count the minutes until she could make her escape.

— ❋ ❋ ❋ —

Morgan eased from the cobblestone street into a dark alley. Kilarny had led Tillie this way, of that much he was certain, but after that? He eyed the row of doors lining the narrow passage. Above his head, shuttered windows with iron balconies stretched three stories. Tillie could be in any one of those rooms.

Casting one last glance at the street, he turned and delved deeper into the shadows. It was a dank place where he ventured, the stench almost unbearable. He could only imagine what the place was like in the heat of the day, when the sun streaming down between the clustered buildings baked the odor into the cobbles.

He took another step, squinting in a futile attempt to penetrate the gloom. Thrusting out his hand, he felt for the wall, found it, and eased his way up the alley. On his left, two doorways gaped black and empty with rusted hinges hanging haphazardly from their jambs. Ahead, the glow of a streetlamp cast a flickering semicircle on the mouth of the alley.

Could they have traveled that far? Indeed, Jacob had the advantage of knowing where he was going, but the fact that he'd managed to lead Tillie so far ahead was astonishing.

Eager to leave the alley behind, he quickened his steps. He was just shy of halfway to the street when he heard the subtle scrape of leather against the cobbles.

Morgan stiffened. The walls of the alley amplified every sound. He had no way of knowing for certain from which direction the sound came. He darted sideways, using the brick wall of the building to his left to protect his flank, then remained motionless, waiting.

Nothing.

He searched the shadows in both directions.

Still nothing.

Separating from the wall, he pressed toward the mouth of the alley. A few feet from it, intuition prickled the skin on his neck and forearms. He was being watched.

No, *hunted* was a better term, for no voice called out in greeting, and no figure hailed him from the darkness. Reaching for his waistband, he pulled out a slim dagger. He carried a pistol as well, but given the confines of the alley and the deep, almost impenetrable gloom that shrouded it, he doubted the weapon would be of much use.

He forged ahead another step and waited. Another three steps and he'd be on the street, yet something warned him that even there, the danger might not be past.

His back flattened against the wall, Morgan covered the last few steps and was just about to cross onto the street when a wooden club came crashing down on his forearm. The dagger clattered from his limp fingers.

The attack had come from the street. Morgan crouched low, but before he could spring, scuffling sounded behind him. He jerked his head that way in time to see a heavyset man barreling toward him.

Neither assailant made a sound as they knocked Morgan to the ground. Rolling into a crouch, he managed to avoid a booted foot, then whirled to grab the man's leg, and with one savage yank dropped him to the street.

He had no time to press his advantage, however. The second man flung himself on Morgan's back. A blade glinted in the pale light. Morgan threw up his arm, felt the bite of steel against his flesh. He twisted. With one hand he grabbed the man's arm. Hunching low, he drove his shoulder into the man's stomach. His legs pumping, he knocked the man against the wall, heard an "oomph" as the air was driven from his lungs.

A fist like a hammer struck Morgan's side just above the kidney. Stars exploded in his vision. He sucked in a breath. Another blow. He felt his knees weaken. If he didn't defend himself, he'd pass out.

He spun, his own back pressed to the wall. Willing his vision to clear, he spotted a familiar glint atop the cobbles.

His knife.

He sensed, rather than saw, when the next blow came. This time it was aimed at his head. He plunged sideways, heard the unmistakable crack of bone against brick.

A howl of pain.

Morgan dropped to his knees and rolled.

A muttered curse.

He groped for his knife and found it.

A shadow loomed.

Raising the knife, he plunged it into the man's thigh. Jerked it back. The man screamed and dropped to his knees.

Morgan struggled to his feet. Wielding the knife, he faced his attackers. The streetlamp cast just enough light for him to make out the jagged scar that marred the first man from his brow to his cheek. Glaring at Morgan, he cradled his shattered fist against his chest. The other man pulled a handkerchief from around his neck and knotted it around his thigh.

"Who are you?" Morgan snarled. "Who sent you?"

Neither man responded.

He stepped closer, the end of his dagger thrust toward them. "I said, who—?"

A thud above his right ear. Pain. Excruciating.

Then the man with the broken hand flashed him a smirk. Morgan sank to his knees. Shoving from the wall, the man bent over Morgan as he slid to his side on the cold, hard street.

The man drew back his foot. Morgan tensed, prepared himself for the next blow.

"Name's Hennessy. Pleased to make your acquaintance."

38

Conversation swirled around her. Tillie did her best to remain hidden in the room's murky corner. Feeling curious eyes upon her, she lifted her head and found a youngish lass, probably around Meg's age, peering at her.

But despite Tillie's attempts to remain unobserved, the girl sidled closer.

"My name's Mary McCloud."

"Tillie," she said, then realized that everyone in the room knew who she was. "Matilda," she corrected hoarsely. "Mc-Grath."

The girl gave a shy bob of her head and motioned toward the crate. Tillie slid over, though in reality she questioned whether it would hold them both.

"I knew Braedon," Mary said.

Shocked, Tillie stared at her, eyes rounded. "You did?"

"I met him back in Ireland; we grew up in the same village. My da used to buy wood from his family. He always seemed like a kind lad. I liked him."

"Aye, that he was."

Mary shifted on the crate to face her. "Do ya mind if I ask how the two of you met?"

Indecision tore at Tillie. She'd come intending to ask questions. She hadn't figured on having to answer any. "He . . ."

She hesitated and looked to Jacob for help, but another argument had broken out between him and Seamus. Neither man even spared a glance in her direction.

She breathed deep. "He was at the market selling wood with his family, and I was there selling eggs. I got knocked down by a stray dog. Braedon saw and came over to help."

She quieted as the memory washed back over her: Braedon's tender chuckle drowning out the mocking laughter of the other village boys; his strong hands gently lifting her and wiping the embarrassed tears from her cheeks.

"I'm dreadful sorry you lost 'im."

Startled to find that Mary still watched her, Tillie clasped her hands and shrugged. "It wasn't long and we were together. Braedon loved me enough for a lifetime."

Warmth flooded her heart as, perhaps for the first time, she realized how deeply she meant the words. Always before, when she agonized over losing Braedon, she'd felt anger toward God for taking him so young. Tonight, she felt only gratitude for having loved him at all.

She smiled at Mary. "Thank you for telling me that you knew Braedon. Glad I am to know he hasn't been forgotten."

Mary returned her smile. "He would be proud of you, I think, for continuing the fight for Irish independence. If I can help, you need only ask."

Discomfited by the turn in the conversation, Tillie managed a self-conscious nod of agreement.

Across the way, the opening of the door let in a draft that set the room's candles to flickering. Tillie intended only a glance, for others had come and gone in the hour or so since she and Jacob had arrived. This time, though, she stared transfixed as a man wearing a gray flatcap wound his way through the throng of people gathered there until he reached a spot near the front.

"Tillie?" Mary leaned over to touch her forearm. "What is it?"

"I . . ." Tillie licked her lips and slid cautiously to her feet. "I need to get a little closer. Will you come with me?"

A bit of the puzzlement cleared from Mary's face. "Of course." She held out her hand. "Come. I'll get you round the other side quick enough. We can see better there. Not as many people standing."

Tillie accepted Mary's hand, and together they inched through the raucous group until they reached the other side. Indeed, she had a better vantage of not only Jacob but of the latecomer staring so earnestly into his face.

He was a broad-set man with a barrel for a chest. Of his face she could see but a little, hidden as it was by the cap, but even that bit set her heart to racing.

The rider who'd attacked them and nearly killed Cass, the same man whose devilish intent had been burned into her memory, now sat just feet away.

"Say, you feeling all right?" Mary prompted. "You've gone all white."

Feigning illness would be no difficult task considering the butterflies in her stomach and the trembling of her limbs. Tillie hunched her shoulders and slunk as far back into the shadows as the walls would allow.

"I . . . I am finding the room a bit stifling. Perhaps if we got some air?" she whispered.

Mary nodded. "Aye, then. C'mon."

Tillie kept her eyes focused in the direction of the latecomer as they eased through the crowded room. For seconds at a time he'd be blocked from view by someone's head or another's shoulders, but then he'd reappear, his profile as forbidding and stoic as ever. Each time she breathed a sigh of relief as she moved one step farther away.

And then a portly Irishman with graying muttonchops lumbered to his feet, drawing them to a halt and blocking Tillie's view while he shouted a call to action, followed by several blustering attempts to incite those around him to even greater ire.

"Are we going to sit by forever while the English ignore our right to be free?" he began, his face reddening. "Or are we going to do something? No more sitting on our haunches waiting for the right moment. Now is the time to strike! Not a year from now, not even a month—"

"Ach, be quiet!" another man yelled. "Sit down and hear what the lad has to say before you go spilling your blarney all over it."

Waving his hand in disgust, the portly man shoved out of the way, his muttering drowned out by the blistering glare that struck Tillie head-on in his wake. She froze, pinned for one horrifying moment by a pair of black eyes.

Like a nightmare unfolding, the latecomer left his chair and raised his hand, his arm hanging in the air like some evil portent as he gestured at her. "Let's go, Mary."

Tugging on her hand, Tillie urged Mary around a table toward the door, but what had seemed easy before was now a path fraught with obstacles. Men, lurching in front and around them, slowed their every step. Chairs, crates, and booted feet formed hurdles for them to cross.

Tillie risked a peek over her shoulder and gasped. How quickly the man in the cap had cut the distance between them! There was no doubting his intention now. He walked pitched forward at the waist, arms flailing and shoulders lowered as he shoved people out of his way.

"This way." Spying a crack in the tightly knit mob, Tillie

hurried toward it, then looked back, confused, when Mary resisted the pull upon her hand.

"What's your rush?" she asked.

Gone was the pleasant smile. Instead, Mary stared up at her from between narrowed eyelids.

Shocked, Tillie dropped her hand. "You . . . ?"

She cast a quick glance around the room. Indeed, the course on which Mary had set them had not been by chance. Neither had it been Tillie's imagination and fear that made it seem as though the route out of the room were much more difficult.

Her gaze fell to Mary, who stood with her hand extended, a grin on her elfish face.

"The ring, Tillie. That's all we want. Give it to me."

"What?"

The man was close enough now for Tillie to sense his menacing scowl.

"I know you have it. Braedon gave it to you, ain't so?" Mary persisted.

Tillie backed away slowly. "I dinna—"

"Give it to me!"

She shook her head. Even if she'd brought the ring, she would not see it placed in this woman's greedy palm. "No."

A growl ripped from Mary's throat. She jerked her head toward the man in the cap and motioned for him.

Tillie spun, pushing through the crowd, away from the door and toward Jacob. If she could just reach him, if she could call out and somehow be heard above all the angry voices . . .

"Jacob! Jacob!"

It was no use. Even to her own ears, her shouting was lost to the masculine voices clamoring for attention. Someone grasped her elbow and she wrenched herself away without looking. If they caught her now, no one would even notice.

She strained against the sea of bodies, begging for passage and receiving only solid backs.

Most of the men had risen to their feet now. She could no longer see around their broad shoulders or raised fists.

Heat fanned her cheeks. Her breath came in rapid, shallow gasps. Inside her chest, her heart pumped a terrified rhythm. She twisted to her left, then her right. Behind her, beside her, more bodies pressing in—men clothed in gray coats buttoned down their chests. White shirts. Brown coats. And somewhere the man in the gray cap. All swirled in a crush that robbed her of air.

"God, please . . ."

Tears blurred the human mass. Then, just as quickly, a path opened.

The door!

Somehow she'd gotten turned around. Lost. She stretched out her hand, reaching for the door, but it swung open before she could get there. Recoiling, she clutched her fingers to her throat and watched, horrified, as two men dragged a third into the room and dropped him with a sickening thud to the floor.

Time ceased. No sound. No raised fists. No press of the crowd. Nothing but the sight in front of her.

The man on the floor was Morgan.

39

"Quiet!" Jacob's roar echoed through the cramped room. From his place high on a table, he craned his neck to see. "Matilda?"

Tillie tore her gaze from Morgan long enough to shoot her hand into the air. "I'm here, Jacob."

He nodded at her, lifted two fingers, and motioned his men in her direction. Almost immediately she was flanked on either side by two dour-faced men, who helped to alleviate the terror she felt.

There was no sign of Mary or the man in the gray cap.

Tillie glanced at Morgan and then back at Jacob. She longed to rush to his side, but having overstepped her bounds once before, she wasn't eager to do it again.

"What in blazes is going on back there?" Jacob demanded, both fists propped on his hips.

He hopped down from the table. The crowd parted, creating a path for him straight to Morgan. He made no sign, no glance or slightest flicker to show that he recognized him. Instead he looked to the two who'd brought him in and frowned. "Where'd you find him?"

"The alley," the larger of the two men replied. "He's been trailing ya since the pub."

Jacob turned to Tillie and looked her squarely in the eyes. "Do you know him, lass?"

"I . . ." she began, her stomach plummeting, her knees turning to water. She read urgency in the lines of strain on Jacob's face. All eyes focused on her, as if she alone had become the object of interest in the room. Despair washed over her. "Jacob, I dinna—"

A groan rose up from the floor. Blood oozed from a gash on the side of Morgan's head and stained the floorboards. Ripping her shawl from her shoulders, Tillie dropped to her knees and pressed it to the wound.

Glancing up at the faces circled around, she said firmly, "He needs a doctor."

Still, no one moved.

Tillie raised her chin, staring at Jacob now. "I know him," she admitted, her voice clear and steady.

For just an instant it seemed relief and an inkling of approval shone from Jacob's eyes. He waved to the same two who'd carried Morgan in. "Get 'im up." To a third man, he said, "Fetch a carriage. Take them anywhere she tells you."

His eyes locked with hers for a brief moment, and then he spun around and returned to the front. Just like that, the shouting, the commotion, everything resumed as it had been before.

Everything, except that Morgan still lay unconscious and bleeding.

A new sort of panic set into Tillie's chest, the likes of which she'd never experienced—not when Cass had been shot, not even when she'd lost Braedon. She grabbed his hand and held on tight while they carried him outside. At the carriage, she scrambled onto the seat and instructed the men to lay Morgan's head in her lap.

"Gently," she cautioned. The moment he was inside, she again pressed the shawl to his head to stanch the flow of blood.

"Ashberry Street," she shouted to the carriage driver. "As quickly as you can."

One of Jacob's men poked his head into the carriage. Holding out the edge of his coat, he revealed the butt of a pistol emerging from the waistband of his trousers. "Just in case there's any trouble," he said. He then climbed aboard and slammed the carriage door shut.

Tillie gripped Morgan's shoulders as the carriage pitched to accommodate the man's weight. He was a large fellow, not the sort she'd normally feel comfortable having accompany her, but at the moment she couldn't have been gladder for another's presence.

The driver gave a whistle, and the carriage jolted into motion. Within minutes they were rumbling at a good clip down the street. The pace was fast enough to leave the fear and danger Tillie had felt at the meeting of the Fenians behind, yet not nearly fast enough to outrun the pain and dread that clogged her chest at the amount of red that stained her shawl.

They passed under a streetlamp. For a precious few seconds, yellow light bathed the inside of the carriage. Just as quickly it faded, and shadows returned once more. Over and over, the scene was repeated. Each time, Tillie used the glow to search Morgan's face, to look for signs of his waking. And each time she was more taken aback as she found evidence of another bruise, another wound she'd not noticed before.

"Oh, Morgan, what were you doing, following us like you did?"

Hot tears burned her eyes, made her throat raw, but at his groan she quickly scrubbed them away.

"Morgan?"

She blew a sigh of relief when his eyes fluttered open, focused a moment, and then snapped to hers.

"Tillie . . ."

He struggled to sit. Still pressing the cloth to his head with one hand, she smoothed his rough cheek with the other.

"Aye, it is me, Tillie. Dinna move—we'll be at the boardinghouse soon."

Confusion and pain clouded his steel-blue eyes. "What happened?"

"You're hurt. What on earth were ya doing, Morgan?"

He grimaced and reached for his head. "Trying to find you."

She gently smacked his fingers away. "Why?"

The carriage bumped and jostled over a rut in the road. Gripping him tightly to her, Tillie waited until the ride smoothed again before peering into his face. "Well?"

Her breath caught as something sweet and glorious flickered in his eyes. Her heart lurched at the sight.

"Your safety is my responsibility. Regardless of what Rourke thinks, or what Kilarny says, I . . . I kinna let you put your life in danger."

His low growl smothered any hope she might have harbored upon seeing the emotion she'd *thought* she read in his countenance. She glanced at the other passenger of the carriage, yet his thoughts were hidden behind an inscrutable mask.

This time when Morgan struggled to sit up, she let him go, then berated herself at the emptiness of her arms without him.

Grimacing, Morgan pulled his hand away from the cut on his head and stared at the stickiness coating his fingers. "What'd he hit me with, a club?"

The man riding with them flexed beefy fingers. "You could say that."

Tillie crossed her arms and said nothing, for she was more

than a little tempted to hit him herself, even if he was still bleeding.

She handed him the ruined shawl. "It could have been worse. You were lucky . . ." She broke off as the vision of the man in the gray cap returned full force.

The shawl held to his head wound, Morgan leaned toward her. "Tillie?"

"I was pretty lucky myself. Your elaborate entrance may have saved my life."

He did not appear amused. "What are you talking about?"

Tillie turned her attention to the other man, her mouth set in a stubborn line. Reading her meaning, he sighed and pounded on the roof of the carriage with his fist. It slowed and then came to a halt.

The man climbed out, turned and faced Tillie. "I suppose you're all right now?"

"Fine," Tillie assured him.

Giving a sharp command to the driver, he stepped back while the carriage resumed its pace.

"Well?" Morgan said once they were moving again. He tried to lower the cloth, but she guided his hand back to the wound. She then told him everything that had happened at the meeting, including her conversation with Mary.

Morgan let out an angry grunt. "I knew it wasn't safe for you there. I never should have agreed to your going."

The carriage swayed, gently tossing Tillie closer to Morgan. "But don't you see? Now we know that the man trying to track me down is tied to the Fenians."

"We thought that before."

"But now we're certain, and we can tell Jacob. The next time I'm at the meeting—"

"There will be no next time, Tillie," Morgan barked, lowering the cloth from his head.

"Morgan—"

"I mean it. It be far too risky and I . . ." He fell silent, his face hard as he stared at her.

"You what?" She held her breath, waiting.

The noise of the wheels over the cobbled street lessened as the carriage slowed. They were approaching Ashberry Street. Soon Meg, Amelia, and the others would be gathered around, and she and Morgan would no longer be alone.

Which was only proper.

Tillie shook her head at her own foolishness for what she'd hoped to hear. Hadn't Morgan proven time and again that his only concern was for her safety, and that out of a sense of obligation?

She eased forward on the seat, ready to disembark the moment the carriage rolled to a stop.

An ache settled in her chest as she lowered her face from view and reached for the door. 'Twas no romantic notion that had sent Morgan out into the street after her tonight, and no amount of wishing on her part would ever make it so.

Though she couldn't admit it to him, the truth was she *did* wish that something deeper had driven him out searching for her, and not anything as trivial as a romantic notion.

She wanted Morgan's love. Nothing less would ever do.

40

Morgan's head felt like a log that had been split in two. Even his hair hurt. And his teeth. He rubbed his bruised jaw. No, his teeth hurt for an entirely different reason.

Pulling the cloth from his head, he grimaced. At least he'd stopped bleeding. Tillie's shawl had served as a bandage, and judging by the amount of blood staining it, she'd never find it useful again. He looked up the walk to the top of the stairs, where she waited. An angel bathed in the glow of the open boardinghouse door.

Ach, but he'd been sorely tempted to admit the truth of his feelings back in the carriage. How easy it would have been to tell of the almost maddening fear that had driven him after her—of the agonizingly sweet relief he'd felt when he'd opened his eyes and seen her face and known she was safe. If it weren't for Cass . . .

He mounted the stairs and paused with his hand on the knob. Immediately she was at his side, her hand a fiery brand upon his arm.

"Are you all right? I can fetch Giles."

"No. I . . ."

Even now, it wasn't too late. The words simmered on his

tongue, longing to be spoken. He turned to her, closing out the memory of the danger that had just passed, the guilt he'd carried over his part in Braedon's murder—everything but the light in her eyes, the tempting silkiness of her hair, even the promise in the curve of her mouth.

"Tillie . . ."

Awareness melted over her face. He saw it in the softening of her lips as she stared up at him.

He stepped closer, letting the shawl slip from his fingers so that he could grip her by the arms. As he pulled her close, she made a sound, so vulnerable and sweet that it sparked an almost primal instinct inside him. How could he have thought for even an instant that he could give her up? Not when being near her made every nerve in his body spring to life.

She tilted her face to his, and her eyes drifted closed. His fingers trailed upward, one hand twining in her hair and the other lingering at her shoulder. For just one instant he wondered what it might be like to put what *he* wanted first, to ignore his duty and think of no one and nothing but himself.

He sucked in a breath. Kissing her now would be selfish, and even were he to forget his brother, he couldn't hurt Tillie. Not ever.

He shuddered and let his hands fall away. "I should check on Cass."

Her eyes shot open, first questioning, and then filled with remorse. "But—"

"I'll let Giles know what happened."

She blinked as if struggling to comprehend, and then her back stiffened and she clenched her jaw. "You should at least let someone tend to the cut on your head." She crossed her arms and glared at him. "Unless you enjoy bleeding all over the carpet."

At least in the face of her irritation, he had room enough to breathe. He managed a grin and followed her inside, where they were greeted by a round of worried exclamations from Amelia, Giles, and Meg.

Amelia rushed to them, an anxious look on her face. "Thank goodness you're safe. Cass is upstairs. He insisted on riding back so he could be here when you arrived." She turned and clutched Tillie's hand, tears welling in her eyes. "He told us about your plan. Oh, Tillie, it was so dangerous."

"How could you have risked it, child?" Giles added with a toss of his gray head. "Don't you know who you're dealing with?"

Tillie shook her head. "We had no choice, Giles. Besides, I'm fine. It was Morgan who was hurt."

Amelia clucked as she examined the bruises on Morgan's face. "Meg, ask Laverne to fetch us some water and then find something to put on these cuts."

"Aye. I'll go straightaway."

Tillie moved to join her. "We'll need bandages, too. I'll get them."

She excused herself while Meg set off in search of the necessary items. Meanwhile, Amelia returned to claim Morgan's hand.

"Come, dear. Sit down and tell us what happened."

Knowing the others would want to hear the story as well, he waited until they'd returned before relaying in detail the events of the evening. While he spoke, Tillie tended to the cleansing of his wounds. Now and then her skirt would brush his thigh or he'd catch the slightest whiff of her perfume. He found it was all he could do to concentrate with her standing so close, her gentle touch sending tremors through every limb.

When he got to the part about the blow to his head, her fingers stilled and he looked up at her.

"That's all I can remember, except for waking up inside the carriage," he finished quietly.

He thought he saw tears gathering in her eyes as she looked at him, but then she blinked and turned her attention to the washbasin.

"I should take care of this," she said.

"I'll see to it, lass." Giles jumped to his feet. "After what we just heard, I dinna think I want you or anyone else outside alone." He shot a meaningful glance at Laverne and Amelia. "That goes for the two of you, as well."

"I agree." Morgan struggled to rise. Surprised at the momentary weakness that wracked him, he steadied himself on the back of a chair. Once it passed, he directed his gaze to Tillie. "I'm going upstairs to check on Cass. After that, I'll ride over to Rourke's place to tell him what we learned. Tillie, you have to promise that you'll stay here with the others until I return. Will you do that?"

Determination shone in the rigid lines of her small frame. "You kinna go alone. You were almost killed tonight."

"Tillie—"

"She's right, lad," Giles said. "Maybe I could go with you?"

"And leave the women to fend for themselves? I dinna think so."

"Cass will be here," Tillie interjected. "Regardless, either Giles rides with you or I do."

She looked as stubborn as a billy goat, staring at him with her fists braced against her sides, with a glower to rival any man's marring her small face. Though he knew it would only make her angrier, he couldn't help but smile.

Raising his hand to ward off another bout of disapproval, he shrugged. "All right, all right. I'll take Giles."

"Good. Then it's all settled," Amelia said, to which Tillie added a muttered, "'Bout time you showed some sense."

His grin widened. At least with her temper he knew a bit of the fire had also returned. The notion also brought with it a renewed sense of dismay, for realizing her mettle only made him love her all the more.

As if that were possible, he mused. Already she occupied most of his thoughts. Even now, he ached at the need to leave her again.

But it wasn't anger he read as their eyes met. In her expression he saw hope, fear, even a bit of pleading. Unable to withstand the draw, he went to her.

"I'll be back as soon as I can."

"Promise?"

The word was like a blow striking at his chest, and though he wanted to close the gap between them, he resisted. "Aye, lass. I promise."

Whirling, he severed the tie that held him bound to her and made for the stairs. Everything would be all right. It would, because regardless of what happened to him, Cass would take care of Tillie and see to it that she came to no harm. As for him . . .

Morgan grimaced and clutched the railing. He would do as he'd always done—what he'd always do.

He would take care of Cass.

— ✳ ✳ ✳ —

Tillie laid her fingers against the door and gave a slight push. Morgan had been at Cass's bedside for some time, and while she felt a bit like an eavesdropper, she couldn't resist checking on them.

Morgan leaned against the window, and Cass watched him from an overstuffed chair near the hearth. A blanket covered him from shoulder to foot, but one corner pooled on the floor as he pitched forward to peer at Morgan.

"You're doing it again. Trying to figure out a way to keep me out of danger while you grab hold of it head-on."

Morgan snorted but did not look at him. "Dinna be ridiculous. You can hardly move. Even if I were worried, which I'm not, I couldn't risk taking you with me."

He moved away from the window then to focus on his brother. "You'd only slow me down, Cass."

He slumped against the chair. "I know."

Morgan pulled a chair over to sit next to Cass. Steepling his fingers, he gave a heavy sigh. "'Tis been good having you on the ship. And here too. I was wrong before, Cass—about the things I said back home in Ireland. You've more than proven it."

"You mean about me being a foolish lad who only cares about himself?"

"Aye, that."

"And about me being green and . . . let's see, how did you put it?" He scratched his head, then held up one finger. "I remember. I believe the words you used were 'dull as ditch-water.'"

"No, I meant that." Morgan ducked as Cass reached back to chuck a pillow at him.

Both men laughed, and then Cass groaned and grabbed for his shoulder, and Morgan his head.

When they quieted, Cass's lips turned in a frown. "We're quite a pair, eh? Tillie probably would have been better off if neither of us had ever showed up on her doorstep."

Morgan hoisted to his feet and clapped his hand to Cass's uninjured shoulder. "Me, maybe. Not so sure about you."

Tillie's breath caught. Did he think . . . ?

"You're wrong about that, Morgan."

Morgan's head lowered, hiding his face from her sight. He shrugged. "Regardless, we have a deal, do we not? I expect you to uphold your part."

Her heart rate quickened. What kind of deal?

"Dinna worry about that, big brother. You just see to it you get the information to Rourke and then head home before anything else happens."

"Right."

Morgan chuckled and started to say more, but Tillie was already padding away from the door, her heart in her throat and her cheeks more than a trifle heated. She lunged into her own room just as he stepped into the hall.

Could it be? Did Morgan keep her at arm's length because he thought she belonged with his brother?

She trembled as she recounted all the reasons why she should not be in love with Morgan, or Cass, or any man. But all of them paled in the hope of one solitary notion: Morgan had feelings for her. He just wouldn't admit it because he cared too much for his brother to risk hurting him.

Joy such as she'd never known lifted her so that she felt her feet barely touched the floor. Morgan knew the truth about her past, and if he could forgive her and love her anyway . . .

She glanced up at the ceiling and smiled. Perhaps God too had already seen fit to forgive her, only she hadn't allowed herself to believe it. Perhaps the only person who had yet to fully forgive Tillie McGrath was . . . *herself.*

41

Giles drove the wagon to the rear of Rourke's home near the carriage house, then set the brake and cast a glance sidelong at Morgan.

"I figure this will be less likely to draw attention than leaving it around the front." He pointed toward Morgan's temple. "How's the head?"

He grimaced in response. The rickety old wagon had been rough enough, but with the hurried pace he felt as if he'd been struck all over again.

Giles chuckled. "That's what I thought. Better let me go in first."

He climbed down and was greeted by a stableboy, who offered to care for the horse. Giles dismissed the lad with a wave. "Best let your master know we're here and let me see to the horse." His brows lowering, he eyed the dark-gray gelding the stableboy had been grooming. "That one new?"

"Belongs to Mr. Hamilton, sir. He arrived earlier today." With that, the boy took off at a jog for the main house.

Morgan hitched a shoulder. "Who?"

"Eoghan Hamilton," Giles said. "Miss Cara's brother. I didn't know he was back."

Guilt rolled over Morgan as the name penetrated his thoughts. "Rourke sent for him. We may not have told you everything that's been going on."

"Ach." Giles clucked his tongue as he ambled for the door. "Dinna worry, lad. I'm not so dense as I make out. I know there's more been going on than what you and that brother of yours have admitted."

Flashing a wink, he led Morgan to wait just inside the door. Rourke appeared a short time later, trailed by another man Morgan had yet to meet. He wrapped Giles in a brotherly hug and then turned to study Morgan.

"So, you must be the captain Rourke has been telling me about."

Morgan stuck out his hand. "And you must be Cara's brother."

Accepting his handshake, he nodded. "Eoghan Hamilton."

"Keondric Morgan."

Motioning toward the hall, Rourke led the group to his study.

"Well?" he said once they'd entered and he'd closed the door behind them. "What happened?"

Morgan gave a concise recounting, then turned to Rourke. "Your men still staking out the boardinghouse?"

"Aye, I've got some there now."

"Good."

"You're worried, then?"

"After what I just told you, aren't you?"

Rourke's face hardened, and he nodded to Eoghan. "There's more you need to know. The man who paid to have Ana's uncle brought to America last winter . . . I have reason to believe 'tis the same one who's been after Tillie."

Eoghan's mouth dropped. "But none of that was about Ana, remember? It was me they wanted dead."

"And why do you think that was?" Rourke crossed to the desk and took up several sheets of paper. He scribbled something on each. Like Eoghan and Giles, Morgan drew closer to read them.

On the first sheet he'd written his own name and Cara's. On the next, Eoghan, and beside that, Ana. On the last sheet he wrote Tillie's name.

Morgan looked them over, confused. "What are you trying to say here, Rourke?"

"Just . . ." He ran his hand wearily over his face. He then drew one final sheet of paper from the pile, but before he wrote on it he looked each of the men gathered in the eyes. "What do all of us have in common? What is the one thing that ties us all together in one way or another?"

Eoghan gave a shake of his head. "I dinna know. I'm guessing you do?"

"Maybe."

Looking down at the paper, he wrote something and laid it in the center of the desk. On the sheet was written *Daniel Turner*.

Morgan shifted his gaze to Rourke. "Your father?"

"Aye, my father. Of course, we know how I'm tied to him. But Eoghan?"

Eoghan glanced at the paper and back. "I was there when he died."

"Aye, and so was Tillie's fiancé."

"Braedon," Morgan said.

"Aye, Braedon."

"But they weren't the only ones." Giles looked at Rourke. "You've said it yourself, lad, your father's death was an accident."

"Was it?"

Eoghan stiffened. "What do you mean?"

"I mean it was meant to appear so, but when that failed, when we found you and realized you had actually been trying to help him—"

"The truth became a liability."

"If there was truth to be found."

"Wait." Morgan lifted his hand. "You think your father's death was planned all along?"

"Why else would someone go to such lengths to cover it up?" Rourke's hand fell to touch each sheet of paper. "Someone has been trying to silence every one of these people. Why? It has to be because they have something in common."

No one spoke for several long seconds. Finally, Eoghan blew out a sigh. "If you're right about this . . . ? Who would want your father, and me, and Braedon McKillop, now even Tillie . . . who would want us all dead?"

Morgan gritted his teeth. "I think I know."

All eyes turned to him. He met them all and settled at last on Rourke. "The ring that Braedon McKillop gave to Tillie, it belonged to The Celt."

Giles's face reddened under the light of the lamp. "Hold up now. Are you saying it was the Fenians what caused all of this?"

"Not the Fenians," Morgan replied. "One of them. Their leader. Why else would he try so hard to bury the truth?"

"Because he was acting alone," Eoghan said. "The Fenians didn't know about his plan to murder Daniel Turner."

Morgan shrugged. "Well? What do the rest of you think?"

Rourke beat the table with his fist. "The Celt. What good does knowing any of this do? We've been trying for months to track him down, and always we're one step behind. We dinna even know who he is."

"But we know someone who might." Morgan glanced over at Rourke. "The man in the gray cap who Tillie said she saw tonight. He was at the meeting with the Fenians. That means Jacob Kilarny probably knows who he is."

Rourke's brows rose. "And if he's working for The Celt?"

"He could be our link," Eoghan said. "I'll meet with Jacob, find out the man's name."

Morgan nodded. "But we'll still need to get close enough to him to ask some questions."

Rourke's nostrils flared as he blew out a breath. "I'll get word to my uncle. We'll set a trap, see if we kinna lure him into the open." He cast a warning glance at Morgan. "It'll mean leaving the boardinghouse unprotected. We'll need all our men if we're to stand a chance."

He didn't like the idea, but Morgan knew Rourke was right. If The Celt discovered their plan, he'd likely disappear, and from that point on none of them would ever be free from the threat to their lives.

Squaring his shoulders, he looked at Rourke, Eoghan, then Giles. "If we bait the trap correctly, it wilna be the boardinghouse they're interested in anyway."

42

The minutes dragged into hours as Tillie paced the library floor, waiting for Morgan's return. Though Amelia, Meg, and Laverne all waited with her, no one spoke. Finally a wagon rumbled around to the stable, and she hurried to the kitchen to unbolt the door.

Morgan and Giles bustled inside, but instead of replacing the bar, Giles took it from her and leaned it against the wall. "I'll see to the door, lassie. We've got visitors arriving shortly."

"Visitors. Who?"

Morgan held out his hand. "Come. I'll explain everything."

Her fingers shook as she slid them into his. When they reached the hall, she tugged him to a halt. "The others are in the library," she whispered. "Before we go in . . . tell me, Morgan."

He turned toward the stairs. "Cass?"

"He's resting."

He hesitated, and then the lines smoothed from his brow. "All right. C'mon. Let's find somewhere to talk."

The light of an oil lamp still glowed beneath the library door as they walked past. At the parlor he slid open the door and took a quick look around before poking his head back into the hall and motioning her inside.

She hurried to a chair and held her breath while he closed the door. "So? What happened? What did you find out?"

Her toes tapped the floor as she waited for him to light a lamp and blow out the match. When at last he joined her to sit, her fingers were red from the wringing.

Bit by agonizing bit he relayed all that had been discussed, including their plan for drawing the man in the gray cap into the open.

"We'll need Braedon's ring, Tillie. With me as the mule and the ring for bait . . ."

She bit her lip. There was no questioning the logic of the plan. What concerned her was the part Morgan would play.

"Tillie?"

His face, already so dear, bore a troubled frown. "You do trust me to take care of the ring?"

"Of course."

Her immediate response eased a few of the worried lines from his face. She leaned toward him, determined to admit a portion of the fear which weighed upon her heart.

"I'm afraid for you. What if this man ambushes you, or if he's not alone? How do you know help will come in time?"

"There is risk involved for sure, but I trust Rourke. Jacob and his men, too. Don't you?"

"I do. But why does it have to be you? Why not one of the others? You're still hurt, and you lost . . . a lot of blood." Feeling her emotions swell, Tillie swallowed and took a deep breath. Looking at him only made the ache in her chest worse. She studied her fingernails, and was surprised when his hand covered hers. "I dinna want you to go," she blurted before he could speak. "I couldn't bear it if . . ."

His thumb lifted to the tears brimming on her lashes and gently wiped them away. "Tillie?"

She shook her head, too miserable to speak.

He sighed and leaned toward her to whisper, "So now you know."

"Know what?" she choked out.

His palm warm against her cheek, he smiled. And to think she'd once believed him incapable of knowing how.

"Morgan?" His name slipped out on a sob.

"You asked me why I went out looking for you. Now you know."

Her heart felt as if it might burst. She closed her eyes against the sudden wash of exquisite hope and tenderness. When she opened them, Morgan's face was hard, and his blue-gray eyes flashed with the intensity of a barely bridled storm.

"Keondric?"

She was pleading, but for what she asked, she couldn't say. He grasped her by the arms and stood, dragging her with him as he rose.

His arms twined around her, pulling her so close she felt cradled against the entire length of him. "I kinna let you go, Tillie," he whispered, his words muffled by her hair. "I thought I could, but . . ." He pulled back, once again holding her by the arms. "I have to know. About Cass. Tell me." With each word his voice grew more ragged.

"What?"

"Do you love him?"

"No! I mean . . . aye, but not . . . I mean, I love someone else." She'd kept it hidden for so long, the truth felt foreign to her. A shiver traveled through her as she peered up at him. "I love someone else," she repeated. She spoke the words slowly, willing him to understand, but instead of the joy she longed to see, he stared at her through narrowed eyes.

His grip on her arms tightened. "Who? Kilarny?" He spat Jacob's name.

Tillie shook her head. "No, of course not."

"Someone else then. Is he in love with you?"

Tears threatened, but she tamped the burning at the back of her throat and whispered, "I think . . . I m-mean I thought . . . I hope so, but . . ."

The words tripped over themselves, and while she tried, she couldn't sort them out. No longer able to stem the rush of tears, they flowed unchecked down her cheeks.

"I love someone else, and even if he"—she forced the words from her mouth—"doesn't love me, it's enough, because I never thought . . . after Braedon, I never thought I could . . ."

A grimace twisted his features. "If? You mean you dinna know if he loves you? How could you ever think that would be enough? You deserve more, Tillie. You deserve to feel cherished."

A fissure formed inside her chest, ripping her in two. He was trying to be kind, trying to find the words to ease the pain he'd caused, because he knew it was he whom she loved and . . .

He did not feel the same.

Shame burned her cheeks. So this was to be her penance— to love a man who would never love her in return. Indeed, Sister Agnes had spoken wisely when she'd accused Tillie of laying a wearisome penance upon herself, for what could be more cumbersome, more unbearable than to long for something one could never have?

Stepping back, she rubbed the dampness from her cheeks. "My thanks to you, for everything you've done."

He moved as though to embrace her, but she shook her head and stepped back from him.

"Please, dinna say more. I appreciate the kindness, but I am not so foolish as to deceive myself."

He drew back his shoulders and braced both hands on his hips. "Deceive yourself? What are you talking about, Tillie McGrath?"

She studied the floor, the buttons on his shirt, anything to avoid his searching gaze. "Morgan, please."

"Keondric."

Startled by the sharpness of his tone, she searched his eyes and then found she could not look away. "What?"

"Earlier, you called me Keondric."

"I'm sorry," she whispered.

"I'm not." He reached over and touched her chin, the warmth of the gesture robbing her of breath. "When he kisses you, this man you love whom you *hope* loves you back," he said, pressing closer to her with each word, "does he make you forget about everything else? Make you feel as though nothing else matters except loving him? Answer me, Tillie."

Even could she have spoken, she never would have admitted the truth to him—that his touch alone was enough to drive all rational thought from her mind.

His hand caressed her cheek. And as he did so, he dipped his head so that his mouth hovered just above hers. "Say my name. I want to hear it again."

She closed her eyes, shutting out the sight of his lips, and was immediately assaulted by the intoxicating scent of his skin. "Keondric . . ."

Before his name had fully left her lips, he was kissing her, his mouth roving over hers in a way that left her weak and trembling.

Once before, she'd been awash with the kind of emotions that now swirled inside her. She'd vowed never to give in to them again, but one kiss from Keondric . . .

Her spine stiffened. Giving a cry, she ripped from his arms and whirled to cover her face with both hands.

"Tillie?"

Anguish resonated in his tone. She felt him move toward her, felt him stop shy of touching her yet reaching out all the same.

"Forgive me, lass. Please, look at me." When she did not, he gave a pained sigh. "I only kissed you because—"

Voices sounded in the hall, interrupting what he'd been about to say—that he'd only kissed her because he felt sorry for hurting her.

This time it was bitter tears that soaked Tillie's eyes and burned her cheeks. Ach, what devastating justice to prove her so wrong. Living without his love was only the start of her penance, but living with his pity?

That was far, far worse.

43

Morgan paced the length of the library, his thoughts as tattered and frayed as a knotted old rope. Behind him, Rourke and Eoghan spoke in hushed tones with Giles and Amelia, while Meg and Laverne hurried to and fro fetching water and sandwiches for Rourke's kinsmen.

His uncle stepped to the center. "All right," Malcolm Turner said, speaking to the room, "we meet at Shanahan's Pub in one hour." He raised an eyebrow in Morgan's direction. "You have the ring?"

"Right here."

Tillie carried the pouch bearing Braedon's ring to Morgan and placed it in his hand. She'd washed her face and combed her hair, but there was no mistaking the redness that rimmed her eyes. He berated himself as a blackguard for having been the cause and laid hold of her fingers before she could move away.

"Tillie."

Her skin was pale, but her eyes were determined as she looked back at him. "Come home safe."

A response burned on his tongue—three words that spoken now would only add to her burden, especially if he could not fulfill her request. But there was one thing he did want her to know.

He squeezed her fingers tight. "I've spoken to Cass. If anything should happen to me, he has promised to look after you and to help you buy that house you want for the orphanage."

The determined mask slipped a bit, and fresh tears welled in her eyes.

Fie, Morgan thought. Did everything he said have to be such a bumbling attempt? "I didn't mean to upset you, lass."

"You didn't." She curled his fingers around the pouch and pressed her hands to the backs of his. "Thank you."

That said, she moved away to join Amelia, Laverne, and Meg. The women welcomed her quietly as the four of them stood watching him with linked arms.

He nodded to Giles. "You have your pistol in case there's trouble?"

"Dinna worry about us, laddie. We'll be fine. It's yourselves you need to be watching out for, you hear?"

"We'll be careful." Rourke turned to Amelia. "You'll say a prayer for us?"

Tremors shook her from head to foot. "Of course. I'm so sorry, Rourke. Perhaps if I'd told you of my connection to the Fenians sooner, you wouldn't be faced with such dire straits now."

He dismissed her protests and wrapped her in a hug. "No. We'd have known nothing of this if it hadn't been for Tillie." He held out his hand to her. "I'm grateful for your courage. I pray we might finally lay some of this to rest."

She smiled as she took his hand and gave it a squeeze. "Please be careful. All of you."

Rourke lowered his head to her and said something Morgan couldn't quite hear before glancing about at the others. "Are we ready?"

Grunts and nods rose from the men gathered. They filed out, some through the front door, others out the back. Morgan waited until the house had returned to a somewhat uneasy silence before giving one last cautious command to Giles.

"Keep the doors locked until morning. If anything happens before then, one of us will report back. Otherwise . . ."

Giles patted a rather conspicuous bulge at his side. "No one'll be getting in here uninvited." He motioned him out the door. "Go on with ya now, so I can get this thing barred up and see to the women."

Morgan clasped his arm and then slipped outside. He waited for the sound of the door being barred before joining Rourke and the others.

Ach, but he was more than ready to get on with the task at hand. Action was always better than idleness in his opinion, and if he could find the men responsible for wanting Tillie harmed?

His stride lengthened with determined purpose. Before the night was done, he'd see to it that those who'd tried to hurt her were punished for it—no matter the cost to him, even if that meant his life.

— ❊ ❊ ❊ —

A sound jolted Tillie awake. For a moment, she thought she'd imagined it, but then Cass stirred in the bed and she knew he'd heard it, too. She put out her hand and laid it on his chest.

He pushed upright. "What was that?"

"I'm not sure. It sounded like something fell." She rose from the chair where she'd been sleeping, the blanket she'd tossed over her shoulders slithering to the floor. "I'll go check."

"Tillie?" His voice rang with caution.

She paused with her hand on the knob. "It's probably just Giles being clumsy as ever. Wait there while I look."

He glanced down at the bandages wrapping his shoulder and made an exaggerated grimace. Hiding a smile, Tillie tugged open the door and stuck her head into the hall.

Except for a single lamp on a table at the bottom of the stairs, the house was dark. Even the sounds emanating from the library had faded as Amelia, Laverne, and finally Meg had given in to exhaustion and dozed despite their worry.

Tillie leaned over the railing and scanned the hall for Giles. The chair at the door where he'd taken up guard duty was empty. Neither did she glimpse any sign of activity from the kitchen. Perhaps he'd gone for something to eat, then dropped his snack while fumbling around in the dark.

She opened her mouth to call out and then paused. If the others were sleeping, she'd only disturb them yelling for Giles. She retreated to Cass's room and poked her head inside.

"Everything's fine. I'm just going downstairs for a minute. Shall I bring you something?"

Cass pushed aside the blanket covering his legs. "It be dreadful quiet down there. Maybe I should come with you."

"Dinna be ridiculous," she said. "The hour is late, and everyone's tired. That's why it be so quiet. Now, I'll be back up in a moment." She wagged a finger toward the bed. "I'd better not hear you moving about while I'm gone."

Though she made the remark in jest, she felt a certain amount of trepidation as she slipped into the hall. Once again, no sound rose from downstairs, and no light escaped from the kitchen or the parlor. She took the first few stairs but was startled to a halt when male voices drifted from the library. Though she couldn't make them out, she sensed they did not belong to Morgan or Rourke.

But if not them . . .

Her breathing became shallow, her hands clammy and cold. Movement from the parlor caught her eye, and without thinking she jerked away from the railing to press her back against the wall.

"What about him?"

The harsh whisper sent shivers coursing over her flesh.

"Tie him up and gag him."

"I dinna have any rope."

"Find some, you fool. Check the barn."

Another voice joined the first two. "And the women?"

At the softer, more feminine tone, Tillie yanked her hand up to cover her mouth. Mary! What was she doing at the boardinghouse? There could only be one answer. But what had they done to Giles?

"Find out what they know. She must be nearby or we'd have seen her leave."

"Unless they disguised her as one of them when they lit out earlier."

"Maybe. You two search the rest of house. The stables too. Move."

Tillie's heart thumped. So they had been watching the boardinghouse all along. She waited till the voices faded down the hall before risking another peek over the railing. As before, it was dark and still, only now angry murmuring drifted from the library.

If she were to have a chance of finding Giles, it had to be now. She wouldn't have long. The intruders would be back to search upstairs. She scurried down the steps, pausing at the bottom to listen for voices, and then dashed across the hallway to the parlor. Holding her breath, she risked a peek through the crack in the sliding doors. At first, the room appeared vacant, but then she observed Giles's booted feet sticking out from behind the settee.

He wasn't moving.

Stifling a cry, she ducked inside and hurried to his side. He was lying on his back, his eyes closed and his mouth slightly agape. "Giles?"

She shook him gently. His head rolled from side to side, yet he made no sound nor showed any sign of waking. Dread settled like a stone in Tillie's stomach.

Remembering the pistol tucked into the waistband of Giles's trousers, she patted his side, found the gun, and plucked it out. He'd not even had time to draw it when they surprised him. No time to wonder how they'd gotten in.

Inching out the way she'd come, Tillie crept up the stairs and scampered on tiptoe down the hall to Cass's room.

"What—?"

Tillie put her finger to her lips. Cass quieted instantly, though the tension showed in his white-rimmed lips and the lines of strain around his eyes. As she eased the door shut, he swung his legs over the side of the bed, then stood and clung to the footboard.

"What's going on?" he demanded in a whisper. "Who's downstairs?"

Trembling took hold of her as she shoved the gun under her blouse and into the waistband of her skirt. Afterward, she hurried to the wardrobe and yanked out one of Cass's shirts. "They've found us. Mary . . . and the man in the gray cap, I think."

Cass paled. "Giles?"

"They must have ambushed him. He's unconscious."

Cass's jaw squared. "I'm going down there."

"No!" Tillie clutched his arm. "Your shirt. Take it. You have to go for help."

"What are you talking about? I'm not leaving you here alone!"

"You have to. They're searching the house for me, but I dinna think they know about you. If you leave now—"

Cass gave a vehement shake of his head. "I wilna run and leave you to face them alone."

"Cass, we have no other choice."

"We can stall. Morgan and the others will be back soon."

"You dinna know that." She grabbed his arm in frustration. "There's no time to argue, Cass. They'll be here any minute—"

She cut off, her eyes wide. By the look on his face, Cass too heard the sound that struck fear in her heart as certainly as any blade. As one, they turned and stared at the door. A moment later, the sound came again, only this time there was no mistaking the source.

It was a creak on the stairs. Shortly afterward, a shadow passed by the crack in the door.

44

Lively music reverberated throughout Shanahan's Pub, originating from the fingertips of a fat fellow seated at an ancient piano and carrying all the way to Morgan's seat. Scattered about the pub were familiar figures: Rourke and his kinsmen playing cards at a table to his left, Eoghan at the bar, and faces Morgan recognized as Jacob Kilarny's men. None of them, however, belonged to the one they all searched for—the man Kilarny had told Eoghan was named Neil Dunahoe.

Morgan caught Rourke's eye and tilted his head toward the door. A moment later, Rourke shoved back from the table, stretched, and begged a reprieve. Though teased for it, he joked good-naturedly before ambling for the exit.

Morgan waited until the card play resumed before joining him outside in the alley. It was dark there, and by the smell of it had been frequented by others in need of a "reprieve."

"Anything?" Rourke asked as he approached.

Morgan shook his head in frustration, though with the gloom it was unlikely he saw the motion. "Nothing. No sight of Dunahoe or the woman who was helping him."

"Mary."

Morgan nodded. "I dinna like it. We've been gone too long."

"I agree, but to leave now . . . we may not have another chance."

"What then? We sit twiddling our thumbs, hoping the man turns up?"

"You have a better idea?"

Morgan whirled and jammed his fist against the bricked side of the pub. Pain shot through his knuckles, but he welcomed the sensation, welcomed the release of tension squeezing his muscles. "I dinna understand! This is the place where Kilarny told Eoghan he'd find Dunahoe. Why isn't he here?" Apprehension trickled over him. "Do you think maybe Kilarny lied?"

"Why would he do that? He has no cause."

"He didn't like us asking questions about Dunahoe. If it hadn't been for Eoghan, he probably wouldn't have told us anything at all."

Shuffling sounded from the street. They fell silent as a bent figure staggered into the alley toward them. The man fumbled for some time before accomplishing his business and then weaving back the way he'd come.

"Well?" Morgan continued once they were alone.

"I say we wait a while longer. If Dunahoe doesn't show up, we'll try another way."

Reaching into his pocket, Morgan pulled out the ring Tillie had given him and held it high. It glinted, even in the deeply shadowed alley. "I have a better idea."

Thinking of his crew, Morgan grinned. For sure and for certain they'd be plenty riled if they knew what he had in mind.

He slid the ring back into his pocket. "Rourke, me lad," he said, clapping him on the shoulder, "how 'bout you join me in a game of cards?"

— ※ ※ ※ —

"Cass, go!" Tillie hissed.

She shoved him toward the window, then darted for the door. Throwing it open, she barreled out and slammed it behind her. She'd gone just a few steps before plowing into a man's solid chest. The impact drove the wind from her. Had the man not reached out to grab her by the arms, she'd likely have fallen.

"Well, well, what have we here?"

The confusion and shock she felt were only partly feigned. Her mouth fell open and she twisted her head from side to side to search the hall.

"Who are you? What are you doing in my house? Where's Amelia?"

The man grinned, revealing teeth that were too large for his mouth and gapped at the center.

"Dunahoe, Mary, come see what I found," he hollered, his raucous voice echoing down the stairs.

Tillie struggled to free her arm, but the man only squeezed tighter. "What are you doing?" she demanded. "Let me go. Who are you? What do you want?"

The man clucked noisily. "Come now, lassie, no need to play ignorant. I think you know what we want."

And what she wanted—nay, what she needed—was time for Cass to make good his escape and for Keondric to return to the boardinghouse.

Raising her foot, she slammed it down as hard as she could on the man's instep. He howled in pain yet somehow managed to maintain his grip on her arm. She kicked again, this time connecting with his shin. The blow was not as effective, thanks to her heavy skirt, but she managed to rip her arm free and tear off down the hall.

"Dunahoe!" the man roared, limping after her.

Tillie started for the stairs, skittering to a stop a couple of feet shy of them. Approaching was the man in the gray cap, with Mary at his heels. Tillie rushed into Meg's room and barely had it locked before a heavy fist began pounding, rattling the door against the jamb.

"Open it, woman, or I'll wring your neck."

The gun she'd snatched from Giles contained one shot— useless against three intruders. Aside from that, a small voice inside told her to wait to reveal it. Tillie cast frantically about the room for another weapon. The fireplace poker!

Yanking it from its stand, she rushed to a nearby window and smashed out the glass. A second later, the door behind her crashed open and three figures with murderous intent carved upon their faces bore down on her. She swung the poker wildly. It made a brief, fleshy connection and then someone snatched it out of her hands.

She let out a scream, but even that was short-lived. The man in the cap drew back his fist.

A second later, everything went dark.

45

The area around the poker table had grown more crowded as the game of cards intensified. With each hand, cheers went up from some, jeers from others. Morgan fidgeted with his collar, tapped his fingers on the table, even tried to appear warm—not too difficult a task with so many bodies pressed up close.

"All right," he blurted, scowling at those seated around the table, "let's see 'em." He jabbed his finger at Rourke. "You! Turner. What have you got?"

His lips stretching in a thin smile, Rourke laid down a pair of eights and three queens. Eyes narrowed, he stared at Morgan across the table. "Well?"

Morgan hesitated a moment, then feigning disgust he threw his cards facedown on the table.

Rourke barked a laugh as he leaned forward and raked in the pot. "Just not your night, eh, fella?" He yawned, then packed up the coins and bills and shoved them into his pocket. "My thanks for the game."

Morgan bolted out of his chair and stood swaying, his finger jabbed at Rourke's face. "Hold up there. You mean to say you're not going to give me a chance to win me money back?"

The instant he rose, several of Rourke's kinsmen also stood and gathered at Rourke's shoulder. Quiet fell over the pub as all eyes swung toward the circle of glowering faces.

"Well?" Morgan demanded. "Are we gonna play or not?"

Rourke gave a snort. "With what? Last I saw, you were nigh unto broke, and I dinna do credit."

Uneasy laughter rippled through the room.

Morgan blustered a bit, then reached into his pocket, drew out the ring and set it on the table. "Broke, eh? Take a look at that. It's gotta be worth something."

He fidgeted while Rourke scooped up the ring and gave it a close examination. Morgan had begun to think he might be overdoing it when Rourke at last laid the ring in the center of the table and gave a nod.

"Nice piece of jewelry. Where'd you get it?"

"None of your business. Are you in or not?"

Rourke scratched his head as though thinking. "I'm not sure. Not all that into rings, even fancy ones. Besides, how do I know you didn't steal it?"

By now, heads had begun to swivel back and forth as people followed the confrontation between the two men.

Good. Now to up the ante.

Leaning forward, Morgan grabbed the ring and then braced both hands on the table, palms down, and growled, "Same way I know you're not a cheater."

Boots scuffled the floor as Malcolm strode forward and threw his coat onto the floor. "Did I just hear you accuse my nephew of cheating?"

Rourke grabbed Malcolm's arm, keeping him from circling around to where Morgan waited. "Easy, Uncle. Not worth the time."

"Not worth the time, or worried I'll kill the old man and then start on you?"

Rourke looked genuinely angry as he shoved back his chair. "That's enough."

"You're a coward," Morgan sneered, "on top of being a cheat."

The whole Turner clan looked mad enough to fight. Hopefully they'd gotten their instructions right or the rest of the scene would play out very badly.

Sucking in a breath, Morgan counted to three, then jumped up onto the table and over the other side. Rourke caught him in midair, twisting so that both of them crashed to the floor. In the same instant, the rest of the Turners descended. Fists flailed and bodies rolled over and past him. Though the fight was staged, more than one of them landed a solid punch. Morgan narrowly escaped a heavy boot to his skull.

Tucking his elbows in tight, he had gotten off a couple of hard licks of his own when a loud boom split the air. Instantly the fight was over, and the men who'd pretended to bludgeon him now stood shoulder to shoulder with him, but what had drawn their attention, he could not see.

Breathing heavily, Morgan straightened and pushed forward until he cleared the crowd. At the door, he drew to a shocked halt. Cass stood weaving at the entrance, his face waxen and covered with sweat, a pistol dangling from his limp fingers.

"Morgan?"

Morgan leapt forward as his brother began to fall. With one arm he caught Cass; with the other he grabbed the pistol from his hand. Rourke hurried over, and together they laid him on the floor.

"What happened?" Rourke said, his voice low.

"I dinna know. Cass?" Morgan grabbed him by the shoulders and gave him a shake. Sweat dampened his body, and the wound that the doctor had taken such cares to stitch had broken open, staining his white shirt.

Morgan lifted his head and saw Rourke over Cass's body. "The boardinghouse."

Cold fingers closed around Morgan's hand. He looked down.

"Morgan," Cass panted, his lips white and his eyes wild to the point of delirium, "they have Tillie."

— ❈ ❈ ❈ —

"Tillie? Tillie, lass, are you all right?"

"You shouldn't have hit her so hard."

"What should I have done, let her scream her head off? How long do you think it would have taken for the neighbors to come a runnin' if I'd not done it?"

Bit by bit, Tillie began sorting the voices out—from Laverne's worried crooning to Mary's strident rasp.

She struggled to come fully awake, and then groaned as pain radiated up from her cheekbone all the way to her eye socket.

"She's waking up." A tremor shook Laverne's voice.

"Praise God." That from Amelia, followed by, "Meg, bring me that water."

"Hold up. I dinna want either one of ya going any nearer."

Tillie managed to peel open her eyelids to see Mary clutching a pistol and holding both Amelia and Meg at bay. Behind her stood the man in the gray cap and two others she didn't recognize.

One, she realized. The other was the man she'd kicked, and he still looked decidedly angry.

Laverne's face bobbed into view. Beads of sweat rolled over her cheeks and neck, and tears welled in her eyes. "Thank God you're all right, dearie. We tried to warn you and—"

Jerking up, Tillie grabbed her hand and gave a frantic shake of her head. The motion caused white spots to flash before her eyes. Dizzy from the pain, she clutched Laverne's fingers.

"G-Giles?" she managed through gritted teeth.

"They've got 'im tied up in the parlor." With each word, Laverne shuddered harder. She turned disapproving eyes to their captors. "Shame on you all, coming in here and terrorizing a bunch of helpless women and one old man."

"Shut up!" Mary screeched, pointing the gun at Laverne. She turned the barrel toward Tillie and waved it at her. "You there. Get up."

"She's hurt, thanks to 'im." Laverne jerked her chin at the man in the cap.

"She'll be hurt a lot worse if she doesn't do what I say."

Placing her hand on Laverne's arm, Tillie tried to will confidence into her touch. "The four of us, and Giles, we'll be all right as long as we do what they say."

Tillie struggled to her feet. She dared not risk a glance at Meg and Amelia, but could only hope as she crossed to Mary that they'd understood her silent message.

"The ring," Mary demanded. "Where is it?"

"I do not have it."

"Neil?" Mary motioned to the man in the cap, who took hold of Tillie's arms and jerked them behind her back.

"Where is it?" he growled, his breath hot against her neck.

Tillie shook her head. "I gave it to Keon—Captain Morgan. He was going to use it to try and lure you out."

Neil's grip on her arms loosened, and he shoved her out of the way. "They lit out of here a while ago. We'll kill the girl and get the ring when they come back."

Tillie's heart leapt to her throat as Mary nodded her agreement. Raising the gun, she said, "You heard him, lass. You're of no further use."

A small part of her brain heard and recognized Meg scream, and Laverne and Amelia gasp, but another part struggled for a way of escape.

The money.

Where the thought came from she couldn't say, only that it was there, and with it a plan.

She held up her hand. "I have s-something else. Something you want." When no shot rang out, she spoke slower, measuring each word. "I have some money . . . hidden upstairs."

"Liar. How would a snip like you come by money?"

"I've been saving it to buy an orphanage." She blinked. "I mean a house. I was going to make it into an orphanage."

"It's true," Amelia said, speaking up for the first time. Though Mary swung the gun her way, she refused to look away. "She works for a milliner on Ashberry Street, just down from—"

"Enough," Mary snapped.

She cut her gaze to Neil. Moving to stand before Tillie, he studied her for a moment. "How much money?"

Nervousness clutched her throat. "Almost ten thousand."

Going by his expression, she'd obviously captured Neil's interest, but Mary hissed over his shoulder, "She's lying. She couldna have earned that much."

"I didn't earn it all," Tillie said. "My fiancé and I brought most of it with us from Ireland." She turned her attention to Neil. "Please, I'll give it to you, all of it, if you'll just leave us alone."

She saw the calculation in his eyes. Finally he nodded and motioned for Mary to step out of the way.

"What are you doing?" Mary asked. "You heard what he said. If he finds out—"

Neil spun, silencing her with a look. "But he wilna find out, because you wilna tell him." He raised his brows at the other two men, who'd watched the exchange in silence. Both men nodded, their eyes gleaming as greedily as his.

He swung back to Mary. "See? He won't find out." He jerked his chin at the men. "Keep an eye on the women." To Tillie, he said, "You come with me."

Though her feet felt carved from stone, she had no choice but to obey. Walking slowly only earned her a cruel shove to the back. She stumbled over the hem of her skirt and nearly fell.

Glancing over her shoulder, she saw Neil eyeing her with suspicion. "No tricks, eh, lassie? Or I'll kill ya with me own bare hands."

"No tricks. But I'm not a fool. You'll kill me anyway."

"Aye, I will. But get me that money, and maybe I'll be quick about it."

His words alone were enough to strike terror into her heart, but added to the matter-of-fact way in which he spoke them . . .

Tillie shuddered and groped for the lamp.

"No! Leave it."

She strained to see his face in the dim light. "'Tis dark down here. It'll be darker upstairs."

"Fine." He picked up the lamp and tipped his head toward the hall. "Move."

Her knees quivering, Tillie ascended the stairs, mentally noting their number.

One. Two. Three.

So this was what a condemned person felt like when approaching the gallows.

Four. Five.

Where were Keondric and the others? It had to have been an hour or more since Cass had gone for help.

Six. Seven. Eight. Nine.

Her throat tightened as she approached the top of the stairs. That money was her last hope. Once Neil had it . . .

His coat rustled. At the top of the stairs she turned and watched him mount the last two. In his free hand, a knife glinted. Surprisingly, the fear she'd felt while climbing the stairs had settled into determined resolve.

"Well?" he demanded.

"I want your word," Tillie said, the waver fading from her voice.

Settling onto his heels, he grinned in the face of her bravado. "My word? On what?"

"Whatever you're doing here, and whatever you intend to do with that knife, I want your word that you will not hurt them. Amelia or Giles or . . ." She felt tears threaten and blinked them back. "You were sent here to kill me. Not them."

She finished on a whisper, the truth of her plea stunning her into silence. They'd been sent to kill *her*. Why? What had she done but sit by her fiancé's side as he lay dying? And what had his death been worth? She realized then she would never know.

Instead of the softening she'd hoped to see caused by her speech, Neil seemed incited by it. He raised the lamp, the flicker of the flame reflected in the depths of his eyes. "The money. Now."

"They dinna know anything," Tillie begged. "They're innocent—"

"Now!" He thrust his face into hers. Gasping, she fell against the wall and jerked her head away.

"Where is it?"

She pointed a shaking finger toward the first bedroom. Grabbing her by the arm, he dragged her down the hall and thrust her through the half-open door.

"Show me."

Averting her face lest he see through her ruse, Tillie made her way past Meg's bed to her wardrobe.

"What are you waiting for?" Muttering curses beneath his breath, Neil shoved past her, set the lamp aside, and threw open the doors. The muttering continued, growing louder as he yanked out shirts and dresses, tossing them on the floor.

The deeper he dug into the wardrobe, the more violent his movements became, until finally he whirled and pointed the knife at her throat.

Cringing, she braced for the agony of the blade. Instead, Neil let out a breath, gathered himself, and then smiled.

Touching his temple with the tip of the knife, he said, "Smart girl, ain't ya? Thought you'd stall for time?" The smile disappeared, replaced by a reptilian coldness that sucked the strength from her limbs.

"You kill me now and you'll never know where the money is," Tillie blurted.

"Aye, you're right about that." He drew so close that she smelled the sweat on his clothes and the whiskey on his breath. "But if you do not show me where that money is, I'll start killing your precious friends downstairs." Angling the knife, he inserted it into her hair and tugged a lock loose from the bun at her neck. "Starting with the old woman."

With an almost lightning flick of his wrist, he ripped the blade free.

She felt the jerk and thought for a split second that he had cut her. Instinctively she screamed and threw her hands up, but instead of blood, she watched in horror as a piece of her hair fluttered to the floor. In the next instant, Neil grabbed the lamp and strode toward the door.

"Wait! I'll tell you."

He stopped at the door and turned on his heel.

"The money is in my r-room," Tillie stammered. "I hid it in a hole in the floor next to the bed. I promise you, the money is there. It's there."

She almost couldn't breathe waiting for his signal. Finally he lifted the lamp and gestured for her to start walking.

Tillie staggered down the hall, blinded by tears and running her hands along the wall to find her way. Bursting into her room, she dropped to her knees and pointed at the rug beneath which lay the loosened board.

"There."

"Get it."

Her chest heaving, she gathered her skirt and crawled forward to haul the rug out of the way. With shaking fingers she pried up the board. Sweat ran over her face and neck. Dragging her sleeve across her forehead, she nodded at the hole.

"Pull it out!"

Tillie rolled onto her backside and used her heels to shove toward the wall. "No. You're going to kill me now anyway. I'll not pay you to do it."

He squinted and, a second later, dropped to his knees. Setting down the lamp, he laid the knife aside and began rummaging in the hole.

Now. The gun.

With him so intent on digging, he'd not even see . . .

Euphoria melted over Neil's face. He pulled his hand from the hole, and dangling from his fingers was the bag holding all the money Tillie and Braedon had worked and scrimped to save. He held it up and gave it a shake, grinning at the resulting *clink* of coins. Shoving the bag into his shirt, he reached for the knife and stood, turning to face her.

For a split second he stood frozen with an almost comical look of disbelief on his face.

Laying her finger to her lips, Tillie pushed to her feet. "Not a sound," she whispered, leveling Giles's pistol at his chest. "There's only one bullet in here, but I reckon that's all it will take."

46

Every evil deed, every possible nightmarish imagining filtered through Morgan's brain, torturing him as he and Rourke raced through the city's winding streets. Bending low over the saddle, he urged the mare's clattering hooves faster, pleading for every ounce of speed the animal could give.

How could he have left them alone?

The same thought pounded over and over in his head, driving him to the brink of madness. If only he'd stayed behind, or left someone besides a wounded brother and an old man to stand guard. If only . . .

He blinked the sting of sweat from his eyes, lowered his chin against the mare's whipping mane.

Please God . . . take care of them.

Never had he felt so helpless, his loved ones so out of reach. Finally, Ashberry Street. At last the shadowy outline of the boardinghouse. Barely had the horse skittered to a stop before he leapt from the saddle.

"Morgan, wait!"

He heard Rourke's voice, knew the others were seconds behind, but he could think of only one thing—saving Tillie.

Flying up the steps, he forced himself to control the rush of adrenaline enough to test the knob. Locked.

"Back here." Rourke motioned from around the side of the boardinghouse.

Morgan vaulted over the railing to the ground, absorbing the fall with his knees. Together, he and Rourke circled to the kitchen, sliding to a halt at the sight of the stable door gaping open and the sounds of a skirmish drifting out.

By now, the rest of his kinsmen had clustered around them in the dark. Rourke jerked his thumb toward the stable. "Two of you check it out. The rest come with us."

At the kitchen door, Morgan scanned the circle of grim faces. Some of them he knew only as Rourke's kinsmen, yet they stared, awaiting his orders.

"We'll go in through the kitchen. There's a door leading to a hall. From there the library is to the right, farther down the hall and parlor. We'll only have a few seconds before they know we're coming. When we get inside, try to split up. I dinna know how many are inside or what they've done with the residents of the boardinghouse, but if we spread out, we should be able to see quick enough what we're dealing with."

Nods came from the four gathered around. Bracing himself, Morgan counted to three, then drew back and gave the door a vicious kick. Splinters flew as it crashed against the wall. He registered the shouts coming from the library and veered that way. Someone jogged at his elbow. He noted his position as he thrust his shoulder into the library door and sent it smashing open.

Two men. A woman—

Morgan saw the gun in her hand and threw himself to the floor, then came rolling up as the report split the air.

Eoghan.

Morgan realized it was he who had followed into the library as he flew at the woman and knocked the gun from her hand. Morgan went in the other direction, tackling the larger of the two men on the run and driving him to the floor. Fists flailing, Morgan landed several blows, then rolled off as the man's head lolled sideways.

Jumping into a crouch, he scanned the room. Rourke had the other man in hand. Eoghan had the woman, and Laverne was clutching her gun. Morgan strode to her, breathing heavily.

"Tillie?"

Laverne shoved the gun at him. "Upstairs. He took her. Go!"

He took off running, shouting Tillie's name as he raced for the stairs.

"Keondric!"

He rushed into her bedroom. Too late, she screamed, "Look out!"

A fist took him on the chin and spun him into the wall. Instantly, Dunahoe was on him, grabbing for his gun. They wrestled for it, Morgan straining to keep the barrel pointed away from Tillie. Away from himself.

Dunahoe grunted. Both their hands locked over the pistol's trigger. A blast echoed through the room.

Tillie screamed . . . and kept screaming.

For a few seconds, Morgan stood blinking—trying to breathe, trying to process what had happened. Shuddering free of his stupor, he rushed to Tillie.

"Are you all right?" He gripped her by the arms and pulled her to his chest. "Tillie . . ."

"He shot you! He shot—"

"No. Tillie, look at him. Look!"

She stared openmouthed at Dunahoe's slumped body, then collapsed into his arms.

"Did he hurt you?" he demanded, his heart thumping.

He clasped her chin and tilted her face to look into her eyes. Her hair was wild, and a bruise covered her cheek. Groaning, he cupped her head to his shoulder and held her tight.

"I'm so sorry, Tillie. God help me, I'm so sorry."

"I'm all right," she sobbed.

"What happened?"

"I dinna know." She looked up. "Amelia?"

"She's downstairs. She, Laverne, they're all unharmed. Except . . . Giles?"

"He's in the p-parlor. They t-tied him up."

Though he desperately wanted to go on holding her, he had to know the rest of the house was secure.

He smoothed the hair from her face. "Tillie, I have to go downstairs. Wait here, do you hear me? Dinna leave this room."

"Keondric—"

The pounding of footsteps on the stairs cut her short. Morgan thrust her behind his back.

Rourke burst through the door, and on his heels was Eoghan. Rourke's lip was bloodied, and one eye looked bruised and purple, but upon spying them, his lips curved in a smile that released the tension from Morgan's muscles.

"You two all right?"

Morgan nodded. "Downstairs?"

"We've got 'em." Rourke pointed down at Dunahoe. "What about him?"

Eoghan went to him, kneeled down and pressed two fingers to his neck. Grunting, he stood back up. "He's gone."

With those words, all of the rage—the panic and fear that had driven Morgan since leaving the pub—drained from his limbs. He blew out a sigh and turned to pull Tillie into his arms . . . except, before he could do so, she was already there.

47

Tears of gladness mingled with relieved exclamations as Tillie and Morgan made their way downstairs to the library. Both Meg and Amelia scurried to her, Amelia patting her cheeks and fingering the ends of her cut hair. Giles sat on the settee, gingerly rubbing his wrists while Laverne fretted over him, but both rose and shuffled close as she entered.

"You all right, lass?" Giles said.

Tillie nodded, repeating her assurance that she was not hurt over and over. She looked toward the wall, where Mary and the other two henchmen sat bound and gagged and guarded by Rourke and Eoghan.

"Did they tell us anything?"

"No, but these two might."

At the sudden voice, she squeezed to Keondric's side. Instantly his arm tightened around her, and she felt tension rumble through him. "Kilarny!"

Holding a gun, Jacob and a couple of Rourke's kinsmen ushered two more in. "Discovered 'em lurking in the stable." He gave a nod to Keondric. "Your brother found me, told me what happened. I came to help."

"And Cass?"

"My men are looking after him."

Keondric said nothing, and for a moment she thought he would not believe Jacob. She twisted to look up into his face.

"Jacob did not do this. I know he didn't."

Though his face was still hard, Keondric nodded. "Fine. Then who did?"

Jacob pointed the gun at one of the prisoners. "Well?"

The man's eyes bounced from the three seated on the floor to the one standing next to him.

"He'll kill you if you talk," the second man hissed.

The hammer on Jacob's gun clicked. "I'll kill you if you don't."

Silence permeated the room. Like the others, Tillie held her breath, waiting. The man's eyes rounded. Sweat slicked his face and neck.

"He . . . he gave us orders," the man began.

"Shut up!" the second man interrupted, but then Malcolm grabbed him by the nape of the neck and forced him to the floor. Driving his knee into his back, he held him there.

"The Celt," Jacob growled, "he's the one what told you to come?"

The man licked his lips and nodded.

"Why?"

He jerked his head toward Tillie. "Her. We were supposed to find some ring, then kill her before she could talk."

Pressing the barrel to the man's forehead, Jacob said, "I want a name. You'll give it to me or I will count to three, and then I will bury a bullet in your skull. Do you understand?"

"Don't give it to him!" the second man groaned from the floor. Across the room, the other three prisoners strained against their bonds.

"One." Jacob's eyes narrowed.

His eye twitched. "No. Please . . ."

Tillie's heart raced. "Jacob—"

"Two."

He would die. And then Jacob would try to force another prisoner to talk. The burden of another man's death would be too much to bear.

She squeezed Keondric's arm. "Dinna let him do it." She lifted her face to him. "Please."

"Douglas Healy!"

Everyone in the room froze, their eyes fastened to the broken man at the center.

He lifted pleading eyes to Jacob. "The man who sent us was Douglas Healy."

Leaving Keondric's side, Tillie rushed to Amelia and grasped her shaking hands. "Amelia?"

"I . . . I kinna believe it. Why would he do this?"

Keondric lifted his hand. After a moment, the room returned to an uneasy silence. He motioned to Jacob, then Rourke and Malcolm. "We need some time to sort this out."

"I agree." Malcolm signaled to his men, spoke quietly to them, and finally turned to Rourke. "We'll wait outside, and take them"—he nodded toward the prisoners—"with us."

"No," Kilarny said. "They're Fenians. My men will take care of them."

Malcolm eyed him a moment. "Fine. Take 'em," he agreed.

"You should go, too." Tillie gave Amelia's fingers a gentle squeeze. She looked to Laverne and Meg. "This has been a shock. I think she should lie down, maybe have something to drink. Giles, will you help take Amelia upstairs?"

They nodded, and within minutes all that remained with Tillie were Jacob, Rourke, Eoghan, and Keondric.

Tillie crossed to him. "Can it be true? Is Douglas Healy The Celt?"

Keondric dragged his fingers through his hair and looked at Jacob. "What do you think?"

Jacob shrugged. "He's wealthy. Powerful. If it *is* him, we'll have a hard time getting close."

Tillie shuddered. "What have I done that he would want me dead? Or Braedon?"

"I think I know," Rourke said. "All along we've suspected that the men who murdered my father were not acting alone. It would make sense that if The Celt were involved, he would want to keep it covered up."

"Why?" Tillie asked.

"Because the plan was always to make sure that Daniel Turner ended up dead," Eoghan interjected.

Rourke nodded. "Healy wanted a parliament seat. He used my father, and the Fenians, to make it happen."

Jacob frowned. "So you be blaming the Fenians now?"

"No." Rourke lifted his hand, palm out. "I'm saying Healy plotted with his son to make it look like it was an accident and the Fenians were involved."

"And the ring?" Keondric asked.

"Sean." Grief etched deep grooves into Eoghan's face. "Sean must have given it to Braedon."

"Hold up. Who is Sean?" Keondric asked.

"Douglas Healy's son," Eoghan said. "Sean must have taken his ring to convince the Fenians that The Celt supported the plan to kidnap Daniel Turner."

"And when Daniel was killed," Tillie said, "Braedon figured out that it wasn't an accident and kept the ring for insurance."

"He must have known something was wrong on the ship," Keondric added. "That's why he gave you the ring and told you to hide it—because he knew he wasn't just sick."

Nausea rolled in Tillie's stomach. "Murder and scheming, even sacrificing his own son—all of this for power?"

She searched their faces and finally settled on Jacob. Of them all, his was the most tortured.

"I'm sorry, Matilda. Sorry for Braedon." Jacob lowered his head. "Healy used our cause—everything we've worked and sweated and bled for—for his own selfish gain."

"We've all suffered," Rourke said grimly. "The question now is how do we stop him? Like you said before, Jacob, we wilna be able to stroll up to the door."

Struck with an idea, Tillie squared her shoulders. "There is a way, if we give him something that he wants."

"Like what?" Jacob said. "The ring?"

"The ring alone wilna be enough to convince anyone what Healy has done." She paused a moment, then said, "We need something more damaging, something like . . . me."

"No!" Keondric said.

"'Tis the only way any of us will ever be free, Keondric. Rourke and Eoghan, even you and Cass now—we're all captives of this man unless we stop him while we still can."

"Morgan, let's listen to her," Jacob began, but he was quickly cut off.

"She was almost killed tonight!" He glared at Tillie. "I dinna care what Healy's done. I won't let you risk your life again."

"What about your life, or Cass's? Do you really think The Celt will stop hunting for you now? We'll none of us be safe again until he is stopped." She placed her hand on his arm. "And I wilna be alone. You'll be with me."

He fell silent. "What?"

Tillie turned to Jacob. "We can disguise a couple of your men, dress them in clothes we take from the prisoners, and use caps to cover their faces."

"What about us?" Eoghan said.

Rourke shook his head. "We're too recognizable, you especially."

"But my men"—Jacob gave a grunt—"we could make Healy think they captured you."

She nodded.

"And if Morgan is with you, Healy will think he was taken in the fight, too," Rourke added.

"We'll need at least one of his own men to lead them," Eoghan interrupted, "or he'll kill them all before they cross the threshold."

"Or one of his women," Tillie said. "Mary. Keondric can walk behind her, force her to keep quiet until we're inside."

"That's still only four," Rourke said. "Five at the most. That wilna be enough to overpower Healy's men."

"We wilna need to," Jacob said. "Some of the men inside that house are loyal Fenians. They're only protecting Healy because they think he's fighting for them. If we can get to Healy, make him confess what he's done, the fight will be over before it starts."

They all fell silent, considering the idea. Finally, Keondric nodded. "All right, but I stay with Tillie the entire time, and if there's any doubt that Healy's falling for our plan, our first concern is getting her out."

Tillie drew a deep breath as all of them nodded their agreement. Once again a trap was laid, only this time she would be the bait.

48

Tension squeezed the muscles in Morgan's shoulders as they approached the ornately scrolled gate surrounding Douglas Healy's house. Though his hands were loosely bound in front of him, he clutched a pistol to Mary's ribs. Behind him, three of Kilarny's men walked disguised as Healy's men. And Tillie . . .

His heart leapt in his chest as he looked at her. One word of warning from Mary and all their lives would be forfeited.

He pressed the barrel tighter to her side and leaned forward to speak into her ear. "I'll not hesitate. Do you hear me? One word, one sound . . ."

She shivered, and he knew she believed him.

They drew to a halt as Healy's guard met them at the gate. The guard glared at Mary. "Where's Dunahoe?"

"Dead. Killed in the fight by these two." She glanced over her shoulder. "I brought the girl."

"Your orders were to kill her."

"My orders were to get the ring, and then kill her. Maybe you can get the information out of her. I couldn't."

"And him?" He looked past her to Morgan.

"He tried to protect her. I figured he might be useful."

Again she looked at them. Morgan held his breath. She then turned back to the guard. "What was I supposed to do? It's almost dawn. I couldn't verra well hang around the boardinghouse. People were going to start stirring."

Her foot tapped the graveled walk. "Well? You want someone to see us standing out here?"

After what seemed an eternity, the guard grunted and waved her through. "Make it quick. He's waiting for ya."

Morgan eyed the layout of the grounds surrounding the main house. 'Twas an expansive estate for the city and no doubt, but what concerned him was the lack of cover for Kilarny's men. He shot a look at Rourke. By his scowl, he felt the same.

"Which way?" Morgan muttered, shifting the gun to jab Mary in the back.

"He'll be in his study," she said. "And no need to remind me about those guns you're all carrying. I'll gladly lead you to him, since we be walking to your deaths. When he finds out who you are, he'll have you all killed."

It appeared she'd be right when several men exited from the back of the house to meet them. The largest of them waited at the door, his arms crossed and an angry frown on his face.

"What are ya doing bringing them here? Have ya gone mad, Mary?"

Morgan increased the pressure of the pistol to her spine.

She fidgeted, then said, "Mad or no, I dinna answer to you, William Byrne. I want to see The Celt. I have a prize for him, one I think will make him most pleased." She jerked her thumb toward Tillie and then pressed her fists to her skinny hips. "Well?"

William's mouth twisted in a sneer. "You always were a grubber, Mary. You think this will make The Celt finally take notice of ya?"

She jutted out her chin. "Just take me to him and shut your mouth."

His scowl deepened, but he led the way. Inside the house, heavy curtains and carved furnishings dominated most of the rooms they passed. Morgan made note of the many twists and turns before they arrived at a set of wide double doors.

Mary narrowed her eyes at William. "Aren't we going in?"

He jabbed his finger toward Tillie and Morgan. "They are. Dinna think there's any need for you. I'd say your job's done."

Morgan tensed. Something wasn't right. Behind him, he sensed the same tensing of muscles from Kilarny's men.

Mary poked out her elbows and stood grinning. "Well, I can hardly go anywhere with this here gun jabbed in my back, now, can I?"

The moment she said it, the doors flew open, and men armed with rifles streamed out. Thrusting Mary aside, Morgan reached for Tillie, but he was too late. William shoved a gun in his face, halting any action he thought to take.

"Ah, ah! No sudden movements now. Wouldn't want your lady here to see you getting your face blown off. Now drop your weapons."

"Keondric!" Tillie stretched out her hand, but he shook his head, willing her to remain still.

Grunts sounded from behind them as more men spilled from the hall.

From inside the study, a deep, booming voice drifted out. "Captain Morgan, Miss McGrath . . . please, come in. I've been expecting you."

— ❈ ❈ ❈ —

Seeing the gun pointed at Keondric's head, Tillie almost couldn't move, couldn't breathe. Arms grabbed her from behind and forced her forward. At the harshness of her handling, Morgan's face darkened, and Tillie resolved to do everything she was ordered so he might not risk his own life trying to protect her.

Despite the hour, Douglas Healy did indeed appear as though he'd been awaiting them. His hair was neatly combed, his shirt collar starched, his vest buttoned. He rolled a fat cigar between his fingers as if relishing the moment.

Leaving the door, Mary sidled to him, a wide smile on her lips. Douglas welcomed her with arms open wide.

"Well, my dear, you were right after all."

"I said he would come back for her, didn't I?" She cocked an eyebrow at Keondric. "I saw how he watched her at the pub. Couldn't take his eyes off her. Knew there was something there." Her mouth drooped in a frown. "Neil's dead." She jerked her chin toward Keondric. "*He* killed him."

Setting down the cigar, Douglas clucked like an old rooster. "I'm sorry to hear that. He was a loyal man." He lifted his head as though thinking. "Aye, and loyalty deserves swift justice." He gestured toward the man Mary had called William. "Take him outside and shoot him."

"No!" Heedless of the danger to herself, Tillie strained against the arms holding her. "No, you kinna kill him!"

But despite her protest, Douglas's men started taking Keondric away. She threw her head sideways to plead with Rourke. "Do something!"

Yet Rourke stared helplessly at her as Keondric was getting farther away.

"Tillie." Even above the din, she heard Keondric's voice— sad and pleading. "I'm sorry."

"No!" Ripping free, Tillie spun so hard she fell in a heap at Healy's feet. "I have your ring!" she shouted. "I know what you did. Stop them now or I'll tell them everything."

Hands grabbed her shoulders and yanked her to her feet,

but she shouted all the louder. "Healy is a liar! And he's using you all to gain power. Ask him for his ring. Ask him where it is." Tears sprang to her eyes. "He doesn't have it, and I know why. Ask him!"

Curious stares turned her way. Healy saw them too, for he lifted his hand above the crowd and signaled for silence. The men dragging Keondric halted at the door.

Tillie grasped the brief reprieve. "Your ring. You gave it to your son the day Daniel Turner died. You knew it was the only way to convince the men with him that you supported the plot to kidnap him, only you never intended it to be lost, did you? That's why you had my Braedon murdered, and why you've been so desperate to hunt down the Hamiltons. You had to cover up what you'd done to Daniel Turner." She spit the words out, half shouting, half crying.

"You didn't want anyone to find out that you'd committed murder in order to steal a seat in parliament for yourself, because you *knew* if the Fenians found out they would turn against you. How many lads died in retribution for something you did?"

To her surprise, Healy made no move to stop her, so she forged on. "Braedon gave me your ring and told me to use it if ever I was in danger. Somehow you learned that I was in possession of it and you . . . you . . ."

Confused by his lack of response, she trailed into silence.

Healy gave a satisfied nod. "Does Morgan here still have the ring?"

"He must. I ain't seen it," Mary interrupted before Tillie could speak.

Striding to Keondric, she ripped open his coat, dug out a pouch, and looked inside it. Holding her prize aloft, she tossed it to William and then sneered up at Keondric. A shudder traveled through Tillie at the murderous look in her eyes.

"I said you was walking to your death, didn't I? You thought you were so smart, so conniving."

"That's enough, Mary," Douglas said.

He took the pouch from William. Reaching in, he pulled out the ring, held it up to the light of the chandelier, and snorted. His gaze fell on Tillie. "It is a rather good reproduction."

Tillie stiffened. "What?"

She watched transfixed as Healy reached into his coat pocket, his long fingers fumbling and finally emerging with a bit of gold clutched tight. "But *this* is my ring." His chin lifted as he addressed the men. "This has been their plot—the Hamiltons and Turners—to create a ring similar to mine and frame me for murder." He held the two rings aloft. "Look for yourselves. Do you see a difference?"

Tillie's eyes widened. "It kinna be . . ."

"He's lying. There is a difference!"

At Keondric's shout, all eyes turned to him. He stared at Tillie, but she shook her head in bemusement.

"The memento mori," he said. Greeted by silence, Keondric repeated the strange phrase, only louder. "The memento mori. Healy's ring has it."

Healy's face took on a look of curiosity. "Remember you must die."

Tillie's heart lurched. At first, she thought he spoke to Keondric, but then realized he'd interpreted the phrase. He lowered the rings and looked at the one taken from the pouch.

There was a disgruntled murmuring in the crowd, and then they parted to allow another larger man to step through. He was one of Kilarny's, disguised in the clothing taken from the intruders at the boardinghouse. He stripped off his cap, revealing a head of graying hair. At his appearance, Tillie looked to Keondric, who sent her a reassuring nod.

Looking at him, Healy's confidence melted from his face. "Patrick Bligh?"

"Aye, that's me. Glad to see ya remember." He lifted a finger to point at the rings still clutched in Healy's hand. "One of those belonged to your predecessor. I know. I was there when he gave it to ya and told ya it had been passed down to him from Fenian leaders all the way back to James Stephens."

A flush crept over Healy's face. "And I've kept good care of it—"

"No." Bligh shook his head. "You haven't. In fact, you weren't even sure where it was, which is why you had that duplicate made." He turned to address the room. "A memento mori is a carving, a depiction of the reminder that death is inevitable." He pointed to Healy's hand, the one clutching Braedon's ring. "That ring has a skull worked into the gold underneath the ruby heart." He scowled at Healy. "Too bad you didn't know that. But I knew, and so did someone else."

"Enough!" Douglas yelled. "William, get them out of here."

"Your anger speaks against you," Bligh said. "Why would you be so determined to end this talk if you had nothing to hide?"

"William!"

Instead of moving to obey, William went to stand next to Bligh, who clapped him on the shoulder. Healy stared openmouthed.

Bligh nodded. "Aye, Mr. Healy. This is he—the other who knew about the ring's secret." He turned to William. "Well? Heard enough?"

For several seconds, no one moved. Only angry muttering filled the quiet room. Finally, William strode to the window. Flipping the latch, he thrust it open and shoved his head out.

"Kil?"

347

"Here." Like a cat, Jacob jumped through the window and landed with a thud.

Douglas's face went white as he stared at William. Around the room, the men who'd seemed to take Keondric, Tillie, and Kilarny's men hostage now stood with their weapons pointed at Douglas.

"What . . . what are you doing?" he stammered.

"It's what *we're* doing," Keondric said, striding over to Tillie and pulling her into his arms. "And we are finishing what you started."

49

Now that the danger was behind them, Morgan's heart ceased its wild racing. He still wasn't keen on letting Tillie out of his sight, however. He knit his arm around her waist and pressed her to his side as the room emptied.

Kilarny sauntered toward them. "I was right—all we had to do was convince the Fenians that what I told them about Douglas was true."

"It still could have played out wrong," Rourke said, joining them from the kitchen. He nodded at Patrick, who gave a respectful nod in return, even though they continued to eye each other warily.

Kilarny barked a laugh. "Still kinna see yourself working with a bunch of Fenians, eh, Turner?" He clapped Eoghan on the shoulder as he too joined them. "We aren't so bad, are we, Hammy, me boy?"

Eoghan chuckled. "I hate to think what will happen to the Fenians when you're their leader, Kil."

This was followed by more laughter, which quieted when William and several of the other Fenians returned.

Anger colored William's features. "We've heard all we need

to." He tipped his head at Kilarny. "I didn't want to believe it, even when you told me about the ring."

The smile faded from Kilarny's face. "None of us wanted to believe he'd betrayed us, William. But I am glad you were willing to listen." He waved toward the door. "What about the rest of his men?"

"The ones who weren't with us are dead. Most of 'em. A few ran off when the fighting started." He drew his sleeve over his sweat-drenched brow. "It's on you now, Kil. The men are waiting to see what you want them to do next. What should I tell them?"

Kilarny's attention shifted to Rourke and Malcolm. "Most of this started with Daniel Turner. I know you've been searching a long time for his murderer, wanting to see him brought to justice, but my concern is for the Fenians. We kinna afford to have Healy's deeds tarnish what we are trying to do for Ireland." He squared his shoulders. "I wilna turn Healy over to the American authorities. I'm asking you plain, will ya trust me to see to it that he pays for what he's done?"

Rourke and Malcolm exchanged a glance, and then Malcolm nodded. "Daniel was my brother. I loved him, but our quest ends here." One bushy eyebrow rose. "Dinna be thinking we're friends now. No Turner has ever broken bread with a bunch of Republicans."

William bristled, but Kilarny laughed. "Fine, no bread breaking."

Malcolm's scowl transformed into a smile. "Even so, that doesn't mean we kinna sit down for a pint."

At this, even William let down his guard enough to smile. He gave one last nod to Morgan and Rourke and left the room.

Kilarny extended his hand. On his finger was a slender gold ring. "Well, Captain, I suppose you'll be setting sail?"

Morgan clasped his hand and, feeling Tillie's eyes on him,

fidgeted uncomfortably. "I'll have to give my brother time to recover, but after that, aye, I suppose we'll be setting sail."

Kilarny turned to Tillie. Taking her by the hand, he said, "You were verra brave tonight, Matilda. Braedon would have been proud. But now I think . . ." He paused, looked back at Morgan, his lips parted in a crooked smile. "Now I think maybe he'd want you to be happy."

"Thank you, Jacob."

He glanced down at the ring on his hand. "You all right with this?"

Tillie only hesitated a moment before returning his smile. "He'd want you to have it."

Nodding, Kilarny pressed a kiss to her cheek before saying good-bye and exiting the room, the rest of the Fenians following in his wake.

A painful tightness filled Morgan's chest as he searched Tillie's face. 'Twas evident she wasn't happy to see Kilarny go, yet it was what he couldn't see that had him most troubled.

He said to Rourke and Eoghan, "The authorities will be here soon. We should go." And to Tillie, "Are you ready?"

"Aye, I'm ready," she replied, her chin held high.

Spinning on her heel, she strode for the door. No doubt it was the pain and the memories that she hoped to leave behind, but for Morgan . . .

Watching her retreating back, he couldn't help but feel that what she left behind was him.

50

The week since Douglas's confession and capture had dragged by as long and slow as a wet Sunday. Combined with a steady drenching of summer rain, it seemed the days would never end—except that with each passing hour, Cass grew stronger and the distance between Tillie and Keondric grew greater.

She released a heavy sigh as she pressed her forehead to the damp, cloudy glass of her bedroom windowpane. Cass had said that given time, things would right themselves. The problem was, time was a luxury she no longer possessed. Tomorrow morning the *Caitriona Marie* would set sail for the Carolinas, and Keondric would be gone forever.

She closed her eyes against the sorrow accompanying the thought. How long ago it seemed that she'd made the decision to put her fate into God's hands, only then she'd never imagined that same choice might mean losing the man she loved.

"I'm trying, Lord," she whispered. "Help me to keep believing."

A soft knock sounded on her door. She left the window and went to answer, surprised to see Cass standing on her threshold, wearing a humble grin. "Did I disturb you?"

She shook her head. "I was just about to go downstairs to help Laverne with the tea. Will you walk with me?"

He stuck out his elbow in answer. Tillie happily took it.

He glanced at her sidelong. "I suppose you've begun making plans for the orphanage?"

"Aye, I've an appointment for the day after tomorrow to meet with the bank. I'm still not certain how I'll afford to run the place once it's open." She shrugged and forced a light laugh. "I guess some things are best left to God."

He made a face she could only describe as peculiar. They reached the bottom of the stairs, but instead of turning for the kitchen, Cass hesitated. "Tillie, have you spoken with Morgan since the other night?"

She looked away, hoping to hide a pang of hurt. "We've spoken, but not privately. Why do you ask?"

He shook his head slowly, and his eyes took on a sad hue. "Devilish hard getting anything through that thick head of his. Can I ask you something? And will you give me your word you'll speak the truth?"

"I'll say as much as I am able. As for true or no, I would never lie to you, Cass. You know that."

He smiled. "I suppose I do. But this . . ." His chest rose and fell as he sucked in a breath. Her hand still rested on the newel. He covered it with his own. "I asked you once if you loved me." A flush rose to her cheeks. "No, Tillie, please listen."

She nodded for him to continue.

"The reason you could never love me, was it because you'd already fallen in love with someone else?"

So much sorrow brimmed in the depths of his eyes, she could not help but be moved. She pulled her hand from under his to caress his rough cheek. "You will always be dear to me, Cass, but more than that?" She shook her head. "How could I love you when I'd already fallen so deeply in love with your brother?"

His shoulders slumped as he smiled. Catching her hand

when she went to pull away, he placed a kiss on the back of it. "Thank you for telling me." He drew away yet continued to watch her with an almost quizzical gleam in his eye. "I'll miss you, Tillie McGrath. Kilarny was right—you're braver than the rest of us combined."

Rather than walking her to the kitchen, he headed for the door.

"Cass, wait. How did you know?" Tillie called.

He didn't answer. Instead, he gave her a small salute, stepped outside, and disappeared from view.

— ✖ ✖ ✖ —

The creaking of the *Caitriona Marie*'s timbers had always been a soothing sound to Morgan's ears. Today, with the wind lashing outside and the rain continuing to fall, it felt more like solitary keening. Or perhaps it was the idea that tomorrow he'd be leaving Tillie forever that had him feeling so melancholy.

He sighed and sank into his father's old chair. It would be different not having Cass on board. His little brother didn't know it yet, but the *Marie* would be setting sail without him—had to sail without him, if he and Tillie were ever to have a chance at a happy life.

Reaching into his coat pocket, he pulled out the advertisement from the land-office window. He wished he could see her face when the man at the bank told her the purchase had already been made in her name.

An old, familiar ache filled him as he spread the page on the table and carefully smoothed out the wrinkles. He could imagine the place with young smiling faces filling all the windows, and a garden for Tillie where she could plant things to grow for her kitchen.

With Cass there by her side, he reminded himself grimly.

It had to be Cass. Hadn't he witnessed for himself how much closer they'd grown over the past week? But that had only happened when he'd put his own selfish desires aside and moved out of their way.

Aye, it would be Cass. He and Tillie would build a life together. And he? He would do what he'd always done. He would take care of his brother.

Pushed by a gust of wind, the door to his cabin burst open and Cass staggered in, his clothes slicked to his back and rain dripping off the bill of his cap. Rising, Morgan helped him drag it closed, then eyed the puddle forming around Cass's feet.

Morgan reached for a towel. "What are you doing here? I figured you'd be at the boardinghouse." He tossed the towel to his brother.

Cass grinned and snatched it from the air.

"Looks like you're feeling better."

"That I am, and anxious to get sailing, too. Feel the wind in me hair and the waves beneath me feet." He ducked under the towel and rubbed the dampness from his hair. "So, how goes the stocking? Bozey said we're packing lighter supplies than normal."

Morgan shrugged. "Aye, well, we're more shorthanded than normal, too."

Finished with his hair, Cass draped the towel around his neck and began stripping off his shirt. "I suppose you're right. We're short Doc and Donal, after all. Still, do you think it's wise not to carry the extra food?"

Squaring his shoulders, Morgan turned and faced his brother. "The lighter load means we'll make faster time."

Cass appeared to ponder that, then gave a one-shouldered shrug. "I guess." Slinging his soaked shirt over the back of a chair, he sat down and laced his fingers behind his head. "I'll be sure to let you know."

Morgan knew his brother well enough to realize there was something swirling about in that wet head of his. Could it be he'd already figured out the plan to leave him behind? He reclined against the table and crossed one ankle over the other. "What exactly do you mean by that? Far as I know, I'm still the captain of this ship."

Cass straightened, and Morgan couldn't help but glance at the puckered scar left on his shoulder. Following his gaze, Cass sighed. "When are you going to stop making me your responsibility, Morgan? Haven't you learned anything from the things that happened? You should know better than anyone, you kinna control people's lives. Only God can do that, and I'm fairly certain He doesn't need your help."

Frowning, Morgan turned aside. He had learned that too well, in fact. "What do you want from me, Cass? You obviously have something to say or you wouldn't be here. So how 'bout you get on with it?"

"Fine."

Removing the towel from around his shoulders, Cass tossed it to the floor and stood glaring at Morgan, his hands on his hips, his legs braced and feet planted. With a couple of days' growth of beard on his face, and the scar on his shoulder, he looked a proper pirate—and right at home on the *Caitriona Marie.*

"You know where I just came from?" he demanded.

"The boardinghouse?"

"Tillie, that's where. I was talking to Tillie, and I'll have you know she's about as torn apart by your leaving as I imagine she was the day you first brought her to the boardinghouse."

All mirth disappeared. Morgan shoved off the table. "What are you talking about?"

Cass nodded. "Aye, that's right, only she's not letting it show because she's too noble, and too . . ." He scowled.

"Well, I was going to say *brave*, but maybe it's not that at all. Maybe she's just as stubborn and pigheaded as you are."

"Watch it, Cass."

He laughed and wagged his finger in Morgan's face. "Ach, that's it. There it is. And you're honestly trying to convince me you dinna care for her? Take a look in the mirror, big brother. 'Tis written all over your face."

He no longer wanted to hide the truth. Clenching his teeth, Morgan started to turn away.

Cass quickly crossed to him. "She loves you, Morgan. She always has. I know you hoped it was me she loved, but that's not how this works." He clasped Morgan's shoulder, and for the first time they looked at each other eye to eye, as equals. "Besides," Cass continued, "this ship was never your dream. Now, Tillie and that farm she's had her eye on for so long? That's your dream. The question is, what are you going to do about it?"

What indeed? Morgan hesitated, looking up and then down as if to study the ship's dark beams above his head to the wooden planks below his feet. In one sense, Cass was right. The *Marie* had never been his dream. But could he just walk away from everything their father had labored so long to build?

"I loved him too, Morgan," Cass said quietly. "But it be my turn now. I'll take good care of Ma and the *Marie*."

His hand fell away from Morgan's shoulder, and with it the burden he'd borne for so long a time.

Cass seemed to sense his answer, for a smile parted his lips. Spinning on his heel, he swung out the door, a merry lilt to his voice as he hollered, "Bozey, get up here! There's been a change of plans."

51

Though the storm still howled and the driving rain appeared to have swollen in intensity, Tillie could no longer bear to stay cooped up behind the boardinghouse walls. Indeed, the wailing wind seemed to call to her, speaking to her in a way only her own troubled spirit could understand.

Grabbing her cape, she tossed it around her shoulders and stepped outside into the pounding rain. Her head she left bare, preferring the cold and shock of the weather against her hair and skin to the thrumming ache she'd been unable to loose for almost a week now.

She turned north, away from the harbor, for though she longed for a glimpse of Keondric, to see the vessel that would carry him away would be a torture too excruciating to bear.

How far she walked, she didn't know. She moved with no sense of purpose, no clear direction, and only drew to a halt when she stood in front of the land office and its dark, empty window.

Empty, except for the ghostly reflection of a bedraggled woman whose pain-filled eyes she dared not meet.

She blinked, as if by closing her eyes she might change the stark image staring back at her. Instead, it only reinforced what deep down she already knew.

Someone had bought the house.

The orphanage—the children whose faces she could picture but whose names she did not yet know—all hope of it crumbled, leaving behind a raw, gaping hole where her heart had been. Tears began to flow, mingling with the rain running down her cheeks.

She threw her head back, her fingers pulling at the sodden cape digging at her neck, but even that barely alleviated the choking stranglehold. Drawing free the knot that held the strings, she let the cape fall to the ground, then stood unmoving as the rain and tears washed her clean.

"Tillie!"

Her chest heaving, she looked around for the source of the voice. Blurred by the rain, a hazy figure moved toward her. At first, she dared not hope the lean body, the broad shoulders and proud head could belong to Keondric. But then he was there, his own eyes red and streaked by the rain.

He grabbed her cape from the ground and threw it around her shoulders. "What are you doing?"

So loud was the rhythm of the rain, he shouted.

Tillie shook her head. "How . . . how did you find me?" she shouted back.

He looked up at the sky and then threw his arm about her shoulders and hurried with her to the shelter of the awning over the land-office window. The storm was only slightly muffled there, but at least she could see his beloved face.

Stripping off his coat, he added it to the cape covering her shoulders.

"What are you doing out here?" he demanded, his breath forming a puffy cloud. "Are you trying to catch your death?"

She shivered. "No, I . . . How did you find me?" she asked again.

He was only inches from her, his nearness and the heat from his body closing out the storm. "I went by the boardinghouse. They told me you'd gone. Somehow I knew I'd find you here."

She said nothing, choosing instead to soak up the sight of his damp lashes clinging so perfectly together, his hair, wet and flattened to his head, his mouth . . .

"They sold the house," she said, pushing the words through lips numb with cold. "The picture's gone."

Keondric puffed out a breath. "I know."

"You know?"

Every breath, every gesture and word, seemed precious. He nodded toward his coat, his lips curving in one of his beautiful smiles. "Check the pocket."

Though her fingers shook, she managed to wrest the mangled piece of paper out. It was the advertisement for the house.

She peered up at him. "I dinna understand."

A look so tender melted over his face, her breath caught. "I bought it for you," he said.

"You"—she shook her head—"you did what?"

"But I've changed my mind." Clasping her hands, he drew them to his mouth and pressed a gentle kiss to the back of her fingers. "I dinna want you to live there alone, Tillie. I want to live there with you. I want to help you run the orphanage, even add a few children of our own. . . ."

He stopped, and she knew he was working up the courage to continue.

"Tillie, I love you. I would do . . . anything for you. And I would like nothing more than to spend the rest of my life making you happy, if you'll have me."

For several heart-pounding seconds, she couldn't move, couldn't breathe for fear of ravaging the blessing that had brought Keondric to her. Confusion flashed across his face, and she knew she had to speak, to somehow force the words out.

"I love you, too." She drew a shuddering breath. "More than I ever thought I'd love anyone again." Fresh tears burned her eyes, but this time they were tears of happiness. "More than that, I never dreamed, never dared hope that you or . . . *anyone* would care for me the way Braedon . . ."

The tension drained from his face. Dipping his head, he placed a kiss to her lips that drove away the doubt and guilt that had plagued her for so long. When at last he pulled away, she knew, finally, she'd found a love that would last forever.

"So," he rasped, his voice thick with emotion, "can you live with others calling you Mrs. Morgan for the rest of your life?"

Tillie laughed, joy such as she'd thought never again to know bubbling up from deep inside. Reaching up to stroke his cheek, she nodded. "Aye, Captain, I believe I can."

Acknowledgments

I am so blessed to be working with the remarkable people at Bethany House. Y'all are amazing! To the entire marketing team—Steve Oates, Debra Larsen, Noelle Buss, and Anna Henke—words cannot express my gratitude for your many efforts. Please accept my humble "thank you." To Paul Higdon and LaVonne Downing, thank you for sharing your talent in art and production. David Long and Luke Hinrichs, my fabulous editors, you know how much I love and appreciate you! Also, to Dave Horton, Jolene Steffer, Jim Parrish, Carissa Maki, Elisa Tally, Whitney Daberkow, Donna De For, Chris Dykstra, and Stacey Theesfield, I never realized how much you do behind the scenes and in front. Thank you for your love of Christian fiction. You have been a blessing to me and I will be forever grateful to you all. I'm sure there are many others whose hands have touched this work in one way or another. May God bless you richly for your faithfulness.

To my awesome critique partners, Jessica Dotta, Michelle Griep, and Ane Mulligan, thank you for your expertise and patient teaching. I love you all so much.

Lastly, to Nina and Cesar Gracia—Mom, Dad, I love you. You're my loudest, strongest, most faithful cheerleaders. Thank you for teaching me to work hard and never give up. I couldn't do any of this without you.